ANNIE CROW KNOLL: SUNRISE

GAIL PRIEST

Published by Hayson Publishing
St. Augustine, Florida

Library of Congress
Registration Number TXu 1-825-233

ISBN-13: 978-0615858869
ISBN-10: 0615858864

TABLE OF CONTENTS

PART ONE
Chapter One: Summer 1955...p 3
Chapter Two: Summer 1956...p 41
Chapter Three: Spring 1957...p 54
Chapter Four: Fall 1958...p 65
Chapter Five: Fall 1959...p 70
Chapter Six: Summer 1960...p 79
PART TWO
Chapter Seven: Winter 1965...p 110
Chapter Eight: Spring 1965...p 119
Chapter Nine: Summer 1965...p 145
Chapter Ten: Fall 1965...p 167
Chapter Eleven: Winter 1965-66...p 173
Chapter Twelve: Summer 1966...p 195
Chapter Thirteen: Fall 1966...p 201
Chapter Fourteen: Spring 1967...p 211
Chapter Fifteen: Summer 1967...p 217
Chapter Sixteen: Fall 1967...p 224
Chapter Seventeen: Winter 1967-68...p 243
PART THREE
Chapter Eighteen: Summer 1980...p 254
Chapter Nineteen: Winter 1980-81...p 261
Chapter Twenty: Fall 1981...p 282
Chapter Twenty-One: Winter 1981-82...p 286
Chapter Twenty-Two: Spring 1982...p 290
Chapter Twenty-Three: Summer 1982...p 310
Chapter Twenty-Four: Fall 1982...p 321
Epilogue: Late Fall 1982...p 333
Acknowledgments....p 335
About the Author...p 337

Also by Gail Priest

ANNIE CROW KNOLL: SUNSET

DEDICATION

For Gary

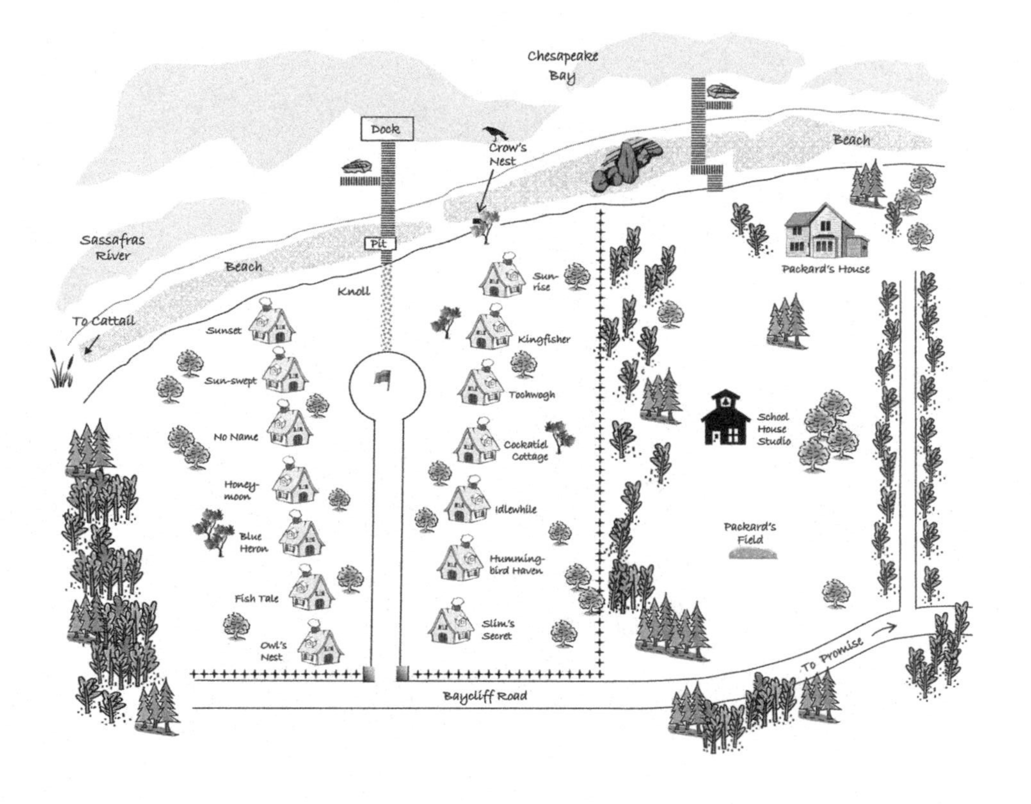

Chesapeake Bay
Sassafras River
Dock
Pit
Crow's Nest
Beach
Beach
Knoll
To Cattail
Sunset
Sun-swept
No Name
Honey-moon
Blue Heron
Fish Tale
Owl's Nest
Sun-rise
Kingfisher
Toohwogh
Cockatiel Cottage
Idlewhile
Humming-bird Haven
Slim's Secret
Packard's House
School House Studio
Packard's Field
Baycliff Road
To Promise

Part One

CHAPTER ONE
SUMMER 1955

NINE-YEAR-OLD ANNIE ATKINSON PEDDLED HER bicycle as hard as she could, but Tommy Reynolds still managed to stay just ahead of her. Several other children watched and shouted as the bikes barreled down the new driveway Annie's father had recently installed between his two rows of summer rental cottages.

As they neared the finish line where the drive circled around a tall flagpole, Tommy pulled away from Annie and screeched his bicycle to a halt. He was about to lift his arms in victory when Annie didn't stop. She hopped the new curb with her bike and kept going across the lawn that edged the steep hill leading down to the beach. Tommy dumped his bike and ran behind her.

"She's crazy!" he yelled as Annie's head disappeared out of sight.

Several cottage tenants had noticed their children cheering on either the Reynolds boy or the owner's daughter, but when the commotion reached a peak, some of the adults joined in with the youngsters following Tommy down the knoll toward the water.

Annie avoided the sandy beach at the bottom and veered her bike right onto the dock. Her father and his friend and employee Big Black Bo were trying to get a boat started for one of the renters. The thump, thump, thump of the bike tires traveling across the planks caught their attention. Luke paused from his job to watch his daughter near the end of their long pier. Surely she was going to brake, he thought. But judging from the crowd, which now included his wife Liz, running down the knoll, it became clear that his daughter had no intention of stopping.

"Annie!" was all her father could get out before she and her bike plunged off the end of the dock and into the bay.

Annie surfaced from the water with a yell of exhilaration. However, her parents' faces staring back at her from the dock above quickly silenced her. More than half a dozen others flanked them, including a smug Tommy Reynolds.

By the time she pulled herself up the ladder and onto the pier, her mother had already headed back up to their cottage. That was not a good sign. Annie's father grabbed hold of her upper arm pulling her back up the dock. He didn't say a word and never loosened his grip, also not a good sign.

The crowd broke up as cottagers headed back to their afternoon activities on the Knoll, the Atkinson's sloping hill property located on the peninsula between the Elk and Sassafras Rivers overlooking the headwaters of the Chesapeake Bay. It was the end of May, and opening weekend of the season. Some tenants were busy setting up housekeeping and getting boats launched. A few were already enjoying the expansive view of the water while sipping lemonade on their front porches, and others sat in beach chairs on the sand, keeping an eye on their younger children, who splashed around in the nippy water.

Tommy Reynolds stayed behind on the end of the dock.

The mixed feelings he had for Annie were beyond his preteen, male comprehension. On the one hand, he was disappointed that she didn't get a good whack on her smart-ass behind, but Luke and Liz never hit Annie like his own parents said they should. At the same time, Tommy felt guilty that Annie's bike was sunk somewhere in the water below. After all, it was a dare between the two of them that had led to all this. He had thought she was joking when she suggested that whichever one of them had the guts to ride their bike down the hill and off the dock was the winner. He felt badly that he never warned her not to do it. She could have gotten hurt.

Tommy slipped off his T-shirt and sneakers and lowered himself into the chilly water. His mother wouldn't be pleased with him for getting his shorts soaking wet, but he couldn't waste time changing into his swimming trunks. If the tide moved the bike, he'd never find it.

The bay at high tide was well over his head, but after spending every summer on the Knoll, Tommy was a good swimmer. He treaded water back and forth where he thought the bike was located. Eventually, he hit the handlebars with his right foot. Holding his breath, he dove under, but he couldn't see the bike in the dark bay water. He surfaced, took a breath and tried again. On the third attempt, he grabbed hold of one of the handlebars but couldn't lift the bike. Running out of air, he surfaced again to find Big Black Bo standing on the end of the dock.

"Want to fish her bike out?" he asked, holding a rope in his hands.

"Sure!"

Tommy didn't understand his parent's objection to Big Black Bo. He worked hard with Mr. Luke but still made time to help the kids out when they didn't know how to bait a hook or put their bicycle chain back on. Mr. and Mrs. Reynolds didn't mind the work that Big Black Bo did on the place, but they did not want to interact with him. They complained in the privacy of their cottage that Annie's parents were too friendly with him.

Bo made a loop at one end of the rope and tossed it down to Tommy.

"When you find the handlebars, slip this over," he instructed the boy.

Tommy took a huge gulp of air and kicked his way down to the bike. His lungs were beginning to hurt, but with the best concentration he could muster, he felt for the handlebars, slipped the loop around them and pulled it tight. When he reappeared and gave the okay, Big Black Bo began pulling the rope. Tommy climbed the ladder back onto the dock to find Annie's bike already there.

"Thanks," Tommy said, hoping that someday he'd be as big and strong.

"You did the hard part," Big Black Bo told him.

"I'll take it up and dry it off."

"You'd better take the chain off and grease it the way I showed you."

"I will."

"And do it right away. I'm guessin' she won't be allowed to ride it for a while, but we don't want it rustin' up in the meantime," Big Black Bo instructed.

"Yes, sir."

Annie stood before her parents in the living room of Sunrise Cottage.

"It's opening day of the season!" her father said. "I'm busy getting boats running. Your mother is trying to get everyone settled into the cottages. You know how hectic it is right now. Why do you have to pick today of all days to make a spectacle of yourself?" He paused only briefly. "Two weeks without your bike."

"Two weeks?" Annie cried.

"Yes, two weeks," Luke repeated. "If you can't treat your belongings with better care, then you don't get to use them. Now I have a bike stuck in the mud right where everyone dives off the end of the dock. No one will be allowed to jump in there until we get it up."

"Why not?" Annie asked.

"Because they could get hurt running into the damn thing," her father said, little patience left in his voice.

"Luke." It was the first word Liz had spoken, a warning about his language.

"Liz, we can't have one of our tenants diving off the dock and breaking their neck on that bike."

"What about Annie's neck?" Liz turned to her daughter, her gray eyes steel with disapproval. "You could have killed yourself." She began clenching and unclenching her fists. She looked as though she were about to say something more, but instead suddenly went into her bedroom and closed the door.

"Oh, for God's sake," Annie said but immediately regretted it when her father started in.

"You need to take your mother's feelings seriously, Annie. She loves you very much. So do I, but I'm not as fearful as she is. I knew you'd be okay. Maybe bruised or a broken arm at the most, but I grew up doing crazy things on my folks' farm."

"If she had her way, I wouldn't be allowed to do anything!" Annie complained.

"Your mother was never permitted to take risks. I think you frighten her."

"I only did it as a dare to that snot nose Tommy Reynolds. He's faster than I am, but I didn't think he'd ride off the dock. It was the only way that I could win."

"Winning isn't everything, Annie," Luke told her.

"I know," she answered half-heartedly.

"Do you? Do you really?"

Suddenly Annie was hit with a brilliant idea. "Next time I'll dare him to ride down the new cement steps and then off the dock."

"Now it's a month!" Her father's voice rose.

"What?"

"Two more weeks without your bike for even thinking about doing that! Even I wouldn't have been stupid enough to try that as a kid. You have some very serious thinking to do, Miss Annie Crow. And you'd better apologize to your mother, too. Now, I have to fish your bike out of the bay." Luke headed out the front door.

Annie felt a chill and didn't know if it was from being in her wet shorts and shirt or from the way her father had looked when he extended her punishment another two weeks.

After getting into dry clothes, Annie looked at her mother's closed door and decided to go outside to think.

The moment Annie sat down on the front porch steps, her pet crow Oliver swooped down from his favorite perch in the big oak tree that stood next to Sunrise Cottage on the edge of the hill leading down to the water. Oliver landed on Annie's shoulder as usual. Anyone watching would have thought the large black bird was consoling her.

"I guess you heard," she said to the crow, who gently pulled at one of her dark auburn curls. "I should look on the bright side. School isn't out for another couple of weeks, so I won't be using it much anyway."

Annie stopped talking when she noticed Tommy Reynolds wheeling her bike over to where she sat. He stood for a moment looking as if he didn't know what to say.

"I greased the chain so it won't rust," he finally announced.

"Well, I can't ride it for a month so what good's that going to do?"

"Wow, a month!"

"Yeah."

"Well, the least you could do is say thanks. Mr. Big Black

Bo and I pulled it out of the bay for you."

"It wouldn't have been in the bay in the first place, if it hadn't have been for you," Annie said.

"This isn't my fault, you stupid, pig-headed girl!"

"Yes, it is!"

"I wish your lousy bike was still down in the bottom of the bay and you were with it, Annie Crow!" He dropped her bike in the grass and stormed away.

Tommy had been the first to coin her nickname. He no doubt thought that she'd hate it, and he could tease her endlessly. However, Annie liked it. Crows were, after all, beautiful and intelligent. He certainly had called her worse things during their summers together.

Oliver called out a piercing cry at the departing boy, as if to make his own allegiance known and then returned to preening Annie's soft, curly hair.

"You're my buddy, aren't you," Annie cooed and reached up to rub Oliver's neck feathers.

Two years before, Annie had found Oliver while walking the beach up river on Cattail, a sandy spit where two small streams emerged from the marsh, creating a paradise of honeysuckle, berry bushes and cattails. At low tide, Annie easily jumped over the first stream that divided the Knoll from Cattail. The Knoll was the last property in the small bay town of Promise, established by Quakers in the early 1800s. Beyond Cattail, there was not much more than woods and marshland.

As Annie had scanned the beach for pretty stones and pieces of sea glass, the engine of their neighbor's wooden workboat shifted into a higher gear, and the loud chugging sound drew her attention toward the water. The angle of the sun hurt Annie's eyes. With her hand shading her face, she squinted and watched dark smoke billow out of the stack of the workboat as the reclusive Mr. Packard moved to his next crab pot.

Suddenly Annie heard a loud plop next to her on the beach. She looked down to find a large baby bird at her feet. It lay stunned for a moment, and then shook its head and partially feathered body. A Great Black-backed Gull overhead gave a disappointed cry at losing a grip on its lunch. Not knowing what to do, Annie stood still for a moment. The strange looking creature with a huge gaping mouth arched its back and rolled right into the water. No longer hesitant, Annie scooped the baby bird up in her hands before it could drown. She felt a terrified heart pounding in her palms as she hurried back down the beach toward home.

Breathless with excitement, Annie rushed with the baby bird to her father and Big Black Bo, who were replacing worn planks on the dock.

"It's best to put it back in the nest, if we can find it," Luke told his daughter.

"What kind of bird is it, Daddy?" Annie wasn't giving up on this too easily.

"Looks like an American Crow or a Fish Crow. Are you sure you weren't near any trees?" Luke asked.

"I was out on the beach. I think a big gull dropped it."

Luke scratched his head.

"Well, then, I suppose you'll have to try to take care of it yourself. Find a box and put leaves and some of this sawdust in it," he instructed.

"What do I feed it?" Annie asked looking down at her new pet's open mouth.

"Try some cat food," Luke said.

"That's ironic," Annie said, proud to use a new word her mother had recently taught her.

Luke smiled at his curly-topped daughter.

"Or some ground beef, but I doubt that your mother's going to give you any of that."

"I'll try the cat food first," Annie assured her father.

"What are you going to name it?" asked Big Black Bo.

"No names, Bo," Luke interrupted. "Annie, wild animals are not pets. You're just a temporary mother until it can fly, if it lives. So don't get your heart set on anything."

Luke headed up the hill to bring more wood down to the dock.

Big Black Bo returned to hammering a nail into a new plank, but when her father was out of earshot, Annie glanced at him and said, "I'm going to name him Oliver."

He paused and remarked, "That's a mighty fancy name for a bird."

"Daddy's told me how smart crows are. And Oliver was smart enough to find me!"

"How do you know he's not a she?"

"I don't know, but he looks like an Oliver to me," she explained.

"Hello, Mr. Oliver," Big Black Bo said to the baby bird, who looked up at his new mother and opened his wide mouth for something to eat. Annie giggled.

Despite Annie's good intentions, by the next morning, the baby crow was weaker. His pale blue eyes were opening less often, and he didn't beg for food like he had the day before.

"Who do we have here?" Maizie Finch said as she towered over Annie on the porch.

Maizie, Jim and Naomi Finch's older daughter from Sunset Cottage, had been dating Sam Waters from Hummingbird Haven Cottage for years. They had attended the same medical school and managed to get a few days off together while putting in long and exhausting residency hours at hospitals in Baltimore.

"Dr. Maizie, this is Oliver, my pet crow, but I think he's dying," Annie said with tears forming in her eyes.

Maizie gave Annie a hug. "Maybe I can help."

"Would you?"

"I'll try."

Next to Dr. Sam, Maizie was one of the tallest people Annie knew. When Maizie sat on the porch next to Oliver's box, her long legs gracefully crossed in front of her, Annie felt some hope for her crow.

"What seems to be the patient's main complaint?" Dr. Maizie asked as she gently felt the bird's breastbone with her fingertips.

"He won't eat. I think that he wants his real mama to feed him," Annie told her. "But he was dropped right by my feet for a reason. I think that I'm supposed to save him."

"Come on. Let's take him over to my cottage," Maizie said unfolding her legs and heading toward Sunset Cottage, located directly across the lawn from Annie's porch.

Annie followed carrying Oliver's box. She had to run to keep up.

"Are you sure you don't mind me bringing him inside?" Annie asked pausing on Maizie's porch.

"Of course not."

"My mother won't let me bring him inside our cottage."

"Old Spic and Span." Maizie laughed and tossed her strawberry blond hair back.

Sam was at the kitchen table eating breakfast. "What's going on?" he asked good-naturedly as Maizie grabbed her medical bag that she took everywhere.

"A medical emergency," Maizie told him with a wink.

"Let's see." He looked into Annie's box to see the baby crow open its mouth. "He's hungry."

"But he's a fussy eater," Annie told him.

"Try these scrambled eggs." He immediately offered his plate.

"We need to soften them up with milk," Maizie said as she took an eyedropper out of her black bag.

Sam's lean, long body moved efficiently and calmly as he mixed milk into the eggs and filled the dropper. Annie imagined Dr. Sam and Dr. Maizie in the hospital saving lives. It sent a thrill up and down her spine.

"Oliver's mother may be softening the food in her own stomach and throwing it back up for him. I'm not sure with crows, but some birds do that," Maizie told Annie. "So if we offer him softer food and poke the point of the eye-dropper down into his mouth, it may work more like his mother does with her beak."

By that Monday morning, Oliver was active again and eating larger and larger amounts. When Liz insisted that Annie go to school, Annie gave feeding instructions to both her parents and Big Black Bo before she was willing to leave Oliver behind and meet the school bus when it came to Baycliff Road.

Running from the bus stop at the end of the day, Annie couldn't wait for summer vacation when she would be with Oliver all day.

Now two years later, here she was waiting again for school to end so she could get back the use of her bike.

When Annie saw her father coming toward their cottage, she knew she had better go in and apologize to her mother before he came in for supper.

"Go on," Annie whispered to Oliver. "I'll see you after dinner."

Liz was in the kitchen cooking their evening meal. Annie began setting the table without having to be told.

"Please don't handle our dishes without washing up first," her mother said with a snap to her voice.

Annie cringed. As usual, her mother wasn't going to make this easy.

"Yes, ma'am."

Liz tore up the lettuce that she had picked from her garden that morning.

"I'm sorry that I upset you, Mama," Annie blurted out while she washed her hands in the kitchen sink.

"What was that? I couldn't hear you with the water running."

Annie turned the faucet off and faced her mother.

"I'm sorry that I upset you. I knew that I wouldn't get hurt."

"Well, you could have very easily. I don't want you acting like a roughneck!"

"Yes, ma'am."

"You're a girl, and hopefully a lady. It is time that you start acting like one." Liz repeated the litany.

Annie didn't argue with her mother on this issue. It was one that would never be resolved between them.

Before Annie's parents had bought the Knoll, it had been a campground. The campers had eventually put up five little one-bedroom cottages and a community outhouse. After Luke returned from serving in World War II, he sold his family's farm and married Liz. They bought the little cottages and the surrounding land. Luke and Big Black Bo had added bathrooms to the older cottages, constructed new cottages, marked the property lines with white fencing and constantly made repairs on everything. Liz managed the rentals and decorated the inside of each cottage. Now the property boasted fourteen pretty cottages painted pale yellow and trimmed with blue shutters, seven on each side of the new driveway.

For as long as Annie could remember, every morning Big Black Bo rode his bicycle to work on the Knoll. When the weather was bad, Luke put Bo's bike into the back of his pick-up truck and drove him back to his home several miles away in Coletown. Annie noticed that he and her father enjoyed each other. They were close in age, loved to work hard and smoked their share of cigarettes while constantly arguing about baseball. She also noticed that some white folks didn't talk to Big Black Bo the way that her daddy and mama did. She knew her parents didn't renew the McIntire's lease this season because they wouldn't stop referring to him as "boy."

Each day when Big Black Bo approached the Knoll at

seven thirty sharp, he and Annie had the same conversation.

"Mornin', Miss Annie."

"Mornin', Mr. Big Black Bo," Annie replied, respectfully using his full name as instructed by her parents.

"You mind your mama now, Miss Annie. She knows what's best for you."

"Yes, sir," Annie always answered.

It was their ritual. But this morning, Annie knew that he was referring to the incident this past weekend when she had ridden her bike off the dock.

Today she asked, "Do you mind your mama?"

He grinned. "I wish I had."

Even in hot weather, Big Black Bo wore long sleeve shirts on the Knoll. He rolled the sleeves no higher than his elbows. But for a moment, he pushed his left shirt sleeve up as high as it would go so that Annie could see the long scar that ran down the inside of his left arm.

"This wouldn't have happened to me if I'd minded my mama and hadn't been where I was, doin' what I was doin'."

Annie's eyes grew as big as saucers. "Where'd you get that?"

"Some place my mama told me not to go."

"Golly, I'll mind my mama for sure. I don't want to end up with one of those on my arm!"

Big Black Bo laughed fully, his big voice carrying across the Knoll. He gave her a wave from his bike as he rode between the two stone pillars that he had helped Luke build at the entrance to the property.

Annie continued toward the bus stop and wondered what he thought was so funny. Having a big, ugly scar on your arm surely wasn't anything to laugh about.

Off-season, Bo and Luke hunted together, and Liz, an excellent seamstress, made custom dresses in order to make ends meet. Soon as the weather broke, usually by March, they began to prepare to open the cottages. In the mornings after greeting

Annie and finishing his cigarette, Bo headed to the picnic table next to Liz and Luke's cottage. Liz always had coffee and fresh corn bread ready, and she and Bo would sit to discuss novels they read. It was an informal book club that took place while Luke happily made his daily run to the post office. Currently, Steinbeck's *Cannery Row* was being discussed.

This Monday morning, however, Bo didn't meet Liz at the picnic table.

"Aren't you coming for coffee today, Bo?" Liz called to him as he headed directly to work.

"There's a lot to do, Miss Liz. Mr. Luke got complaints about the kitchen faucet in Idlewhile Cottage."

"It can wait a bit," she insisted. "The library finally got Steinbeck's latest book *Sweet Thursday*! We can read that next."

Liz looked forward to these talks with Bo. All Luke did was express his concern that her feminine sensibilities might be upset by Steinbeck's subject matter.

"I don't want you to get into any trouble with your customers," Bo answered.

"But they've all gone home for the week."

Bo shook his head. "Now that you've opened the season, no telling when someone might take a weekday off to come in, and it only takes one to start trouble."

Liz guessed that Bo was tactfully referring to the McIntires who used to rent Cottage 4 for an entire season.

"No one else is as bad as Mr. McIntire," Liz reasoned.

"I can count, Miss Liz. You got an empty cottage on account of me."

"The McIntires didn't leave because of you. They left because Luke told them they weren't welcome back."

"But your husband insisted we go ahead anyway with all the improvements this year with the stone pillars out front, the new drive and steps leading to the beach."

"Your concern is very thoughtful."

"I'm concerned about my stomach," Bo said.

"What do you mean?" Liz asked, confused.

"Any other cottagers get it in their heads that you're a nigger lover, they won't rent. They don't rent, and you don't have the money to pay me. I don't get paid, and my stomach's empty."

Liz didn't like that word. She silently took the coffee mugs back into the house. She looked forward to shutdown season in the fall when Bo would feel free to behave again like the friend he had become to her.

On the second Saturday morning of the season, Annie was out front longing for her bike. She was keeping herself busy with Oliver when she saw Dr. Maizie's mother crossing the lawn coming to Sunrise Cottage.

"Good morning, Miss Naomi," Annie called to her.

"Do you feed him enough?" Miss Naomi asked, as the crow poked at a box of saltine crackers that were on the picnic table.

"Daddy says to let him find his own food so he can be independent, but I feed him a little so maybe he'll leave the songbird eggs alone."

"See if you can get him to leave my beach bag alone, too. I had snacks for my grandchildren in there, and when I went into the water with the kids, he stole a cookie out of the bag!"

"Apologize to Miss Naomi," Annie instructed Oliver.

The crow looked up with a cracker in his beak and shook his head.

"I'm sorry, Miss Naomi. I just can't seem to control him."

Naomi smiled. "After three children and now five grand-children, I understand."

"When is Dr. Maizie coming to the Knoll?" Annie asked.

"Not for a while, honey. She and Dr. Sam are both so busy with their new practices in Baltimore," she said with obvious pride. "Is your mama in?"

"Yes, ma'am," Annie answered.

"Come on in, Naomi," Liz called from inside.

"Any nibbles on Cottage 4?" Naomi asked as Liz handed her a cup of coffee.

"None."

"If the McIntires threaten to give you any legal trouble," Naomi warned, "you just remind them that our J.J. is a lawyer."

Liz couldn't help but smile at how Naomi loved reminding people of her son's accomplishment as well as Maizie being a doctor and her youngest Birdie giving birth to twins.

"You just tell those bigots that J.J. Finch is representing you."

"Thank you, Naomi, but I'm sure that will not be necessary," Liz said.

"The reason I came over is Birdie phoned this morning. She has neighbors in Baltimore, Barry and Mae Lipton, who might be interested in renting Cottage 4. They have a little girl Annie's age. They won't come until school is out."

"Cross your fingers that they take it. I guess there are others who feel the same as the McIntires," Liz added with concern.

"Not many and at least they don't say anything to Bo."

"Let's trust that the Liptons are better people," Liz said.

Summer vacation finally arrived. The new girl, Grace Lipton from Cottage 4, sat with Lois Renker and her younger sister Connie on a blanket spread out on the lawn in front of Idlewhile Cottage.

"I named this doll Elizabeth after Queen Elizabeth," Lois said, lifting one of the several dolls she owned and highlighting the word "Queen" with her voice.

Ought to be Queen Lois, Grace thought to herself.

It was her first morning on the Knoll, and the Lipton girl hoped that some of the other kids would be more interesting.

"Don't you have any dolls?" Lois asked.

"I left them at home," Grace told her.

She didn't play with them much anymore, and her mother had told her only to bring what she absolutely needed. The cottage was small, and if she wanted to bring her cockatiel bird, which she did, she'd have to sacrifice other amenities. Grace had put Pete's cage out on the screened porch of Cottage 4, and he was singing and chirping happily.

"You can play with one of my dolls," little Connie said and handed Grace the shabbiest one.

Grace, who held the doll in her lap, smiled at the kind gesture.

"Hey, who's that?" Grace asked when a girl about her age flew past on her bike with a crow clinging to her shoulder and a pair of binoculars swinging from her neck.

"Oh, that's Annie Crow," Lois said with her chin lifted. "You don't want to play with her."

But Grace did. Instinctively she knew she wanted to meet the girl with the crow.

"I'm going for a bike ride," she announced and handed Connie's ragtag doll back to her. "I'll see you later."

Grace grabbed her bike that she'd left leaning against a tree and took off after Annie, who had turned onto Baycliff Road and was heading into town.

"Hey!" she said breathlessly when she caught up with Annie Crow.

"Hi," Annie said, eyeing her.

This girl with the crow didn't seem to want anyone slowing her down. Grace peddled faster.

"Is that your crow?" Grace asked.

"Yeah."

Sensing her defensiveness, Grace said, "He's beautiful. What's his name?"

"Oliver."

"I have a Cockatiel named Pete," Grace explained and then continued, "Lois called you Annie Crow."

"Yeah, that's okay."

"Because of Oliver?"

"Yeah." Annie slowed her pace.

"I'm Grace Lipton. Your daddy helped my mom and me unload the car last night."

"And my mama will be over later with a pound cake or angel food cake before the morning is out. She loves to bake and always brings something over to new renters," Annie explained.

"That's nice."

"You staying all season?" Annie asked.

"Yep."

"Good."

The girls rode in silence for a while. Grace liked the town of Promise. Many yards were filled with flowers, and the air smelled like water. Nothing like the tightly packed form-stone row houses of her neighborhood in Baltimore.

"Where are you going?" Grace finally asked Annie when she turned onto a road lined with cornfields.

"Over toward the Elk River to look for owls at Quaker Point," Annie told her.

"How do you do that?"

"When Oliver finds one, he calls and I follow with my binoculars. Dad says it isn't good to disturb owls because most of them are sleeping during the day. But I'm allowed to let Oliver chase one out once a month. I missed last month."

"Why?"

"I wasn't allowed to ride my bike for four weeks."

"What'd you do?"

"I rode it off the end of the dock."

"Wow." Grace was impressed and a little intimidated.

"You want to come with me?"

"Sure." It beat playing with dolls.

As soon as they reached the woods at the end of the last cleared farm field, Oliver took off and disappeared into the trees. Leaving their bikes behind, Annie and Grace began walking. Annie seemed to know where she was going, so Grace followed.

"Shh," Annie said, although Grace wasn't talking.

Grace paused and listened.

Then Annie asked, "Hear that tapping?"

"Yeah." Grace liked this.

Annie put her binoculars up and looked at a dead tree.

"What do you see there?" Grace asked.

"Here," Annie handed Grace the binoculars. "There's a Red-bellied Woodpecker working his way up the left side of the Y."

Grace lifted the cumbersome binoculars up to her eyes. After a moment, she located the bird. "I see it!"

A short distance away, Oliver began calling.

"Come on," Annie instructed without taking her binoculars back.

The sound of Oliver's *caw, caw, caw* grew louder as Grace followed Annie through the woods.

"He was definitely on something. Maybe a Red-tailed Hawk, but hopefully an owl," Annie explained.

Then she stopped.

Caw, caw, caw. Oliver lifted his beak straight up with each call.

Grace found the crow in an oak tree.

"All right, all right, Oliver. You can calm down now," Annie whispered up to her crow. "Don't scare him off."

"Scare who?" Grace asked.

Annie pointed to a spruce tree next to the oak where Oliver still stood calling out, but even through the binoculars, all Grace could make out were pine needles.

"I don't see a thing," Grace said, frustrated.

"Here, move over this way," Annie said and tugged at her shoulders. "See that cluster of pine cones with the white stuff behind them?"

"Yeah," Grace located the white gooey stuff that she'd later learn were the owl's droppings.

"Raise the binoculars up about one foot."

The small Eastern Screech-Owl opened its huge eyes just as Grace focused on its form.

She was silent.

"Do you see it?"

Grace nodded as she stared into the yellow eyes of the first owl she'd ever seen.

"Amazing," she finally whispered.

Oliver jumped a few feet closer on the limb, and the owl swooped silently out of the cover of the spruce tree. Oliver took chase for a moment, but Annie whistled. He came back and landed on the surprised Grace's shoulder and began pulling at her blond pigtail.

"God, he's heavy," Grace said undisturbed by the bold bird.

"He doesn't go to anyone but my daddy and me. He must like you," Annie said.

Oliver lifted his tail, and a large dropping ran down Grace's back.

"Oh, yeah, he likes you!" Annie said laughing.

"Gross!" Grace shivered but laughed, too.

"Bigger than Pete's?"

"And warmer!"

"I'm sorry about that. I'll wash your shirt," Annie offered.

"Thanks, my mom may take you up on that."

As Liz approached Cottage 4 with a homemade pound cake, she saw Lois and Connie dressing their dolls on a blanket outside Idlewhile Cottage.

"Good morning, girls." Liz moved toward cottage porch. "Hello, Miss Agnes."

The screen door opened a crack. "I'm still in rollers this morning, Liz, or I'd come out," Agnes explained.

"I didn't mean to disturb your quiet," Liz apologized. "I'm going over to welcome your new neighbor."

"Hope that caged bird isn't going to be chirping out on the porch all the time!" Agnes gestured her curler covered head toward Cottage 4.

"I'm sure your new neighbor will be happy to meet you once you've done up your hair," Liz said calmly.

The screen door snapped shut.

When Liz moved on toward the screen porch of Cottage 4, the sweet gray bird with a yellow head and orange cheeks hopped excitedly from perch to perch in its cage.

"Hello?" Liz called in.

Mrs. Lipton came out onto the porch with a cigarette in one hand and a cup of coffee in the other.

"Hi." She set the cup down on the porch table and proceeded to open the door for Liz. "I was just taking a break from unpacking. Come on in."

Mrs. Lipton called out to the girls on their blanket. "Where's Grace?"

"She took off on her bike after Annie Crow," Lois answered.

"Be nice if she told me where she was going," Mrs. Lipton mumbled.

"If she's with Annie, she's fine," Liz said.

"She could be anywhere. Drowned out in that water or

lost in some cornfield," she said, taking another drag on her cigarette before putting it out in an ashtray on the porch table.

"You're accustomed to the city," Liz said.

"Yes."

"How'd you sleep last night?"

"Not great. Too quiet."

"You'll get used to it."

"I'm sorry. I'm Mae Lipton. This is Pete." She gestured to the cage, and the bird lifted his crest as if to say hello. "And apparently Grace has met your daughter. Annie Crow, is it?"

"Yes. That's a long story. I'm Liz Atkinson. Welcome to the Knoll." She held out the pound cake.

"Thank you. How did you know I needed breakfast? Want some coffee?"

"Sure."

Liz and Mae wandered into the cottage, which consisted of two bedrooms, a bathroom, a living room and kitchen.

Mae took a coffee cup and saucer and two small plates out of the china cupboard that stood in the living room near the archway into the kitchen.

"I love the dishes here. The pattern is real cute," Mae remarked.

"I hope it's not a bother to keep the dishes in the living room. There's just no space for the cupboard in that tiny kitchen," Liz explained.

"It's only a few steps away, and the china looks nice displayed out here," Mae said, carrying a cup of coffee to her guest.

"We're happy you could take the cottage for the whole summer," Liz said.

"Me, too. Good to get Grace out of the city. A break from…I mean for her dad."

Liz noticed Mae glance away. "Will Mr. Lipton be coming out on the weekends?"

"No, not this weekend." Mae took her first bite of pound

cake. "Hmmm, this is delicious. It's a good thing that Birdie is my neighbor, or I wouldn't have found out about this place. Now tell me about Annie Crow."

As the girls and Oliver headed back to the Knoll, Annie began pointing out the significant places in Promise. There weren't many.

"There's our church." Annie gestured toward the Promise United Methodist Church on the right. "My daddy helped put the new roof on it last year. That's Turner's Market." She pointed to the only store in town. "They've got most everything you'd need, including our post office. If you want to go to the movies or do clothes shopping, you have to drive over to Chester Landing."

Pointing toward the water at the bottom of Center Street, Annie said, "Down there is the public beach, but I like ours better."

They turned onto Baycliff Road.

"That's Doctor Brown's office on the corner."

Nearly a half a mile down, as the peninsula began to curve, the road narrowed at the property before the Knoll.

Grace pointed to the house set back in the trees. "Who lives there?"

"Mr. Packard Marlboro. He's sort of a hermit."

"Is he old?"

"Kind of, but not as old as my parents," Annie explained.

"What's he do all day by himself?"

"He fishes, and my father says that he paints."

"Houses?"

"No, paintings, you know, that you hang on a wall."

"I love to draw. Maybe we can go see his paintings sometime," Grace suggested.

"I don't think so. Dad says that he likes to be left alone so we don't bother him, and we keep the other kids off his property."

"Is he mean or something?"

"No. Dad just says that we have to respect his privacy."

As the girls neared the cottages, Grace pointed to where Baycliff Road came to a dead end just past the Knoll property.

"Are there any owls in those woods?" she asked Annie.

"Sure. We'll go out there next time."

"Why didn't you just go there today? It's closer."

"Daddy asks me to rotate between here and Quaker Point so I'm not disturbing the same owls."

"What would happen?" she asked.

"They might stop nesting."

Oliver gave a cry and flew off Annie's shoulder when they turned into the entrance to the Knoll.

"Must be hungry," Annie said as she slowed her bike to a stop.

Grace stopped next to her. "Do you feed him?"

"A little, but now he mostly scavenges for himself. Crows eat just about anything."

"Is that your cottage up there?" Grace pointed to the one closest to the water on the right. Oliver landed in the oak tree next to it. He began picking at a small lizard he had snapped up quickly from the beach below.

"Yes. We call it Sunrise Cottage because it has a great view of the sun rising over the water. My daddy built it for us. It's the only heated cottage. And we have a separate dining room and a fireplace in the living room, too."

"Who is that?" Grace pointed to a middle-aged woman coming out of the next cottage on the left. Three teenagers poured out after her.

"They're the Millers in Kingfisher Cottage."

Grace looked confused.

"A Belted Kingfisher is a bird that hovers over the water

and dives in headfirst to catch fish. You'll see. It's my dad's favorite bird. Next is Tockwogh Cottage. That's the Indian name for the Sassafras River. It's a weekly rental so different folks will be in and out of there. And you're in Cottage 4."

"No Name?" Grace asked.

"No one's ever named it," Annie said simply. "And in Idlewhile Cottage, we have the 'charming' Lois and Connie Renker and their parents Miss Agnes and Mr. Augy."

Grace smiled. "Yes, I met Lois and Connie."

Annie waved to the girls who were still sitting on the blanket with their dolls.

Connie gave a weak wave back, but Lois purposely ignored her.

"What is Lois' problem?" Grace asked.

"I'm not sure, but I think she might be an alien."

Grace laughed, and Lois looked right at her.

"Well, she's not going to like you now," Annie assessed.

"Doesn't matter."

"Mrs. Waters, from Hummingbird Haven, is some distant cousin of Miss Agnes or Mr. Augy, I don't remember which," Annie continued.

"She has a pretty garden."

"She gets the most Ruby-throated Hummingbirds with all those flowers."

Grace nodded.

"Slim and his wife are in Slim's Secret." Annie pointed to the last cottage on the right. "They came here because they are best friends with Mrs. Waters and her husband. The four of them did everything together until Mr. Waters died right before his son Sam went to medical school. Oh, and Dr. Sam is in love with Dr. Maizie from Sunset Cottage."

"I need a chart to keep this all straight!" Grace exclaimed.

"I'm half way through." Annie turned Grace to face the other side of the drive and pointed to the first cottage on the left by the entrance.

"Across from Slim's is the Owl's Nest, and it's a weekly."

"Weekly?" Grace asked.

"Weekly rental like Tockwogh."

"Oh."

"And in Fish Tale Cottage we have the monsters Tommy and Jack Reynolds with their parents Mr. Bob and Miss Jean. It's spelled t-a-l-e not t-a-i-l because of the tales Mr. Bob tells about the size fish he catches. Tommy's aunt and uncle are next door in Blue Heron Cottage. They have a new baby, who cries a lot. Then there's the Honeymoon Cottage."

"It looks a lot smaller than the others."

"Daddy and Mama lived in it when they were first married and building our cottage. Daddy says that it's the tiniest cottage and only happy newlyweds could cope in such close quarters. This season it's a weekly, and so is Cottage 12."

"No name for Cottage 12 either?" asked Grace.

"Not yet."

Annie pointed to the last two cottages back toward the water. "The Finches take up Sun-swept and Sunset."

"Big family?"

"Mr. Jim and Miss Naomi picked Sunset Cottage the very first summer my parents opened the Knoll. With their daughters Maizie and Birdie, their son J.J. and his wife and kids, it was getting crowded. Now Birdie and her husband have twins so they took Sun-swept Cottage, too."

Another voice chimed in. "Finally allowed to ride your bike, Annie Crow?"

It was Jack Reynolds. Behind him, Tommy banged out of Fish Tale and ran over.

"Do you always have to let that screen door slam?" Mrs. Reynolds' voice called out.

"We're going over to Cattail to work on the fort," Tommy said breathlessly.

"You want to come?"

"Sure," Grace answered impulsively. Then she looked to

Annie, who was silent.

"Come on," Jack said and headed toward the beach.

"Thanks for getting my bike out of the water," Annie said sheepishly.

"That's okay," Tommy answered and then took off after his brother.

All was forgiven. Boys didn't hold grudges. Annie appreciated that about them.

"They don't seem like monsters. They're cute!" Grace said.

"They're okay, I guess. Let's go."

Leaving their bikes in front of Cottage 4, Annie and Grace ran to catch up with the boys.

Grace and her mother had been on the Knoll a month and Mr. Lipton had yet to show his face. Some of the cottagers were beginning to wonder if Mae really had a husband.

"Maybe the girl's a bastard," Agnes Renker said, while rocking on her screened porch.

Jean Reynolds wished that she wasn't having this conversation while standing outside Idlewhile Cottage, because Mae Lipton was right next door in Cottage 4. But no one ever went into Miss Agnes' cottage, and she rarely came out. Augy, her husband, brought food on the weekends, and Agnes sent Lois and Connie into town to Turner's Market for the little things in between.

"Mr. Lipton is supposedly coming this weekend," Jean whispered back through the screen.

"That's what she told us last weekend, and he never showed up," Agnes said in between rocking in her rocker and sipping her iced tea. Agnes was only thirty-five, but seemed much older.

Grace came out onto her porch, and her Cockatiel went into full song.

"That bird never shuts up," Agnes complained to Jean.

"Good morning, Miss Jean, Miss Agnes," Grace said cheerfully as she changed Pete's food and water dishes. The small bird climbed out of his cage, hopped onto Grace's hand and lowered his head. Grace knew it meant that he wanted his head scratched.

"Do you want tickles?" she asked Pete.

The bird looked up at her and then impatiently put his head down again.

"All right, hold your horses," Grace said to her pet. "Let me finish putting clean food in your dish."

"Come on, Grace," Annie called from the yard.

Grace put Pete into his cage.

"The tide's out," Annie said holding up a beach pail.

The girls walked up and down the beach, gathering tiny pieces of glass worn smooth from years of tumbling in the surf and sand. Annie kept hers in a large glass jar in her room. Grace said that she might like to glue hers into some kind of design on a piece of wood.

The pail quickly filled up with pieces of frosty white, green and amber glass.

Annie, who had wandered farther down the beach, hollered, "I found gold!"

Grace ran to where she was and looked down to see a small piece of blue glass in Annie's hand.

"That's blue, not gold," Grace said.

"Of course it's blue. That's why it's gold. It's rare. Precious. I hardly ever find it."

"But the edges aren't completely smooth."

Annie had taught her to only select the pieces that were "ready."

"Doesn't matter with blue. When you find blue, you have to keep it anyway. If I throw it back, I may never find it again."

Miss Naomi came down the new cement steps to the beach with her little twin granddaughters in tow.

"Morning, girls."

"Morning, Miss Naomi."

Before she could set her canvas beach chair down, the twins were running across the sand to see what the older girls were doing.

"What do you have?" the blonder of the two five-year-olds asked.

"We're looking for sea glass. You want to help?" Annie asked.

"Yes," the other twin chimed in.

"Go get your pails. You can keep any color you find, but I'll give you a red licorice for every blue piece you give me."

"You're always thinking," Grace observed.

By the time Mr. Lipton arrived the next night, half the cottagers were lined up to make his acquaintance.

"Friendly people, aren't they?" Barry Lipton said as he stepped into the living room of Cottage 4.

He was tall and blond, like Grace, with beautiful, piercing blue eyes.

"Hi ya, Barry," Mae started to light up a cigarette, but Barry took her in his arms before she could strike the match. He put his hands on her hips and pulled her to him.

"God, I missed you, Mae," he said while smelling her hair. "You know I can't live without you."

Grace hung back by the archway to the kitchen. Her father's eyes met hers.

"What's the matter, baby? Come on, give your old man a hug."

Barry Lipton let go of his wife and knelt down on one knee. Reluctantly Grace crossed to her father and gave him a quick hug.

"Hello, Daddy."

Barry held on to her arms and looked into her eyes.

"Daddy is very sorry, and you don't have to worry now. Everything is fine."

The weekend Grace's father arrived, one of those spontaneous Knoll parties developed with almost everyone barbecuing together and having a few beers around the new fireplace. Along with the drive and cement staircase down to the beach, Luke and Big Black Bo had dug out a level area half way down the hill and poured a cement patio. They had also constructed a large stone fireplace at one end of the cement landing.

This area was soon referred to as "the pit," and it was the perfect place for the adults to gather after dark while the children chased lightning bugs and toasted marshmallows.

It was Luke's birthday, and although Liz hadn't planned a party, everyone sang "Happy Birthday" which was followed by a chorus of "For He's a Jolly Good Fellow."

Barry Lipton called everyone to his attention by standing on one of the picnic benches. "I'd like to thank you all for making my family and me feel so welcome. Here's to Luke and Liz." Barry raised his glass of cola.

"Here, here." Various voices chimed in and folks raised their drinks as Barry stepped down.

"Mind if I have one of those?" Barry asked Tommy Reynolds' dad and pointed to the ice chest of beers.

"Of course not. They're for the taking," Bob Reynolds said, tossing him one.

"Barry?" It was Mae, who hadn't said much all evening.

"It's just one, for Christ sake," Barry said with a tone no one had heard before.

Quickly catching himself, he laughed it off. "Little woman is watching my every move."

Mae left to find Grace and get her ready for bed.

The party began to slow down as the other children also needed to be cleaned up and put to bed. Bob Reynolds, Jim Finch, Barry Lipton and Luke stayed to talk baseball as the embers in the new outdoor fireplace continued to glow.

Barry eventually rose and stretched. "I guess it's time to call it a night. Think I'll take one for the road, if you don't mind."

Bob, who was in a deep discussion with Jim and Luke over the current Philadelphia Phillies pitching staff, just gave him a wave, and Barry disappeared up the stairs and into the darkness.

After reaching an impasse of opinions, Luke started poking the fire down.

"Well, if you two are planning on going out fishing with me at the crack of dawn, we'd all better get some shut eye," Luke said.

Bob grabbed his ice chest, which felt empty. "Guess we all drank more that I thought. See you at 5 AM, boys."

"You'd better be up, or Liz won't appreciate us banging on your door at that hour," Jim joked and headed up the stairs, too.

Luke stayed behind to finish a cigarette before dousing the last coals with water. Smoke poured out of the front of the fireplace and up the chimney. He stirred it a bit with a stick until he felt sure it was safely out.

When he came up the steps, he heard a loud voice coming from Cottage 4. Nearly every other cottage was dark, but the lights burned brightly at the Lipton's. Instinct told him to go over.

As Luke approached, something crashed to the floor, and Grace, wearing only her pajamas, came running through the front porch and out the door.

"Go to Sunrise Cottage," Luke told her, and then he bolted onto the screened porch. Through the living room doorway, he saw the china cupboard lying down on the floor. Pieces of dishes were scattered across the floor. Barry was standing with his back to Luke, and he was brandishing a table lamp. Mae was up against the far wall with her hands covering her face.

Luke knew he had to act quickly before the drunken Barry

Lipton knew what hit him. He stepped into the room, swung Barry around by his shoulder and punched him soundly in the face. Barry went down cold, and Luke managed to catch the lamp before it hit the floor.

Mae stood frozen for a moment, and then as if someone flipped a switch, she started picking up pieces of broken dishes. Tears streamed down her face as she frantically grabbed at sharp edges of china, and she cut her finger. "Damn, Liz's pretty dishes," she muttered and wiped her nose, streaking blood across her face.

Liz appeared at the doorway in her bathrobe.

"My God, he hit you!" Liz cried.

"No!" Mae stood to her full five foot three inches. "He has never hit me or Grace."

Luke, who had been silent, finally spoke. "He's not welcome on the Knoll."

"We'll leave tonight," Mae said.

"No, you're not," Liz said and then looked at Luke. "We're not letting her and Grace go back with him."

"Leave that," Luke said as Mae started to lift the cabinet up. "Here's what we'll do. He's out cold and shouldn't give us any trouble. We'll put him in the back seat of his car, and I'll drive him back to Baltimore. Mae, you follow in my truck, and after we get him settled at home, you and I will ride back here where you'll be safe."

"That's too much to ask. I can't let you do all that. I can manage him all right, if Grace can stay with you tonight," Mae insisted.

"Of course Grace can stay, but you're not going to be alone with him," Liz said.

"Come on, help me get him into his car," Luke instructed.

"First you'd better wash up, Mae, honey," Liz told her.

"I must look a sight."

"You look like you lost a boxing round with a kangaroo. We'll bandage your finger, too."

When they began to lug the unconscious Barry Lipton to his car, Augy Renker from Idlewhile Cottage suddenly appeared. He was returning from one of his nightly walks to town and back.

"Need some help?" he asked, as if it were normal to find three people carrying what might be a dead body out of Cottage 4.

August Renker was one of the quietest Knollers. He was remarkably pale, and although he wasn't more than forty, he had almost no hair on his head or any other visible part of his body for that matter. Avoiding the sun, he spent most of his time inside with Agnes, who rarely left her rocker on the porch. They played Parcheesi endlessly.

After Augy helped them secure Mae's husband in the back seat, he said one thing. "Looks like I missed the party."

Mae's face turned white.

"Don't worry, my wife and girls sleep though everything, and I certainly wouldn't tell her. Otherwise, I'd have to hear about it for the next three months."

"Thanks," Luke said, and the men shook hands.

"Will you be all right from here?"

"Yes, we can manage."

Augy said nothing more and quietly disappeared into his cottage.

Liz had slept little more than an hour after Luke and Mae returned from depositing Barry Lipton in Baltimore. It was barely dawn when she noticed her neighbor Packard Marlboro climbing over the fence behind her cottage and lumbering across the Knoll on his way to Cattail. The high tide prevented him from staying down on the beach. Otherwise, Liz rarely saw him. Instinctively she stepped back from her window. After all these years, she knew he'd prefer not to have to wave to her. After he passed, Liz went to the window again.

At twenty-six, Packard struck a vivid picture as his large figure hulked across the lawn, silhouetted by the growing pink of the rising sun up river. His wild black hair was blown back by a gust of wind that moved up off the water and over the edge of the Knoll. Then he disappeared down the cement staircase to the beach.

Liz had just sat down with a cup of coffee to watch the sun continue to rise when there was a knock at the front door.

"Get up, you lazy bum!" Bob Reynolds hollered.

"You're the one organizing this expedition," Jim Finch added.

Liz poked her head out of the front door.

"Hey, you fellows better quiet down out here. You're going to wake the entire Knoll," she said, trying to appear casual.

"Sorry, Liz. It's just that Luke started this whole idea of fishing this morning, and we haven't seen hide nor hair of him," Jim explained.

"He was sick during the night," Liz decided to say. "Too many marshmallows."

"Too much beer, I'm guessing," Bob said and laughed.

"Now you know that Luke isn't much of a drinker," Liz said.

"Well, somebody drank a lot of beer last night. My ice chest was almost empty."

"You all probably had a few too many. Lost count," Liz told him.

"Yeah, I don't feel so great, myself. Maybe I'll go back to bed," Bob decided.

"You have to be kidding!" Jim fumed. "I got up before dawn to go fishing, and you're going with me whether you want to or not."

"Could you boys take this some place else? I need Luke back on his feet later today and Annie is still asleep, too."

"Oh, right. Sorry, Liz."

Hearing the men's voices as they headed toward the stairs for the dock, Oliver decided to follow them. When a bag of marshmallows left behind down in the pit caught his eye, he landed there to investigate. Jim paused to watch the crow pick at the bag with his beak. Bob continued down to the dock.

When Oliver successfully pulled out a marshmallow, Jim scolded, "Hey, that's not bird food."

"Quit talking to birds and unhitch that line, will you?" Bob instructed from down in his boat.

Oliver flew to a piling with his prize and began to eat.

"Hell of a breakfast," Jim muttered as he grabbed the remaining marshmallows for himself.

From his perch on a piling, Oliver called to the men as they pulled away from the dock. Then he noticed the big man walking the beach further up river. The curious crow took off after him. When Oliver got closer, he saw the man drop something out of his pocket so he landed on the beach to inspect. Finding that it wasn't anything to eat, Oliver left the small piece of blue glass where the man had purposely dropped it.

"Good bird," Packard said. "Leave it for Annie to find."

Annie rolled over when she heard Grace whimper in her sleep. Instinctively she wrapped an arm around her friend.

"Shh, it's okay," Annie whispered. Grace became quiet and then opened her eyes.

"Bad dream?" Annie asked, propping herself up on one elbow and looking intently into Grace's blue eyes.

"I guess so," Grace answered. "Do you know what happened after your mother went to my cottage last night?"

"No, I fell back to sleep."

"Me, too."

Grace remembered how warm and safe it felt when she crawled into Annie's bed after running in her pajamas and bare feet from Cottage 4. Liz had told the girls to stay in bed while she went to see what was going on. Even Annie wouldn't disobey her mother when she had that look on her face, and Grace was glad to stay away from the frightening commotion between her parents. She felt guilty leaving her mother with her father out of control, but Annie's parents would make sure that everything was okay. They seemed to have a knack for that, Grace realized.

Now the smell of bacon cooking got them both up and dressing. Annie let her guest use the bathroom first, and when she came into the kitchen, Liz was alone at the stove.

"Where's Grace?" she asked her mother.

"Good morning to you, too, my precious daughter."

"Sorry. Good morning, Mama," Annie said and gave Liz a kiss.

"Grace wanted to see her mother."

"What's going on?"

"Grace's parents are having problems. Mr. Lipton is back in Baltimore."

"Does Grace have to go back?" Annie asked, concern rising in her voice.

"No, honey. She and her mother are staying here."

"Good."

"Make sure that you treat Grace with special care right now. Compromise once in a while for a change."

Annie nodded. She liked doing things her own way. Perhaps that was why she'd never had a best friend before, but now she knew that she did.

With Liz's encouragement, Mae landed the job at Turner's

Market. At first, it was difficult, due to her notoriety as a woman whose husband had disappeared in the night and never returned. Certainly Liz hadn't told anyone, but news of Mae's situation was all over Promise anyway. People made extra trips into the store, saying that they had forgotten this or that, just to see the city girl who was leaving her husband, the drunk.

"Don't give it a thought," Letitia Turner, who ran the store with her second husband Elwood, told Mae on her first day. "I try to keep it quiet, but my first husband was a drunk. You're better off without him."

Mae bit her lower lip when it began to shake.

"Enjoy it while it lasts," Letitia continued. "Most news in Promise only lasts a couple of weeks, and then, you become old news. People are like that. They need new stories to spread, and if nothing happens, they'll make something up." She fussed with her red hair a moment and then leaned closer into Mae. "And if they're the type to enjoy the occasional spotlight, they start a rumor about themselves." Then she laughed her belly laugh and patted Mae on the back.

It seemed as though Mrs. Turner had been right. Around the middle of the second week, things were settling down for Mae, until her car disappeared from behind the market in broad daylight while she was inside working.

Cars were rarely stolen in Promise. When they were, it usually involved some kids looking for a joy ride, and the county police quickly returned the vehicle. However, this car was Mae Lipton's, and that fact created a telephone party line overload.

The police found no trace of it in the county. Mae knew they wouldn't unless they extended the search to include Baltimore City. But they weren't about to do that.

"If your husband paid for it to begin with, then it isn't really stealing if he takes it back," the police chief told her.

As summer came to an end, Mae packed up their meager belongings to move to Philadelphia where Grace would now attend school.

"Why can't you live here and then you could go to school with me?" Annie asked her best friend.

"I wish we could," Grace said. "But Mom says that we have to save money, and there's no way we can rent here again next summer if we don't live with Grandmother during the school year."

"But you'll be all the way up in Philadelphia, and we may never see each other again," Annie whined and didn't like the sound of her own voice.

Grace threw her arm over Annie's shoulders as they sat side by side on the curb by her grandmother's car.

"Don't worry. I think Grandmother will help us so we can come back next summer. Believe me, she is not happy about having a bird in her car, much less in her house."

Grace stood and covered Pete's cage with a tablecloth to keep him calm before wedging it into the back seat where she would sit for the drive to her new home.

CHAPTER TWO
SUMMER 1956

THE FOLLOWING SEASON BEGAN WITH doings of monumental proportions. Maizie Finch and Sam Waters' wedding was to be held on the Knoll. Liz had been hired to make the bride's gown, the matron of honor's gown, and two dresses for the flower girls.

When Maizie and Birdie came for their final fittings, Annie helped her mother by holding the pincushion and yardstick.

"My sister and J.J. got all the brains, but I got the looks," Birdie teased as Liz adjusted the darts in the bodice of the sky blue matron of honor gown that set off Birdie's turquoise eyes and blond hair.

Annie watched Birdie admiring her reflection in the full-length mirror Liz had set up in the living room. Birdie Finch had always had an hourglass figure. After having the twins, and then her third child last year, Annie noticed that Maizie's sister was even more voluptuous. Annie liked the sound of that new word Liz had taught her. Voluptuous. She enjoyed how it felt on her tongue when she said it out loud.

However, when Maizie Finch came out of Liz's bedroom in her wedding gown, she took Annie's breath away. The doctor was taller than her sister and moved with confidence. *Like a queen,* Annie thought. Her strawberry blond hair flowed to her shoulders, and her green eyes sparkled.

"Annie. Annie, the yardstick, please," Liz said, as she knelt to check the length of Maizie's gown.

"Sorry, Mama."

"I love the gown, Liz. It's perfect!" Maizie bubbled. "It must have taken you forever to sew on all these pearls."

"I enjoyed it. Made the winter pass," Liz told her.

"I'm so glad I didn't cave into friends who thought I should get my gown in the city. No one else could have done a better job."

Annie noticed her mother blush.

"Or even that dressmaker over in Chester Landing," Birdie said, smiling into the mirror next to Maizie. "You know us, Liz. You really know our figures and what works."

And Liz did. Even at ten, Annie noticed how the lines of Birdie's gown made her appear taller. She became the perfect complement to her sister.

"Did you realize that the dressmaker in Chester Landing is somehow related to Packard Marlboro?" Birdie said.

Now reaching for more pins from the pincushion Annie held, Liz said, "She's his cousin."

"I heard that she's the only relative he has and about the only person he talks to," Birdie added.

"We saw him walking along Baycliff Road when we drove in today. He's quite handsome, in a rugged sort of way," Maizie remarked.

"If you like the unshaven, mountain man type," Birdie squealed. "Besides, you're not supposed to be looking at other men! You're going to be a married woman soon!"

"I've been surrounded by smart, good-looking men all

through med school, and I've never been unfaithful to Sam."

Annie felt excited by this grown woman talk.

"You can always look. There's no harm in looking," Liz advised.

Annie was surprised by her mother's remark and let out a little gasp.

Maizie turned to her. "And what do you think of all this talk, Miss Annie Crow?"

Annie stared at her heroine and couldn't find words.

"That old gossip Miss Agnes remarked to Mother that you and Sam were a bit long in the tooth for a traditional wedding," Birdie teased her sister.

"And she told Sam's mother that we'd be starting a family right away since I'm a pediatrician and Sam is a, and she whispered the word, gynecologist," Maizie laughed.

"Maybe she won't leave the porch for the wedding," Birdie added with a twinkle in her eye.

"I'm sure she'll want a closer view of her daughters in the pretty dresses I made them," Liz said diplomatically.

Maizie carefully leaned down to look Annie in the eyes. "I wish I could have asked you and Grace to be my flower girls instead of Lois and Connie, but they are Sam's relatives, and blood is thicker than water."

"Thanks anyway," Annie finally spoke. She beamed and couldn't wait to tell Grace when she arrived for the summer that Maizie wanted them in her wedding and not Lois and Connie.

"Maybe we could get Oliver to fly in with the rings or something," Birdie joked.

"Don't you worry, that bird won't be bothering the wedding. I'll tether it if I have to," Liz said. "Now, Maizie, straighten up before you muss the gown. I think we're done. You can both get changed."

Annie didn't like the sound of the word tether. She'd have to try to keep Oliver out of the way on the wedding day.

Grace and Mae arrived just in time to join in on final preparations for the wedding day. Annie and Grace helped Luke and Big Black Bo set up the chairs on the lawn for the ceremony and tables for the reception while Liz and Mae dealt with the caterer, who was quite temperamental about working out of the tiny kitchen in Sunrise Cottage.

After the ceremony, Annie and Grace quickly took their seats with Tommy and his brother Jack at the children's table located under the big oak tree near Sunrise Cottage. Birdie's twins were impressed to be seated with the older kids and not stuck with their baby brother at their grandparents' table. Connie Renker joined them in her organdy flower girl dress.

"Where's your sister?" Tommy asked.

"Lois wants to sit at the main table with the bride and groom, like Birdie and J.J. are doing," Connie answered with a roll of her eyes. "I told her that it'd be boring up there, and we'd have a lot more fun with you."

"Here comes Miss Snooty Pants," Jack teased Lois as she flounced over to sit by her younger sister, clearly unhappy to be missing the limelight of the bridal party table.

Once all the guests were settled at tables, Annie noticed the caterer's staff bringing food out of her mother's kitchen. Big Black Bo was nowhere in sight, and she realized she hadn't seen him since they had finished setting up. She wondered why he wouldn't want to stay for the party.

A beautiful woman with skin the color of cocoa and long, dark lashes framing her black eyes brought a platter of fancy sandwiches with the crusts cut off to the children's table. Birdie's twin girls politely took one sandwich each from the tray. Jack and Tommy both took three each because although the sandwiches looked elegant, they were tiny.

Before Grace or Annie could select from the choices of

tuna, chicken or egg salad, Lois Renker said to the woman holding the tray, "I want what they're having at the other tables."

"I'm sorry, miss. I was told to bring these special sandwiches to the children's table," she said politely.

"Well, I don't want these baby sandwiches. I want the grown-up food!"

"Don't be rude, Lois," Annie interrupted.

Lois glared at Annie but turned back to vent her disappointment at not being seated with the rest of the wedding party on this innocent woman who was serving.

"Listen, girl, you bring me the regular food, or I'll get your boss."

The woman was silent, but Annie noticed the fire in her eyes and wished that she'd speak her mind.

As usual in tense situations, Grace was the one to attempt to smooth things over.

"Don't pay any attention to her, miss. She's just unhappy to be stuck at this table with us."

"I should be with Maizie and Sam!" Lois whined and smacked the hand of her hungry little sister who reached for one of the delicate sandwiches.

Connie Renker let out a wail. Jack and Tommy both broke into laughter while the twins looked around nervously for their mother. The situation was falling apart quickly when the bride suddenly appeared.

"Lois, what's going on?" Maizie asked.

"This girl won't give me what you're eating."

"Sam and I thought you'd be happier sitting with your friends," she said while stroking the hair on each of her niece's heads. The twins smiled and began eating. The Reynolds boys settled down as well.

"I don't want to eat these stupid sandwiches!" Lois snapped.

"Bring her my dinner," Dr. Maizie said to the server.

"Oh, no ma'am. You'll need your strength for your wedding night."

The bride gently laughed and offered her hand to the woman. "Hello, I'm Maizie."

For a moment, Annie watched the woman hesitate while holding eye contact with Maizie.

"I'm Viola," she finally said and shook the bride's hand. "And I'm serious. I remember my wedding night. You're going to want to eat now while you can."

"I appreciate your advice, but go ahead and bring my chicken dish to Lois. I'm much too excited to eat anyway."

"Well, if you're sure," Viola said, as Maizie returned to her guests.

While everyone else was busy enjoying the fancy sandwiches with potato salad and pickles at the children's table, Lois sat smugly, waiting for vindication by being given the bride's lunch.

Oliver gave a call from the oak tree above their table just as Viola placed the chicken dish down in front of Lois. When she stepped away, a splat was heard. A large bird dropping gushed between the leaves of parsley garnishing the lovely chicken dish. Lois' face went red with horror, and she ran screaming from the table. Little Connie followed her out of habit, but not without taking an egg salad sandwich with her.

After the wedding, it poured rain for seven days straight. The girls were getting restless so Liz gave Mae money to pick up paints and paper down at her job at Turner's Market.

When Grace saw the paints, she said, "Let's paint signs for each of the cottages!"

"Can we, Mama?" Annie asked with the first real excitement in her voice since Maizie's wedding.

Relieved that the girls would have a project so she could focus on her Knoll responsibilities, Liz said, “I’m sure your father can give you some small pieces of scrap wood to use for signs.”

“I can paint the easy stuff like a sunrise and a river for Tockwogh, but you’ll have to paint the birds,” Annie admitted.

“We can’t just have you paint a number 4, Grace. What would you like to name your cottage?” asked Liz.

“May we call it Cockatiel Cottage, after Pete?”

“That would be very nice.”

“What about Cottage 12?” Liz asked.

“Bluebird?” Grace suggested.

“No, we already have Blue Heron,” Annie reminded her.

“We’ll think of something.”

“You’d better check with Mr. Slim about Slim’s Secret before you make the sign. With his coconut head collection, he might prefer Coconut Cottage,” Liz suggested.

“Coconuts?” Grace asked.

“You’ll see.” Annie grabbed her father’s big umbrella. “Come on.”

“Well, what are you two up to?” Mrs. Slim asked when Annie and Grace arrived in the rain.

“Come in before you drown,” Mr. Slim called out from the living room where he and his wife were in the midst of a hot card game of double solitaire.

Mrs. Slim dashed past the girls to return to the card table.

“You moved a card!” she said accusingly. “I said ‘freeze’ when I left to let the girls in and you moved a card!”

“Can’t get away with anything around here,” Slim sighed. “She’s clairvoyant, you know,” he added with a wink.

Grace gaped at what looked to be about fifty different faces carved into coconuts that lined several shelves of the walls in the living room. The images ranged from animals to clowns to people and each was hand painted which added to the artistic effect.

"What can we do for you, girls?" Mrs. Slim turned her attention to them but kept one eye on the card table and her husband's hands.

"We wanted to know what you'd like to name your cottage," Annie said.

"We've always called it Slim's Secret. I like the alliteration. Do you know what alliteration is?" Mr. Slim asked.

"Yes, the repetition of the beginning consonant sounds," Annie answered.

"Slim's Secret," Grace said and wrote it down on a pad of paper she'd brought.

"Is it okay if we make up a sign for you?" Annie asked.

"That would be very nice. Make it official. Are you making signs for all the cottages?" he asked.

"Yes, sir."

"Make sure you spell Mr. Reynolds' cottage correctly."

"F-I-S-H-T-A-L-E, yes, sir."

Slim smiled.

When the girls headed back out into the rain, they heard Slim say, "Ouch! You have got to file down those lethal fingernails of yours, Margie, if you want me to keep playing double solitaire with you."

Once outside under the huge umbrella, Grace said, "When I saw all those faces carved in the coconuts, I thought Coconut Cottage was a better choice."

"They're sort of eerie, but I like the monkey face."

"My favorite is the pirate with the tiny pipe sticking out of his mouth."

"Dad said Mr. Slim carved them all when he was stationed in the South Pacific," Annie explained.

"Why should the tenants have a vote anyway? They're your cottages. You should be able to name them anything you want," Grace told her.

This idea took Annie by surprise. Her cottages. She had never considered this before. The Knoll belonged to her father and mother, but one day, it would be hers.

Grateful when it stopped raining, the girls set up on the picnic table to paint the signs outside.

"What should I paint on Sun-swept?" Annie asked.

"How about a sun and a broom?" Grace suggested.

"Okay. What about Idlewhile Cottage?"

"I was thinking of Miss Agnes' rocker."

"You'd better paint that one. I think a rocker is too hard for me," Annie said. "And Cottage 12 still has no name."

"That's it. No Name Cottage," Grace declared.

"What'll we paint on the sign?"

"Question marks."

"Question marks I can handle," Annie told her.

As planned, Annie painted and lettered the more straightforward signs while Grace tackled the ones requiring more artistry. She had a relatively smooth time with the Belted Kingfisher and Blue Heron. Naturally a Cockatiel was easily done because she had made drawings of Pete many times in the past. However, she went through three boards and still wasn't satisfied with her Ruby-throated Hummingbird for Hummingbird Haven.

"We're going to run out of wood before you're happy," Annie teased, admiring Grace's perfectionism.

Oliver flew down to visit the girls at the picnic table. Annie wouldn't stop painting to scratch his head, so he flew off with Grace's favorite thin brush, dripping green paint as he took off.

"Come back here, Oliver," Annie yelled.

Oliver landed several yards away in the grass. He dropped the brush and called out to tease her. *Caw, caw, caw*.

As Annie approached, he grabbed the brush with his beak

and flew several more feet away. He landed and repeated his mischievous cry.

Knowing there was no way she could win, Annie gave up and went back to the picnic table.

"But I want that brush," Grace complained.

"Get it yourself," Annie joked.

"If he won't give it back to you, he sure isn't going to let me have it. Stupid crow."

"He just wants some attention," Annie explained.

Oliver picked up the stolen brush, flew over the table and dropped the brush directly into a surprised Grace's lap. After a few aerial displays, the crow landed next to Annie and waited for a rewarding head and neck scratching. This time Annie obliged.

"You spoil that bird," Grace remarked as she returned to painting the humming bird.

"Oh, and you don't spoil Pete?"

"Not as much as you do."

"Hogwash."

"It's Oliver this and Oliver that. You'll probably marry an Oliver," Grace quipped.

"Wouldn't that be funny if you married a Pete and I married an Oliver?"

Annie's mother came out the door with a load of laundry to hang on the line.

"Can we have some glue?" Annie asked.

"'May we?" Liz corrected her.

"May we have the glue? We want to put shells and glass and drift wood around the borders of the signs."

"It's in the junk drawer."

Noticing the two rejected hummingbird signs cast to one side of the picnic table, Liz said to Grace, "I know who could help you with that hummer."

Tossing her brush into the water pail, Grace was all ears.

"Mr. Packard might be willing to take a look at it for you,"

Liz continued.

"Mr. Packard?" Annie asked in disbelief.

"We're not to bother him," Grace said.

"He's a hermit," Annie added, her eyes wide.

"We want you children to respect Mr. Packard's privacy, but you don't need to be frightened of him. We'll go over after dinner," Liz told them. Both the girls were speechless.

That evening, Annie and Grace reluctantly followed Liz over the fence behind Sunrise Cottage. The ever-curious Oliver, of course, flew along. The girls carried their paints and the sign through the field toward the Marlboro house where it sat in a grove of trees overlooking the bay. Liz carried surplus vegetables from her garden.

When Luke and Liz first moved to the Knoll eleven years ago, they had initiated the neighborly exchanges of vegetables and fish with Packard's parents. Shortly after that, Mr. and Mrs. Marlboro had died within a year of each other, leaving their nineteen-year-old son to fend for himself. Packard continued the occasional neighborly exchanges but seldom any conversation.

As they neared his house, Mr. Packard was standing at his easel on the front porch. Oliver flew ahead, landing gracefully on the porch railing next to the artist. Packard didn't seem to mind Oliver coming to pay a visit, but when he turned and saw Liz and the girls trailing behind, his dark eyes flashed. Then he turned his easel away from them, and Annie's stomach lurched.

"Good evening, Mr. Packard," Annie's mother said from the lawn.

"Miss Liz, Miss Annie Crow," he responded and looked at Grace.

"This is Annie's friend Grace," Liz told him.

He nodded and stood stiffly.

"Nice to meet you, Mr. Packard," Grace managed to say.

Liz nudged Annie's shoulder to inform her that she was

being rude.

"Good evening, Mr. Packard," Annie stammered. She was glad to be standing down in the yard between her mother and Grace.

Liz cleared her throat. "Here are some tomatoes and a zucchini."

"Thank you." He moved to the steps, took the sack and began lining the tomatoes up on his porch railing so that Liz could take her sack back with her. Oliver hopped along the railing to inspect the first juicy tomato.

"That's not for you!" Annie scolded her crow.

"Best to let him have one," Packard conceded. "Then maybe he'll leave the rest alone." And with that, Oliver began poking a hole in the tomato.

Liz explained that the girls were making up signs and asked if he could help with the one for Hummingbird Haven.

"The hummers won't stay still long enough for me to get a really good look," Grace explained.

"Do you know that the males and the females are different?" he asked.

"Yes, the males are a little smaller and have a ruby patch on their throats."

"Do you have access to a bird book?"

"Why didn't I think of that?" Liz interrupted nervously. "Of course. We have a book, and you can copy the picture from there." She picked up her sack and began to move the girls away.

"Let me see what you've done so far," Packard said to Grace.

Grace walked up onto the porch with her work.

Packard's large, bear paw hands held up the sign. His dark eyes studied Grace's efforts at the ruby throat. After a good look, he placed it on one of the several rockers that lined his long porch, facing the water.

While Annie wondered why Mr. Packard had so many

rockers when no one ever visited him, suddenly, he picked up his own brush and pallet and began painting a humming bird directly on the white clapboard wall next to his front door. With his brush in hand, the large, stiff man became agile and fluid in his movements. Annie noted that among the paints on his pallet were various greens, along with black, white and red as if he were expecting them to arrive this evening and ask for help painting a Ruby-throated Hummingbird.

In a few moments, he was done.

Grace was awestruck. "I wish that I could paint like that."

"You're on your way already," Packard told her as he picked up her sign again.

"See the body line here? And the eyes?" He pointed to her painting and then to his. "You're very close."

"Would you paint it for us?" Annie found her tongue.

"That won't be necessary," he said. "Grace can do it herself if she can borrow Miss Liz's bird book."

"Of course she can," Liz said.

"She *may*," Annie whispered. But Mr. Packard overheard and Annie noticed him smile a little.

Then she saw her mother shoot her a reprimanding look before adding, "Of course she may borrow the book."

"Thank you, Mr. Packard. I see what I need to do now," Grace added.

After Liz, Oliver and the two girls disappeared into the trees, Packard turned back to his painting of the climbing rose against his porch column, but the light had changed. As he organized his paints to clean up, he laughed quietly at the male Ruby-throated Hummingbird now on his house.

CHAPTER THREE
SPRING 1957

IT WAS JUST AFTER DAWN when Packard Marlboro tossed his satchel containing a sketch pad, plenty of pencils, a thermos of coffee, and corn bread wrapped in wax paper up into Luke and Big Black Bo's deer stand in the woods above Cattail. He climbed up and settled in to draw.

Annie wasn't up yet, so Oliver, as he often did, followed the man and perched in a nearby tree. Pack started with a pencil sketch of Oliver staring back at him. The previous day, he'd done a drawing of Oliver dive-bombing an eagle. Earlier that spring, Oliver had taken up the dangerous habit of tormenting the local Bald Eagles that fished the waters above Promise. Pack guessed the reason for these daredevil antics might be that the crow was trying to impress potential mates. Pack had also seen two mature bald eagles lock talons and spin perilously close to the water only to separate at the last moment and fly off. He was sure they had mated and were feeding their young now, which made Oliver's game a perilous one.

The sun had risen up above the treetops now, making the inky colors of the crow's feathers glow. Suddenly, as if Oliver knew that he was the center of attention, he fell forward and hung upside down from the branch, swinging like an acrobat.

Pack sighed and took it as a sign to eat some corn bread. He loosened the string he'd tied around the wax paper. This interested Oliver greatly. He righted himself and hopped from the tree into the deer stand. Pack tossed a few crumbs over, and the crow gobbled them down. Then he started pulling at Pack's bootlaces for more. The bread had to last Pack a while, so he shared one more morsel and put what remained into his bag.

"Hunt for yourself," he said aloud to Oliver, who cocked his head and flew off. *Annie is probably up*, Pack thought to himself.

"Go ahead. I know I'm only second fiddle," he said teasingly after the crow.

From the clear picture he had in his mind, Packard continued his drawing of Oliver until the familiar sound of what always reminded him of sneakers squeaking across a gymnasium floor took his focus off his work. It was an eagle screeching. Pack realized that he'd been hearing Oliver calling for a while, but in his concentration had tuned it out. The eagle screeched again.

Packard stood for a better view from the tree stand and spotted Oliver following an eagle. In hot pursuit positioned just over the eagle's tail, Oliver chased the huge bird out over the trees and toward the beach. Once clear of the treetops, the eagle flipped upside down in the air, and snatched the crow in his huge talons, silencing the intruder for good. Oliver dropped onto the sand below.

Back at Sunrise Cottage, Annie came outside the front porch to greet Oliver. Each and every morning, Oliver flew directly to her shoulder, but not today. She felt a knot in her stomach. She began calling to him and scanning the trees. Her father had repeatedly warned her that Oliver might one day find a mate and disappear.

Annie remembered when she made the decision to let Oliver fly. After nursing the baby crow back to health, he would no longer stay settled in his box on the screen porch. The curious young crow began testing his now fully feathered wings by hopping up onto the top of one of the porch rockers and flapping vigorously, rocking the chair back and forth until he had to take flight, smacking right into one of the screens and crashing to the floor in a heap.

"You're going to have to let that bird off the porch before he hurts himself," her father warned.

"But I'm afraid that he'll fly away and never come back."

"I told you that he isn't a pet, but since he is so clearly attached to you, you could clip his wings so he can't fly. They do that to the ravens at the Tower of London."

No, she decided, she couldn't take the joy of flight away from Oliver. So with the crow on her shoulder, she bravely walked off the screened porch. Her father watched with admiration as his curly-topped daughter and her black crow crossed the grass. Then Oliver took off.

"Oh, God, let him come back to her," Luke whispered as he followed with his pipe and tobacco pouch in his hand.

Annie watched Oliver take his first flight out over the water. Her heart pounded in her chest. She could live with him not returning to her, but prayed he wouldn't fall in the water and die. If he did, she'd never forgive herself for allowing him his freedom.

Oliver landed, not too gracefully, on a piling down on the dock. He called for Annie, who ran down the hill toward the pier. When she reached the bottom, Oliver took off again. This time with more confidence, he pounded his wings up and over the edge of the Knoll and landed on the porch roof.

"He's playing with me," Annie hollered to her father, as she started back up the hill.

Oliver called for her again and threw himself back into

the air.

Sensing that things were under control, Luke sat down to have a smoke at the picnic table.

As Annie's head appeared at the top of the knoll, Oliver swooped down and snatched Luke's tobacco pouch from the table.

"Hey!" Luke hollered.

"Looks like he wants you to quit smoking," Annie said breathlessly when she reached the table.

Oliver cried out from his new home in the oak tree. *Caw, caw.*

"That crow may win points with your mother after all," Luke told Annie.

Now, years later, when Oliver failed to greet her first thing in the morning, Annie worried that he had finally flown off for good.

Packard stood over the dead bird and saw Annie coming down the beach toward him. Then she began to run. What could he possibly say to her? He wanted to hide the crow's body from her, but he knew Annie would want to see what had happened to her pet.

She stopped a few feet away and stood staring down at Oliver. Then she looked up at Packard.

"The eagles have young. Oliver got too close to their nest, and one of the eagles killed him," he told her directly.

Wordlessly she approached Oliver and scooped his lifeless body up into her hands, holding him much as she had the day the gull dropped him at her feet in the sand. This time she felt no heartbeat against her palm. Annie looked up at Packard again. Her eyes were huge, brown, watery saucers. A limp, black wing cascaded over her white fingers. Then she turned and walked back toward the Knoll. Pack noticed her shoulders shaking as she carried her dead companion home.

Suddenly a portrait was in his head. Pack went back to the deer stand and stayed until nearly sunset, making preliminary sketches.

On his way back home, he once again cut across the Knoll so this time he could leave the sketch of Oliver he had done that morning for Annie. He rolled it up and tied it with the string from his corn bread wrappings. He quietly slipped it onto the front porch. He could hear voices inside but headed directly across the field to his house and up to his studio on the third floor to paint.

It was late morning. Packard had painted all night. He heard a faint knocking from deep in the house but ignored it. It was harder, however, to ignore the growling in his stomach. He hadn't eaten since the corn bread he had shared with Oliver the day before. But nothing could interrupt him.

The painting was there in the canvas before he started. All he had to do was release it. Or the painting was inside him, and he had to release it onto the canvas. Pack wasn't sure which was true, but he knew he had to paint until it was finished. He had worked through the night with lamps. The sun had been up for hours now, and he finally turned out the lights, and looked at the painting from a short distance. In it, Annie stood staring at the observer with Oliver dead in her hands. Her eyes. He hadn't gotten her eyes right yet.

Then the faint knocking sound came again.

"What the hell?" he muttered aloud.

Pack crossed to the open windows overlooking the water. He leaned out one window.

"Yeah?" was all he shouted to whoever was under his porch roof two floors below.

No answer.

"Who is it?" he yelled down, annoyed.

The mass of dark auburn curls appeared out from beneath

the front porch roof.

Annie had come off the porch and was now looking up at him from the lawn. She was holding a box.

"It's Annie, Mr. Packard."

"Wait, I'll come down," Pack said more softly and then banged his head on the window frame pulling himself back in. "Shit," he muttered and rubbed the back of his head as he climbed down both sets of stairs and crossed the living room to open the front door. Annie had never come over here by herself, and Pack felt a little alarmed.

"What is it, Annie, are you all right?" he asked as he crossed his porch to the steps.

She took a gulp, dug at the ground with one sneakered toe and then spoke.

"I want to bury Oliver at sea." She gestured with the shoebox, which Pack presumed held the remains. "My folks don't understand this at all. They said to bury him in the yard. Daddy even offered to dig a hole someplace special on the Knoll, but it isn't right."

Pack scratched his head and then winced from touching the spot that he'd hit on the window frame.

"Oliver flew," Annie continued. "He doesn't belong in the ground. I can't bury him in the air, so I thought the water was the next best thing." She paused. "I was wondering if you'd take me out in your boat so I could bury him at sea."

Pack hadn't slept in thirty hours and hadn't eaten in twenty-six, but he found himself explaining how Oliver could be returned to the air and have a burial at sea as well.

When Annie's face lit up at the idea, Pack told her to wait in the yard while he ran back up to his studio. Once there, he opened a can of linseed oil and poured some into the glass Mason jar he kept by his easel. He tossed the wet brushes in and put the lid back on the can. Along with the can of linseed oil, a set of matches and some string, he grabbed a primitive looking toy boat he'd made as a boy. It was nothing more than a flat board for the bow with a wooden dowel nailed on to hold a drooping handkerchief sail. He'd noticed it in the corner gathering dust a few weeks ago and wondered why the hell it was still there. Pack's house was filled with "I'll need that someday" but this time it was true. He knew just how this old toy could serve its final purpose.

Packard led Annie down his dock toward the skiff with the outboard motor. Next to it was his thirty-eight-foot Chesapeake Bay deadrise workboat. The name *Sophie* was painted in black on the round stern of the white boat Packard used to carve out a living from the bay.

"Who is Sophie?" Annie asked, as she sat down on the front seat of the skiff.

"My younger sister Sophia," Pack answered while tossing the lines into the bottom of the boat and stepping in with great agility for such a big man.

"That's a pretty name. I didn't know you had a sister."

"She died when she was a baby," he added.

"We're both only children," Annie said.

At twenty-eight, Packard hardly considered himself a child anymore, but the little girl's sincerity was so genuine that he couldn't help but smile.

"It's not so bad," he told her.

"No, I've gotten used to it," she answered.

"So, do you have any place in mind for Oliver?"

"Off Cattail," Annie said with certainty. It was where she had found Oliver and where he had died.

Packard tugged at the rope and the outboard motor started with a jolt. Annie clutched tightly to the shoebox holding Oliver's remains.

Packard was glad that the tide was going out as he maneuvered up river past the Knoll and toward Cattail. If there were any crow remains that didn't burn, they would go out into the bay and not be discovered later along the shoreline where Annie played.

In a couple weeks, Packard would be setting the stakes for his pound nets up river past Cattail, just as his father and grandfather had done before him. It was a two-man job, so he usually hired Big Black Bo to help him.

"This is good," Annie interrupted Packard's concerns when they reached the spot that suited her.

Pack cut the outboard motor and told her to secure the shoebox onto the small boat with the string. Then Pack held the burial boat over the water and poured linseed oil over the box and toy boat. He set it in the water and lit the match.

"Are you ready?" he asked Annie.

She nodded.

Pack held the match to the funeral pyre. The box went up in flames as the tide carried Oliver out toward the bay. The sail caught fire, too. They watched for some time as smoke and ashes floated up into the air.

Annie turned to Packard. When she moved her eyes from the burning shoebox to his face, he recognized in his portrait of her what he had yet to capture in her eyes. He first glimpsed her soul when she held the dead crow on the beach yesterday. At this moment, he saw it again.

Then suddenly, Annie moved next to him and threw her arms around his waist, burying her face in his shirt. Instinctively, Pack covered her shaking shoulders with his big arms. He worried for a moment how long she'd cry, but as quickly as the tears came, they stopped and Annie moved back to the front of the skiff.

They had drifted a distance from the burial boat, and she asked, while wiping her face with her sleeve, "Can we follow it to make sure he's all gone?" Always practical, she needed to be sure.

Packard started up the outboard and moved toward the still burning boat. The sail, the box and Oliver were gone. A small flame was still gnawing at what remained of the dowel and danced on the top of the charred board. Soon the water would extinguish it.

"I'm okay now. Would you please drop me off at the Knoll dock?" Annie asked.

Pack was relieved that she wanted to go straight home. He had to get back to the painting now that he knew what needed to be done with the eyes.

After she stepped up onto her dock, Annie squinted in the brilliant morning light. She shielded her face with one hand and looked directly down at Packard.

"You would have made a very nice brother," she told him.

Afraid that his voice would crack, Packard smiled and didn't say anything but nodded as he pulled away from the dock.

Annie noticed that *Sophie* was gone from Mr. Packard's dock the next morning. She worried when the workboat still didn't return by the following evening. She'd never taken any notice of his comings and goings before, but now they interested her very much.

After the second night with no sign of *Sophie*, Annie finally spoke to her father.

"He's fine," Luke reassured her. "He has to go where the fish are. You know that."

But she didn't. Not until she saw him standing over her precious crow, looking like he might cry himself, did she give much thought at all to what Mr. Packard did.

The next morning, Annie was the first one out the door. She found a bucket of fish on the porch step. She didn't go over to see how Mr. Packard was doing. She knew better than that. But it was a comfort to see *Sophie* back in her slip at his dock.

Luke started hammering lengths of wood up the trunk of the

oak tree where Oliver used to perch. The noise of his hammering brought Liz to the kitchen door.

"What are you doing, Luke?" She hollered at him while pulling her wind blown hair out of her mouth.

"Building Annie a crow's nest."

"A what?"

"A lookout, a tree house," he answered as he drove in another nail while standing on the already finished lower rung.

"Out over the water?" Liz asked with concern.

"She'll be all right. You can keep an eye on her from the kitchen window."

"Yes, a perfect view to give me a heart attack every time she's up there!" Liz slammed the door behind her.

Despite Liz's protests, the tree house was built. Luke labored every free hour he had, creating the floor, walls, and roof of the little house nestled up on three large limbs that served as the main supports. He made openings for windows and two doorways, one at the top of the ladder and one on the opposite wall, overlooking the water. A large, strong branch crossed directly over the door opening facing the river, and Luke secured a thick rope to it so Annie could swing out over the river and drop into the water.

He even painted a sign for the tree house that read "The Crow's Nest."

Annie watched the progress with wonder, but she missed Oliver desperately.

"Why do you look so glum?" her father asked as he was driving nails into the sign to hold it to the base of the oak tree.

"Maybe I shouldn't be up in Oliver's tree."

"Just remember that when someone dies, they don't expect us to stop living or living joyfully."

"You mean you think that Oliver would want me up there?"

"What do you think?'

Annie suddenly smiled and nodded. "I think he'd like me

to be having fun in his tree. Besides, his spirit might get lonely up there."

When her father went into the house to wash up, Annie climbed up the lengths of wood that created a ladder to her new tree house. She adored having Oliver's view of the world. In one direction, she had a view of Cattail and up river. In the opposite direction, she saw Mr. Packard's field and the woods where his house was now completely hidden by budding trees. Out the door-opening facing the water, she had a view of the Knoll beach and dock, as well as Mr. Packard's dock. Stretching out before her was the Chesapeake Bay.

Directly below, the water lapped at the shoreline. It didn't take her long to grab hold of the rope and take her first swing out over the river. She loved being suspended for a moment, during which she was truly flying, and then letting go and dropping. The pressure filled her head and lungs as she plunged deep into the cold water.

Chapter Four
Fall 1958

ANNIE LOADED A THERMOS OF hot cocoa, a blanket, her binoculars, a copy of *Romeo and Juliet*, and a new letter from Grace into a large wicker basket. When she reached the top of the ladder, Annie pulled on the rope that hauled her basket up to the Crow's Nest. She had everything she needed for the rest of the day.

She could hear the loud honking of migrating Canada Geese and the subtle lapping of the water on the beach. A breeze rustled the dry leaves still clinging to the branches around her. Their russet reds contrasted the brilliant blue sky above.

Annie cuddled under the blanket and read Grace's letter. The school year without her best friend seemed endless, and this was only the beginning of their long separation.

Deeply engrossed in the last paragraph of the letter, the sharp report of a shotgun from the marsh distracted Annie. She assumed that her father and Big Black Bo were hunting, but when she heard a cry for help, she looked out to see someone limping on the beach of Cattail. Annie grabbed her binoculars and focused them on the figure that then collapsed onto the ground. It was Bunky Watson, a boy a grade ahead of her in school.

Annie quickly scrambled down from the Crow's Nest, ran across the lawn and down the stairs to the dock. She stood for a moment and called to Bunky. She waved, and he waved back. Annie untied the lines to her father's skiff and jumped in. With three tugs, she started the outboard motor and pulled away from the pier. As Annie moved closer to Cattail, she saw Bunky look up in the sky with one arm over his eyes to block the sun. She looked up, too. The outboard motor had drowned out the sound of another flock of Canadas flying overhead.

Annie cut the motor, lifted it up and let the boat glide to shore. She hopped out, grabbed the front end and tugged it up onto beach, making a rasping sound over the sand.

"What happened?" Annie asked Bunky as she approached him.

"I shot myself in the damn foot!" he snarled.

That's what he'd been doing. Trying to shoot one of those poor birds. Annie wondered how the edge of the shot pattern hit Bunky's foot when he was aiming at the geese in the sky. However, there wasn't time to ask questions.

"Well, come on. Throw your arm over my shoulder so I can help you to the boat," she instructed.

Annie could barely pull him up onto his uninjured foot. Blood trailed behind them as she labored with the husky boy toward the skiff.

"What about my daddy's shotgun? I dropped it back there in the marsh," Bunky suddenly asked with concern.

"Leave it for now. We've got to get you to the doctor."

"But I wasn't supposed to take it by myself. He's going to kill me."

"Not if you die from loss of blood or lead poisoning first.

Now get into the boat."

"All my friends got their own shotguns long before now," he complained.

"I'll come back for it later with my father."

"Don't tell your father! He'll call my daddy!" Bunky whined.

"Judging from your foot, your father may be able to guess that you took his gun."

Annie's face was wet with sweat after getting big Bunky Watson to the boat. The air felt cool on her skin as she steered past the Knoll and toward the town beach. She hoped someone would be there to help her get him up the street to the new doctor who had just taken over for the retired Dr. Brown. There was blood in the boat now, and Bunky was getting pale.

When Annie pulled up to the town pier, she began blowing a series of three short blasts on the whistle that her father kept in the boat.

Miraculously, Mr. Packard appeared on the beach and came striding across the sand as she cut the motor.

Wordlessly, Pack lifted Bunky and cradled him like a huge toddler.

"Go back and get the shotgun, will you, Annie? It's my daddy's new Winchester, and he's going to skin me alive if anything happens to it," Bunky pleaded.

"You're lucky that you didn't blow off your damn head, Bunky Watson!" Annie shouted at him as he and Packard headed off the beach and up the street to the doctor's office.

Annie drove the skiff back to the Knoll to find her father. They went together to retrieve the shotgun from Cattail.

As Luke unloaded the shells and put them into his pocket, he said, "Annie, I'm very proud of you. You did the right thing. All the right things."

Annie blushed. Praise from her father meant everything to her.

By the time Annie got back up into the Crow's Nest, her

cocoa was cold. In her rush to get to Bunky, she'd left the lid off the thermos. So much for her quiet afternoon alone, reading. She was no longer in the mood to enjoy tragic *Romeo and Juliet*.

Annie wrapped the blanket around her shoulders and looked out the bay side door of the Crow's Nest. In the distance, several lines of geese were crossing the bay. The sound of their honking grew louder and louder as they traveled past the Knoll and up river. Annie enjoyed shooting when her father set up old tin cans for target practice, but how could anyone want to kill one of these beautiful creatures, she wondered?

"Phone, Annie," her mother hollered out the cottage door.

Annie hated leaving this cacophony of their calls, but once again she scrambled down the ladder and in the kitchen door.

"It's the new doctor," Liz told her.

"Why does he want to talk to me?" Annie whispered.

"Ask him yourself," Liz said, handing her the phone.

"Hello?" Annie wondered if Bunky had died or something.

"Miss Annie Crow?"

"Yes."

"This is Doctor Linden. You are quite the heroine today."

"Is Bunky all right?" Annie asked.

"He wouldn't be, if you hadn't gotten him here as quickly as you did."

"How's his foot?"

"Well, I didn't have to amputate," the doctor joked, "but there won't be any more football for him this season."

"I'm glad he's okay," Annie said, not knowing what else to say.

"I'd like to meet you soon, and hopefully not because you're sick. Come by to say hello to my wife Miss Linda and me sometime, won't you? We're new here, and we're trying to get to know everyone."

"Sure," Annie said. She liked having an adult talk to her

like she was grown up.

"Mr. Watson said to thank you for saving Bunky's life."

Saving his life? Annie didn't think that she'd done anything quite that significant, but still she enjoyed the attention and thought about the exciting letter that she'd be writing to Grace tonight.

CHAPTER FIVE
FALL 1959

WHILE COTTAGES WERE BEING CLOSED up for the season, Annie's mother and Big Black Bo were discussing *Moby Dick* in the mornings at the picnic table, and in the evenings, her mother was reading *Macbeth* with Annie in her bedroom.

"I liked *Hamlet*, but *Macbeth* is more disturbing," Annie told her mother.

"What do you find disturbing?" Liz asked with interest.

"For one thing, why would Lady Macbeth say she would kill her own children for power?"

"Well, it's not natural for a woman to feel that way, and the play explores the natural, unnatural, and supernatural," Liz began.

"When did you start reading Shakespeare?" Annie asked.

"I don't remember exactly. When I was younger than you, my mother read plays by Shakespeare, Moliere, and Shaw aloud to me. She played all the characters' voices and emotions much better than I do because she actually studied acting."

Liz rarely spoke of her mother so Annie was eager to know more.

"What was my grandmother like?"

"She was lovely. She had curly, dark auburn hair, like yours."

"What happened to her?"

"She died before you were born. She was a very special person, which is why you are named for her."

"Where did you and her live?"

"You and she," Liz corrected.

"Where did you and she live?"

"I've told you before, Annie, with your great-grandmother Delia in the big brick house up river in Kingstown," Liz answered impatiently.

"You and Grandmother Ann never lived anywhere else before your father died?"

"No, and Mother wasn't well. Delia had to take care of us." Liz's voice had a finality that put an end to any more discussion of this topic.

"Do I have to visit her again this year?" Annie asked, with a roll of her eyes.

"For her birthday, yes."

"Why don't you ever go with me?"

Annie's mother ignored her question. "You can pick something out for her at Turner's Market before Mrs. Turner takes you up there."

"I don't like the way Great Grand's house smells," Annie said, wrinkling up her nose.

Tolerating Annie's nickname for Delia, Liz asked, "How does it smell?"

"Old and doggy."

Annie noticed that her mother tried not to laugh. She probably remembered how smelly those Pekinese lap dogs of Delia's could be since they had to be a hundred years old.

As the date of her great-grandmother's birthday visit approached, Annie complained in a letter to Grace that she was never comfortable going there. She shared her suspicions that her mother was hiding something.

Grace responded:

Dear Annie,

Your mother isn't the only one with secrets. I found out by accident that my mom has been seeing my dad. Grandmother found out, and I heard her arguing with Mom about him. But don't say anything about this to your mom. Okay?

As far as your mom hiding something about your grandmother, ask your dad. Maybe he knows the truth...

Annie had never thought to approach him. She had always asked Mama, who gave her the same limited, carefully rehearsed version of her own mother's life. Maybe her father did know and would be willing to tell her something.

She waited until her mother's weekly quilting night held in the church basement. She approached her father as he was reading the paper and purposefully asked him about his family first.

"What's on your mind?" he asked, as she sidled close to his armchair.

"Is it true that your great grandparents helped fugitive slaves escape?"

Without putting his paper down, Luke said, "I've told you that story a million times."

"Tell me again."

"My family was Quaker. They were against slavery, and during the Civil War, they helped slaves across the bay to the Susquehanna River and to Pennsylvania."

"Is that why Great Grand won't let you in her house?"

"Something like that."

"Why won't Mama talk about her mother?"

Luke put down his newspaper.

"What's this really all about?"

"Well, I can tell that something weird must have happened because Mama never wants to talk about her."

"It might be because of how she died," Luke answered.

"What do you mean?"

"I want to be honest with you, Annie, but your mother should be the one to tell you this."

"But she won't. I've asked and asked. Was Grandmother Ann murdered or something? Did Great Grand do something to her?"

"Your grandmother drowned in the river, Annie," Luke said carefully.

"Which river?"

"This one," Luke said, hesitantly. "Up in Kingstown."

"Did they find her body?" Annie asked.

"Yes." Luke answered.

"Good," Annie said, relieved that there was no chance of her running into Grandmother Ann while swimming.

"Are you okay?" he asked.

"Yep." Annie went into her room, pausing in the hall to take her parents' wedding album from the bookshelf.

As Annie held the album in her lap, she remembered the first time her mama had allowed her to open it many years ago. It contained a music box built in the cover, which played "*Let Me Call You Sweetheart*" when opened. Annie had looked carefully at each photograph, and when she finished, she had asked, "Why aren't I in any of the pictures?"

Annie flipped quickly now to find a picture of her mama in her gown, standing outside the First United Methodist Church in Chester Landing. Grandmother Ann was next to her.

Annie studied the photograph closely. Her grandmother was beautiful, but there was a sadness to her eyes. She looked tired.

Annie heard her parents talking when her mother returned from quilting. Her father's voice rose.

"If she's old enough to ask, then she's old enough to know the truth, Liz. All of it."

Annie looked up from the wedding album when her mother appeared in her bedroom door.

"She looks more like your older sister than your mother."

"You resemble her," Liz said.

"You think so?"

"Definitely. You have her lovely curly hair and her perfect nose."

"Where's your father?" Annie asked.

"I never knew him."

"Did he die when you were a baby?"

"Now, Annie, it's time for bed. You have a big day tomorrow."

"Mama, I don't want to go tomorrow."

"It's Delia's seventy-fifth birthday. She's your only living relative other than your father and me," Liz said and began to leave to put the album back in its place on the hall bookcase. "Besides, I've already made arrangements with Mrs. Turner. As usual, she will drop you off on her way to visit her sister and pick you up on her way back."

"How old would your mother be now if she hadn't drowned?"

"I don't know. Go to sleep," Annie's mother said as she walked out and closed the door.

On the morning of her great-grandmother's birthday, Annie searched Turner's Market for a gift.

"I can't believe it's that time of year again," Mrs. Turner remarked when Annie asked to smell the lilac cologne in a pretty purple bottle at the front counter.

"Afraid so," she answered as she put the bottle to her nose.

Mrs. Turner smiled and said, "Do you like that cologne?"

"It'll do. I don't think she likes or uses anything I give

her."

"Delia Witherspoon doesn't deserve what you give her every year." Mrs. Turner rang up the sale and wrapped the bottle in tissue paper with a pretty ribbon.

"What did she do, anyway?" Annie asked.

"Do?" Mrs. Turner seemed to realize that she'd said too much and patted her graying red hair in her customary way. "Nothing. She's just undeserving, that's all."

"Can't I stay here at the store while you visit your sister and then you can drop me off at the Knoll as if I visited my great-grandmother?" Annie asked.

"I'm afraid not, but let's take some cookies to eat on the way. You never know what you'll get at your great-grandmother's. Everyone knows how tight Delia Witherspoon is. You'll be lucky if she feeds you week-old crackers."

Unwilling to go directly to the Witherspoon house, Mrs. Turner always pulled over at the corner so Annie had to walk up the block to one of the few remaining pre-nineteenth century structures that the British didn't burn when they advanced along the Sassafras River in 1813.

Annie guessed that Mrs. Turner was full of hot air and was actually afraid of Great Grand. A lot of people were.

As usual, when Annie rang the doorbell, Walter answered the door. His ancestors had been slaves on the Witherspoon properties, and his mother had been the housekeeper. Walter had been born here, and as far as Annie knew, he had never left.

"Good afternoon, Miss Annie," the older gentleman said with perfect diction.

"Good afternoon, Mr. Walter. How are you?"

"Starting to feel my age, Miss Annie."

Unsure of an appropriate response, Annie said, "Sorry to hear that."

Then she handed him a carefully wrapped package from her mother. Liz always sent some treat along with Annie for

Walter's sweet tooth.

Walter smiled. "Tell Miss Liz thank you."

"Yes, sir."

"I'll let Miss Delia know that you are here."

Annie was left standing in the huge central hall, which was flanked by solid mahogany double doors on either side. A grand staircase, starting on the left, led to a beautiful stained glass window on the landing before the stairs disappeared up to the right. Under the right side of the stairs was another door that led out to a garden room. That was where Delia always took Annie. Annie realized that she'd never even seen behind the double doors or up the stairs. She hadn't ever used a bathroom in this house. She was grateful for a strong bladder.

Suddenly three nasty Pekinese dogs raced out from behind the door located under the stairs. They barked and snarled at Annie. When one nipped at her ankle, Annie pushed at it with her foot.

"Don't kick Sweet Pea!" Her great-grandmother's voice boomed from the end of the hall.

The dogs kept barking, and Annie couldn't hear herself think.

Delia picked up the offending dog and cuddled it in her large chest. "Oh, my poor baby. Don't let this mean little girl scare you."

The other two dogs settled down next to Delia's swollen feet, which poured over the edges of her tiny tan pumps. The dogs eyed Annie as if they'd rip her apart when given the command.

"Oh, my Sweat Pea," Delia said, kissing the dog's flat face on the lips.

Annie was glad that her great-grandmother never kissed her.

"Happy Birthday," she said, holding out the wrapped bottle of lilac cologne as a peace offering.

"Well, come on then," Delia said and walked back into the

garden room.

Annie followed the dogs, the gift still in her hand.

After battling the Pekinese dogs, offering another ignored birthday gift and being ushered onto the sun porch for tea, Annie had had enough. She wasn't seated for long before she burst out.

"How did you feel when my grandmother drowned?"

Delia's stern face turned fierce, and Annie felt a knot turn in her stomach.

"Who told you that?" her great-grandmother demanded.

"My father—and mother," Annie answered, fiddling with the napkin in her lap.

"It was an accident. Ann fell into the river and couldn't swim," Delia said.

For a moment, Great Grand looked as if she might actually cry. Annie saw her face turn soft and her eyes glisten.

"I didn't mean to upset you," Annie said quietly.

"I'm not upset," Delia said, pulling herself together in an instant. "You'd better go now. I don't want you here."

"But Mrs. Turner won't be back to pick me up for another hour," Annie explained.

"I don't care. Get out of here!" she shouted as she hauled her large body out of her chair and raised a hand to Annie.

Annie's parents never hit her, and she wasn't going to let anyone else do it either. Her napkin fell to the floor as Annie scampered out of her chair and ran to the hallway. She could hear the dogs barking in hot pursuit. She bolted out the front door, being sure to shut it, and dashed across the lawn. The dogs were left scratching at the other side of the big door.

Then there was silence. Annie half expected the door to fly open, but nothing happened. She heard a cardinal chirping from one of the dogwood trees that lined Great Grand's front yard.

A face appeared at one of the first floor windows. It was Walter. Annie hadn't said goodbye to him. He raised a hand with a gentle wave and then disappeared behind the lace curtain.

Tears burned in Annie's eyes and a hard knot lodged in her throat as she walked down to the corner, turned onto the main street of Kingstown and headed toward the bridge that spanned the river. A breeze picked up at the water. It felt cool on her hot face and the flood of emotions she felt began to subside.

Once Annie made it halfway across the bridge, she leaned on the railing and looked up to where she could see Delia's brick house on the hill. The perfectly manicured lawns flowed down to the water's edge.

Annie pictured her grandmother floating under the very bridge where she now stood watching the current swirl beneath her. She thought of *Hamlet*'s Ophelia and hoped that her grandmother had had flowers in her hair.

Chapter Six
Summer 1960

FROM WHAT ANNIE COULD FIGURE, the tension between her parents began right after she told them that Delia Witherspoon had said to get out and never come back. Annie had added the instructions not to return and tried not to feel guilty about this embellishment, despite the fact that her parents seemed to be walking on egg shells ever since.

Annie's mother changed after that day. She apologized for everything and nothing. Luke said not to apologize and then she'd apologize for that. After Annie went to bed, she overheard them speak in angry whispers.

"If you're not going to tell her the truth, then let it go, Liz," her father said. "Forget about it until it comes out on its own, which it will someday."

When Annie wrote about it to her best friend, Grace didn't respond with her usual sympathy.

Hey Annie,

Welcome to the club. I don't remember a time when my

folks weren't fighting. I wished they'd just get divorced. I know my grandmother would prefer it. But Dad still drives up here and takes Mom out on dates! They are a pair of nuts. But you're lucky. Your parents are probably just going through a phase. They'll get over it... .

The season was opening in one week, and Annie had never witnessed such chaos and disorganization with her parents. For the first time, they might not be ready for the tenants.

On top of an endless list of repairs to the cottages, the roof of Sunrise Cottage had leaked in the spring. Luke and Big Black Bo had patched the roof but hadn't had time to repair the damaged and stained plaster ceiling of the living room.

While Annie poured cereal into a bowl, she heard her mother say, "I know that you and Bo are up to your necks with the season about to open, but I can't have tenants coming in here and seeing this mess. Let me do something about it."

"You don't know how to plaster, Liz. I'd teach you, but there just isn't time," Luke explained as he sat down to put on his work boots.

"Bo said that the two of you working together could get it patched in a day. Then I'd paint it. You'd only be giving me a day, Luke. Please."

"That was before I turned the water back on for the rest of the cottages yesterday, and the water heater in Fish Tale leaked. I had water all over, and I have to replace the damn thing, which means a trip to Chester Landing to buy a new one, and that'll eat up more than an hour." Luke felt in his coat pockets. "Have you seen my keys?"

"While you're buying the water heater, couldn't Bo and I start working on this embarrassment?" Annie's mother gestured to the stained living room ceiling.

"If it'll get you to stop complaining, go ahead," Annie's father snapped.

Her mother looked like she was on the verge of tears. She glanced at the kitchen clock and said to Annie who had stopped eating her cereal, "You're going to miss the bus to school."

"I'll drive her," Luke said, having found his keys on the counter.

"No, I'll be all right," Annie told him and dashed to get her books from her bedroom. When she emerged, her father's truck was gone.

"Hurry up," Liz called.

Annie nearly ran into Bo as she raced down the front steps.

"Sorry, Mr. Big Black Bo. Hope the bus waits for me."

Annie hurried along the drive, and when she reached the entrance to the Knoll, she saw the school bus disappearing down Baycliff Road. She hollered and ran after it as far as Mr. Packard's property, but the bus driver never saw her. She paused to catch her breath before turning to trudge home. Now her parents would be angry with her for missing school, but then again, maybe she could help her mom and Big Black Bo repair the ceiling or her father install the water heater. Her father had been teaching her how to use tools and fix things, and she was proud to be able to do a lot more now.

With that cheery thought, Annie picked up her pace back to Sunrise Cottage. When she opened the door, they didn't hear her. She watched her mother wrap her arms around Big Black Bo's waist and hug him. He hesitantly put his arms around her shoulders, as he was a good foot taller than she was. They were still for a moment before they both seemed to realize at the same time that they were not alone. They looked toward the door and saw Annie.

Annie dropped her schoolbooks in the doorway, bolted out of the cottage and took off for Cattail. Her mind was reeling as she ran down the steps to the beach. Her mother's voice calling out to her sounded foreign. Nothing was going to stop her from escaping what she'd seen.

What had she seen? Annie wasn't really sure, but it didn't feel good. Her mother didn't belong in anyone's arms but her father's. That was a certainty.

When she reached the end of the beach, Annie realized that the tide was high. She would have to pick her way through the briars above the tide line. Usually she did this with care, but she couldn't slow down. There was a force pushing her away from her mother.

Annie didn't feel the thorns cutting into her bare ankles. Nor did she notice the blood dripping down her legs. She was out of her body.

The same body that betrayed her with changes she couldn't understand. Her shape was transforming, and this drew the attention of the boys, who treated her differently now. They wanted to kiss her and even tried to touch her. Annie felt awkward and less agile. This was painfully obvious to her as she attempted to leap over the stream separating her from Cattail at high tide, and her ankle twisted into the soft sand on the far side. Annie came crashing down onto the cool, damp beach.

She just lay there, the pulse beating in her temples. Her breathing hurt her lungs. Her mother had stopped calling. Or perhaps Annie was just far enough away for the rush of water to drown out her past, her childhood, her innocence as well as her mother's voice.

Just before dinnertime, Annie came in limping, with dried blood on her ankles and socks.

"What the hell happened to you?" Luke asked as she walked gingerly on her swollen ankle.

"I fell over on Cattail."

"Looks like a raccoon attacked you. Are you all right?" Luke asked.

"Fine."

"Better let your mother put some ice on that."

Liz moved to help Annie but when their eyes met, Liz

froze.

"I'll get the ice myself," Annie snapped. "I'm a big girl now."

"Stay off it for a couple days. You should have gotten ice on it sooner, but this bandage will help support it. The swelling will be gone in time for the weekend," Doc Linden said as he finished with the elastic bandage.

His fingers had squeezed her ankle when he'd examined it, and Annie had shivered. He was so young and so handsome. He made coming to the doctor's office dangerous and fun. But today, it didn't feel like an adventure. It felt like a trial, and Annie was on the witness stand with information she could not reveal. She wanted someone to hear what she had seen and explain it to her.

"Annie, did you hear what I said?"

"Yes," she answered automatically. She guessed he must have been telling her about how to use the crutch.

"All right then. Off you go with the crutch. Just keep most of your weight on the other foot."

When Annie hobbled out the door of the examination room, she was relieved to find that her father was the only one in the waiting room.

Doc followed her. "She'll be fine. Just a sprain. Nothing's broken," he told Luke. "Maybe it's time you stopped racing around like a boy on Cattail, Annie. Be more of a lady like your mother."

Oh sure. If he only knew, Annie scowled to herself.

There was a sudden splash over the end of the dock as Tommy and Jack Reynolds wrestled and then pushed each other into the bay at the same time. The cold water stung Annie's skin. She was hot from lying on her towel in the sun.

Boys were so immature, she thought to herself when the icy spray hit her. Her ankle was no longer swollen, but she just didn't feel like the usual horseplay with the boys. She threw an arm over her eyes to block out the piercing sunrays.

Things got quiet, and then she felt water dripping on her skin. She opened her eyes and discovered Tommy standing over her, his legs straddling hers. He was grinning down at her as droplets from his wet body fell on her.

"What do you think you're doing?"

"Peeing on you." Tommy sneered.

"Gross!" Annie pushed on his legs but he didn't budge.

"Where's your sidekick gone?" Annie noticed that Jack had disappeared, and she and Tommy were alone.

"He decided to swim to the town beach. See what's going on down there."

Annie could see Jack's head bobbing in the water as he swam the half-mile to town. She rolled over so her butt was facing Tommy.

"Why didn't you go with him?"

"I prefer the scenery here."

"Oh that's original."

Tommy sat down close to her. His wet skin felt cool next to her.

"Come on, Annie. Meet me tonight to go skinny dipping."

"You've got to be joking."

"I'm dying to get a look at you. I won't touch you or anything."

"Damn right, you won't."

"Then you'll do it?"

"I didn't say that."

"You're dying to see me, too. Admit it."

"I am not!" Annie got up, grabbed her towel and headed up the dock toward the stairs.

Tommy gave an appreciative whistle as Annie walked away from him in her two-piece bathing suit.

"It's a full moon tonight. I'll be here at midnight…waiting," he called after her.

Annie walked into Sunset Cottage just in time to hear Tommy's mother say to Liz, "Surely Luke was in here helping Big Black Bo do the work on the ceiling."

"No, Luke was too busy replacing your water heater," Annie's mother replied.

"Well, I sure wouldn't want to be alone in the house with Big Black Bo," Mrs. Reynolds sniffed, as she handed over her rent check.

"Why wouldn't you?" Liz snapped.

"Well, look at all those riots and lootings. You certainly know those people can't be trusted."

Annie cleared her throat. Her mother and Jean Reynolds both turned to see her standing there.

"Well, isn't that a cute suit," Mrs. Reynolds said as she examined Annie. "How old are you now?"

"Fourteen," Annie answered.

"You certainly are developing a figure," she added, as she headed to the front door. "I bet the boys can't take their eyes off you."

Annie felt compelled to follow Tommy's mother out the door. She stopped on her front porch though and watched Mrs. Reynolds head straight next door to Mrs. Miller, who was watering her newly planted geraniums. They stood in front of Kingfisher Cottage talking about Liz allowing Big Black Bo to work right inside her cottage without Luke being there.

At that moment, Annie decided she would go skinny dipping with Tommy Reynolds at midnight. She wondered what Grace would think. But Grace and Mae weren't due on the Knoll for several more days. Annie considered trying to call, but after some thought, she decided it was best not to ask for anyone's opinion on this. She'd just do it.

The full moon provided more light than Annie expected at midnight. The idea of seeing Tommy's private parts floating unencumbered in the water made her want to gag so she kept an inner tube floating between them. Because Tommy had nothing on, she finally felt obliged to slip off the bottom of her bathing suit.

"Come on, Annie, the top too."

"That's not fair. All you had to take off was the bottom."

"That's right. You get to see my sexy chest anytime. Now show me yours."

"You'd better not tell anyone," Annie warned knowing that this would make him need to tell even more.

She tied the bottom of her suit to the inner tube, then reached around and unsnapped the back of her top and let it float off her shoulders. Tommy stared longingly over the inner tube at Annie's breasts, shimmering just under the water.

"You're beautiful, Annie."

She hated herself for it, but she blushed.

"I'll never forget this, Annie. Never."

Tommy dove under the inner tube and circled her like a shark. The moonlight hit his body beneath the surface. Annie hadn't seen a man nude before. She was fascinated as she watched him holding his breath for what seemed like forever as he admired her from his underwater vantage. Then he stopped in front of her, his hair floating around his face like a halo from a religious painting. He reached his hand out under the water, one finger extended toward her belly. Annie held her breath, but he stopped less than an inch away and broke the surface of the water with a wolf call.

"Shut up!" Annie whispered loudly.

He stood in the water with that silly grin of his. Their eyes were locked, and then he looked down at himself, and she followed his gaze to below his waist.

"Holy cow!" Annie gasped.

Tommy laughed and swam to the dock where he'd left his suit. He didn't bother with the ladder but lifted his body right out of the water with his strong arms flipping himself around to face her. Her effect on him was still apparent.

I caused that! Annie realized. The power of it flooded her senses. She tied the top of her suit to the inner tube and swam away imagining herself as a mermaid. She felt the caress of the water all over her naked body, caresses of a lover.

When she looked back to the dock, Tommy and his suit were gone.

Silly boy, she thought. When the time came, he would never be her lover. He was beautiful, but not worthy. By morning his ego would have him bragging to everyone how he'd seen Miss Annie Crow naked. No, someone else would be her first lover, someone who deserved her.

It was barely noon when Annie's mother heard the news. Tommy must have made quick work of it, since he rarely got out of bed before lunchtime these days.

"How could you, Annie? These people are our customers, our livelihood," Liz scolded.

"Don't talk to me, Mother."

"Everyone on the Knoll is talking about you!" Liz retorted.

"At least they've stopped talking about you being alone in here with Big Black Bo, which is much worse for business, if that's all you're worried about. And they don't even know the half of it."

"Annie, please let me explain!"

"There's nothing to explain, Mother. I saw you!" Annie's voice rose.

"Please, your father is just outside. He'll hear you," Liz begged.

"You are a hypocrite!"

The color drained from her mother's face, and Annie knew she had landed the punch. Before Annie could say anything more, Liz walked outside with her head down, joining Luke.

When Annie saw her parents talking, she moved closer to the window.

"Did you talk to her about it, Liz?"

"Yes."

"Does she understand that these people are our customers?"

"But Jean Reynolds is acting like Annie demoralized her little boy!" To Annie's surprise, it sounded like her mother was defending her.

"Even so, why can't she play 'doctor' with one of the locals? Then I'd be free to take the little shit down to the end of the pier and adjust his smug attitude. But Tommy would run to his mommy, and then she'd pack up her cottage, and her brother and his wife would inevitably pack up their cottage, too, and we would be in worse financial trouble."

"Is that all you care about? Our fourteen-year-old daughter is being … seduced by Tommy Reynolds, who is nearly two years older than she is, and you're thinking about what it'll cost you!"

Uncharacteristically, Annie's mother turned defiantly toward the other cottages and put her hands on her hips. Her father grabbed his wife by the arm and pulled her around to the side of Sunrise Cottage away from anyone's view. Annie quietly moved toward a side window and knelt down on the floor.

"What's happening to us, Liz?" Her father sounded sad.

"It's like we're living in a fish bowl here sometimes," Liz complained.

"And?"

"You work very hard, Luke, and I appreciate it so much."

"So do you. I don't run the place by myself."

"But sometimes—a lot of times, you act like you do. It's always about the Knoll and the other cottages and the tenants. Frankly, I don't know where Annie and I fit in anymore."

"Then let's sell it. We'll find something else to do," he blurted out in a desperate tone.

"Sell the Knoll? I don't want to do that!" Her mother paused. "It used to be fun, Luke. Remember the first year when we lived in the Honeymoon Cottage? It was freezing cold in there, and we didn't have two extra dimes to rub together, but we were happy."

"We still don't have two extra dimes to rub together."

"That's not true. We have to be careful, but we are financially better off than we were fifteen years ago. We're just not happy."

The frankness of her mother's voice startled Annie.

"You and Annie come first. The Knoll comes second," her father said.

"That's easier said than done, Luke."

"Maybe you should do a cross-stitch of it to remind me," Luke tried to joke.

"Maybe you should get it tattooed on your forehead," Liz retorted.

It was quiet. Then Annie heard her mother coming back inside, so she dashed into the kitchen and tried to look busy. After hearing her parents' bedroom door slam shut, she peered out at her father who sat on the back stoop with his head in his hands.

Annie wondered how Mama could do this to him. The anger she felt toward her mother burned in her throat. And Big Black Bo was her father's best friend! But Annie didn't feel the same rage toward Bo. Perhaps because she clearly remembered her mother hugging Bo first, while he had hesitated. Annie didn't understand it, but she was sure that this was entirely her mother's fault.

Annie thought if one more person talked to her about her reputation that she was going to kill them. Why wasn't anyone concerned about Tommy's reputation? Instead, he seemed to grow in stature on the Knoll after their skinny dipping escapade.

"It isn't fair," she complained to Grace on the first morning she arrived for the summer.

"Guys get all the breaks."

The girls sat together in their bathing suits on the end of the dock. Their feet dangled near the water.

"No one is thinking any less of Tommy, but they sure are of me."

"I don't think less of you," Grace told her.

"Neither do I," Maizie said. She had walked down the dock unnoticed and took Annie and Grace by surprise.

"Good morning, Dr. Maizie," the girls said nearly simultaneously.

She sat down with them. When she dangled her long legs off the dock, her feet reached the water.

"I appreciate that you don't think I'm some sort of fallen woman or anything," Annie said.

"Obviously the talk isn't fair to you, Annie, but was the experience?" the older woman asked.

"What do you mean?" Annie wasn't clear.

"Did he push you to do anything you didn't want to do?"

"Oh, no!"

"Good," Maizie said with relief in her voice.

"All anyone is talking about is that he saw you, but—"

Grace paused. "Did you see him?" she asked with a blush.

"Oh, boy, did I!"

"Oh, my God!" Grace rolled right off the dock and into the cool water with a splash. When she surfaced and pulled herself back up onto the dock, she asked, "Why did you do it in the first place?"

"I don't know," Annie lied. She couldn't bring herself to reveal wanting to shift the gossip from her mother and Big Black Bo to herself.

"Natural curiosity is healthy," Dr. Maizie said. "But do you both know what can happen when a man and woman have sex?"

Grace looked about to throw herself back into the river, but Maizie reached across Annie and grabbed Grace's arm. "This is serious now."

Grace stayed where she was.

"The same as any mammals like dogs, cats, horses or deer. They get pregnant," Annie answered.

"Yes, and you don't want that until you are much older," Dr. Maizie advised. "And there are ways to keep from getting pregnant so you talk to me before you do anything. If I'm not around, go to Dr. Linden up in town."

"Doc?" Annie gasped. "I couldn't talk to him about this stuff."

"He was in medical school when Sam and I were residents. He's a good guy. You can go to him, but let's hold off for several more years."

"Why didn't you come to be our doctor here in Promise?" Annie asked.

"I don't think the Eastern Shore is ready for a woman doctor."

"My mom says it's like we're going back ten years in time when we come down here," Grace said.

"More like twenty, but then, that's part of its charm," Maizie admitted.

"Did you want to become a pediatrician, or was it because, you know, women and babies?" Annie asked.

"That's an excellent question," Maize said unruffled. "If I'd wanted to be a brain surgeon, I would have done that. However, I thought I could do more good working with women and children. I love babies, and it was perfect with Sam going into gynecology. After a baby is born, he passes the patient right next door to me. We're also starting a clinic to work with young, unwed mothers."

"That's important stuff you're doing," Annie told her heroine.

"Thanks. It's important to do what you love."

"I love art," Grace said. "I want to be an artist, but one that makes money. You know, do drawings for magazines, or maybe photography. I don't want to depend on my husband for my money."

"That's smart. What about you, Annie?" Dr. Maizie asked.

She thought for a moment. "I know what I don't want to do."

"What's that?"

"I don't want to learn to sew and cook. Mama has signed us up for Mrs. Turner's Young Ladies Club." Annie wrinkled her nose.

"We're going to make pillows and bake cookies," Grace said with excitement.

"Oh, please," Annie moaned.

"It's only once a week and not until next month," Grace explained. "I'm looking forward to it."

"You would!" Annie rolled her eyes.

"Hey, you have to eat, so cooking can be helpful. And don't knock sewing. Look at the gowns your mother made for my wedding," Dr. Maizie remarked.

"I'm all thumbs around her sewing machine. But I do like to help Daddy and Mr. Big Black Bo. They've been teaching me carpentry and plumbing. I helped Daddy replace the screens on your cottage this year."

"And you did a fine job, too," Maizie praised.

"You'll end up running the Knoll," Grace told Annie. "Your future is all set."

"Would you like that?" Maizie asked.

"Yes. Yes, I would."

"And you'll marry someone named Oliver and live happily ever after," Grace joked.

"Wasn't that the name of the pet crow you had years ago?" Maizie asked.

"Yes."

Grace chimed in, "I'm going to marry a Pete, like my Cockatiel and Annie has to marry an Oliver."

"No, I'm swearing off boys. They're more trouble than they're worth."

"I wish I had some boys to swear off," Grace complained.

"With your blond hair and pretty blue eyes, I'm surprised you don't have to beat them off with a stick," the doctor remarked.

"But I don't have hardly any boobs yet! It's awful. I'm four months older than Annie, and she's already got a shape!"

"Everyone's body is different. Don't worry. You're blooming fast enough. And remember, both of you, real men are interested in more than hair color and cup size. And on that note, ladies, I mean, women, I'll leave you to your own devices."

When Maizie was gone, Grace exclaimed, "She's so cool."

"When I first found Oliver, she helped me feed him."

Grace instinctively put her arm around Annie's shoulders.

"Three years and I still dream about him flying to me when I whistle. I wake up feeling the weight of him on my shoulders." Annie's eyes began to tear up.

"This is progress."

"What?"

"You are showing your emotions."

"I'm about to get my period. I cry at anything, and I hate

it."

"Girls are supposed to cry."

"Exactly." And with that Annie pulled Grace into the water with her.

"You sneak!" Grace hollered when they surfaced.

Annie relished the awareness that Grace had finally arrived for the summer as they swam up river toward Cattail.

After a short distance, Grace switched to a sidestroke. "So any progress on your mom's big secret?"

Annie lost her breath for a moment before remembering that Grace had no idea about what Annie has witnessed between her mother and Big Black Bo.

"No, my mother still hasn't told me the big family secret about Grandmother Ann. I think there's something fishy about my grandfather, too. I've heard my father practically beg her to just tell me the truth," Annie explained.

"Parents are crazy," Grace mused. "I think that mine might be getting back together."

"Really?"

"Yeah. Dad is paying for the cottage so Mom doesn't have to work at Turner's Market this summer."

Annie flipped over onto her back and floated.

"Do you want them to get back together?"

"Sure—I mean, if Dad's okay, which Mom is constantly preaching that he is. I've only seen him on my birthdays and holidays with Mom and Grandmother there, so I don't really know."

"Bald Eagle!" Annie shouted and pointed while treading water.

The bird soared over them with a confused fish dangling from its golden talons.

"There aren't so many eagles anymore. We don't know where they've all gone," Annie explained.

"You're amazing, Annie Crow. I mean one killed Oliver and you still care."

"It was just protecting its babies."

They floated quietly for a moment, the current pulling them along.

"I'll race you back to the dock," Annie suddenly declared.

And like a shot the girls were plying the water with their strong, solid bodies.

The first Young Ladies Club meeting was spent sewing patchwork pillow covers in the back room of Turner's Market. Annie was struggling to line up the tiny squares of fabric evenly. She glanced over at Grace, who was already sewing entire rows of squares together with no difficulty and felt annoyance at her best friend. The least Grace could do was offer to help Annie, but she was deep in conversation with another girl in the club. When it was time to leave, Annie knew she couldn't go home without something that slightly resembled a pillow cover.

"May Grace and I stay and use one of your sewing machines today?" Annie asked Mrs. Turner as the other girls were leaving. "I need extra time."

"All right, dear. I'll be right out in the store if you need anything."

After Mrs. Turner left the room, Annie held up her mismatched squares and said, "Grace, you have to fix this."

"You really are a mess, you know."

"I can't have my mother nagging at me about this stupid pillow!"

"All right. I'll do it. Get the scissors."

As Grace cut apart the mismatched squares, Annie said, "Don't make it too perfect or she'll know I didn't do it."

"What's the matter with you? I'm helping you, and you're still mad at me," Grace told her.

"I'm not mad at you."

"Look, I can't help it if you won't talk to Tommy Reynolds anymore, so he's flirting with me instead. He's only doing it to make you jealous, which is working, I might add," Grace said as she pulled another square loose.

"I might add," Annie repeated in an exaggerated imitation of Grace.

"I don't even like him," Grace told her.

"I don't care if you do."

"Yes, you do."

"I hate him!"

"If you hate him, why do you care that he's talking to me?"

"Because I hate him," Annie said. "How can you be so thick?"

"Then I won't talk to him."

"Really? You'd do that?"

"How can you be so dense? No boy is worth our friendship," Grace insisted.

Annie smiled.

"I'll even let you have Pete when I go back to my grandmother's this fall," Grace blurted out suddenly.

"Are you crazy? You love that bird."

"Maybe I am, but I know you still miss Oliver."

"I'll ask you to give up an occasional boy for me, but never Pete. Never," Annie told her.

"Maybe your mom would let you have another crow?"

"Who are you trying to kid?" Annie groaned.

Grace stopped working for a moment and looked directly at Annie. "You have always been hard on your mom, but this summer, you act like she's some monster."

"I've been hard on her?" Annie scoffed.

"Look, I don't know what happened between you and your mom since last season, but I think she's just about perfect."

Annie moaned again. She felt a mixture of guilt and pain.

She'd never had a secret that she couldn't tell Grace, but she would never say anything about her mother and Big Black Bo.

"What happened?" Grace asked as she sewed Annie's squares of material back together.

"I can't tell you."

"Will she?"

Although Annie wondered what her mother would say if asked, she shouted, "No! Don't ask her!"

"Okay, okay. Geez, don't blow a gasket. I won't say a word."

"I'm sorry," Annie said quietly. "Look, thanks for fixing this stupid pillow cover."

"You owe me."

"I know. What's it going to bc?" Annie asked with dread.

"Let's go to the dance at the town beach tonight," Grace suggested.

"You just want to look at boys." Annie rolled her eyes.

"Well, don't you?"

"Not like you do. You're obsessed!"

"I am not. It's just that I heard Pete Ferguson's sister talking about it during club, and she said he was going to be there."

"He's Bunky Watson's best friend, and we know what a brain trust Bunky is after he managed to shoot himself in the foot with his father's shotgun."

"But Pete is cute, and we agreed that I'm supposed to marry someone named Pete."

"I'd kill you before I'd let you marry that loser. I don't care what his name is," Annie argued.

"But you owe me," Grace said holding up an improved patchwork pillow cover.

"Oh, all right."

When Annie and Grace walked down to the town beach that night, they saw lit Hawaiian torches lining a wooden dance floor set up on the sand. Some kids were dancing while others were hanging out at a nearby table covered with chips, pretzels and sodas.

Bunky Watson and a few of his other buddies caught sight of Annie and Grace and started toward them.

"I can't believe you talked me into coming," Annie complained.

"What is your problem? This is great! I'm going to have fun, and you can just be a crab if you want to," Grace said, swaying to dance music pounding from a pair of large speakers set up on the back of a pickup truck.

Bunky walked with a swagger now that he had grown out of his baby fat. He was used to girls giving him attention because he played sports.

"Hey," he said to Annie and Grace.

"Hello, Bunky," Annie said with a monotone voice. Grace smiled nervously.

The other boys just nodded. Too cool to actually talk, they seemed to wait for Bunky to let them know what to do. Finally, Pete Ferguson said something after Bunky gave him the go-ahead.

"Hi, Gracie."

"Hi, Pete," Grace blurted out.

"I'm going to dance the first slow dance with you, Annie," Bunky announced.

His friends all snickered as Bunky grinned at his proclamation.

If he'd asked her to dance, Annie might have been willing, but being told, as if she were a piece of property waiting to be claimed didn't sit well with her. She wanted to ask Bunky if he could dance after shooting himself in the foot, but she knew that would be going too far, even for her.

"Not if you were the last boy on earth," Annie said instead.

Bunky's friends sort of coughed and cleared their throats. When Bunky regained his composure, he led his pack off to scout out more receptive girls.

"What are you, nuts?" Grace asked. "Bunky is a star football player!"

"I don't care. He's a jerk."

"I'll never understand you, Annie. You're going to end up an old maid because no man will ever be good enough."

"I'd rather be an old maid than marry the first Neanderthal who grunts at me."

"You've got guts. I'll give you that," Grace conceded.

Just then, Pete returned with a couple of sodas. He handed one to Grace, and they drifted off together.

Annie felt stupid standing there alone, so she looked around for someone to ask to dance. Most of the boys didn't interest her. And then she noticed Doc Linden on the edge of a group of other grownups who had sponsored the dance. When he stifled a yawn, Annie thought he looked a little bored, so she walked over and asked him to dance with her.

Doc's face turned red as a slow song began to play, but he took her hand and moved with her onto the dance floor.

Although Doc kept a respectable few inches of air between them, Annie hadn't been this close to a man before. She remembered how she had felt when he had wrapped her ankle last May, and now her hand was in one of his while his other hand rested gently on her back.

"Your ankle seems to be doing fine," he said.

"Yes." Annie couldn't think of anything else to say.

"Are you having a good summer?" Doc asked.

"Yes. How is Miss Linda?" Annie asked about Doc's wife.

"She's doing well. Her parents are visiting so they're up at the house."

"They weren't up for this shindig?"

"I think they'll come down a little later."

Annie didn't see him coming, but she heard Tommy Reynolds' voice.

"May I cut in?"

"Certainly, young man. Say hello to your parents for me, Annie," Doc said as he turned her around to face Tommy.

"Hi, Annie Crow."

He held her closer than Doc.

"I thought I should rescue you from the older man." He smiled, his teeth very white against his tan skin.

"Maybe I prefer older men." Annie tried not to look at him. She watched the other couples slow dancing around them.

"Well, that's perfect because I am older."

"Not even two years."

"Now, Annie. Grace told me you had forgiven me."

"When did she tell you that?"

"I was just dancing with her. She was getting mauled by some townie and was very grateful when I cut in."

"Where is she now?" Annie asked with concern.

"Don't worry," he whispered in her ear. "She's dancing with my brother."

"Oh, that's very reassuring."

"He's a perfect gentleman."

"Unlike you!"

"You should have been complimented when I bragged about skinny dipping with you. If you weren't the best looking girl in town, why would I brag?"

"Your logic is lost on me."

"You know what you do to me, Annie," he said, making eye contact.

When did his eyes get so green? Annie wondered when she looked into them.

"Well, you'll never know more because you can't keep your mouth shut!" she retorted.

"My loss," he said with a laugh. "Maybe you'll give me another chance."

"Not until hell freezes over."

He laughed again. Nothing seemed to throw him. Annie was relieved when the song ended and Grace was right by her side.

"You want to go back to the Knoll?" Grace asked.

"Yes."

"Bye, Tommy," Grace said, but Annie just started walking.

"I can't believe you asked Dr. Linden to dance!" Grace said to Annie when they cleared the crowded dance floor and crossed the beach.

"Why not?" Annie asked. "He's better looking than Bunky Watson will ever be!"

"But he's married! And he's old!"

"He's not that old. I bet he's barely thirty yet."

"What was it like having his hand on your back?" Grace asked.

Annie hesitated. Then she smiled. "It was nice."

"Well, Pete Ferguson was creepy. He kept fiddling with my bra hook right through my blouse like he could get it loose while we were dancing!"

"Did you tell Tommy that I had forgiven him?" Annie asked, shifting topics.

"Absolutely not."

"I figured he was just giving me a line."

"Boys are losers," Grace declared.

"Men, on the other hand, are preferable."

"Definitely."

"How old is Doc?" Annie asked her mom before the next meeting of the Young Ladies Club.

"It's not polite to ask people's ages," Liz told her.

"I'm not asking him, I'm asking you."

"I don't know." Liz began rinsing the breakfast dishes.

"Guess."

"About thirty three."

"That old?" Annie said, disappointed.

"You said to guess. I'm guessing. Why do you care about his age all of a sudden?" Liz asked.

"Just curious," Annie answered.

"Get going. Grace was out front calling for you a while ago."

Annie wandered out the door and didn't see Grace. She had probably already left.

In no hurry to get down to the club meeting, Annie slowly walked into town. As she passed Doc's house, which held his practice on the first floor and the living quarters he shared with his wife on the second floor, Annie thought, *He sure is cute.*

Because Annie had missed the beginning of their meeting, Mrs. Turner made her stay longer and take the last batch of cookies out of the oven. Grace had offered to wait for her, but Annie told her to go ahead. She'd been planning something all morning while they'd mixed the batter for chocolate chip cookies.

When Mrs. Turner finally released her, Annie had a full dozen cookies wrapped up for Dr. Linden. She crossed the street from the market and walked into his office. Usually Doc's wife was behind the desk in the waiting room, but the room was empty when Annie walked in.

"Doc? Miss Linda?" Annie called out.

"Yeah," Doc said from the examination room. "I'll be right out."

Annie sat down uncomfortably in one of the waiting room chairs. A moment later the young doctor came out into the doorway.

"Well, Annie, this is a surprise. I was just about to go upstairs for lunch before my afternoon hours."

"Here. These are for you. I made them in the Young Ladies Club." She held out the paper plate of cookies covered with wax paper.

"Well, that was very thoughtful of you."

She could tell he was surprised to see her under these circumstances. *What must he think,* she wondered nervously?

"Miss Linda just loves chocolate. We'll have some of these for dessert tonight. But, come to think about it, she likes chocolate so much, she'll probably eat them all, so what if you and I eat a couple before I take them upstairs?" Doc suggested.

"Sure that it won't ruin your appetite for lunch?" Annie asked.

"I think I can handle one cookie, don't you?" He gave her a wink, and she felt flushed.

Doc removed the wax paper and held the plate out to Annie. She noticed how clean his hands were. Each nail was flawless and trimmed neatly. Annie took a cookie, and so did he before putting the plate down on the waiting room chair next to Annie. Then he sat two chairs away from her leaving the plate of cookies between them.

"Hmmm, this is delicious," he told her.

"Yeah, not bad for my baking," Annie admitted.

Doc gulped the last bite and said, "Annie, are you all right? Is there anything bothering you?"

Annie hadn't expected this and lied. "Well, I had a sore throat this morning."

"Let's take a look."

Doc rose and crossed over to her.

"I don't have any money to pay you." Sensing her red cheeks, Annie hoped they would help to make her look feverish and not embarrassed.

"Well, I only charge a plate full of chocolate chip cookies for examinations done out in the waiting room. Now open up and say 'ahh.'"

Annie obeyed as Doc peered down her throat. His hazel

eyes were lined with fine brown lashes.

"Okay, you can close now."

He felt around her neck gently with his warm fingers.

"Does this hurt?"

"No," Annie refused to lie again.

Doc smiled at her revealing adorable laugh lines around his eyes. She didn't care how old he was. Doc was a dish.

"Do your folks know that you are here?"

Annie tried not to sound alarmed, but for a moment, she thought that he was reading her mind.

"No! I mean, I didn't want to bother them. They are so busy running the Knoll."

"That's thoughtful of you, but your health is very important to them, and you should never keep secrets from your parents."

"What secrets?" Annie was sure that he knew that she had lied.

"About your sore throat."

"Oh, yeah, that. Well, it feels much better now."

"You'd be smart to gargle with warm, salt water tonight just to be safe."

"Yes, Doc. I will."

"All right then. Thank you for the cookies."

"You're welcome," Annie said as she hurried out of his office and up the street toward the Knoll.

When Annie came through the stone pillars, she recognized Grace's mother's stolen car sitting in front of Cockatiel Cottage. She hurried past to Sunrise Cottage.

Her parents were both standing on the porch staring.

"I don't believe it," her father said.

"It might not be Barry Lipton," her mother told him.

"Of course it's him. Who else would have that car?"

"Maybe the police finally found it."

"They stopped looking for that car years ago. I'm going over there."

"Please don't, not yet. Give him a chance," Liz requested.

"To what? Turn over another china cabinet?"

"Who's to say that he's drunk?"

"Who's to say that he isn't?" Luke paused. Then his voice rose. "Has Mae been seeing him?"

"She hasn't said."

"Annie." Her father took his eyes off the car and looked at her. "Aren't Grace's parents divorced?"

"I don't know." Annie felt like she was on the witness stand.

"What do you mean? She never divorced that creep?"

"Luke, why are you so angry?" Liz asked.

"Didn't you say that she was divorcing him?" Luke asked her.

Annie watched her mother selecting her words carefully. "I just assumed they got a divorce, but Mae never really said one way or another."

"What do you women talk about all the time? I thought you told each other everything," Luke said in exasperation.

"She never stopped loving him."

Luke looked at her, dumbfounded.

"You know how Joe Esposito was sweet on Mae last season?" Liz asked.

"A fine man, too," Luke noted.

"Joe would drive all the way down from Kingstown just to shop here at Turners, but Mae wouldn't give him the time of day."

"I guess not, if she was still married."

Despite Annie's anxiety about what was going on, she smiled at her father's sarcasm.

"Well, I like Joe, so I asked Mae about it," Liz went on. "I asked why she didn't try a date with him, and she said she couldn't get over Barry."

"Women."

"Wouldn't you want me to love you no matter what?" Liz

asked earnestly.

"Not if I was an alcoholic who drank away all my money and stole your car! And I sure wouldn't want Annie putting up with that either."

"Thanks, Dad," Annie said.

"Yeah, well." His voice faltered a moment. "Don't distract me from keeping my eye on Cockatiel Cottage."

But there was no need. Barry and Mae Lipton were heading straight to Sunrise Cottage.

"Annie, go see how Grace is," Liz instructed.

Annie did as she was told, only briefly saying hello when she passed Mr. and Mrs. Lipton.

When she reached Cockatiel Cottage, Annie called Grace's name. No answer.

"Grace?" she called louder.

"In here."

Annie opened the screen door and from the porch, she saw Grace sitting on the floor of the living room. She was crying while Pete stood on her shoulder preening wisps of her blond hair from her ponytail.

"What happened?" Annie asked, coming in and sitting on the floor next to Grace.

"We're moving to California!" Grace sobbed.

Annie couldn't speak.

"My dad got a new job there. He came here to ask us to go with him, and my mom said yes."

"Oh, Grace," Annie finally got out.

"He's gone up to apologize to your parents for the mess he made here years ago. Part of his program or something."

"Yeah, I saw them so I came here."

"I'm afraid I'll never get to come back to Cockatiel Cottage again and . . ." Grace hiccupped, gasped for air and added, "I'll never see you again, Annie Crow."

Grace threw her arms around Annie, and Pete fluttered to his perch.

Grace never stopped crying the whole time she watched her parents load the car with all of their possessions, including Pete in his cage. She still stood crying in front of Cockatiel Cottage while Mae was hugging Liz goodbye and her father climbed behind the steering wheel and started the car.

"Just think about all the gorgeous guys you'll meet in California. All tan and sexy," Annie encouraged Grace.

"Don't you care that we won't see each other anymore?" Grace asked.

"Of course I care!"

And Annie did. Holding in her pain did more harm to Annie than Grace could ever understand.

"It'd do you good to cry for once, Annie," Grace told her.

Annie hugged Grace and whispered, "I will miss you very much."

The girls were still hugging when Mae gently put her hands on Grace's shoulders.

"Come on, honey."

When the car taking Grace to California disappeared up Baycliff Road, Annie took off in the opposite direction. She ran down the cement stairs, onto the beach, and up toward Cattail.

Mr. Packard was coming back from Cattail when Annie passed him on the beach without a word. Her face was red. He wanted to ask her if she was all right, but her rigid demeanor warned him off.

He turned to watch Annie as she continued along the beach. Her shoulders shook as they had when she walked away with dead Oliver in her hands. Unable to help her, Pack searched his pocket and felt the dull edge of a piece of blue glass that had tumbled for some time in the sand and water. He pulled it out and dropped it on the beach as he headed home.

Part Two

Chapter Seven
Winter 1965

THICK SNOW PELTED THE WINDOWS on the bay side of Sunrise Cottage. Annie looked up from her Principles of Photography textbook, and in the darkness outside, she saw a red pulsing light bouncing off the white-blanketed landscape. Classes at the community college Annie attended had been cancelled for three days due to the weather.

Restless from being stuck inside, her folks had gone to Chester Landing for dinner, so there was no one else to ask what they thought the red light could be.

Annie crawled out from beneath the quilt she cuddled under on the sofa. The floor felt cold through her socks as she walked to the front door to see a police car stopping in the circle at the top of the drive. Annie opened the front door. There was no siren. In fact, there was little sound at all, except the icy snow hitting the dried leaves surrounding the front steps of her cottage. The swirl of red light stopped, and Bunky Watson stepped out of his patrol car. Annie shivered as his boots crunched along the path to her door.

"Good evening, Annie," he said standing on the steps.

What was Bunky Watson doing in a police uniform? Annie wondered.

"May I come in?" he asked.

"Sure." Annie stepped aside.

Bunky stamped his feet on the mat just inside the door and took off his hat. Annie closed the door.

"There's been an accident, Annie," he said with his back toward her. Then he turned to face her. A fine line of wet snow dripped off his hat and onto the mat. Annie stared at him.

"Your folks ran into ice on that curve on Swamp Road, and they lost control of their car." Bunky swallowed hard. "They were both killed. I'm sorry."

Annie shivered again, and Bunky stepped over to the sofa, picked up the quilt, and draped it around her. She continued to stand next to his puddle of melted snow by the doormat.

"Annie, did you hear me?" Bunky asked.

"When did you become a police officer?" Annie asked.

"Three months ago," Bunky answered.

"That's not possible. You were in high school with me last year," she said.

"No, Annie, you graduated two years ago, and I was a year ahead of you."

Embarrassed by her confusion, Annie muttered, "Still, you're awfully young."

"Annie, can I call someone for you?" Bunky asked.

"No. Why would you do that?"

"I don't want you to be alone."

"I'm not. You're here, and my parents will be back—"

"Annie?" Bunky interrupted.

She noticed the panic in his voice. This was likely the first time he'd had to break news like this.

"No, you're right. They won't be home, will they?" Annie

said.

"No, they've been killed in an accident," Bunky repeated. "I'm sorry."

Annie nodded. Bunky put his arm around her shoulders and guided her to sit on the sofa.

Annie's mind was in a complete fog. Why had her parents gone out when they knew the weather conditions were so bad?

"My parents were getting cabin fever the last couple of days and decided they could use a night out," she explained more for herself than for Bunky.

"Hell of a night," he said and then looked down at the floor and cleared his throat. "Is there a relative or friend I could call for you?"

Big Black Bo was the only person who came to Annie's mind as someone she'd want to comfort her. However, she hadn't seen him since the weather turned bad back in December, and he wouldn't be welcome in town at this hour anyway. Annie realized that Bunky could contact her great-grandmother, but Annie hadn't seen her in years. She certainly didn't want to see her now, even if Delia would be willing to come.

"No one," Annie answered.

"What about Grace Lipton?"

"She's at college in California."

Annie was beginning to feel sorry for Bunky. She sensed that he didn't want to be stuck with her all night. Annie couldn't think of anyone who could relieve the poor guy of his duty.

There was a sudden knock at the door, which made Bunky jump.

"I'll get it," he said with authority.

But before he reached the door, Mrs. Turner burst in.

"I saw Bunky speed past with those red lights going so I called over to the station, and they told me why he was coming out here. Annie, dear, I'm so sorry." She took off her scarf revealing her unnaturally red head of hair. "Now, I'm here to take care of you, sweetheart."

Annie was reminded of the many years that Letitia Turner had driven her up to Great Grand's house in Kingstown. And although Annie felt she had never measured up to Mrs. Turner's Young Ladies Club expectations, the woman had always been kind to her.

"Thank you, Mrs. Turner," Bunky said as he put his hat back on and headed for the door. "I'm sorry for your loss, Annie."

"Thank you," Annie heard herself say.

Bunky nodded and closed the door behind him.

Letitia put her coat and scarf on the coat rack where Liz's and Luke's coats should be hanging. She sat on the sofa and patted Annie's knee, making a tsk, tsk sound that reminded Annie of the noise parents make when the baby has spilled the milk.

Annie never felt so alone in her life.

Early the next morning, Packard Marlboro was sawing up a huge, dead branch that had fallen down with the weight of the ice at the front edge of his property along Baycliff Road. It was a chore that could have waited until the ground was clear of snow, but Pack needed to get out of doors. He'd been cooped up in his studio painting for two days, during which more snow and ice and fallen, but now in the morning sun, the trees were dripping.

Reverend Johnson drove by on the wet road. Packard didn't hear the car over the sound of his chain saw, but he noticed it heading toward the Knoll when he finished the cut.

About a half an hour later, when Pack was loading small pieces of the branch into a wheelbarrow, he heard someone calling to him.

"Did you hear about Luke and Liz Atkinson?" the voice

asked.

Lost in his own world of thought, it took Packard a moment to realize that the voice was coming from a different car now stopped on the side of Baycliff Road. He wiped his hands and sweaty forehead with a bandana as he walked toward the road. Judging from the direction of Letitia Turner's vehicle, he guessed she must have just come from the Knoll.

"Did you hear about Annie Crow's parents?" Mrs. Turner asked when Pack leaned down to the opened window.

He shook his head.

"They were both killed last night in an automobile accident," she said.

When his face disappeared because he bolted up like a rod into a straight position, Letitia leaned out the window so that she could see him.

"Now that the roads are clearing up, Reverend Johnson and Doc are going to take her to identify the bodies. Doc offered to do it, but Annie wants to see them. Late last night, when Bunky Watson flew by with his flashing red lights . . ."

Guilt overwhelmed Packard as Mrs. Turner yammered on, not noticing or perhaps not caring that he wasn't responding. *I should have known. I should have been with her last night,* he told himself. *What must she think of me?* The last thought caused him to actually move. He walked away from Mrs. Turner's car without a word.

By the time Packard reached his house, he began to think more clearly. As much as he wanted to go to her, Pack realized that Annie would not be expecting him. The last time they had actually interacted was when she was a child and had asked him to bury her pet crow Oliver at sea.

Grace and Mae flew in from California and stayed with Annie. They reluctantly slept in Luke and Liz's bedroom because there really wasn't any alternative in the tiny two-bedroom cottage.

"When you're ready to talk, I'm here for you," Grace reminded Annie.

"Your parents would want you to finish your community college program," Mae insisted. "Now if you need money to do so, Grace's father said to tell you that he'd take care of it."

While Annie appreciated their company, at times the two of them were so emotional Annie felt obliged to comfort them. She was quickly running out of energy, and although being alone on the Knoll for the first time in her life was a little frightening, she longed for time to herself. She needed it to think. With all the funeral arrangements to make and well-meaning neighbors and friends keeping her busy, Annie hadn't begun to let it sink in that both her parents were dead.

The actual funeral service held at the United Methodist Church in Promise seemed more like a bad dream than reality to Annie. She felt as if she were outside her body observing the mourners walk to the caskets and then giving her their condolences.

Among them were Jim and Naomi Finch, Maizie and Sam Waters and their two children, Birdie and her family, and J.J. Finch and his family.

"I have all those guest rooms in our big house in Towson, since the children left home long ago. You could come and stay anytime you want," Miss Naomi told Annie.

When Mrs. Waters arrived with the Slims, Sam brought his mother directly over to Annie.

"I'm so sorry, my dear. You must let me or Sam and Maizie know if there is anything we can do for you."

"I will," Annie replied.

As Sam and his mother moved away, Annie overheard him tell his mother, "I can't imagine how Annie will cope. It was so difficult losing Dad. If I'd lost you at the same time, I couldn't have made it through medical school."

Mr. and Mrs. Reynolds came from Philadelphia, and while Jack sent flowers from Connecticut where he now lived with his wife and baby boy, Tommy drove down from New York University. He said all the right things to Annie with great poise and sincerity.

When Tommy moved into the crowd, Annie whispered to Grace, who never left her side, "I have him to thank for all I know about keeping the Knoll running."

"What do you mean?" Grace said, letting her eyes linger on Tommy as he politely spoke to Miss Agnes, Mr. Augy, Lois and Connie.

"If he hadn't told everyone about skinny-dipping with me, I might not have been lectured to death about a girl's reputation and maybe wouldn't have followed Daddy and Big Black Bo around to learn all the 'manly' trades as revenge."

"You do know every pipe and shingle on the place."

But even her father hadn't done it alone, Annie realized. He had had Mama and Big Black Bo to help. Luke, Liz and Bo had kept the Knoll going and their friendship intact despite what Annie considered to be the deepest of betrayals on her mother's part.

"No signs of your wicked witch of a great-grandmother," Grace pointed out as they left the church and walked along the snow lined path to the car.

"No, she didn't send flowers, not even a card."

When the mourners gathered at the gravesites in the cemetery, Annie noticed Packard Marlboro standing on the edge of the crowd. Big Black Bo joined him there. Neither man had come to see her after the accident nor had either attended the church service, but Annie felt comforted to see them now. Then Grace took her cold hand as Reverend Johnson began to speak.

The day after Grace and Mae returned to California for college and work, Annie sat opposite her great-grandmother's lawyer in the living room of Sunset Cottage. The wiry little man with bushy eyebrows and enormous amounts of hair poking out of his nose and ears seemed to know that now Annie would be on her own with no one to support her.

"Of course your great-grandmother understands that your parents left the Knoll to you, but she also realizes that you are very young to be handling a business like this on your own."

"I'm nineteen," Annie said. "I've been helping my parents run it for years."

"Yes, but helping isn't the same as handling it on your own," he told her. "Now, Miss Delia is willing to buy you out, which will pay off the second mortgage your father took out last year for the new bulkhead and pilings for the dock. It's a sizable debt, but there'd be enough left over to get you into college or settled into a place of your own in town."

"Dad had no choice but to put in the new bulkhead after the run-off last spring," Annie said defensively. She didn't like the lawyer making it sound like her parents had foolishly left her in debt.

"Of course he did. And I'm sure that he assumed that he'd be alive for many years to pay off the debt. But God saw it another way," he said adjusting his glasses.

Annie felt her temper rising. *What did this man know about God's will?*

"Why is my great-grandmother interested anyway? She didn't even come to her own granddaughter's funeral."

"She's not well. But she is concerned about your welfare."

"Yes, I'm sure that my welfare is of the utmost importance to her next to the tidy sum she'll make when she turns around and sells the Knoll to a developer. Why should I sell it to her first? I could make a great deal more if I sold directly to a developer myself."

"But you won't. Miss Delia said that you wouldn't. Will you?"

Annie shook her head. Great Grand certainly knew her.

Then the lawyer began gathering up his papers and then delivered his trump card.

"Miss Delia wanted me to make it perfectly clear that her offer is only good now. If you refuse it and then can't pay the loan, she will not bail you out later."

"How kind of her not to pressure me in any way."

Annie felt hot tears welling up in her eyes as Great Grand's lawyer drove off the Knoll.

"No." Annie scolded herself out loud. "There is no time for tears."

Immediately she went to the desk her parents shared in the running of the Knoll. She poured over the copious notes that her father had kept on what needed to be done to the cottages before opening another season. Seeing the familiar bold loops to his handwriting felt strange to her. How was it possible that they outlived him?

Her mother's perfectly aligned bookkeeping figures were even more painful to examine. For as often as her mother had tried to bridge the gap between them since having been discovered hugging Big Black Bo, Annie had held the grudge firmly. Now tears burned again in her eyes, but she wiped her face angrily. I can't afford a single moment of self-indulgence right now, Annie told herself.

Chapter Eight
Spring 1965

AFTER INSPECTING EVERY INCH OF the cottages, Annie added to her father's list of repairs to be done before the new season. She couldn't do all this on her own, but she hadn't seen Big Black Bo since the funeral. She decided to ride her bike the eight miles to Coletown and find him.

As Annie neared the little town where Big Black Bo lived, she wondered if she'd made the right decision to bike and not drive. Over the years, she had heard the warnings. White women didn't go there alone. She brushed that thought aside, knowing that she had nothing to fear in Coletown.

When Annie saw a group of women sitting on the front stoop of a house with little children playing in the yard, she stopped her bike and greeted them. The women nodded, nothing more.

"I'm looking for Big Bo," Annie said.

"You mean Big Black Bo?" the youngest-looking one of

the group asked.

Even they referred to him as black. Annie was surprised for some reason.

"Yes, Big Black Bo."

"What would you be wanting with him?" The woman eyed Annie up and down.

"I need to ask him a favor."

The group just laughed at her.

This was not going well so Annie decided to move on. He couldn't be that hard to find; after all, it was a tiny town.

Annie turned yet another corner on her bike, and she saw Big Black Bo leaning under the hood of his old car.

"Why, mornin', Miss Annie. What are you doin' way out here on your bicycle?"

Big Black Bo put out his cigarette and wiped his hands on a rag.

"I'm looking for you, Bo." Annie decided to call him Bo like her parents had. Maybe he'd be more likely to see her as an adult.

"Thank you for coming to the funeral."

"I'm sorry, Miss Annie," Big Black Bo said with true emotion in his voice.

"I need your help," Annie said.

"My help?"

"I want to keep the Knoll, and I can't do it without you."

"Are you sure about that?"

"They're trying to take it away from me. Force me to sell," Annie said.

"Now calm down, Miss Annie. Who is trying to take it?"

"My great-grandmother."

"The old lady up in Kingstown?"

"That would be the one."

"What's she doin' still alive?" Bo smiled, and Annie laughed.

He added, more seriously, "Your folks would want you to

keep the place for yourself."

"I can't do it alone. Will you help me?"

Bo ran his hand across his forehead. "I don't know about a nineteen-year-old white girl and a Negro man running a place together," he said.

"You're the only person I can trust." Annie tried not to whine. She wanted to sound like a woman who knew what she was doing.

"Well, I am out of work since your folks passed. I don't care to work any other place than out there," Big Black Bo admitted.

"Great. Then we have a deal. Can you come tomorrow morning?"

Big Black Bo smiled at her. "I'll be there if I have to walk."

"What's wrong with your car?"

"I don't know yet, but now I've a reason to make sure I fix it today."

When Annie saw Big Black Bo's car pull on to the Knoll, she grabbed a thermos and her list and went outside to meet him.

"Morning, Miss Annie," he said, stepping out of his car.

"I know Mama always had corn bread for you. I'm sorry, I only have coffee."

"Thank you. I ate, but I'll take the coffee."

"Here's a list of everything that needs to be done," Annie said, handing the paper to Bo as he sipped from the thermos cup. "I thought we'd start by replacing the screening on the porch of Owl's Nest Cottage. It's one of the first cottages people see and having torn screening isn't a very good advertisement."

"You're thinking like your daddy."

Annie blushed and ran her hand along the collar of the over-sized flannel shirt she wore with her T-shirt and jeans. It was one of her father's favorite work shirts, and she wondered if Big Black Bo recognized it.

They'd begun removing the old screening when Annie suddenly asked, "Look, can I just call you Bo?"

"What bothers you about Big Black Bo?"

"I feel like I'm ten years old again. I don't want you calling me Miss Annie, either. Just Annie will do."

"You can't change that I'm black," Bo said as he pried loose a resistant nail.

"My parents called you Bo."

"You'll have some troubles with a black man out here workin' without your parents or any cottagers on the place."

"I've got worse troubles than the color of your skin," Annie remarked, pulling the brittle screen off a frame they needed to reuse.

They said no more about it but worked like two people on a mission.

At the end of the day, Bo started packing up the tools.

"I best be going, Miss Annie, before it gets dark."

Annie decided not to argue, even though she could have used his help for at least another hour. The town ordinance not allowing colored people in Promise after dark was no longer on the books, but everyone still followed it anyway.

"I'll see you in the morning," Annie said.

Bo nodded and began walking to his car.

"I'm sorry that we argued," Annie called after him. "It was your first day back. I meant for it to be nice."

"We're finding our way without your father. That's all. It'll smooth out," Bo said and smiled. "You're the boss now. I have to remember that."

"But I want to have your opinion. Daddy always trusted your opinion, and so do I."

"Thank you, Miss Annie. I'll see you tomorrow."

"Good night, Mr. Big Black Bo."

After he turned his car around, Big Black Bo stopped in front of Owl's Nest Cottage and called over to Annie.

"Just Bo is okay."

Annie smiled and waved good night.

The image of her mother and Bo hugging flitted into mind. Annie remembered her mother trying to explain the situation, and Annie refusing to listen. Whether her father ever knew or not, the three of them had gone on as usual. Now it was too late. Her mother was dead, and she couldn't imagine asking Bo. The bottom line was her dad had always trusted Bo and Annie did, too.

The next morning, Annie and Bo stood staring at the foundation in the back of Hummingbird Haven. It was beginning to sink.

"We can't put this off, Annie," Bo sighed.

"It's bad, isn't it?"

"Well, we don't want Mrs. Waters' bathroom dropping off the back of her cottage, do we?" He slid a cigarette out of the pack and lit it.

"Is it something we can handle?" Annie asked, not wanting to be told that she wasn't strong enough to hold up her end.

"I'm not sure the two of us can lift this part of the building to replace the foundation underneath."

"How do we do it?" Annie asked.

"We get that big wood chopping stump and a long piece of pipe. It works sort of like a seesaw. With the stump as a support, we put the short end of the pipe under the building. When I push down on the long end of the pipe, the short end eases the bathroom up off the foundation."

"What do I do?"

"Climb under the building to put in temporary bracing." Bo shook his head. "This isn't going to work, Annie. I don't fancy holding up the bathroom with you under there. "

"I have a couple of old bottle jacks we could use," Packard said from a few feet away.

Annie and Bo both jumped with surprise.

"Mr. Packard," Annie managed to say.

After the men shook hands, Packard said, "Annie, I'm sorry for your loss."

"Thank you for coming to the funeral."

"I'm sorry I haven't come over sooner, but…" he trailed off like he'd run out of energy.

Bo put his cigarette out. "So you have some bottle jacks?"

Packard seemed to come alive again. "Yes, they'll hold up both back corners while we dig and pour new footings."

"That's thoughtful of you, Mr. Packard," Annie said. "But don't you have fish to catch?"

"Fish aren't going anywhere," Pack replied and headed back to get his jacks.

With the help of three long two-by-sixes, the jacks and some muscle, the back end of Hummingbird was lifted off its two sinking cinder block pilings. Annie mixed cement to lay new footings while Packard and Bo dug down below the frost line.

Recalling how Birdie and Maizie teased about Mr. Packard being attractive in a rough, mountain man sort of way made Annie smile as she watched him working silently with Bo. He seemed comfortable with them, and she sensed a quiet comradery between the two men, but she missed the banter that had usually gone on between Bo and her father.

At the end of the day, Annie asked Packard, "What can I do to repay you?"

"You don't owe me, Annie. If you need anything, let me know." He climbed the fence separating the Knoll from his property and crossed the field to his house.

"Don't you think I ought to pay him a day's wages?" Annie asked Bo, who was washing off his arms and hands with the garden hose.

"If you want to insult him, sure, do that," he told her.

"But he's losing money helping us and not fishing."

"I suppose a grown man knows his own financial situation."

"Okay, but I don't like it."

"You just don't like owing anybody." Bo turned off the hose faucet. "He said that you didn't owe him anything, so just be grateful."

As usual, Bo was right. Owing anyone made Annie uncomfortable.

"How's it going, Annie Crow?"

"Grace!" Annie almost couldn't believe her ears when she heard her best friend's voice on the phone. "Okay, I guess."

"You sound down. Any more word from that wicked old witch of a great-grandmother of yours?"

"No, thank God. But I still don't have all the cottages full, and we open in less than seven weeks."

"Who's coming back?"

"The ever faithful Finches, of course."

"They taking Sunset and Sun-swept as usual?"

"Yes. However Jean and Bob Reynolds are bailing out. Miss Jean said with Jack married and Tommy in New York City, she can't see the sense of it anymore."

"I bet Mr. Reynolds wants to come back. He's going to miss his fishing."

"But you know who calls the shots in that family."

"Miss Jean."

"And because Tommy's parents aren't renting Fish Tale, of course his aunt isn't taking Blue Heron Cottage either."

"I'm going to miss Tommy. He's turned into a huge hunk."

"Well, he won't be here, and neither will you," Annie said glumly.

"Don't be so sure about that!"

"I'm sure that Tommy Reynolds has better things to do this summer in New York City than to waste his time on the Eastern Shore."

"But I don't."

"What are you saying?" Annie was afraid to believe what Grace was suggesting.

"How would you like a roommate this summer?"

"I'd love it!" Annie shouted.

"I already called Letitia and Elwood Turner, and they're hiring me to work in the grocery. I'll help you with the turn-arounds on the weekly rentals. I can paint anything that you need painted—"

"Hey, hey. Just come. You don't have to earn your keep."

"And my parents are giving me enough food money to feed both of us all summer. They said that it's the least they can do for all the meals your parents fed me when I was little."

Annie stifled a sob.

"Annie, are you crying?"

"No," Annie answered with a sniffle.

"Yes, you are!"

"You're uninvited if you're going to nag me about showing my emotions," Annie said, getting herself under control again.

"Too late, you can't un-invite me when you didn't invite me in the first place. I invited myself. I'll get there as soon as I can."

"Thank you, Grace. Thank you for coming. I didn't know how I was going to manage without my folks," Annie said.

"It'll be fine. You'll do great."

"I miss them so much."

"I know. Me, too."

"I feel much better knowing you're coming."

"So bottom line. How many cottages have full season rentals?"

"Five."

There was a pause. "How many with down payments?"

"Four."

"No wonder you're crying."

"I'm not crying."

"Have you advertised?"

"My father never did."

"Times have changed, my dear. Leave it to me. I'll have something out to the Philadelphia and Baltimore papers in a couple of days."

"What will it cost?"

"Don't worry about that."

"I don't want you to pay for things like that."

"Let's just say it'll cover my bed for the summer."

"Can't I at least proof it first?"

"Trust me. You'll love it."

"Trusting and owing. You really know how to get on my nerves," Annie remarked.

"I'll see you right after I finish taking my exams."

It paid to have an artistic best friend studying advertising and graphic design.

Grace drew a silhouette sketch of Sunset Cottage with the leaves of the big tree in front lacing the top edges of the ad. The Chesapeake Bay filled in the background.

The ad read: *Waterfront cottages for weekly, monthly and seasonal rental at Annie Crow Knoll on the Chesapeake.*

Annie Crow Knoll! Annie was stunned, then embarrassed. However, when the phone started ringing with inquiries, she was happy to answer, "Annie Crow Knoll."

As Annie headed out to the post office one morning a few days after the ads were released, she discovered a beautiful sign hanging on the front gate. It replicated Grace's design, but was done in color.

It read: *Welcome to Annie Crow Knoll.*

Added to Grace's original were a male Ruby-throated Hummingbird and an American Crow in each lower corner.

Annie turned to Bo, who was brushing a fresh coat of paint on the front of Slim's Secret.

"Did you do this?" she asked him, pointing to the sign.

"No, this is the only paint brush I know how to handle."

"Well, I'm grateful enough that you can paint these clapboard cottages even faster than my father."

"Thank you. But the picture painting is up to Miss Grace."

"I doubt that she had time to do this and the ad with her final exams. How would she have gotten it here anyway?"

Annie looked again at the detail on the sign, first at the hummingbird and then the crow. It was Oliver. Maybe crows all looked the same to most people, but she'd know Oliver anywhere. It was the glint in his eye and the cock of his head. Mr. Packard was the only other person who knew that crow. Annie remembered the sketch of Oliver Packard had left for her after she found him standing over the crow's lifeless body on Cattail.

If Mr. Packard weren't so shy, Annie knew that he would have given it to her personally and not hung it up at the crack of dawn when no one was around to thank him. Years ago, he had left that sketch of the crow with no word as well. She wanted to march right over there with a pineapple upside down cake, but since she had neither the time or the talent to bake, and he'd find that kind of display embarrassing, she'd wait until he showed up to help Bo. He'd been doing that pretty often lately.

But Packard didn't show up. For several days, his workboat was out. Annie found herself checking for *Sophie* as she had after he helped her bury Oliver at sea. She vaguely remembered her father reassuring her that Mr. Packard was all right out on the bay for days.

Reflecting on the last few weeks, Annie realized that Packard was helping her with her parents' deaths as he had with Oliver's. She found it comforting to see the lights flicker through the trees from his house across the field since she was alone on the Knoll. She began to miss them when he was out fishing.

Annie pulled into the parking lot of Wilson's Hardware, with a lumber list and no money to pay for any of it. There'd been several more inquiry calls and interest expressed in renting the remaining cottages, but no checks in the mail yet. Annie had used up the last of this month's cash to pay Bo's salary. If he'd been aware of the situation, she knew that he wouldn't have taken any pay, so she lied to him. She told him that there was money for the lumber they needed to repair the porches on Sun-swept and No Name.

Annie planned on using her father's line of credit. She tried to reassure herself with the power of positive thinking. If she assumed they'd give her credit, then they would.

"Hey there, Annie Crow," she heard when she walked into the store.

"Hey, Carol Sue. How are you?" Annie tried to be pleasant but felt her stomach tighten up. She and Carol Sue went all through school together but never saw eye-to-eye.

"I'm fine. Say, I'm awfully sorry about your mama and daddy."

"Thank you."

"How you managing out there all by yourself, Annie Crow?"

"I'm fine. Now here's what I need to get." Annie handed her the list.

"My, my. This is quite a list! You and your darky must be

keepin' busy."

Annie tasted bile in her throat but kept her mouth shut as Carol Sue picked up the phone to read the list to the owner who was out in the lumberyard.

"Mr. Wilson wants to know what you're building," Carol Sue told Annie while she held the receiver.

"We're repairing the porches on two cottages," Annie answered, hoping there weren't too many more questions to this inquisition.

"She says that her and her darky are repairing two porches, Mr. Wilson," Carol Sue said to her boss.

Annie slammed her hands down on the counter. "Listen you, bitch, if you call him that again, I'm going to take that phone and ram it down your throat!"

"Sweet Lord!" Carol Sue yelped and dropped the phone.

By then a crowd had started to gather closer to the commotion. Among the usual customers were two young men. They looked nearly the same age and wore similar T-shirts and jeans on this Saturday morning, but Annie noticed the one who wore glasses. He was staring at her.

Suddenly Carol Sue, who seemed to have collected herself, handed Annie the order total.

Annie told her to put it on the Knoll's credit.

Carol Sue smiled. "Don't you have the cash?"

"No," Annie said quietly, not wanting to draw any more attention to herself. "I want to use my father's credit."

"Well, I don't think that I can do that, Miss Annie Crow. Your daddy's dead."

"What the hell is going on up here?" Mr. Wilson hollered as he came in from the lumber yard. "Carol Sue, what are you doing dropping the phone like that? Is there a problem?"

"Well, yes there is, Mr. Wilson. Annie Crow called me a bitch and now she's trying to use her dead daddy's credit," Carol Sue whined.

Mr. Wilson turned and looked at Annie. The crowd that

had now taken up permanent residence near the counter was silent and waiting to see what would happen next. The young man with the glasses had a sympathetic look on his face.

Mr. Wilson spun back around to Carol Sue. "Annie called you a bitch because you deserved it, and of course we'll accept Luke's credit. Her daddy bought all his lumber here and that was quite a lot for all those cottages over the years. Now process that bill and get this young lady on her way. I'm sure she's got plenty to do out there on the Knoll."

Annie was relieved to head out to her truck. As she pulled around back to the yard to pick up her lumber, she could see though the front plate glass windows that the crowd around the counter hadn't broken up yet. Mr. Wilson seemed to be talking to them.

Probably telling them what a nut I am, she thought.

It was getting dark when Annie heard a boat pulling in.

Packard is back, she thought, and felt herself relax.

Catching up on some liability insurance reading was not her idea of an evening's entertainment, but it was how she spent her nights now, dealing with Annie Crow Knoll paperwork before collapsing into bed after working all day with Bo.

A sudden rap on the porch screen doorframe surprised her.

"Hello?" An unfamiliar man's voice followed another knock. "Anyone home?"

Annie threw on the porch light and opened the cottage front door.

"I'm sorry to bother you, but I saw your lights on. I'm having trouble with my boat, and I was wondering if you'd let me use your phone?"

All Annie could make out was the dark form of a man standing on her front step beyond the porch screen door.

"What's wrong with your boat?" Annie asked.

"I don't know. I'm not very mechanical," he laughed.

"Is the motor dead?"

"Yeah."

"But I heard the motor," Annie told him.

"Is this Annie Crow Knoll?"

Annie didn't like how he avoided her observation by changing the subject. Something didn't seem right, and she squinted into the dark edge of the screen door to see if the latch was hooked. Not that it was any serious deterrent, but it would buy her some time, if he tried to get into the porch. She couldn't remember if she had locked it.

Packard probably should have stayed in Rock Harbor after delivering his last haul and gotten Bud Nelson to look at the engine on *Sophie*. It wasn't running smoothly, but he'd wanted to get back. He'd been out fishing for a few days and wanted to check on Annie. Knowing that Bo was out there nearly every day helped, but Packard had gotten into the habit of making sure his young neighbor was safe and helping out whenever he could. He nursed *Sophie* back up the bay, figuring he could solve the engine problem himself the next day.

When Packard pulled into his dock, he noticed an unfamiliar boat in one of Annie's slips. Instinct took over as he headed up his pier. People didn't visit by boat this time of year and certainly not at this time of night.

Following that instinct, he made a quick detour to the house and grabbed his father's shotgun. It wasn't loaded, and Pack hadn't fired it since he was fourteen. On his first and only hunting trip, he'd brought down a Canada Goose, much to his father's pleasure. However, when his dad pushed on the poor dead bird's chest and the escaping air made a honk, there was no joy in it for young Packard. He never hunted again. *I shouldn't have left her alone for so many days*, Pack chided himself while crossing the field, feeling foolish carrying an unloaded shotgun. But if his gut was telling him the truth, and Annie was having a problem with an unwelcome guest, at least he could give the intruder a good whack on the head with the butt of the shotgun.

"Maybe you could use some help around here?" Pack heard the man's voice as he rounded the back of Sunrise Cottage. He held back, though, giving Annie the chance to handle it herself if she could.

"No, I don't," Annie said.

"Ah, come on. You must need a hand. I could use a job, but I'd be happy to work a deal."

Packard's hands tightened around the shotgun.

"I'm not hiring anyone."

"Well, then. Why don't you show me your cottages? Maybe I'll rent one," he added.

"We're all booked."

"That surprises me since I've seen your advertisement."

"Look, if you're really interested, come back in the daylight," Annie said.

"So you're not all booked?"

Annie didn't respond.

Packard wanted this guy out of here.

"There's a nice moon out this evening. Why don't you show me what's available now?"

"Get off my property," Annie told him.

"My boat engine won't start. Just let me use your phone, and I'll get out of here."

He pulled on the screen door handle and discovered that it was locked.

Annie slammed her front door shut.

Packard stepped out into view.

"Hey, buddy." The man stammered at the sight of big

Packard Marlboro holding a shotgun. "I'm going."

But the guy wasn't half way across the distance to the steps leading down to his boat when the front door swung open again and a shot rang out. Then he ran in earnest down the steps.

Beyond shock, Pack turned to see Annie holding Luke's gun and examining the huge hole she'd blown right through the screen.

"Great, something else to repair," she muttered, and then noticed Packard standing on her lawn. "Hey, Pack," she said. "Thanks for the sign. It's real sweet."

"Sure," he managed. "Hell of a hole you've got there."

"Yeah. I would have saved myself the effort if I'd known you were out here with a gun."

"It's not loaded."

"Your daddy's?"

"Yes. I haven't shot it in years. I don't hunt. Don't have the heart for it."

"Neither do I," she said. "But Daddy and Bo taught me to shoot tin cans when I was little. It comes back to you, like riding a bike."

"The fellow was giving you some motivation, too."

"Yes, he was aggravating me."

They heard the boat motor turn over and tear out quickly.

"I don't think he'll be back," Annie added.

"I sure wouldn't, if I were him."

"If I'd wanted to hit him, I would have."

Packard wanted to talk some more but couldn't think of anything else to say.

"Thanks for coming over to help," Annie said.

"I don't think you actually needed it."

"You make quite a picture standing there with your daddy's shotgun, Mr. Packard. Right out of *Field and Stream*."

Packard couldn't catch his breath.

"Well, good night," she said.

"Night, Annie."

On his way back across to his place, everything seemed new to Packard. His entire world had somehow changed when Annie took notice of him. Suddenly he felt a sense of possibility.

Annie and Bo were digging down to the septic pipe on Tochwogh Cottage when a VW Bug came up the drive, sounding like its muffler was hanging on by a thread. A stiff wind was blowing across the water, and the flag snapped loudly atop the pole at the circle where the Bug stopped. A young man stepped out of the car and stood staring for a moment at the view of the bay. Then he walked over toward Annie and Bo.

The sun was in Annie's eyes when she heard, "Are you Annie Crow?"

"Yes." She adjusted her stance so she could see this stranger more clearly.

Surely it wasn't that jerk from last night. He couldn't be that stupid. No, this man had a different build, and his voice wasn't the same.

"I'm Drew Bidwell." He shook her hand even though it was filthy with questionable matter. "I heard that you could use some volunteer help out here."

"Where'd you hear that?" Annie asked, still a little suspicious.

"At Wilson's Hardware. I teach at Queen Anne College. One of my students and I were there buying lumber for the spring theatre production. Mr. Wilson said that you're trying to save this place, and I'm always a sucker for a good cause."

Annie recognized him now. "You were there when I made quite a scene."

"I thought you had every right."

Annie stared at him. She liked how he looked, and she hoped she didn't have dirt on her face.

Bo cleared his throat.

"Oh, God, I'm forgetting my manners. This is Bo," Annie said.

"Hi, Bo. I'm Drew." He took Bo's hand and shook it firmly.

"Nice to meet you, Mr. Drew," Bo said. Annie's mouth was a bit open, but no words were coming out so Bo continued. "We sure could use some extra hands. What kind of work can you do?"

"I'm a pretty good carpenter," Drew offered.

Annie still couldn't find words and was relieved to hear Bo say, "Well, Mr. Drew, the front door on the Honeymoon Cottage got water damage over the winter, and it's all swollen shut. Do you mind takin' a look at it?"

"Sure. I have to get my tools out of the Bug," Drew answered.

"Why don't you show Mr. Drew the Honeymoon Cottage, Annie?" Bo gently nudged her with his shoulder.

"Oh, yeah, okay," she heard herself respond.

Drew turned back to Bo. "No need to call me Mr. Drew. Drew is just fine."

Annie saw Bo smile. She could tell that he liked this young man. Then she heard Bo chuckle as she and Drew Bidwell walked to his car.

When they reached the cottage, Drew pointed at the battered sign of a moon circled by honeybees and asked, "Why is it called Honeymoon Cottage?"

"Because it's so small, and my parents lived in it when they were first married."

"I'm sorry for your loss."

Drew's sincere statement caught Annie off guard. She felt the now familiar lump rise in her throat. Refusing to cry, Annie looked down and dug at the ground with the toe of one workboot.

"Thanks," she said after she was sure she had control again.

Drew pulled at the swollen door and forced it open. Annie liked the look of his strong, clean hands as he ran them over the edge of the wood.

"Thank you for helping," she said, struggling with owing yet another person, especially a stranger.

"No problem," he said and quietly set about working.

Annie didn't understand it, but she believed that this man just wanted to be there. He wasn't going to want anything from her in return. She stepped away to go help Bo but turned back to see Drew put his tool belt around his waist. He hitched his jeans up around his nonexistent hips. He was thin. Not skinny, but thin with a strong, broad back.

Then she felt it, the melting in her very depths. He might not want anything from her, but Annie wanted something from him. She'd waited longer than most girls had, and now she wouldn't have to wait too much longer. Instinct told Annie that Drew was the one worthy of her, and she started humming as she headed back to the septic problem at Tochwogh Cottage.

Packard hadn't been able to get *Sophie* running properly and nursed her down the bay to his mechanic. Between the repairs done and a storm, he had been stuck in Rock Harbor for two days. The entire trip down the bay and back, Pack kept thinking about Annie saying that he looked like a picture out of *Field and Stream*. It certainly seemed like a compliment. Her tone had been flirtatious. As much as he told himself not to expect anything, he couldn't deny that what he was feeling was in fact, hope.

Immediately after unloading his gear and cleaning up, he

headed over to the Knoll with that hope lodged between his throat and his heart. Climbing over the fence behind Sunrise Cottage, he heard voices on the front porch. When he reached the side of the screens, he saw Annie laughing with a young man he didn't know. Before they could turn and notice him, Packard stepped back out of view.

Hating himself for doing it, but unable to move, his heart raced as he listened.

Pack couldn't make out what they were talking about, but her voice sounded different. She was flirting! The young man laughed.

"You look like a picture," she had said to Packard in the same tone he heard now.

Unable to live with himself if he eavesdropped any longer, Pack bolted toward the fence but saw Bo wave to him from the back end of the roof on Cockatiel Cottage. Unable to make a clean escape, he walked behind Kingfisher and Tochwogh Cottages to where Bo was checking for loose shingles atop Cockatiel.

"I thought I saw you hop over the fence a bit ago," Bo said.

"Was going to see Annie, but she had company."

"Oh, that's Professor Drew Bidwell. He teaches over at the college." Bo paused to nail a loose shingle in place. "Storm blew these off last night. Had to check all the roofs today."

"What's he doing here?" Packard asked.

"Who?"

"That fellow with Annie?"

"Heard over at the lumber yard that we could use some help, so he volunteered. He worked all day yesterday and came back out after his morning classes today." Bo hammered another nail. "Might be nice for Miss Annie to have a beau. Give her something else to think about besides losing her folks and keepin' this place goin'."

Packard's ears were ringing, as if he were deep under water. Bo kept talking, but Pack couldn't hear him.

"I said, did you find your bottle jacks all right?" Bo asked, picking around in his pocket for the last roofing nail. "I put 'em over on your porch."

"No, I must have missed them."

"They did the trick. Thank you."

"Sure. I'll see you later," Pack muttered and then practically ran along the fence to where he was accustomed to climbing over.

Bo didn't see Packard again for a long time. No one did.

Sitting on the porch of Sunrise Cottage while Annie went inside to get more iced tea, Drew marveled at his good fortune. Last night, Annie had fed him dinner as a way of thanking him for his work on Honeymoon Cottage, and today he had been invited back for lunch after his morning classes. Although she belittled her cooking, these were the first home cooked meals Drew had had in ages. The family of one of his UCLA buddies owned a home in Chester Landing that they only used during the summer, and during the school year, Drew lived there alone. He took most of his evening meals at Randi's, the local pub several blocks off campus. In between, he grabbed sandwiches here and there. The last two days, he had found both Annie and her cooking delicious. Drew quickly realized that Annie Crow was no damsel in distress, either. She would be saving her Knoll with or without his help or Bo's for that matter. She was determined, bright and very appealing.

It concerned Drew a little that he was seven years older than Annie, who was only nineteen, the same age as many of his students. However, she was wise beyond her years and thankfully not enrolled at Queen Anne College in Chester Landing. Otherwise, it would be hands off. And he most definitely wanted to get his hands on her. He sensed that she felt the same way about him.

"Put a little meat on those bones," Annie had joked during dinner last night.

Drew was lean, but he could tell from her glances that she found that attractive.

"How did you end up on the Eastern Shore?" Annie asked when she returned with a fresh pitcher of iced tea.

"Honestly, at first I wasn't sure why I wanted to accept the position at Queen Anne College. My parents weren't wild about it."

"Why?"

"They assumed I'd be happier at one of the larger universities that had offered me a position. I gave them all the superficial reasons. Growing up on the West Coast, I couldn't live too far from a coast, any coast. The Chesapeake Bay is beautiful, and I appreciated that Baltimore, DC, Philadelphia and New York City are only a day's travel to museums, theatre and opera. I think they were also concerned that I wouldn't fit in at a small East Coast college."

"So what made you decide?" Annie asked.

"My instinct guided me to the Chesapeake Bay," he told her.

The payoff for Drew had been a culture steeped in American Folklore, which was his passion. Despite his parents' misgivings, he was glad that he had listened to his own voice. It was the same voice that told him two days ago to show up to help at Annie Crow Knoll. Not that the attractive Annie wasn't a motivating factor. She was, but he didn't really have any spare time to do volunteer work so a young woman whom he didn't even know could hold onto a property that he hadn't ever seen.

Everything had fallen into place, however, when Drew stepped out of his VW Bug and took in the astonishing view of the Chesapeake Bay. Then he met Annie and Bo, who were both knee-deep in Lord knows what working on a septic pipe. Instantly Drew felt affection for these two oddly matched people and at home on the Knoll.

"How did your instinct pay off?" Annie asked.

"In many ways, but primarily, I'm writing my doctoral dissertation on American Folklore, and the Eastern Shore of Maryland is steeped in lore," Drew answered.

"You make us sound quaint."

"Rich with tradition," he said, sensing Annie's defensiveness. "The watermen, the Black culture, the American Indians who once fished here. It's a magical place filled with wonderful people with fascinating stories."

It made Drew happy to see Annie relax after his response. He truly appreciated her home and hoped she knew that he appreciated her as well.

As the weeks prior to the opening of the Knoll approached, Annie and Drew talked non-stop whenever he came out to help, which he did frequently. Sometimes their conversations lasted into the wee hours of the morning when he should have been home grading papers and she catching up on the endless paperwork that her mother had seemingly managed with very little effort.

Their conversations ranged from literature to politics to carpentry.

"But do governments need to support the arts?" Drew asked one evening.

"History makes that clear," Annie replied. "What would have happened to Shakespeare without the patronage of Queen Elizabeth I or Moliere without Louis XIV?"

"Are you going to go back to the community college in the fall?" Drew suddenly asked.

"No."

"A local public high school education isn't enough. You'd benefit from college." Drew noticed her eyebrows go up. "Everyone does," he quickly added.

"You're a snob!"

"You're right. I'm sorry."

"Well, at least you admit it."

"I don't like confessing it, but you have rather skillfully, albeit surgically, exposed my prejudice. However, it is based on experience. Some of the local students who make it into my classes need tutoring to catch up," Drew explained.

"You find it hard to believe that an Eastern Shore high school educated country bumpkin has read Shakespeare, Ibsen, Hellman, and Steinbeck," she retorted.

Annie wasn't going to admit that her mother's tutelage was the primary force in her exposure to the classics. Never let the truth get in the way of a good argument.

"You haven't simply read them, you're equipped to debate the finer points more intelligently than most of the collegiate English majors I've met," Drew said with a smile of delight.

That was why she wanted to rip those cute professorial eyeglasses off his shockingly blue eyes. He had apologized and then complimented her, but only after making glaring assumptions about her education. How could she want to make love with him? Yet she did. Despite his flaws, Drew Bidwell did something to her that no man had ever done, and this was without even having touched her yet.

Besides, she didn't want to end up as Grace had predicted. "You're so picky that no man will ever be good enough for you," her best friend had said. Annie could live with becoming an old maid, but not a virgin old maid. She wondered when Drew Bidwell would finally make a move.

Just two weeks before the Knoll opened and ten days before Drew's semester grades were due, he drove out to see Annie. Since he was under the end of the semester crunch, he hadn't been able to come out to work for several days. But he had stayed up late every night that week grading papers so he could give her a full day's work on Sunday.

"Are all the cottages rented now?" Drew asked that evening after spending long hours repainting the blue shutters on most of the cottages. Bo, Annie and Drew had worn themselves out on the project, but Drew lingered past dinner, not wanting to leave Annie. They sat together on the dock, watching the sun set.

"Nearly."

"Do you still have anything open for the season? The house in Chester Landing is going to be too noisy and filled with people this summer to concentrate on writing my dissertation."

"You can rent Honeymoon Cottage. I'll give you a break on the cost for all the work you've done here."

"I can't let you do that. I volunteered. I'm not expecting anything in return."

"Well, if you want to keep helping in the future, it has to be taken off your rent," Annie insisted.

"You mean you won't let me volunteer if I'm paying rent?"

"No."

"You're not the shrewd business woman I thought you were."

"Maybe I like cutting my nose off to spite my face."

"And what a lovely nose it is."

"Then what are you waiting for? I mean, for what are you waiting?"

"Nothing."

"So kiss me, Drew Bidwell."

Drew didn't need to be invited twice.

After several lingering kisses, he asked, "Is this how you land all your rental agreements?"

"Hmmm. Maybe."

Drew took Annie into his arms and held her while twilight melted into darkness. Feeling her close to him, he suddenly wondered if moving into the Honeymoon Cottage was such a good idea. Would he be able to concentrate on his paper with Annie only a few steps away?

"Seriously," he said.

"Oh, I'm serious," Annie glanced up at him.

"I am too." He moved a bit so that he could look at her straight on. "You charge whatever rent you'd get from a regular tenant. I'll help out when I want and only on a volunteer basis. I have serious work to do this summer on my dissertation. I have to be ready to defend it back at UCLA by January. I can't be expected to fix a leaky faucet because I'm paying less rent."

"I can fix that myself!"

"I realize that. But I need you to understand that I'll be writing."

"My God, you're uptight for a Californian."

"I'm from Oregon."

Taking on the heaviest, stereotypical Eastern Shore accent she could imitate, Annie said, "I dun thought they was the same thing."

Annie stood to dash up the dock, but Drew caught her wrist, and they fell back into each other's arms, laughing and kissing. They spent the rest of the evening on the dock talking and watching the stars in the clear Chesapeake sky.

Chapter Nine
Summer 1965

THE DAY THAT ANNIE DROVE to the Philadelphia airport to pick up Grace, she felt like she was going to burst from excitement. The Knoll season opened in three days; nine of the cottages now had season rentals, and the other four were about seventy percent rented by the week. Annie and Grace would have hectic Saturdays getting four cottages cleaned in only three hours, but Annie knew that if anyone could pull it off, they could.

As she waited at the gate for Grace's plane, Annie couldn't have been more nervous. It was the closest thing she had to bringing Drew home to her folks. What if Grace didn't like him when they met tonight?

Before they had even pulled out of the airport parking lot, Grace asked, "Have you slept with him, yet?"

"No!"

"What are you waiting for?"

"He's a slow mover, I think."

"I'm just teasing," Grace said. "There's nothing wrong with waiting. It's better to be sure."

"I'm sure."

"But you'd better not marry him," Grace said with a deadpan expression.

"Who's talking about marriage? You haven't even met him yet. How do you know I shouldn't eventually marry him?" Annie said a little defensively.

Grace enjoyed baiting her and now pulled the hook. "His name isn't Oliver."

"Very funny. My God, you had me worried there for a minute."

"Does he know that you're a virgin?"

"I'm not the only one left, you know."

"So he knows."

"I haven't a clue."

"I was just wondering if maybe that's why he's taking it slowly," Grace suggested.

"Well, we've been seeing each other for over a month. I can't stand it much longer."

"Maybe he's moving slowly because he's a virgin, too!"

Annie almost ran her father's truck into oncoming traffic.

"Look, I haven't really driven in this kind of traffic. You'd better not say anything else like that or I'm going to end up killing both of us, and I'll die a virgin!"

"What if he is?"

"Then we'll figure it out together, but I don't think he is." Annie tried to sound confident.

"Why?"

"He's been to college in the same state as you!"

"California? Oh, then, he's definitely not a virgin!"

"Plus, he seems to know what he's doing so far."

"Good?"

"Very!"

Opening weekend, everyone remarked on how prepared Annie was. The lawns were manicured, every cottage was spotless, and all repairs were completed. Drew enjoyed watching Annie beam with pride as she greeted each tenant. In celebration, he presented her with two cement crows.

"Where did you find these?" Annie said with delight as they placed them atop the two stone pillars at the entrance to Annie Crow Knoll.

"We made them at the college theatre. I found an old prop crow and had the kids make a mold from it. Then we poured two castings with it."

"They couldn't be more perfect." Annie smiled. "Thank you."

In the Honeymoon Cottage, Drew decided to set up his typewriter, files and piles of endless note cards on the table in the kitchen area, located at the back of the tiny, one room building. Since he was invited to eat most of his meals with Annie and Grace, this afforded him the best view of the east side of the property as it sloped down to the river and toward Cattail while he worked.

After writing all morning, Drew decided to stretch his legs. When he saw Grace on the beach raking up debris washed ashore from the previous night's thunderstorm, he grabbed a rake from the tool shed and went down to help. The exercise would clear his mind, and he wanted to speak to Grace privately.

"Like some help?" he asked her.

"Sure."

They worked in silence clearing the beach. Eventually Grace said, "You seem to have something on your mind, Drew."

"As a matter of fact, I do." He enjoyed her perceptiveness. "I know we've only known each other a few days, but you're still not sure about me, are you?"

"I'm sorry that it shows."

"Don't be. It proves your love for Annie," Drew assured her.

Grace looked at him. "A few professors at my college date students. I guess it can be okay in certain situations, but my roommate got hurt pretty badly by one."

"That's unconscionable. I have never and would never get involved with a student."

"I don't want that to happen to Annie."

"Annie isn't my student."

"She's young enough to be."

"Look, even though I'm seven years older than she is, I view her as an equal."

"Annie wouldn't accept anyone who didn't."

"True." Drew smiled. "What I'm saying is that there can be an inequality when an authority figure, such as a teacher, dates someone who looks up to him or her, such as a student. We didn't start with that relationship, so Annie and I are on equal ground."

After a moment Grace said, "I like you."

"But?"

"Well, I'm confused."

"How?"

"On the one hand, I think it's admirable of you to be so respectful of Annie, but on the other hand, I'm wondering what's wrong with you that you don't make a move!"

Drew laughed. "And I thought Annie was honest."

Grace blushed. "I probably shouldn't have said that. Annie'll kill me."

"I'm waiting for her," Drew said simply.

That evening as Annie was getting ready for bed, Grace appeared in her bedroom doorway. "Annie, you have my blessing."

"To do what?" she asked while putting on her pajamas.

"God, you're dense." Grace nodded in the direction of Drew's cottage. "He's waiting for you, and I think he's a wonderful guy, so if you're ready, you have my blessing."

"How do you know he's waiting for me?" Annie asked suspiciously.

Grace simply replied, "Trust me," before disappearing into Liz and Luke's bedroom, which she'd taken over for the summer.

Annie certainly felt ready. Doc had put her on the pill a week after she met Drew, but she was a little nervous now that it might actually happen. She looked out the front window across to Honeymoon Cottage. The lights were out. He was probably already asleep. She hesitated. Maybe Grace was right, she thought. So she dressed again in just her skirt, halter top and flip flops and quietly snuck over in the dark. She guessed that he wouldn't bother to lock the door. No one did on the Knoll.

When Annie entered, Drew sat up in bed naked only a few feet away from her.

Now that she stood in front of him, she didn't know what to do exactly.

"I couldn't wait any longer," she finally said.

Drew reached his hand out to her, and Annie fell on him. At first they kissed hard and fast. With urgency, she tugged off her skirt while Drew pulled the two bows to remove her halter top.

Then Drew stopped. For several moments, he simply looked at her.

She felt completely comfortable under his gaze.

"Annie, you're beautiful," he finally whispered.

Then he leaned over her, kissing her slowly and softly on the lips. Annie felt her toes curl as he began running kisses down her neck and shoulders.

This is it, she thought as she gave herself over to the wonderful things Drew was doing, a rite of passage and with the right person.

As the season continued, all the regulars supported Annie's management of the Knoll. If Jim and Naomi Finch had any concerns about how things were going, they never questioned Annie in front of other tenants. Maizie and Sam Waters gave her their unconditional support. They made sure that their two children, Sammy and Sarah, treated Annie with the same respect they'd shown her parents. The Slims, Mrs. Waters and other returning renters regarded Annie as the owner.

Annie clung to those regular, friendly faces with tremendous gratefulness. Even the new full-time renters were settling in pretty well. However, the weekly renters, or "transients" as Annie and Grace teasingly referred to them, in Owl's Nest, No Name, Blue Heron and Fish Tale often didn't seem to understand that Annie was in charge.

One afternoon, a snake appeared with its sleek form slicing through the water and its head held up above the surface. It came up onto the quiet beach to sun itself when two "transient" boys from No Name Cottage noticed it from the dock.

"Throw stones at it," their grandfather instructed as he lit another cigarette.

Given an assignment to attack, the boys jumped into action, neither one of them considering whether or not this was the right thing to do.

They screamed with excitement as they threw pebbles by the handful cornering the snake on the beach. Their wild yells caught Annie's attention as she and Grace were weeding along the top of the knoll.

"Stop it," she shouted from above.

Perhaps the boys couldn't hear her for the wind or their own thirst to hurt something, but they persisted. Annie ran down the stairs, yelling for the boys to stop it. Grace followed.

"Leave the snake alone," Annie hollered again. The boys ignored her.

"Hell, we used to kill snakes when I was their age," the old man said as he took another puff on his cigarette.

Annie knew not to waste precious time asking this man to stop his grandsons because he clearly didn't care what she wanted. The oldest boy was aiming a large rock, and Annie swiftly knocked the rock out of his hand. It landed with a thud in the sand.

The snake made a mad dash back into the water and disappeared.

"What the hell do you think you're doing?" another man standing nearby snapped. "That's my son!"

"He was trying to kill the snake," Annie said, looking the man right in the eyes. "I told him to stop, but he ignored me. I had no other choice."

"She hurt my hand, Dad," the boy whined.

"That's not all I'll do if you don't respect the wild life on the Knoll," she said, standing with both hands on her hips and her feet firmly planted.

"It was only a stupid snake," the grandfather chimed in.

"You're the stupid one for telling the boys to throw stones at it. What if one of these boys goes hiking with a scout troop, and he sees a rattlesnake or a copperhead? Is he going to know the difference between a harmless snake and a venomous one?

No. Has he been taught to attack snakes instead of giving them a wide girth? Yes. And what happens when this misguided boy riles a rattler and the snake goes after him to protect itself?" Annie turned to the boys. "Either of you ever been bitten by a snake?"

The boys looked at her with wide eyes.

"It can kill you. You could die. So leave the snakes, all snakes alone."

The boys nodded.

"I'm sorry if I hurt you. But you weren't listening to me, and I own Annie Crow Knoll. What I say goes."

"Yes, ma'am."

"Come on, boys. I've had enough of this," their father said.

The grandfather tossed his cigarette butt on the beach.

"There's an ash can for that," Grace said as he passed her.

He ignored her and followed his son and grandsons up the stairs.

"They won't be return customers," Grace remarked to Annie.

"I don't care. My father wouldn't have put up with that."

"No, but they'd take it better from a man."

"Well, to hell with them." Annie saw no signs of the snake. "I hope the poor thing is all right."

Once a week, Drew left his dissertation work on the Knoll and spent the day in his office at the college, preparing for the fall semester and catching up on mail.

During his second visit in July, his office phone rang.

"Can you stop by before you leave?" Dr. Leonard asked over the phone.

"Sure. I can come over right now if it's convenient."

"That's fine."

Since Dr. Leonard's office was only down the hall and other department members weren't in their offices today, Drew wondered why his Department Chairman hadn't just stopped by. There had to be a reason for the conversation to be in Dr. Leonard's office. As he made his way, Drew hoped there wasn't going to be a change in his schedule since he'd already done a good deal of prep work.

"How's the dissertation coming?" Dr. Leonard said, as Drew took a seat across from his boss.

"Fine. Quite well, actually. I'm on the schedule that I set for myself."

"We'll be calling you Dr. Bidwell before long."

"I don't want to appear rude, sir, but you seemed to have something on your mind when you asked me to come in."

"Yes, I do, Drew. It's kind of a delicate situation."

"Please, go on."

"Do you know who Delia Witherspoon is?" Dr. Leonard asked.

"No, I don't."

"She's your landlady's great-grandmother and a key benefactress of the college."

Drew found it odd to hear Annie referred to as his landlady.

"Annie's great-grandmother?"

"Has Miss Annie mentioned her to you?"

Drew wondered why the wealthy relative wasn't helping Annie out financially at the Knoll.

"No, she's never mentioned her."

"Mrs. Witherspoon has felt it necessary to inform me that you are having a romantic relationship with her great-granddaughter."

Drew tried to check his anger as he said, "I didn't know that my personal life was of concern to you."

"Not me, necessarily, but it is of great concern to Mrs.

Witherspoon."

"Why does she care? I haven't even met the woman," Drew said, as calmly as possible.

"Apparently she and Miss Annie's mother had a falling out when Mrs. Witherspoon didn't approve of Annie's father."

"And now she doesn't approve of me?" Drew was incredulous.

"No, she doesn't disapprove of you at all."

"Annie? She doesn't approve of her own flesh and blood?" Drew was figuring out very quickly why Annie never mentioned her great-grandmother.

"Mrs. Witherspoon doubts her great-granddaughter is suited to be the wife of a professor at Queen Anne College."

"I don't believe this!" Drew said, running his fingers through his hair. "Where has she gotten her information? Does she have someone spying on Annie?"

"Mrs. Witherspoon did not reveal her source to me, Drew."

"This is sick."

"Nevertheless, Delia Witherspoon carries a great deal of power at Queen Anne, and she doesn't want to see you getting into a relationship that might harm your career."

Unable to find a way to be diplomatic, Drew asked, "Are you threatening me?"

"Of course not."

"Because you might as well fire me right now before the fall semester begins."

"Please, Drew, you're overreacting."

"I won't have my personal life controlled by some mean-spirited money bag who donates to the college so that she can run people's lives."

"Well, for not having met her, you certainly seem to have her number," Dr. Leonard said with a smile.

"I'm serious about this. I love it here, but I'll type up my resignation right now if I'm not free to date whom I please and marry who pleases me."

"I don't want to hear any more about resignations," Dr. Leonard said firmly. He removed his eyeglasses and rubbed his brow. "I wasn't going to mention this just yet, but once you get your doctorate, I'm recommending you for a full professorship early." He didn't pause for Drew to respond. "Why don't you bring Annie over for dinner one night this summer? We'll have a few other professors and their spouses over, too. That way we can get to know her. Make her part of the family here. Then her great-grandmother's opinion won't be the only one tipping the scales."

"She has to pass some kind of approval test?" Drew asked.

Unflustered, Dr. Leonard said, "Just think about it. That's all I'm saying."

During his drive back to Promise, Drew replayed his conversation with Dr. Leonard. He had surprised himself. "Marry who pleases me." Somewhere deep inside himself, he realized he wanted to ask Annie to marry him but hadn't said it out loud.

When he reached the Knoll, Drew found Annie in Cockatiel Cottage with her head and torso in the cabinet under the kitchen sink and her legs and feet sprawled out across the floor.

"How'd it go today?" she asked from under the sink.

"Interesting," Drew answered and then asked, "Is there a leak?"

"Not anymore." Annie pulled herself up, holding a wrench in her hand. "What was interesting?"

"Well, Dr. Leonard called me in to discuss your great-grandmother who is a major Queen Anne College benefactress."

Drew watched a darkness come over Annie's face.

"I have no idea who she gives her money to, and I don't care."

"But it sure isn't to you, is it?" Drew asked.

"No."

"Why? Why isn't she helping to save this place from development?"

"Because she's the one who wants to develop it."

"That must be terrible for you."

His sincerity must have cracked something open in Annie because tears began to form in her eyes.

She turned away and put the wrench in her tool bag. "I've new tenants coming in here soon."

"Honey," Drew said. "It's okay to tell me and to cry if you need to."

Annie ran a hand roughly across her burning cheeks.

"I don't want to cry!" she shouted.

"But you already are." Drew took her into his arms.

When she could get the words out, she said, "I miss my parents. They would know how to handle Great Grand for me. Just because she owns half the county she, thinks she can run my life."

"But she doesn't own the Knoll," Drew reminded her while passing her his handkerchief.

"No, and I'll die before I'll let her get her greedy hands on it."

"Why is she so vindictive?" Drew couldn't help but ask.

"Great Grand wants to control everyone," Annie said and blew nose. "I haven't seen her or spoken to her in years."

"Even when your parents died?"

"Most definitely then. They were dead to her years before."

"Why didn't you tell me about her trying to get the Knoll?" Drew asked.

Annie pulled away again. "My finances aren't your concern."

"How do you do that?"

"Do what?"

"Let me in one moment and shut me out the next?"

"I'm sorry. I just don't see how it's your business."

"It's not. But I'm your friend, aren't I? I'm your lover, for God's sake. Grace knows about Delia, doesn't she?"

"Yes."

"I'll bet Bo knows, too."

"Well, yes."

"You don't trust me like you do them?"

"I've known them longer."

"Oh."

Annie paused and then said, "When I really listen to my heart, I do trust you, Drew. I just don't always have time to let myself listen."

But it was too late. Drew felt hurt and confused. He was risking his career while Annie didn't even trust him enough to tell him about her great-grandmother.

"I think, that under the circumstances, we need to be more discreet," he told her coolly.

"What circumstances?"

"Your great-grandmother has a lot of power, and somehow she's connected the two of us. She could cause you more trouble."

"Look, everybody knows everything out here. It's impossible to hide anything, so why try?" Annie argued.

"What about your reputation?" Drew asked.

"I lost that years ago when I went skinny dipping with Tommy Reynolds," Annie said with a laugh.

"You're not a kid anymore. You're a grown woman with a business to run and protect."

"I don't care what people think!"

"Well, I suggest that you start caring! It can and will affect your business."

She picked up her tool bag and gestured with it. "This is what affects business, not my precious reputation." And she was gone.

Annie infuriated Drew. How could he possibly be thinking about marrying this irresponsible teenager? It hit him square in the face; she was still a teenager! After some consideration, however, Drew had to admit to himself that he had called Dr. Leonard's bluff because he didn't like being told what he could and could not do. He hadn't done it only for Annie or because he loved her, though he did. Actually it had been a knee-jerk reaction to feeling manipulated by the college system and Delia Witherspoon. Perhaps Drew wasn't so different from Annie Crow. He was more polished and, yes, discreet. There was that word again. But underneath, they were more similar than Drew had realized.

Annie felt miserable. She and Drew had had their first fight, and she didn't appreciate the way it made her feel. He had sounded judgmental like her mother, and she resented it.

After all, Annie told herself, *I run a respectable establishment. Annie Crow Knoll is a nice, family place. What I do after hours is my business.*

Annie did, however, want someone's honest opinion. Grace was still at work at Turner's Market, but fortunately, Maizie was there for the week with her children. Sam had stayed in the city. Annie felt sure she wouldn't shock Maizie with this question and that she'd get a straightforward answer. So she went directly to Sun-swept Cottage to ask her.

"Is it obvious to you that Drew and I are sleeping together?"

"It's obvious that you're in love," Maizie said with that Finch twinkle in her eye.

Annie didn't know what to say. She hadn't factored that into the equation of her life quite yet.

"You think so?"

"I know so."

"Then why don't I know it?"

"You will when you're ready."

Annie sat for a moment pondering.

"Drew and I had our first fight today."

"That's inevitable."

"It was awful. He thinks we need to be more careful about our relationship. If it's so obvious to you, then I guess everyone knows that we are having sex."

"I didn't think that would matter to you."

"It only matters if people find it offensive and don't rent the cottages."

"I see. Well, you haven't been that obvious about it."

"I don't think so either. I mean, ninety percent of the time, one of us sneaks over to the other's cottage after dark, and then sneaks back before dawn. Once in a while, we get lazy and stay. I suppose that's not a good idea."

"Most people are going to think what they will," Maizie said. "We both know that there are no secrets on the Knoll. But Sam and I went through a similar thing before we were married. We both had to protect our reputations as doctors. We were careful. It was such a relief after we got married, and we didn't have to hide it. But, in some ways, things are more relaxed nowadays."

"I don't like hiding and sneaking. It's ridiculous!"

"But a lot of people still feel that sex should wait until after marriage, and if they are trying to instill that moral in their children, they don't want their kids exposed to adult role models who are obviously not waiting."

"It's stupid that women have to worry about their reputations!" Annie said.

"I was thinking about Drew. He's teaching young people as his career. Parents could be very upset if he isn't living, or doesn't appear to be living, a certain lifestyle."

"I hadn't thought about Drew. I'm so self-centered sometimes."

"It's not easy to start thinking about another person's feelings all of a sudden."

"But I have to if I want to have a relationship."

"If you want it to last, you do."

Annie impulsively hugged Maizie.

She found Drew sitting on the steps of her cottage. She didn't think that she could cross the lawn to him fast enough.

"I'm sorry. I'm so sorry!" she said, as she reached him.

"So am I," Drew said, putting his arms around her waist.

"You are? What do you have to be sorry about? I'm the one who was being selfish."

"Hey, I like this," Drew joked. "Is this how it'll always be when we fight? You'll admit that you're wrong and apologize?"

"No." Annie gave him a gentle nudge in the arm. "I hadn't thought about you needing to protect your reputation at the college. I don't mind protecting your reputation. It kind of makes me feel like—"

"A man," Drew interrupted.

"No, like I'm taking care of you," Annie said, as Grace arrived from Turners with a bag of groceries.

"I don't know what this is doing for my male ego!" Drew teased Annie.

"Come on, maybe dinner will help counteract whatever has bruised your male ego," Grace said.

As Annie and Drew followed her into the cottage, she added, "And it's Drew's night to do the dishes. That should just about send him into therapy!"

"Don't worry, I'll restore his precious male ego later tonight," Annie said with a laugh.

Drew awoke to the sound of birds. Light began to creep in through the window.

"Shit!" he whispered.

Annie didn't wake.

He'd fallen asleep in her bedroom when he should have gone back to Honeymoon while it was still dark. He threw his clothes on and crept out the front door onto the porch. It didn't look like anyone was up yet. As quietly as he could, Drew opened and closed the porch screen door, making sure that it didn't slam shut. He ran down the steps and almost collided with Packard Marlboro.

"Oh!" Drew said, startled.

He recognized the man as the waterman he'd seen on the dock of the property next to the Knoll. He looked much bigger to Drew as he stood here next to him by Annie's cottage. The tall man simply nodded and then continued on his way along the edge of the Knoll toward the steps to the beach. His body language indicated anger, and Drew wondered what the man had to be angry about on this beautiful morning.

On the weekend, Annie and Drew took the skiff out to see what was biting. Annie couldn't believe that Drew had never fished as a kid. It was most apparent when they returned and the catch had to be cleaned.

"How did you grow up on the West Coast and never learn to fish?" she asked, as they sat on the end of the dock.

"We surfed."

"Poor excuse."

"Wait until you've surfed to make that call, especially now when it's time to clean these stinky things."

Annie watched with amusement when Drew closed his eyes as he cut the head off the first fish. She had tried a number of times to teach him how to handle a knife on a fresh fish, but he just couldn't get it right.

"Give it to me before you butcher the whole thing, and we don't have anything left to eat," she chided him.

"Hell, no. I can do this."

Annie heard a boat and looked up to see Packard pass by in *Sophie* on his way to his dock. She waved, and Pack tipped his hat.

"Why don't you ever talk to him?" Drew asked and pointed with the knife.

Annie reached for it unsuccessfully. "Will you give up?"

"Don't try to change the subject. What's with that guy?"

"That guy is Packard Marlboro, and you're starting to sound like a local."

"I know. I'm going to have to concentrate when I'm back in the classroom."

"Your students will like you better if you talk like you do here."

"They like me fine, and you've done it again. Changed the subject. Why don't you speak with your neighbor Packard Marlboro?"

"What do you mean? Of course I speak to him."

Annie realized how little contact she had had with Packard since last spring.

"No, you don't."

"I just waved to him."

"But you never spoke."

"Why are you trying to start trouble?" Annie asked.

"It's not natural to never speak to a neighbor," Drew insisted.

"He doesn't want to talk. He never has," Annie tried to explain.

"Never?"

Annie knew that that wasn't completely true. He was a wonderful neighbor. She felt a little guilty that she had let him drift back into his solitude, but he must have wanted it that way. After all, he had stopped coming over.

"How do you know? Did you ever ask him?"

"Drew, he likes to be left alone."

"Well, I'm going over there. The man obviously makes his living fishing. He'll know how to teach me to filet one of these." Drew rinsed his hands in the bay water and grabbed the bucket of fish.

"Tell him hello from me, will you?" Annie asked.

"Tell him yourself," he called back on his way up the dock.

At the top of the stairs, Naomi and Jim Finch, who were sitting on the porch of Sunset Cottage, intercepted Drew. They wanted to know how his dissertation was coming. They offered him a cup of fresh coffee and threw ice on his fish in the bucket. As was typical on the Knoll, one thing led to another, and by the time Drew crossed the field to the Marlboro place, Packard sat in his yard painting a picture of a chocolate brown Labrador retriever. A photograph of the dog was clipped to the top edge of his easel.

"You paint!" Drew said, startling first Packard and then himself when the big man jumped up nearly knocking over his easel. "Sorry."

Packard said nothing but settled back down to continue painting.

Uncomfortable with the silence, Drew asked, "Your dog?"

"No."

Maybe Annie was right, Drew thought to himself, but he persisted.

"It's a beautiful dog," he said, as Pack continued painting. "Who took the photograph?"

"My cousin."

"His dog?"

"No."

Wow. Four words so far. Drew took this as a challenge

now, as he might with a student who wouldn't speak up.

"His friend's dog?"

"Her neighbor's dog."

"You've really captured the dog's expressions. It's in his eyes."

"I have to finish this so I can go fishing tonight," Packard finally said.

"Ah, fishing. That's why I came by." Drew lifted up his bucket. "I wondered if you'd show me how to filet these fish Annie and I caught?"

"No, I can't."

"Of course, you're busy. Maybe some other time," Drew said. "Oh, I'm Drew Bidwell, by the way."

When Drew extended his hand, Packard sighed. Realizing that the artist would have to put down his brush, Drew withdrew his hand.

"I'll leave you to it then," Drew said.

As the college professor retreated back to the Knoll, Packard wondered what Annie saw in that skinny guy with the glasses, anyway. Didn't even know what to do with a fish he managed to catch.

However, Packard couldn't waste time on this. He had to finish this painting before his sometimes pushy, but caring, cousin Elsie Trommer called again asking when it would be done. Several years ago, Elsie had gotten him roped into painting people's pets, horses, homes, and estates. She took ten percent for finding the client and taking the photographs. That way Packard didn't have to deal with the actual clients. It was a nice additional income to Elsie's dressmaking business, and it gave Pack welcome work in the winter. However, it was inconvenient when she found a commission during the height of the crabbing or fishing seasons.

"But it's Bosco's master's birthday this month, and his wife, the owner's, not the dog's, wants Bosco's portrait as a gift," Cousin Elsie had insisted. So here Packard was painting with a deadline, and now this college professor had taken up valuable time. He hoped he had seen the last of Drew Bidwell.

But like a bad penny, Drew showed up again about a week later when Packard was pulling up to his dock after spending several days and nights out on the water. All he wanted to do was take a shower and crawl into bed.

"Hey!" Drew called, as he walked down the dock toward the workboat.

Pack still had to unload his gear and wash down the deck before he could sleep, and this guy, with the lousy timing, was back.

"Been out for a few days?" Drew asked.

"Yep." Packard gave his usual monosyllabic response in hope of discouraging this guy.

"Must be tired," Drew said and reached for the lines and tied them to the piling.

"You have a knack for observing the obvious."

"I'm persistent, too."

"More than one annoying trait."

"Tons. You can ask Annie."

"No, I don't need to ask Annie," Pack said pointedly and then disappeared into the wheelhouse of his workboat. Through the window, he saw Drew step onto the deck.

"This is a beautiful old boat. I noticed you named her *Sophie*."

"Yep."

"Short for Sophia?"

"Yep."

"Your sweetheart?"

"My sister."

"Does she live around here?"

"She died."

"Sorry."

Packard came out of the wheelhouse with a load of gear.

"Here, let me help you with that stuff." Drew lifted the duffel bag and jumped back onto the dock. "Hand me that," he told Pack, pointing to the ice chest.

"You know much about boats?" Pack asked, as he handed off the ice chest off.

"I don't know much about fishing, but I've been around boats."

"Pleasure boats," Pack remarked.

Drew shrugged his shoulders and smiled.

Packard didn't want to like anything about this guy, but he did admire how Drew refused to back down.

When Packard leaned over the deck with a bucket and pulled up bay water to wash down *Sophie's* deck, Drew hopped back on board, grabbed a nearby mop and began cleaning.

"I put a basket with a fresh blackberry pie in it on your porch. Annie and I baked it from berries we picked on the edge of the woods."

"Thank you." Packard realized he wasn't going to get rid of Drew so he leaned up against the wheelhouse and watched him mop.

"Can you get another bucket of water?" Drew asked.

As he emptied the bucket on deck, Pack found himself asking, "Want to go crabbing on Sunday?"

"Sure. That'd be great."

CHAPTER TEN
FALL 1965

IT WAS GETTING CLOSE TO dusk as Packard prepared for Drew to arrive for their weekly game of chess. Before he knew what was happening, Drew had started coming over from the Knoll one night a week to play chess on the front porch of the Marlboro house. At first, Pack was a bit resistant, but he enjoyed it, despite himself. He liked spending the evening on the porch drinking imported beers, smoking cigars and calculating the next strategic move with this bright young man. As the summer progressed, the ten year age difference between them disappeared. Packard surprised himself and began considering Drew his friend.

Having learned to live with impermanence, however, Packard hadn't expected these weekly games to continue once the fall semester started for Drew and he moved out of the unheated Honeymoon Cottage and back to the house in Chester Landing near campus. He felt sad rather than relieved that his new friend might stop coming by on a weekly basis. But Drew had no intention of stopping.

The professor was due to arrive at seven o'clock, and his host busied himself with setting the chessboard up in the living room. Tonight was the first time that they'd be playing inside Packard's house. It was getting too cool to stay on the porch, and the sun was setting much earlier as well.

When Packard made one last trip toward the kitchen to get an ashtray, he glanced again at what he considered the largest hurdle of the night, which was having Drew see the portrait of young Annie with her dead crow. It hung on the dining room wall, adjacent to the living room, and was impossible to miss. Pack wondered what Drew would say. Would he tell Annie? What would she think?

As usual, the punctual Drew Bidwell arrived five minutes early. He parked his car in the drive by the back door, but since he'd never been inside Packard's house, he walked around to the front porch, which overlooked the bay. The sun no longer met the horizon over the water but set farther in the southwest now, causing the trees to create long shadows across the lawn.

"Getting dark much earlier," Drew noted, as he shook Packard's hand.

"It's bound to happen. Come on in."

The front door of the old house entered directly into the living room, the walls of which were lined with shelves of books. Along the windowsills sat old jars filled with pieces of different colored sea glass. There were more glass-filled jars set along the mantelpiece of the fireplace.

Although the books and jars fascinated Drew, he was immediately drawn to Packard's paintings, which covered any space not occupied by book cases. He spent time carefully examining and appreciating each one, beginning with a portrait of Packard's parents which hung over the fireplace. When he turned and entered the dining room and saw Annie with Oliver limp in her hands, he only said, "She was a beautiful child."

As autumn progressed, Annie and Bo took on the tasks of winterizing the cottages with great enthusiasm. Managing to stay one step ahead of the loan payments and Delia Witherspoon, they held closing up the first season at Annie Crow Knoll as a celebration.

Several families had already made down payments to hold their cottages for the next season. However, Annie still needed additional income over the winter. She hadn't realized the difference that her father's hunting and handyman work and her mother's sewing had made until she looked over Liz's ledgers.

"I'm not going to be able to keep up with these payments without a winter job," she told Grace on the phone. "I asked at the market, but Mrs. Turner didn't need anyone. She and Elwood can pretty much handle it themselves after the summer season ends. I guess I'm going to have to go into Chester Landing and see if I can find anything."

"You should write," Grace told her from the phone in her dorm hallway.

"Write? Are you out of your mind? Drew is the writer, not me."

"Open your eyes, Sunshine."

"Sunshine?"

"It's a California thing…Listen, I have an older sorority sister who graduated the year I pledged. Her parents are loaded, in publishing, from Atlanta, and she's started a magazine for women called *Elegant Southern Life*. Patsy contacted all the sorority sisters looking for articles on stuff like five ways to make the perfect plantation punch and crap like that."

"What's that got to do with me? I don't know how to write magazine articles for women," Annie said.

"But you write letters to me all the time, hundreds of them over the years, all about life on the Knoll."

"Letters are different."

"That's where you're missing it. Letters are perfect! When I go home to visit, Mom loves it when I read your letters out loud to her."

"I hope you haven't read all of them!"

"Don't sweat it. I don't read the juicy parts to her. Well, until you met Drew there weren't any juicy parts. But seriously, what you write is funny, informative, and well, Southern."

"Gee."

"So pretend that you're writing to me when you write for the magazine," Grace advised. "Contact Patsy and tell her I recommended you submit something for her fancy ass magazine."

"Can I quote you on that?"

When Drew arrived for the weekend, Annie told him about writing an article for the magazine.

"Patsy told me to 'whip up something on spring gardening or Easter dinner tips.'"

"Why don't you take a writing course first?" Drew advised and then regretted it when the enthusiastic look on Annie's face immediately disappeared.

"You don't think that I can do this, do you?"

"Of course you can. You can do anything in the world, Annie. But you didn't just pick up a hammer or a wrench and know how to do carpentry or plumbing. Your father taught you."

"And my mother crammed grammar and literature down

my throat until I thought I'd gag. Maybe this is the gift for having endured her good intentions."

"Go ahead. Submit an article. Just don't be surprised if your first time out, you get a refusal. Writers submit articles by the hundreds before they have one accepted."

"I stand warned," Annie said coolly.

It was Drew's custom to withdraw early on Saturdays to work on his dissertation. He had made Annie's parents' bedroom into a sort of den for studying and reading during his weekend visits. Annie liked it when Drew was close by in the next room and totally absorbed in his own world. However, after last night's suggestion that she take a writing course before submitting anything to *Elegant Southern Life*, she wished he hadn't come at all.

Annie had to get her first article written, and with Drew using the spare room to work, she found herself pacing in the next logical room to write, the dining room. She didn't realize there'd be so much pacing involved in writing. The first problem was that she couldn't decide what to write. Every idea seemed trite. She wondered how she could possibly concentrate when Drew had been so negative. Why hadn't he been excited for her when she needed him to be supportive? She thought if he hadn't put doubt in her mind, she'd be writing by now. But Annie kept pacing. She considered marching into Drew and demanding to read his dissertation and finding fault with it. It dawned on her that he had never asked her to look at any of his writing. She even worried that he thought she wasn't capable of understanding it.

Annie fumed about this for almost an hour. Then she decided it was time to stop blaming Drew. He had said that she could do anything in the world. She had saved the Knoll so far, hadn't she? Annie remembered Grace saying to write as if she were composing a letter. She could certainly do that. She sat down at the table and began to write.

"Dear Reader, I want to tell you about springtime on An-

nie Crow Knoll ..."

By the time Drew emerged for lunch, Annie had written a charming article about all the signs of spring on the Knoll. She'd talked about the different flowers and birds. Drew actually laughed out loud when he read her description of the antics of a little Carolina Wren determined to make a nest in the clothespin holder out on the clothesline.

"It's sweet," Drew told her. "I really like it."

She was relieved and tried not to expect more. After all, it was only a silly little article for some women's magazine. But she had written it, and she was proud of her first attempt.

Patsy accepted the article, after her editor cleaned it up some, and told Annie that she was looking for a gardening piece and a spring-cleaning piece. Annie said she could do both. However, when she realized it would be her mother's skills and habits that gave her the information she needed to write these two articles, the old resentment resurfaced followed by tears.

Annie missed her parents desperately, but she felt relief that her every action wasn't being evaluated by the ever vigilant Liz. What would her hypocrite mother think of Annie sleeping with Drew without the benefit of matrimony?

In the long run, Annie knew the articles needed to be done, so she buried the hurt along with her pride and wrote to the readers about the beginning stages to her mother's glorious flowers and vegetables. Then she wrote the article on spring cleaning, using her mother's tips and routines and included humorous mistakes that Annie herself had made while trying to emulate her mother's perfect approach.

Annie could hardly believe it when Patsy decided to give her a regular monthly column in the magazine called *Notes from Annie Crow Knoll*. She promised to send out a photographer to take some shots of Annie Crow Knoll for the design team to use in creating the layout.

CHAPTER ELEVEN
WINTER 1965-66

THE PHOTOGRAPHER FROM *ELEGANT SOUTHERN Life* was scheduled to come out to Annie Crow Knoll in a few days. Annie had yet to make the garland her mother constructed every year for the front gates, using evergreen boughs, pinecones and wild mistletoe.

Annie hoped that Big Black Bo would come out to hunt so she could ask him to shoot down bunches of mistletoe that grew high in the trees behind Cattail. Her father had always done this for Liz. However, the first winter following Luke's death, Bo didn't appear. Maybe he didn't like to hunt by himself, or perhaps he went elsewhere now with other buddies. Either way, Annie was going to have to load up Luke's shotgun and head up the beach to Cattail by herself.

Annie's boots crunched in the first snow of the season. A sudden image of Bunky Watson's patrol car in the snow made the crisp air burn in her lungs. Tears again? She felt annoyed and rubbed a gloved finger under each eye. *I won't be able to shoot straight*, she told herself but hiked on up river determined to bag some mistletoe.

Packard heard the gunfire. He was in the woods taking photographs from which he'd select pictures to paint during the worst winter weather. Annoyed when the following shots were closer, Pack decided he'd better alert the hunter to his presence.

"Hold your fire," he bellowed in the direction of the last shot.

Pack's breathing tightened when he saw Annie round the bend of trees. The morning sun lit up the auburn in her dark curls. Her father's orange hunting vest hung loosely on her frame.

He let out a deep breath. "Good morning, Annie."

"Hey, Packard," she smiled. "Looks like we meet again while aiming to shoot something."

"But I only have my Nikon," he said good-naturedly and lifted his camera up a bit.

"My folks gave me a Nikon last Christmas. The camera I was using on loan from the community college for my photography classes was pretty bad."

"I'm sorry this will be your first Christmas without them," Pack said gently.

"Thanks."

Pack hadn't been much older than Annie when he lost both his parents within several months, but when she said no more, he changed subjects.

"So why the shotgun? Have you taken up hunting?"

"Only mistletoe, and let me tell you, it's a lot harder to hit the stem of a bunch of it than it is to hit a tin can."

"Or a terrified intruder running for cover."

"Yeah, well ..." She smiled again and blushed a little.

"If it's mistletoe you're wanting, there's a fair amount of it within reach at the top of your father's old hunting stand. What we can't cut down, you can shoot from a closer range from up there."

Annie unchambered the shells and dropped them into the pocket of her dad's hunting vest. They hiked through the blanketed landscape. When they reached the stand, Pack went up first to make sure that the unused and weathered ladder rungs were stable.

Annie handed him her shotgun. Pack gave her a hand up. He knew she didn't need it, but he wanted to touch her. Then Packard took a knife out of his pocket and opened it. He began harvesting clumps of wild mistletoe that clung to branches surrounding the platform and handed them to Annie.

"Would you like to come to Christmas dinner?" she asked.

"Oh...thanks, but I don't want to intrude on your holiday."

"The Finches are coming, too, Jim and Naomi, Maizie, Sam and the children. J.J. is going to his in-laws, but Birdie and her crew may come, too."

"I'm not so good with crowds. I told Drew that on Wednesday night when he invited me."

"Oh?" Annie sounded surprised.

"You knew that he was out to play chess," Pack said.

"Yes. I just didn't know that he had invited you already," Annie explained.

"Is this enough, or do you want to reload your shotgun?" Pack asked, as he closed his knife and put it back in his pocket.

"No, this is more than enough. Thank you."

Packard and Annie gently dropped the boughs of berries down to the ground.

He went down from the hunting stand first, and Annie handed down the rifle and Nikon.

When she reached the bottom of the ladder and turned to

take the rifle, Packard couldn't take his eyes off her.

She met his gaze. He didn't look away. They were only inches apart, but after a moment, she said, "Well, I'd better get all this mistletoe back to the Knoll." And she began gathering the branches from the ground.

"I'll help you," Packard said.

Laden with bunches of mistletoe, Annie and Packard left the woods and started up the beach together. The receding water had melted the snow below the high tide line, and they walked in the sand along the river's edge.

"Thanks for not minding that Drew comes out to play chess," Packard said, as they started up the steps to the Knoll.

"Of course not."

"I mean, some women . . ."

"Don't even finish that stereotypical comment."

"You could be lonely, that's all. With your folks gone and Bo done for the season."

"I miss my parents, but I'm getting used to being alone. I'm glad to see Drew on the weekends, and I'm glad that he has his own life as well." She thought for a moment and then added, "I enjoy my time to myself."

"Better be careful or you'll turn into a recluse like me," Packard said and smiled.

Annie laughed. "Maybe we're two of a kind."

After unloading his clumps of mistletoe onto Annie's porch, Pack turned to go.

"At least think about Christmas. We'd both like to have you," Annie said.

"I'll think about it," Packard said and headed back out for more photographs.

Sunrise Cottage smelled of sugar cookies, pine needles and a roasting turkey. If Annie hadn't woken up in Drew's arms that morning, she wasn't sure she could have faced the first Christmas without her folks. Now that the Finches were there, too, she was distracted enough with food preparation and general merry spirits, and she felt calmer.

Naomi was finishing her famous sweet potato dish while trying to keep Jim's fingers out of everything that she, Annie and Maizie dished up. Annie checked the turkey that was filled with her mother's delicious chestnut stuffing, and Maizie was putting the finishing touches of icing and candies on her double-decker chocolate cake in the shape of a Christmas tree.

The door opened and a blast of cold air accompanied Drew and Sam, who had taken Sammy and Sarah down to toast marshmallows in the fireplace in the pit. Their cheeks were rosy from the cold air.

"Go wash up now," Maizie instructed her children. Then she turned to her husband. "I hope you didn't let them eat too many, Sam. They'll ruin their appetite for dinner."

"Only a dozen," Sam said, holding up what was left of the marshmallows in a plastic bag.

"A dozen!" Maizie cried.

"Each," he said with a wink.

"Would you carve the turkey?" Annie asked Mr. Jim as she carried glasses out of the kitchen. "My dad's carving knives are on the counter."

"With pleasure."

"Be sure to put on an apron, Jim," Naomi instructed.

Annie took a look at the crowded dining and living room. All one big space really, with an open arch between them. Sunrise Cottage was the biggest cottage on the Knoll but still tiny for this many guests.

"It's a good thing Birdie couldn't come. I'm sorry the twins came down with the flu, but I don't honestly know where we would have put everyone," Annie said.

"Your tree is lovely, Annie," Naomi remarked.

"Drew picked it out himself and brought it as a surprise for me."

"So many lovely ornaments. Didn't your mother make some of these?" Maizie asked.

"Most of them. And she gave me a new one every year. Felt funny not opening one this morning."

"I wish you had told me," Drew said, as he put his arm around her. "Next year, I'll be sure to give you one."

"You gave me the tree. That was more than enough."

Naomi and Maizie exchanged glances, but Sam was the one to ask what they were wondering.

"Sounds like you're becoming a permanent fixture here, Drew."

"If Annie will put up with me," Drew said and pulled her closer into him.

Annie felt safe and warm in Drew's arms. She missed him the minute she had to go back into the kitchen to check on the gravy.

As the dishes of food were being brought to the table, Drew leaned closer to Maizie's husband. "Sam?"

"Yes?"

"Would you be willing to give the blessing this evening?"

"Of course."

"Annie had asked me, and I'm honored, but I didn't have the privilege of knowing her parents as you did. I'd really appreciate it, if you'd make some reference to them."

"Certainly, Drew."

Annie's voice called from the kitchen, "Would someone bring the gravy boat in here?"

"Where is it?" Drew asked.

"On the buffet."

"The turkey is carved," Jim announced, walking in from the kitchen wearing one of Liz's old aprons.

"Don't you look cute, Dad," Maizie said with a laugh.

"Hey, just following orders."

The last of the food was placed on the table, and everyone finally gathered in close quarters and stood behind their chairs. Maizie's youngest, while eyeing the delicious food spread out in front of her, noticed an extra place setting.

"Who's going to sit there?" Sarah asked.

"Mr. Packard is invited," Drew told her.

Sam, who was next to the empty chair asked, "Would you like me to clear it? We'd have a bit more room."

"No, please leave it," Annie interrupted. "He may still come."

Everyone joined hands as they stood circling the feast.

"Our heavenly Father," Sam began. "We thank you for the blessing of this holiday and the meal we are about to share. We thank you for the coming together of these friends and our family. We ask you to bless the souls of our dearly loved and sorely missed Liz and Luke."

Maizie squeezed Annie's hand tighter.

"Please comfort us in our loss on this first Christmas without them. We are grateful for our trust that they are well provided for in your kingdom, as we are blessed with your bounty here on earth. Amen."

"Amen," everyone chorused and they began to take their seats.

Just as they settled, the front door burst open and in the doorway stood a clean shaven Packard Marlboro dressed in new jeans, a madras plaid shirt, navy sports jacket and a red tie. He carried a small gift-wrapped package in one frozen hand and balanced a large covered dish in the other hand.

"I'm sorry I'm late. I didn't time my grandmother's Christmas pudding recipe properly."

Drew rose and rushed toward him with so much enthusiasm that Pack nearly dropped the pudding.

Suddenly Sam, Maizie, Jim and Naomi were all up and talking to Packard.

"Merry Christmas."

"Come in, come in."

"You must be frozen coming over here without an overcoat."

"Did you walk in this cold?"

"Get the man a drink."

Packard forgot that he didn't own a dress coat to wear over his new clothes. He was late, and hadn't even bothered to wrap a scarf around his neck when he bolted out of his door and across the field to Annie's cottage. But seeing her now, standing at her place at the table across the room, Packard didn't feel cold or even hear the voices swimming around him. Looking at her made him realize that accepting this Christmas dinner invitation was correct. He'd done the right thing pushing past his fears and misgivings.

His eyes and Annie's locked long enough for him to see her face burst into a smile which made him certain that, at the very least, she was clearly glad that he had arrived.

"You only missed the blessing. We were just about to start dinner," Drew said as he guided Pack to the table.

Someone had taken the covered dish out into the kitchen, but he still held the small gift.

"Merry Christmas, Annie," Packard said, and he handed her the box.

As people settled into their seats, including Packard, Annie carefully lifted the lid of the prettily wrapped box. Inside she found a hand carved black crow with a gold ribbon attached to its back. She held it up for all to see.

"For the tree?" she asked.

Packard nodded.

Annie crossed to hang her new ornament on the Christmas tree, and Mr. Jim gave a whistle of admiration. "You carve that yourself, Packard?"

"Yes, sir."

"You do nice work."

"Thank you."

"Can we eat yet?" young Sammy asked.

"Mind your manners," Maizie instructed.

"But you always say to eat our food before it gets cold."

"Yes, everyone, let's get started," Drew said, and glanced at Annie, who stood at the tree for a moment admiring the tiny Oliver whose shiny black paint reflected all the colors of the lights and other ornaments.

"Thank you," she said as she briefly put her hands on Pack's shoulders on her way back to her place next to Drew.

Food was being passed at a furious pace. Conversation was humming, and Annie felt content.

After the chocolate Christmas tree cake and Christmas pudding were polished off, Packard made his excuses, making sure to thank Annie and Drew for a wonderful time.

"I'll walk out with you," Drew told him.

Once they were out on the porch, Drew said, "Keep an eye on Annie while I'm on the West Coast, will you?"

"Sure," Pack said.

"Between visiting my parents and grandparents and going through the whole dissertation process, I'll be gone nearly a month. I'm even going to miss her birthday, and I don't like her out here by herself."

"She'll be fine."

"I won't worry so much if I know you're close by…I'm…I want you to know that on Valentine's Day, I'm planning on asking Annie to marry me."

Packard sat down on a porch chair. He held his empty covered dish in his lap.

"I know it's soon, which is why I didn't pop the question for Christmas. It's her first one without her folks. I'll be away on New Year's and her birthday. Besides, I wanted to discuss it with my mom and dad. I'm going to ask my mother to help me select the ring while I'm out there. She and Dad haven't even met Annie, and I thought they'd like to know about my plans first. And you. I haven't told anyone, but you. You'll keep it a secret, right?"

"Yes," Pack said and got to his feet. "Congratulations." He palmed the dish in one hand and shook Drew's hand with the other.

"Thanks!" Drew's smile was huge. "I'm very happy about it."

"I'm sure Annie will be, too."

"Gosh, I hope so."

"It's cold. I'm going to get going."

"Yeah, sure. Goodnight, Pack. And Merry Christmas."

"Merry Christmas, Drew."

When Packard cleared the fence, he began to run. His warm breath made clouds of smoke in the air. When he reached his back door, Packard slammed into his kitchen. Tossing the covered dish onto the table, he sat down to catch his breath and think. However, there was no reasoning to be discovered.

"My God, I love her," Pack said aloud. "I love Annie."

Annie paced in front of the phone. It was 5 PM, and Drew had gone in to defend his dissertation at 11 AM West Coast time. That was two hours ago. He had promised to call as soon as it was over. Annie had no idea how long these things took. She worried that the committee might be tearing it to shreds, but Drew had said that they had already done that. He had told her this was more of a formality than anything else. He'd made all the changes they had required. He expected things to go well, and that he'd be receiving his doctorate at the May commencement services.

Suddenly the phone rang, and Annie instantly grabbed up the receiver.

"Hello?" she said.

"Were you sitting on the phone, dear?" It was Letitia

Turner's voice.

"Sort of," Annie said, trying to keep the disappointment she felt out of her voice.

"I haven't seen you down at the store all week, and with the weather we've been having, I thought I'd check in on you."

"I appreciate that, but I'm fine."

What if Drew got a busy signal and couldn't call back, Annie worried.

"Mrs. Turner, I have to keep the line free. Drew is out in California defending his dissertation, and I'm expecting him to call any minute."

"Oh, well. Big doings. Okay, then. I'll talk to you soon. Give me a call after you find out how he did, will you?"

"Yes, of course. I'll call you right away."

"All right then. Good luck."

"Thanks," Annie said and decided to make some tea to calm herself down.

The tea in her cup was cold, and she was beginning to think about dinner when the phone rang again.

"Hello?"

"It's me," Drew's voice said over the line.

"Well?" Annie almost shouted.

"Everything is fine. They approved it."

"Oh, Drew, that's so wonderful! I'm thrilled for you!"

There was a disturbance on the line, and Annie heard him mumbling to someone in the background.

"Drew?" she asked.

"Sorry, hon, that was my dad."

"Are you in Oregon?" Annie was confused.

"No, of course not."

Then he spoke to someone else. It sounded like he was at a restaurant or bar.

"Where are you?" she asked.

"I'm sorry, Annie, what did you say? I couldn't hear you."

Where are you?" She spoke louder.

"At my grandparents' house."

"What's your father doing there?"

"He and Mom came down to LA with me," he said over the din.

"It sounds like a party."

"What?"

"I said, it sounds like a party," she shouted.

"Listen, Annie, I have to go. My little sister just got here from San Francisco. Crazy kid! I can't believe it. I'll see you soon."

The line went dead.

Annie stood with the phone still in her hand, wondering what the hell she was doing all alone on the Eastern Shore of Maryland. At this important moment, Drew was surrounded by his family and loved ones. She wasn't included among them.

Suddenly resentment and jealousy welled up in Annie. Drew had a mother and father and grandparents and a sister who loved him. She was angry with the man she loved for having a family! It was irrational. However, she couldn't help herself. He had everything she missed so much.

There was no one waiting to hear from Annie Crow, except old Mrs. Turner.

Annie made the call.

Drew drove straight from the airport out to Annie Crow Knoll. He decided that he couldn't wait another two weeks until Valentine's Day. His great-grandmother's diamond ring, which his mother had had refurbished while he was out west, was in a box inside his pocket.

The moment Drew walked into Sunrise Cottage, he sensed that something was wrong. Annie seemed happy to see him but tense. Although he usually listened to his instincts, Drew decided not to read more into that and chalked it up to an initial nervousness after being apart almost a month.

Annie presented him with an exquisite leather briefcase to commemorate his successful dissertation. Still, there was something between them that didn't feel right. He was about to ask her when Annie spoke.

"Why didn't you ask me to go with you to defend your work?"

"It never crossed my mind."

This obviously wasn't the answer she wanted to hear. Actually, there was no good answer to that question, and Drew realized this early on in their discussion.

"I need to know where we stand, Drew. I'm not trying to pin you down or anything, but having your entire family throw a party for you while I'm on the other end of the phone made me feel like I'm not that important to you." Annie looked about to cry.

"I didn't know that my parents were going to fly down with me, but when they offered, I appreciated the support. It was nice to know that they and my grandparents were outside that room when I was in front of the committee. I had no idea that my crazy sister would skip classes and drive down, and the party, if that's what it was, was totally spontaneous. If I'd known that any of this was going to happen, I would have invited you to be a part of it."

Annie's tears wouldn't abate.

"Honey, please, don't cry," Drew said. "I'd never intentionally hurt you."

"I know," she said between sobs. "I've cried more since I met you than I have in my entire life."

"Great."

"I didn't mean it like that exactly."

He took her in his arms.

"I felt so alone when everything was happening for you. I just wanted to be a part of it all."

"I understand."

"This is crazy. I've never cared what anyone thought of me before, whether they liked me or didn't, whether they'd include me or not. I was fine on my own." Annie paused to wipe her eyes with a tissue. "But with you, it's like some big hole is inside me when I'm not with you. I don't mean every twenty-four hours—God, I'd get a gun—but when you were far away, and I thought maybe you didn't want me there, I couldn't breathe."

"I'm guessing that some of this has to do with grieving your parents, too. My timing isn't so great. And for the record, I wanted you there. I want you with me all the time."

"You do?"

"With all my heart. Maybe things got a little screwed up with this trip, but I don't ever want to have another important or regular day, for that matter, go by without you being a part of it. In fact, there's something I want to discuss. We're talking about a life together, but Annie, I'm not going to be like your dad. You have to understand that from the beginning."

"I wouldn't want you to be!" Annie interrupted.

"I think, in a way, that you wish I would be. You'd like it if I worked here on the Knoll helping you full time."

"I can handle it on my own, but I wouldn't mind if you worked here with me," Annie admitted.

"But I would mind. My day can't be about how many roof shingles are needed to repair Blue Heron Cottage. I have to teach. It's what I love. I need to have a part of my life that's my own. I want to drive off the Knoll every day and know that my students are waiting for me to have heavy academic discussions. I need to be Doctor Bidwell, Professor of English," Drew said without embarrassment.

"I'm okay with you driving off the Knoll every day, as long as you want to come back every night," Annie said.

"Of course I do." Drew took her into his arms and kissed her. "This is my home now, if you'll have me," he whispered in her ear.

"You mean it? You'll live here?" Annie asked with enthusiasm.

"I believe it is customary for married couples to live together," he teased.

"Married?" Annie looked astonished.

"All we need then is the ring," Drew said as he pulled the small, black velvet box out of his pocket. "Will you marry me, Annie Crow?" He revealed a lovely antique diamond ring.

"Yes," Annie answered with more confidence than she realized she could feel.

Drew slipped the sparkling diamond on her finger.

Annie cried with delight, "It's perfect!"

"Let's have the wedding here on the Knoll," Drew said, which only made Annie even happier.

On Drew's second evening back from the West Coast, he made time to go over to visit Packard. It wasn't a chess night, but still Drew expected his friend to be at home. He longed to tell him all about his dissertation, the trip and that Annie had accepted his proposal. However, Packard was nowhere to be found. The house was dark and his truck was gone from the drive.

When Drew shone the flashlight he'd used to cross the field between the Knoll and Packard's house up onto the porch, he noticed a package leaning up against the front door. It had his name written on it.

Drew couldn't wait, so he sat on the porch step, in the cold night air and balanced his flashlight between his knees. He tore open the wrapping to find a first edition, signed copy of Walt Whitman's *Leaves of Grass*.

A note fell out of the first pages.

Dear Drew,

Congratulations on your dissertation.
Your friend, Packard

But Annie had told Drew that she hadn't seen Packard to tell him that Drew's dissertation had been approved.

Dr. and Mrs. Leonard were hosting a cocktail party for the entire English Department faculty and their wives. Since the gathering was in honor of Drew Bidwell and Hugh Snyder, the two youngest department members who had recently completed their doctoral dissertations, as Drew's fiancée, Annie had to attend.

"Are they going to want to inspect my teeth, too?" she asked, as she struggled with the clasp to her mother's pearl necklace.

"What?" Drew asked.

He stood waiting in the doorway of what used to be her parents' bedroom. Now that they were getting married, Annie and Drew were taking this larger room and turning Annie's smaller bedroom into a study and guestroom.

"You know, like a horse." Annie turned to him and grinned showing him all her teeth.

"Very amusing."

"Would you help me with this?" Annie asked, giving up on getting the clasp to hook on her own.

"You look lovely," Drew said and moved behind her. He enjoyed her reflection smiling at him in the vanity mirror as he concentrated on hooking the clasp. "There."

"Bet you didn't think I owned a dress."

Drew admired Annie in the mirror. She wore a classic black sleeveless dress. The pearl earrings and necklace were the perfect, elegant touch.

"You didn't, at least not this dress," he told her.

"How do you know?"

"You didn't take off the tag," Drew said holding it out from the back neckline. "Unless you were planning to return it after tonight."

"No, of course not. I just forgot to cut it off. Here." She handed him manicure scissors from the drawer.

"There we go," Drew said. "Come on. I don't want to be late."

The Leonards' large Victorian house was located in Chester Landing, just one block off campus, and boasted a glorious wrap-around porch with a great deal of gingerbread.

Drew and Annie were on time but the last to arrive. Annie expected that Drew would introduce her to everyone. However upon arrival, he was quickly sequestered into one parlor where the other five male faculty members were drinking and talking, and she to the adjacent parlor where their wives were gathered. The introductions fell upon Mrs. Leonard, who headed the hierarchy of the English Department wives. Mrs. Gramble's husband was senior member after Dr. Leonard and so she held the same position here. The wives of Doctors Webber and Mercer were, as their husbands, in the third and fourth positions. When Annie received a particularly cold reception from Shelly Snyder, she quickly recognized that as the two newest professors, Drew and Hugh were vying for the fifth seat. The loser would be sixth. Despite Annie's competitive nature, she didn't care about her position as fifth or sixth wife; however, she did care about Drew.

"Your home is lovely, Mrs. Leonard," Annie said, as she was handed a martini.

"Please, call me Iris."

"And so conveniently located," Annie added.

"We all live in Chester Landing," Mrs. Mercer said.

"That way it's easier for our husbands to meet the demands of their work," Shelly Snyder remarked.

And that was how it started, a series of subtle but well-aimed insults.

"Tell us about your little column in this new magazine," Mrs. Leonard said.

"You're lucky that Drew lets you write this column," Mrs. Webber added.

"I hadn't realized that I needed his permission," Annie said with a smile.

"How will you handle your name change in your articles after you marry?" Mrs. Mercer asked.

"Won't the readers find it confusing if you switch from Atkinson to Bidwell after several issues?" Mrs. Gramble asked with fake concern in her voice.

With all that Annie was juggling, she honestly hadn't given this a thought. She instantly recalled how hard Maizie worked to become Doctor Maizie Finch, only to turn around and be known to many people as Mrs. Sam Waters after her wedding.

"I'm keeping Atkinson for my writing," Annie announced boldly.

"Oh, dear," one of the ladies gasped.

"I think that your point needs to be taken seriously, Mrs. Gramble. I wouldn't want to confuse the readers," Annie added and felt triumphant for the moment although she would have preferred the opportunity to belong rather than this battle she was being forced to join. Worst of all, the situation smelled of Annie's great-grandmother Delia Witherspoon.

Eventually the conversation turned to the two dissertations. Relief spread through Annie as she had insisted on reading Drew's paper in preparation for meeting his colleagues. Up until that point, she had only vague notions about his American Folklore research.

"It surprises me," Shelly Snyder said pointedly, "that Drew is considering extending his folksy topic into an entire book."

While prepared to discuss the merits of her fiancé's work,

Annie had had no warning of this. She hoped that her face hadn't revealed her surprise and hurt.

"A text book," Shelly continued and then giggled. "What college class would need a text on Eastern Shore Folklore?"

"An American Folklore class," Annie recovered quickly.

"We don't have any such class," Iris Leonard said.

"We will and so will many colleges and universities in the near future," Annie announced.

Then Annie set down the martini that she hadn't touched and excused herself.

Much to the surprise of both the women and the men, Annie crossed into the next parlor and took Drew's arm.

"Would you be kind enough to introduce me to our host and your other esteemed colleagues, dear?"

As the introductions were made in the exact hierarchy as before, Annie was sure to specifically compliment each man's wife. She had no doubt, however, that these same women were tearing her to shreds in the next room.

Annie felt Drew gently but firmly pull his arm away from her grasp. She must have been digging her fingernails into him.

Upon the final introduction, Annie said, "I'm very impressed with your wife's knowledge of American Folklore, Dr. Snyder."

"Really?" Hugh Snyder seemed surprised.

"Yes. She is apparently quite interested in Drew's dissertation and his plans for a text book."

"Annie!" Drew said in a tone that forced her to look at him. His eyes told her that she'd made a mistake.

It had started to rain when Drew pulled the car away from the curb in front of Dr. Leonard's house. Annie thought the party would never end. Finally alone in the car and free to speak her mind, Annie said, "Shelly Snyder knew about your book before I did!"

"I haven't discussed it with anyone but Dr. Leonard." Drew sounded like he was trying to keep his anger in check.

"Well, he either told his wife who told Shelly Snyder, or he told Hugh Snyder who told his wife. Either way, you'd better watch your back. In case you hadn't noticed, mine is bleeding all over the upholstery from the daggers."

"You didn't give them much of a chance, Annie."

"Thanks for assuming the fault is mine!"

"I'm not saying that."

"They didn't give me a chance, Drew. They criticized where I live, my column, my name and your 'folksy' dissertation. It was unbelievable. And then to be made the fool when I have no idea about your future plans. What was your purpose for keeping me in the dark like that?"

"What the hell did you think you were doing blurting it out in front of the entire department?"

"Because I assumed they all knew."

"Why would you make that assumption?"

"Because Mrs. Snyder made it sound like it was common knowledge."

"If I hadn't told you, why would I have discussed it with any of them?"

"I don't know, Drew. You tell me. You tell me why you hadn't shared this major decision with me."

Drew was silent.

"If you'd told me that it was privileged information, then I'd have known what to do when Shelly Snyder set the trap, but you let me walk into that trap!"

"You know that I've been under pressure to publish. Dr. Leonard and I began discussing a text book, but I had no way of foreseeing that my vague and sketchy ideas about it would be a topic of conversation this evening!" Drew said sharply.

Annie felt the tears welling up but willed them back

down. She absolutely would not allow herself to look weak at this moment.

"Shit," she said.

"Annie!"

"Shit, shit, damn it to hell!"

"Annie, please."

"What? Is cursing not faculty 'wifey' enough?"

"Now you're being childish."

"No, I'm being angry."

"And childish!"

"Look, maybe I'm just not Queen Anne College wife material."

"What are you saying?" Drew pulled the car off the road and put the brake on. Softly he asked, "Are you saying that you don't want to marry me?"

Annie found Drew's whisper more frightening than his screaming would have been.

"Are you?" he asked again quietly.

"Nobody else seems to think we're suited."

"I need to know what you think."

At that moment, Annie desperately wanted her parents. They'd know what she should do. Ironically, Annie had always thought that she had a mind of her own. Most of the time, she thought that she hadn't listened to her folks or anyone else. But she must have gauged their feelings in some delicate, obscure way. She felt totally adrift without them.

"My God," Drew muttered when Annie didn't answer.

Then he gestured, which made Annie look directly at him. She saw that Drew had taken off his eyeglasses and was holding the bridge of his nose between his index finger and thumb.

The wind shifted causing the cold rain to batter the windshield. She couldn't clearly make out his face in the darkness, but Annie thought he looked about to cry. Impulsively she threw her arms around him.

"Don't cry! I do want to marry you!" She stroked his hair

as he leaned his head into her chest. "I love you, Drew."

"I love you, too, Annie."

Under the dim streetlight, he looked much younger in her arms.

"Tonight sucked," he said quietly and then sat up.

"Yes, pretty much."

Drew put his glasses back on. "I'm sorry, Annie. There's just so much pressure on me."

"I understand."

"There was one good moment tonight."

"When was that?" Annie asked.

"When you made Hugh Snyder look like a fool by implying that his wife was more interested in my dissertation than her own husband's."

Annie laughed. "As well she should be."

"I thought you were brilliant!" Drew said. Then he put the car back into gear and pulled onto the road.

Chapter Twelve
Summer 1966

THE WEDDING DIDN'T SEEM REAL to Packard until the day the ivory colored invitation arrived in the mail. Before then, he had managed to separate Drew, his friend, from Drew, Annie's fiancé. But once he held the request for the honor of his presence, Packard felt his throat tighten. How could he reconcile this ambivalence in himself? He wanted Drew to be happy, but not with Annie. He wanted to support them by attending the wedding but wished that he were the groom. Nothing seemed right or comfortable. Packard talked himself into believing that it was a better match. After all, he was too old for Annie. While holding a pen, he stared at the place for a response on the small matching card and tried to make himself check off that he would attend. Then his palms began to sweat, and he tossed down the pen and buried the invitation and response card in a drawer.

However, even if he couldn't face the ceremony, Packard felt a responsibility to support the couple in some way. He decided to paint a portrait of Annie in her wedding gown as a gift for both of them. Finding Annie on the canvas wasn't an issue, but he had no idea what her gown was going to look like. Surprisingly during one of their chess games, Drew mentioned that Annie had gone over to Chester Landing for a fitting.

"Is Elsie Trommer making her gown?" Pack asked, trying to sound nonchalant.

"I think Annie said it was someone named Elsie or Essie," Drew said while concentrating on his next move.

That was all the information Packard needed.

Along with securing pet portraits and estate paintings for Packard, his cousin Elsie Trommer had always made a living as a seamstress. Knowing how much Elsie loved to talk, all Packard had to do was call and mention his neighbor Annie Atkinson and his cousin took over the conversation.

"Oh, Packard, it is going to be beautiful. The gown is sleeveless with a scoop neck. The bodice is covered with lace. Since it's an outdoor wedding, she's going to forgo a veil. She's pulling her hair up in a loose knot and putting baby's breath around it."

Packard saw the painting now in his mind. Annie would be standing on the edge of the Knoll with the waters of the Chesapeake behind her. He'd let a few of her wild curls loose from their pins and dangle them lightly around her face and neck.

"Pack? Packard, are you still there?" Elsie's voice brought him back.

"Yes, Elsie, I am but I have to go now. It was good talking to you."

Before she could say another word, the line was dead.

As is often true with the weather patterns around the north

bay region, the thunderstorms predicted for the wedding day came though during the preceding night, leaving the special day pleasantly cool and sunny.

Bo arrived bright and early to set up the chairs, tables, decorations, and floral arrangements, just as he had for Maizie and Sam's wedding ten years before. However, this time he wasn't going to miss the ceremony. His Sunday suit, white shirt, tie, shoes and socks were all waiting in his car.

Annie had offered to hire someone to take care of the wedding preparations and other unforeseen tasks so Bo could arrive in his suit and be a guest the entire time.

He wouldn't hear of it. Bo wanted to make sure everything was perfect.

"I don't know that I'll stay for the reception," he warned her, as they inspected the final touches before the service.

Annie was confident that the world she created on the Knoll was different. The guests were all relatives, Knollers and friends, along with some students and colleagues of Drew's. At best, Bo would be treated with respect. At the worse, he'd be ignored. However, she would go along with whatever he decided about staying for the reception.

"I understand, Bo. But I am looking forward to seeing you all dressed up in a suit," she teased.

"I'm looking forward to seeing you in your wedding gown, little girl! I don't believe I've ever seen you in a dress, let alone a gown!"

"I wore a dress to Maizie's wedding."

"You were ten years old."

"I guess it's about time then."

Later that morning, as Annie and Grace dressed for the wedding in Sunrise Cottage, Annie asked, "What do you think of my hair?"

"It looks fabulous pulled up. You should wear it like this more often, but you've got too much baby's breath in the back."

"Well, I couldn't see what I was doing."

"Sit down. I'll fix it." Grace gestured to the vanity chair.

"Elsie told me not to sit too much once I put on the gown," Annie said.

"All right then, stoop down."

As Grace adjusted the baby's breath, Annie blurted out, "I had Doc fit me for a diaphragm."

"But you've been on the pill since you met Drew."

"I'm so emotional all the time."

"No, you showed no emotion your whole life, and then your parents died, you nearly lost this place, and you fell in love and started having sex. I think you're acting normally for the first time."

"Aren't you done yet? My legs are cramping."

"One more second."

"My moods are all over the place. I couldn't take it anymore, so I talked to Maizie a few weeks ago and she said it could be the pill and to try a diaphragm."

"There. I'm done. You can stand up." Grace looked at Annie. "It's perfect. You look beautiful."

"I do?"

"Take a look."

Annie walked over to the vanity mirror and turned this way and that while examining the flowers around the soft and full bun she had made of her hair.

"Here." Grace picked up a hand mirror so that Annie could see the whole way around.

"I like it."

Grace put the mirror down. "I'd better get into my gown. It's nearly time."

"Wait a sec." Annie took Grace's hand. "I know things are changing between us."

Grace's eyes filled up.

"Now, don't you start!" Annie insisted. "I'll cry, too, and we're going out there any minute. I want to look good for at least the first moments."

"I can't help it. Things are changing because you're getting married."

"Yes, but I'm not going to need or love you any less."

Grace carefully dabbed at her eyes with a tissue. "I'm all right."

"You are my best friend."

"Drew is your best friend."

"He's another best friend, but not like you. You're my best girlfriend. That will never, never change."

"Okay." Grace didn't sound convinced.

"When you marry Pete, you'll understand," Annie said.

"Pete who?"

"I don't know."

They both laughed.

"Anyone home?" A man's voice came from the living room.

Annie emerged from the bedroom to find Doc waiting for her.

"All the guests have arrived," he told her.

"Oh, God. Grace, hurry up," Annie called back to her.

"Annie, you look beautiful," Doc said as he moved to her and lightly kissed her cheek. "Thank you for asking me to give you away. I am honored to stand in your father's place."

"I'm so grateful, Doc. For everything. You have been wonderful to me since the day I first talked to you when Bunky Watson shot his foot."

"Yes, I remember calling to tell you that he'd be fine, but also I wanted to talk to this little girl who had kept her head during an emergency. Now you're all grown up."

As Drew walked down the white wedding runner that traveled

between the seats, he smiled at students, colleagues, friends and all the cottagers whom he'd come to know in this whirlwind year. He beamed at both of his parents, his sister and grandparents. When he reached Rev. Johnson and the temporary altar positioned with a dazzling view of the bay, Drew looked over to Packard's dock. There was no sign of his friend or the old workboat. A few days before, a gorgeous wedding portrait had been left crated on the porch before dawn.

Drew wanted to accept Pack's disappearance but didn't understand it. He turned back toward the congregation as Grace walked down the aisle. She smiled at him and gave him a wink. Then the bride made her appearance on Doc's arm, and when Drew saw her coming toward him in her gown, nothing else existed in his mind but Annie Crow.

CHAPTER THIRTEEN
FALL 1966

PACKARD COULDN'T STAY STILL LONG enough to paint. He hadn't been able to work since finishing Annie's wedding portrait. Each time he stood in front of the canvas, his mind would drift, with his body eventually following. His third floor attic studio felt cramped and dark. It was impossible for him to work patiently though the subtle details required of someone's eyes or the light on the hair.

Although he didn't understand what was happening, Pack felt a significant shift taking place in his work. He wanted something bigger. Huge. Forget the tiny details for a while, the voice inside him said.

Just when he was struggling with this upheaval, Elsie telephoned with another commission, a portrait of someone's thoroughbred. The idea of painting another horse or dog added to Packard's resolve.

"No more pet portraits?" she exclaimed.

"I'm sorry, Elsie."

"But why?"

"I don't want do to it anymore."

"You're going to stop painting?" she asked with obvious pain in her voice. "You're too talented."

"Thanks, and no, but I'm searching. I think that I need to be working on a larger canvas, with less detail." Pack struggled to explain something that he didn't yet understand himself.

"Do you have room for that in your studio?"

"Not really." Another question Pack couldn't answer.

"What will you live off?" she asked with concern for her unpredictable cousin.

"The bay."

"But most of the watermen are complaining that it's getting harder to make a living."

The income from the estate and pet portraits had been welcomed. It was a relief not to have to rely totally on calm waters and bountiful fish to survive. Pack would have to cut back, which was easy for him to do. Except for his passion for books, he was comfortable living without things. He didn't need much.

"Don't worry about me, Elsie, something will come along. It always does."

"I'll tell people that you are working on something new. That'll create interest, and if you change your mind, they'll give you commissions like crazy."

"No," Packard told her firmly. "You deserve every dollar you've earned finding clients for me. You go ahead and locate another artist and work with them."

"Lucy Jo Webster, from the Arts League, has expressed an interest."

"Great," Pack said relieved. He felt badly that his decision would impact Elsie's income as well.

"But she's not as good as you."

"She will be."

"I think that she needs the income, too. She's having a

hard time of it since Stan died last year. She put the Locust Creek parcel of her farm on the market and got a buyer too, some Philadelphia businessman with no sense of history. He told her that he's going to build a hunting cabin out there, but he's planning on tearing down the old Locust Creek Schoolhouse first."

Packard knew the building well. He had done a painting of the post and beam schoolhouse for an art class assignment back in high school. His art teacher and mentor Mrs. Weyand had entered Pack's painting into the local historical society art show and it had won first place.

"That building should be preserved," Pack said.

"Lucy Jo refuses to sell the land now if the man won't save the schoolhouse."

"Stay right where you are. I'm coming over."

"Why?"

"The old schoolhouse is going to be my new studio."

Aside from the front vestibule lined with cloakroom cupboards and another small room off the back of the building where the first teacher lived in the 1800's, the post and beam schoolhouse was basically one large room measuring twenty-five feet wide and forty feet long. Chalkboards still lined the front and back walls, and ten large windows, five located along each of the two longer walls, allowed for plenty of fresh air and sunshine. All the desks had long disappeared, but a pot belly stove that had served as the students' source of heat in the winter still stood in the front of the room near where the teacher's desk would have been. The open ceiling peaked at twenty-eight feet with large wooden joists crossing to support the structure. Packard loved the space. It was all the room he needed.

When Annie heard about Packard purchasing the schoolhouse from Lucy Jo Webster, she saw great potential in the preservation project and gave Patsy at *Elegant Southern Life* a call. Since the magazine's largest expense would be sending a photographer to cover the weeks and weeks of work, Annie suggested submitting her own photographs. She had studied photography at the community college and had a decent eye. The editor jumped right on board.

After much persuasion, Packard reluctantly gave Annie permission to take photographs of the entire process, which would accompany her column documenting the saving of this historic Southern building.

Along with Drew, several of Drew's students and Bo, Pack disassembled the structure in order to move it to its new location in the field between the Knoll and his house. Beam by beam and board by board, every piece of wood was numbered and listed. As they worked, word spread and more people came to give volunteer help. Quickly Packard was becoming somewhat of a local hero for saving the building. Although he was uncomfortable with the attention, he appreciated the support resulting from it.

When planning where to place the new foundation, Packard debated on the exact location of the schoolhouse in the field between his house and Annie Crow Knoll. He walked and paced the meadow for a long time. Obviously he wanted the large double doors that led into the vestibule to face the water. He looked forward to leaving those doors wide open and reaping the benefits of the bay breezes while he worked. But the exact location on the field was tricky. Briefly, he toyed with placing the schoolhouse near the bluff so he'd be as close as possible to the bay. Although it might be the optimum spot when the weather was good, nothing would protect the building from the fierce bay winds in the winter.

Walking back to his house, he also noticed that putting the studio right on the bluff would block his view of the lights flickering though the trees from Annie's cottage. He appreciated that view especially after her parents' accident because it enabled him to keep a supportive eye on Annie without being intrusive. But now she didn't need it. She was married to Drew.

Perhaps blocking out Annie's cottage would help him to separate from the pain of losing her to his dearest friend. Packard quickly realized, however, that that was an illusion. The pain had to be felt and dealt with over time, and the young couple showed no intention of leaving him alone anyway.

Finally, Packard laid the new stone foundation for the Schoolhouse Studio further back into the meadow. He nestled it in, just clear of the small woods bordering his side of the field. The view was spectacular. The winds wouldn't be so harsh in bad weather, and he'd get all the benefits of the sights, sounds and smells of the meadow as well as the water.

As autumn waned, and the primary structure took shape in the field, the number of volunteers slowed. Big Black Bo was busy over on the Knoll closing up the cottages for the winter, and Drew, who had helped frequently for the first several weeks, had to concentrate on his teaching again. Even the chess games were postponed for a while. Although Pack enjoyed his regained solitude, he noticed that he also missed the company.

The exterior of the one-room building would look as it had for over a hundred years, but the interior was changed to meet Packard's studio needs. He put insulation in the floor and walls before reinstalling the old pine boards but left the ceiling, with thick wooden joists crossing it, open. Two huge mobiles were forming in his mind, and he planned on hanging them up in the ceiling rafters. When winter arrived, he'd lose some of the heat from the new wood-burning stove he put in, but Packard rarely felt cold when he painted, and he preferred the sense of space that the open ceiling provided. Both the space and light in this new studio made Pack wonder how he'd ever painted in his well-loved but rather cramped, dark third-floor studio over in the house. Now light and bay air poured in through the large schoolhouse windows, and Packard framed out the old vestibule wall without replacing it so that when he propped open the double doors, he had a glorious view of the Chesapeake.

The closed-in feeling Packard had experienced ever since Annie and Drew's wedding was lessening. The worry of when he'd ever be able to paint again lifted. The adrenaline was now flowing, and Pack couldn't wait to throw paint across a huge canvas. However, first he built the mobiles.

Annie paused inside the doorway of the completed Schoolhouse Studio. At first, she had thought the huge room was empty. Then her eye caught movement up above. He looked like an angel, like Gabriel, if he'd only had wings, standing high up on a beam in white painter's pants and a long sleeved, white shirt that hung loose and open at his chest. She watched him inching his way barefoot on one of the thick joists that crossed the width of the open ceiling. With total grace and confidence, he balanced as he released the pulley system that had raised the second of two giant mobiles into place.

The centerpiece of the mobile Packard had just installed was the earth, which looked vulnerable and fragile hanging in space. The earth was surrounded by six large crows, which teetered out on the ends of long bamboo poles. Each crow was in a different position of flight. When the gentle wind current coming through the open doorway and windows passed through the mobile, the earth spun in place and the crows flew around it. Annie didn't want to take her eyes off it, but now the breeze moved the second mobile hanging directly above her. She turned and looked up. The centerpiece of this one was a preening crow. The shiny, black feathers appeared distinct. Six planets orbited the large crow: the earth, sun, moon, Venus, Uranus, and Saturn, with its flowing rings.

How did he do it? she asked herself.

Packard settled down on the beam. An extension ladder leaned next to his dangling legs. He wasn't sure if Annie had seen him up there. Her back was toward him as she stood below and looked up at the universe controlled by a preening crow. She was the first to see the work completed and installed. He wondered what she was thinking. He thought he heard a sigh. Her shoulders had lifted and dropped again. Annie looked tiny and fragile down there. He wanted to fly down, lift her into his arms and carry her up into the heavens of his studio.

Annie put her camera to her eye and took a photograph of the mobile directly above her. Then she turned and started shooting the one hanging closer to where Pack sat. She saw him tense up. He was perched in the frame, to the left of the crows flying around the earth.

Packard leapt onto the ladder and headed down. Within a moment, he was at the bottom and crossing the space toward her. She focused solely on him. Pack didn't run, but his shirt was flowing open with his pace. His large torso was solid muscle from years of hard work. Annie kept shooting. He was saying something to her, but she was too busy refocusing to hear him.

When only his face and shoulders filled the frame, he laughed, and she caught his smile. Then he was upon her, and a hand covered her lens.

She pushed the shutter one more time in the darkness.

"Annie, stop it." His voice was firm.

She lowered the camera and met his serious, dark eyes.

"No pictures of me in the magazine." His huge hand was still over her lens.

They stood close.

"Let go of my camera," she said.

"Only when you promise that none of these photos of me will end up in *Elegant Southern Life.*"

"Okay, I promise," Annie gave in.

"Hey, you two," Drew said from the door startling Annie and Packard so much that they both stepped apart.

"You look like you are in serious negotiations," Drew added and crossed to give Annie a kiss on the cheek.

"Your wife is taking advantage of my generous nature. Photos of the schoolhouse are fine, but now she's trying to take shots of me for her magazine."

"The camera won't steal your soul," Annie quipped.

"How about some dinner?" Drew asked, deciding not to get into the middle of this battle.

"The light should be just right outside. I'm going to shoot a roll of the exterior of the completed Schoolhouse Studio, and then I'll be over."

"Here, have some chips to hold you," Pack said, pointing to a bag on the worktable.

Drew grabbed a handful and looked up at the mobiles.

"Hey, these look fabulous," he said between bites.

As the men wandered between the two mobiles discussing the technical points of how Packard assembled them to move the way they did, Annie went outside. The late afternoon sun bathed the old walls in a warm glow.

Walking around to the back of the building, Annie liked hearing the men's voices humming through the open windows. She framed the schoolhouse with the bay in the background.

When Annie came around to shoot the double front doors, she was suddenly inspired. She set her camera down on the steps and dashed across to the Knoll. Moments later, she was pushing a wheelbarrow full of mums and pumpkins to dress up the front steps of the schoolhouse.

Using her parents' slide projector, Annie edited slides of the shots she took of the schoolhouse studio before sending the best to Patsy. When she came to the shots of Packard and his mobiles, she felt surprised. He looked different to her. At twenty years of age, she finally comprehended what Maizie and Birdie Finch had said about Packard Marlboro years ago. She recalled her mother's smile and the girlish laughter of Maizie and her sister.

Packard was beautiful, in a mountain man sort of way. The lines of his big, sturdy body were art. His dark eyes, wild hair and beard could be interpreted as dangerous. His infrequent smile was open and wise. Annie turned the slide projector off and started writing the article to go with these photographs, but an hour later she was back projecting Packard's image up on the screen.

She looked at the one with his shirt flowing open and realized that she couldn't have planned it better, if she wanted to.

As Annie reviewed the pictures of the mobiles, she felt strongly that she had to ask Packard's permission to use them in the magazine. His mobiles should be featured as a part of the completed project. The one of Pack sitting up in the rafter next to his creation was perfect, and even though he was barely recognizable in it, she knew that he'd never agree.

Well, he couldn't refuse her getting a print made for her own home. Annie selected the close up of Packard smiling to be printed and framed. It would be placed on the table with her parents' wedding photo, her baby picture, a shot of Annie fishing with her dad, another of Annie and Grace and her own wedding photo with Drew.

Sitting in front of the wood-burning stove in his new studio where Packard and Drew now resumed their weekly chess game, Pack looked at his friend with a warm glint in his eyes.

"Since when did you start doing your wife's dirty work? Oh, checkmate, by the way."

"Give me a break!" Drew said exasperated.

"It was a fair move."

"No, I mean about Annie. She knew that you'd say no to her so I offered to approach you."

Drew had shown Packard prints of the two slides Annie wanted to submit to the magazine. He didn't point out that Pack was pictured sitting up on the joist in one of the shots. The less said the better.

Drew agreed with Annie that along with the restoration of the schoolhouse, Packard's art deserved to be highlighted. They both hoped that with some exposure perhaps Packard could make a name for himself as an artist. It was risky, though, because they knew how much Pack treasured his anonymity. The man would rather break his back fishing all day and night to make ends meet than be forced into a suit and drink champagne at a gallery opening.

"Oh, what the hell," Packard said uncharacteristically.

"You won't regret this," his young friend reassured.

"Don't push your luck, Drew. I may very well regret it, but my gut is telling me to throw caution to the wind. So tell Annie she can put these photos in her column."

Chapter Fourteen
Spring 1967

ANNIE AND BO WERE BUSY preparing to open the cottages for the season. Annie had so much on her mind that it took ten days before she realized that her period was late. She had always been like clockwork, so hoping that this was all a bad dream wasn't going to change anything. After waiting another two weeks, Annie reluctantly made an appointment with Doc.

"Congratulations, you're expecting your first child," he told her on her return visit.

"Oh, God."

"What's the matter?" he asked surprised.

"What's the matter? What the hell good was that diaphragm you gave me?" Annie snapped.

"I explained that diaphragms are not a hundred percent foolproof," Doc took a seat, realizing that this could take some time. "I'm sorry that this isn't happy news."

Annie's voice rose. "Since I came here for birth control,

we obviously weren't planning to have a child so soon!"

"You're angry with me," Doc said gently.

"I'm sorry. I don't mean to take this out on you." Annie made an effort to calm down.

Doc sat patiently.

"I just don't know what Drew is going to say. It's so unexpected. We've only been married for eight months."

"Did you discuss having children?" he asked.

"Yes, eventually."

"You both want a family?" Doc rose and walked around the desk to Annie.

"Of course, but we aren't even used to each other yet!"

"First, I hope that you never get used to each other. Linda is still surprising me, and it keeps the marriage alive. Secondly, most married men are thrilled when their wife first gets pregnant. I'm betting that Drew will be very happy. You just let me know if he isn't, and I'll set him straight for you." He winked and patted her hand.

The sun was setting as Annie walked up Baycliff Road toward the Knoll. She felt a chill growing in the air, which helped to clear her mind. She had to find a way to tell Drew about the baby.

While Doc was trying to be like a second father to her, and she appreciated his efforts so much, he didn't know the pressure Drew was under regarding his early tenure and professorship. Drew said that he wished that Dr. Leonard hadn't convinced him to apply to move up so soon. Now the wait for the decision, which could come any day, was agony.

Since the wedding, Annie had attempted to maintain a delicate balance. She had attended large student events such as the homecoming dance and the winter theatre production but avoided small faculty gatherings. All this was done in the hopes that maintaining a low profile would keep her great-grandmother off the back of whomever it was that held Drew's future in their hands. However, Annie's limited involvement could be interpreted as a lack of interest, and this could also hurt Drew's chances. It was ridiculous to Annie. Her husband's work should be the issue, not whom he married. When she reached Sunrise Cottage, Drew was sitting on the front steps gazing out at the water. He looked as if he'd been there some time.

"It's cold, honey, what are you doing out here?" Annie asked pulling her coat collar up around her neck against the damp March wind.

"Where have you been?"

"For a walk." Annie didn't want to mention seeing Doc with Drew acting so peculiarly. "Come on, let's go inside and get warm."

Drew didn't move. "The decision came down today," he said and paused.

Annie felt her spine tingle from the icy air off the bay.

"I didn't get it."

"Oh, Drew. I'm so sorry," Annie sat on the step next to her husband.

"Dr. Leonard reassured me that my job is secure, but there's no professorship, yet. I shouldn't have tried to move up early."

"I'm guessing that Hugh Snyder was moved up," Annie said.

"Yes, and he should be. He's been there six years, and he deserves it."

"But so do you!"

"Annie, don't."

"You're writing a groundbreaking text book which is going to establish a new course curriculum in most of the universities and colleges in the country."

"I'm going in to get a beer," Drew said.

Annie followed him into Sunrise Cottage. "It's my great-grandmother, isn't it? If you weren't married to me, you'd have gotten the promotion."

"Dr. Leonard didn't say, but I know that he fought hard for me despite the risk to himself," Drew said, looking for a bottle opener.

"I'm sorry, Drew."

"It's not your fault. It's the politics of academia. Delia Witherspoon contributes major money so she can call the shots."

"She's punishing you for marrying me. I hate her. I truly hate her."

Drew took his beer into the living room and turned on the television. He plopped down on the sofa. Annie stood wondering if telling him that she was pregnant would make him feel better or worse. She couldn't risk making him worse, so it would have to wait.

The phone rang, and Annie answered it. It was Doc's wife Linda.

"I've done something terrible." Annie heard Miss Linda say over the phone.

"Drew stopped in to find out if Doc had any open time tonight to see you. Drew was worried about you having a stomach virus that won't go away. But before he could get all this out, I assumed that he was here about your morning sickness."

"Oh, no," Annie groaned.

"Yes, I'm afraid so."

"Drew knows that I'm pregnant?"

"I had no idea that you hadn't told him," Linda explained.

"Is he still there?"

"No, he left in kind of a hurry. Honey, I'm so sorry. I can't tell you how very sorry I am."

"Linda, I have to go." Annie hung up the phone on the verge of tears. As she reached for another tissue, she wondered what was happening to her. She had gone through entire boxes in the last several days.

How could Linda be that stupid? Annie asked herself and pounded the kitchen table with her fist several times, and then sucked on the side of her sore hand. She started to telephone Grace but didn't want to come off as a sniffling, twenty-one year-old who had gotten herself pregnant long before she was ready. So Annie decided instead to wait for Drew, but he didn't come.

"Annie is pregnant," Drew blurted out to a paint spattered Packard, who stood stunned in front of a huge canvas of blues and greens. A brilliant red was dripping from the brush he held limp in his hand.

Drew dropped onto the sofa by the wood-burning stove. He sank low into the tired springs and threw one arm over his face.

Packard sighed before putting down his wet brush and pulling over a stool to sit opposite Drew.

"I'd assume that congratulations are in order, but you don't look too happy."

"No. She doesn't even know that I know."

"She didn't tell you herself?"

"No." Drew lowered his arm and met Pack's gaze. "She hasn't told me yet."

"How do you know?" Pack asked.

"Doc's wife let it slip."

"Oh."

"Yeah, a real banner week for the Bidwells."

"Why hasn't Annie told you?"

"Hell if I know."

"Maybe she's concerned that you're too upset about not getting the promotion."

"I am."

"Maybe she's afraid that you won't be happy about the baby."

"I'm not."

Pack felt a surge of anger in his chest and throat. He clenched and unclenched his right hand. "Well for God's sake, Drew! No wonder she hasn't told you."

Drew threw his arm back over his face again. "I don't know what to do," he moaned.

"You're going to pull yourself together and go home and take her into your arms and tell her that you're thrilled."

"Oh, God."

"You've got to take care of her, Drew. She's pregnant with your baby. You're her husband. It's your job to convince her that everything will be fine."

"Okay, okay," Drew hauled himself up off the sofa. "You're right. I'm being childish."

"And selfish," Packard added and stood, slapping a big hand on Drew's back. "Go take care of your wife. She's frightened. That's why she hasn't told you."

Drew dragged himself toward the studio doors. He raised a hand, a gesture of thanks, without saying a word or turning to look back at his friend.

As Packard threw red over the cool blues and greens, he pictured himself taking Annie into his arms, reassuring her, comforting her, and awaiting his baby. Then he shook the image out of his head. Packard would have to trust that Drew could do the job.

Chapter Fifteen
Summer 1967

PACKARD WAS FIRST AWARE OF her high heels clicking across the floor of the Schoolhouse Studio. He felt the hairs on the back of his neck stand erect, but he didn't turn around immediately. He was intent on the next stroke of his brush in a new abstract series reflecting the civil rights movement. It was hot, and once he lifted the brush off the canvas, Pack turned, wiping his brow with a forearm.

She stood on legs that ran from the Eastern Shore to Canada and then disappeared in the tight skirt of her New York designer suit. With the matching three-inch heels, she was nearly as tall as Packard. Her silky black hair turned up in a sophisticated flip on the ends. A copy of *Elegant Southern Life* dangled between two perfectly manicured pink finger nails.

"Packard Marlboro?" she asked, raising the magazine up to the page with his picture.

"Yes."

"I'm Sheila Van Bruen, and I want to buy these two mobiles."

"They aren't for sale."

"They're in the magazine."

"It's a column, not an advertisement."

"Well, one assumes."

"Don't assume anything about me, Mrs. Van Bruen."

"Miss Van Bruen."

She was the opposite of any woman he had ever slept with and certainly couldn't be more different from Annie. He'd been with his share of women in his youth, all very casual, of course, with no commitments. But his reclusive nature and his feelings for Annie had led him to a monk-like existence for a long time. He was tired of it. It wasn't healthy. He wanted to bed Sheila Van Bruen this instant.

"Well, they still aren't for sale," he said, admiring her tall, lean stature as she stood looking up at the planets spinning around the crow.

"I'm a corporate art dealer. I have a client who wants both of them for the lobby of his new building in Manhattan."

"But he hasn't even seen them."

"I know what he wants."

"I bet you do," Pack heard himself say.

"He's willing to pay $100,000."

Packard couldn't speak.

"Each," she added when he didn't respond.

"I won't sell them."

"Listen," Miss Van Bruen said, with a soft but deliberate stamp of one high heel. "Let's cut to the chase. Do you want more money, or would you consider making replicas for the price I offered?"

She was smart. He admired that.

"Exact replicas," she added.

"They aren't made from cookie cutters, Miss Van Bruen. I'm not working an assembly line here."

She seemed to change tactics. "I'm sorry. I didn't mean

to insult your obvious talent. Would you be willing to create two more mobiles on the same theme with similar figures for $120,000 each?"

"Yes." Pack said and surprised himself.

He'd make the crows into ravens. It would be a small enough change to pacify his artistic integrity and still earn more money than he usually did in years of fishing and painting estate and pet portraits.

"I assume that you won't sell these two because of some personal attachment?" she asked.

"There you go assuming again." Packard avoided her inquiry.

"And are these for sale?" Miss Van Bruen clicked her way over to his first abstracts, which were leaning against the far wall. Packard admired the shape of her calves as she stood balanced atop those impossible shoes.

"I don't know," he said honestly. "I hadn't thought about it. They're my first abstracts."

"What did you paint before these?"

"Portraits, mostly."

"I have a ton of corporate clients who want their portraits done for the board room wall and so on."

"No dogs, I hope."

"Not literally," she said, a bit confused. "A few wolves though."

Pack laughed. *Sharp*, he thought. *She's sharp*.

"Would you like to have dinner some time?" Packard asked. He had no idea what was going to come out of his mouth next.

"Yes, I would," she said, without any hesitation.

"How's next Saturday?"

"No good, I'll be in Paris. I'm back the following week."

"Then the next Saturday."

"Great. I've never been to the Eastern Shore before. Are there some nice restaurants?"

"Do you like crabs?" he asked.

"Love them."

"Come casual. No high heels," Pack said, glancing at her shoes.

After she left, Packard immediately grabbed his sketchpad and pencil and began drawing her face and figure while planning the seduction of Miss Van Bruen.

Sheila Van Bruen made quite a picture coming down the stairs with sleepy eyes and tousled hair, wearing one of Pack's huge chambray shirts.

Packard had done a meticulous job of hosing down *Sophie's* deck and cleaning out the wheelhouse. He hadn't thought to do anything but leave his rather musty old sleeping bag on the bunk because he never imagined Sheila Van Buren would be so comfortable on a boat. However, after years of competitive sailing as a teenager, she was right at home on any vessel. It wasn't long before they took advantage of the cozy wheelhouse for their initial plunge into tantalizing exploration, but they soon discovered that between the two of them, they took up too much room in the boat's bunk to be comfortable. Pack brought Sheila home to his big bed where they had plenty of room to enjoy one another fully all night.

This morning Pack was enjoying the view of his shirt just covering her thighs. She wore nothing else. He wanted to sweep her back into bed, but they were both starving. The crabs they'd caught before getting distracted by other things were still in a trap Packard had tossed overboard by the dock.

"I'm about to fix some breakfast and coffee is already on."

"I know. The smell is what pulled me out of bed."

As they walked through the dining room, Sheila noticed the portrait of a little girl holding a dead crow.

"How sad," she said, looking at the work carefully.

Pack continued into the kitchen to start breakfast.

"Who is she?" Sheila asked, still analyzing the portrait.

"My neighbor," he answered while taking eggs out of the refrigerator.

"What's her name?"

"Annie Crow. I mean Annie Atkinson. Well, Bidwell now."

"She writes the column in the magazine where I found your mobiles."

"Yes," Pack said, as he took a bowl out for whipping up the eggs.

Sheila noticed the details in the crow. The same as the mobiles, she noted.

"How old was she here?" she asked.

"Eleven."

A knowing smile came to Sheila's face. *He's in love with Annie Crow*, she thought. But there was no jealousy. For Sheila Van Bruen, it was just as well. She wasn't looking for anything serious. Pack was easy on the eyes, talented, bright and delicious in bed. That's all she wanted in a man.

"Hi, Preggies. How's it going?" Grace asked cheerfully over the phone.

"Doc says the baby is doing well."

"That's great! Oh, Patsy was out here for our spring alumni fund raiser, and she went on and on about the terrific job you did on the schoolhouse restoration series for her magazine. It was a big hit with the readers. In fact, some fancy-ass art dealer called Patsy's office about Packard's mobiles."

"That's his girlfriend!" Annie almost shouted.

"Packard is sleeping with the art dealer?"

"Yes, and according to Drew, it's about time."

"What's she like? Give me the details."

"I haven't met her, but I've seen her," Annie said carefully, not wanting to reveal that only yesterday, she had hauled her pregnant self up into the Crow's Nest to get a better look at Sheila Van Bruen down on Pack's dock.

"So?" Grace asked curiously.

"She's gorgeous—an Amazon. She has to be close to six feet tall. She's slim with shiny, shoulder-length, black hair that always turns up into a perfect flip. Her clothes are perfect, too. Can you tell that I hate her?"

"Are you crying?" Grace asked surprised.

"No. Yes. I cry over everything anymore."

"Oh, honey, I'm so sorry that I can't be out there with you this coming summer."

"It's okay. I understand. Here I am crying over nothing and haven't even asked how the internship of a lifetime is going?"

"It's great. I love every minute of it. I think they may hire me full-time after I graduate!"

"That's wonderful."

"But I'm really worried about you."

"Don't be. Everyone says that it's all in my head."

"How's the season at the Knoll going?"

"Fine. I had to hire someone to turn over the weekly rentals. And Bo is working constantly. I can't seem to keep up with it all," Annie admitted.

"How's the *Elegant Southern Life* column going? What are you going to do to top the schoolhouse series?"

"I don't know." Annie paused. "Grace, I can't seem to concentrate long enough to write."

"Annie?" Grace asked with alarm in her voice.

"But it's okay. Patsy said that we can rerun earlier columns if we have to."

"What's Drew say about all this?"

"He pats my hand and tells me that he's heard that all pregnant women get a little nuts."

"Hey, why not write the column about being pregnant? Grace suggested helpfully.

"That's a good idea," Annie said.

However, the truth was that no one would want to read about how awful and out of control she felt. People believe that this is the happiest time in a woman's life. Annie wanted to believe it, too. But if she did, then she'd have to face that there was something very wrong with her.

Chapter Sixteen
Fall 1967

DREW WAS ON CAMPUS TEACHING, and Bo was draining the water heater in Fish Tale Cottage for the winter when the phone rang. It took Annie a moment to find her feet. Her center of gravity had shifted during this her eighth month of pregnancy, and she found that she had to carry herself differently. It seemed like she was constantly moving in slow motion. Her mind still reached the point of destination quickly, but her body was always behind.

"Hello," Annie said a little out of breath.

"Miss Annie?" a timid voice said over the phone.

"Yes?"

"It's Walter Barns, Miss Annie."

"Yes, Mr. Walter." Annie was cheered to know that the dear man was still alive.

"Your great-grandmother has passed."

"I see." Annie felt nothing.

"It was peaceful. The nurse kept her comfortable."

"I'm glad that you weren't alone."

"The nurse moved in two weeks ago."

"Now what happens, Walter?"

"She'll be buried the day after tomorrow. Her lawyer is taking care of all the arrangements."

The baby kicked inside Annie.

"Has he called you about her will?" Walter asked.

"No, the lawyer hasn't contacted me."

"Well, I asked him to call you. Mrs. Witherspoon done left everything to me and I don't want it, Miss Annie!" he said.

"You've lived in that house your entire life."

"But I'm seventy-eight years old. What am I going to do in this big, empty house?"

"Sell it and buy whatever you want," Annie told him.

"It's not just the house. There's all the land and several businesses and stocks. I don't know what to do with any of it," Walter said, sounding more like a little boy than an older man. "It should really go to you," he added.

"But I want you to have it. You deserve it. Your great-grandparents and grandmother were slaves, and I'm sure that your mother was paid next to nothing."

"There'll be trouble if I own it. I don't want no trouble."

"They wouldn't dare." Annie knew that he meant the local Klan members.

"I'm afraid Mrs. Witherspoon did this just to spite you. I'd be better off signing it all over to you."

"You just sit tight."

"But you're the next of kin," Walter reasoned.

"Who's to say that you're not, too?" Annie realized.

"No! Mrs. Witherspoon's grandfather wasn't that kind," he insisted. He didn't like lying to Miss Annie when she suggested that he was a blood relation, but he wasn't going to let her open up that long, buried Pandora's Box.

"One way or the other, Delia Witherspoon named you as the beneficiary, and I support that decision."

It was getting dark earlier and earlier every day. The baby was due in a few weeks, and Annie felt her entire being shifting with the season. Annie had promised to visit Walter, but by the time she got around to getting into the car, it was late afternoon. She wondered if this last stage of pregnancy was slowing her down even more, or if she'd procrastinated all day purposefully. She hadn't been back to the brick house in Kingstown since she was a little girl.

Old Walter's warm welcome calmed Annie as she stood in the large foyer of her great-grandmother's house. Since the only other room she had ever been allowed in was the garden room, Walter insisted on giving her a tour of the downstairs. He still kept all the doors to unused rooms closed and all lights off as Delia Witherspoon had instructed. He moved slowly with arthritic knees and hands as he opened the doors to the two large parlors off the center hallway. Each had marble fireplaces and was filled with antiques, oriental rugs and oil paintings. The focus point of the huge formal dining room was a crystal chandelier, which loomed over the Chippendale dining table and chairs.

"I was never allowed in any of these rooms," Annie reminded Walter as she took in all the faded grandeur. "I feel like I'm breaking the rules and that Great Grand will appear any minute to reprimand me and sic her darn dogs on me."

"There's only one dog left, and he's in no shape to hurt you," Walter said as he led Annie back through the butler's pantry, which was lined with glass cabinets filled with six different sets of china.

The kitchen smelled of herbs and freshly baked bread. Annie's stomach growled.

"Was that you or the baby?" Walter teased.

"Both."

"Want some soup? It's hot."

"Yes, please."

The pleasant smell of the kitchen reminded Annie that she had brought a treat of chocolates for Walter. She rummaged in her shoulder bag for the box.

"I remember your mother always sent sweets to me. Thank you," Walter said and placed the box on the table. "Have a seat."

As Annie lowered herself into a kitchen chair, she saw into Walter's room through an open door past the stove. It was clear that he was still staying there and had no intention of moving to one of the bedrooms upstairs.

Then an ancient Pekinese wandered out of Walter's room. The dog's overgrown nails clicked on the tile floor, and his eyes were cloudy with cataracts.

"Come here, baby," Walter said to the dog, which followed Walter's voice toward the bowl of warm broth just set on the floor.

"His teeth are gone," Walter said and gave the dog a gentle pat on the head.

After they ate, Walter insisted on showing Annie the rest of the house. Due to his arthritis and Annie's ever-expanding belly, they made their way slowly up the grand staircase. The wiser old dog stayed curled up on the rug down in the foyer.

Walter led Annie to the rear of the house first. There was a back staircase without any ornate balustrade which had once been the servants' route from the kitchen below to their beds on the unheated third floor.

Walter moved to open a nearby door that had a bolt on the hall side of it. Inside was a small, empty bedroom.

"This was your mother's room when she was growing up," he told Annie.

"Way back here?" Annie asked, looking at the barren room.

Walter nodded. "Yes, this was Liz's bedroom—back

here."

"Where was my grandmother's room?"

"At the front of the house, across the hall from Mrs. Witherspoon's bedroom. She kept your mother as far away from your grandmother as possible. She even insisted that Liz use the back staircase instead of the main one in front."

"My mother never told me much about her childhood."

"It wasn't a happy one," Walter admitted grimly.

"Why isn't there any furniture in here?" Annie asked.

"Your grandmother helped Liz escape the morning of her wedding."

"Escape?"

"Your great-grandmother locked Liz in here with the intention of keeping her from marrying your father. Your grandmother Ann slipped some of her own sleeping pills into the old lady's coffee, and while she was asleep, freed your mother who left here with only the clothes on her back. After the wedding, Mrs. Witherspoon threw away all your mother's belongings, including the meager furniture and an old rug that she had provided for her."

Annie was shocked. She had had no idea how difficult her mother's life had been. "I saw pictures of the wedding. Everything looked normal. My mother wore a wedding gown, and my grandmother was with her in the photographs."

"The gown had belonged to your father's mother. I drove Miss Ann to the church. There was hell to pay when your great-grandmother finally roused herself, but I didn't care. I wasn't going to let the sweetest, kindest creature on the earth miss her own daughter's wedding."

Walter seemed startled when Annie touched his arm and leaned in to kiss his cheek.

"May I see my grandmother's room now?"

Walter led her past a number of doorways. As they neared the front rooms, Annie noticed a study completely lined in solid cherry paneling. She paused.

"That was Mrs. Witherspoon's grandfather's study, and then her father's office and finally hers."

"It still looks so masculine," Annie noted.

"She never changed anything after her father died and she took over running the estate."

"What about her husband?" Annie asked.

"She divorced him after their honeymoon train trip across country. Just long enough for Mr. Witherspoon to discover that his new bride wasn't going to sign over her assets like an obedient wife. And just long enough for the bride to learn that her husband was so interested in her assets because he had none. They parted company at the end of the train tour, but she was already expecting your grandmother."

The next door was Annie's grandmother's room. It was cornered between Delia's own bedroom and office. Ann could go nowhere without crossing the path of her mother's watchful eye.

Lilacs clinging to lattice graced the wallpaper of Annie's grandmother's room. The windows, which overlooked the front lawn and side gardens, were secured with two set of locks.

"I'm surprised that there aren't bars on the windows," Annie said.

Then she turned and saw a portrait of her grandmother Ann. It looked to have been painted when she was about seventeen years old.

"That was done the year before she ran away to New York City," Walter explained.

"Before she did what?" Annie couldn't believe her ears.

"Your grandmother wanted to become an actress. Mrs. Witherspoon wouldn't hear of it and forbade her to even audition for school plays. Always obedient to her mother, Miss Ann secretly memorized roles, hoping for the right opportunity to change her life. After high school graduation, a girlfriend of hers was going to live in New York City and wanted her to come along. Knowing that her mother would lock her in her room if she asked to go, she did the bravest thing she ever did in her entire life."

"She ran away." Annie looked again at her beautiful grandmother in the painting.

"Yes. Unfortunately, Miss Ann had been so sheltered her entire life that she wasn't prepared to cope with the real world. A man, who claimed to be a producer, made promises that he would get her on stage. He got her pregnant and abandoned her. She was expecting your mother before anything came of her acting career. She had nowhere else to go so she came home in disgrace."

"My mother was illegitimate!" Annie reached for an armchair. Her knees felt weak.

"Are you all right?" Walter asked.

"Yes. I just need to sit."

Walter helped her into the chair.

"Please don't think less of your mother." Walter looked stricken.

"I don't even know who my mother was!"

"Liz was a wonderful girl," Walter defended. "Why, there were whole stretches of time when her mother couldn't even get out of bed. Miss Ann wanted to see your mother. I'd hear her call for Liz, but Mrs. Witherspoon said that no one should see her in that state."

"State? Do you mean she was mentally ill?"

"Depressed," Walter said with some hesitation and then added, "There were happier times too, when Miss Ann would read plays aloud to your mother."

"Yes, my mother replayed those scenes with me many times when I was growing up."

"I guess she wanted to relive the times when her mother was well."

"Delia said that my grandmother died in a drowning accident."

"It was no accident," Walter said with tears in his eyes. "About a month after your parents were married, Miss Ann left your great-grandmother sitting at the dinner table, walked out to the river and jumped in. I think she knew Liz was free then, out of that house, and she could finally let go."

Annie couldn't respond.

Suddenly the silence was pierced with the sound of breaking glass, as a brick flew between Annie and Walter, landing with a thud on her grandmother's bed.

Walter reached the window first followed by Annie, who had difficulty pulling herself up out of the chair. When they saw a large wooden cross being lit down on the lawn surrounded by twenty or so figures wearing white robes and hoods, they both stepped away from the window. Walter shut the drapes.

"I'm calling the police," Annie told him.

"They won't do anything," Walter told her as he followed her down the grand staircase to the main hall. Delia's ancient Pekinese was now barking furiously at the front door. Walter moved as quickly as he could to lock it.

"They're trespassing on and vandalizing my great-grandmother's property," Annie snapped and starting looking for the phone.

"No, they're vandalizing my property." Walter spoke firmly.

"Where's the damn phone?"

"The police can't stop them."

"Why the hell not?"

"Because half the police force is probably out there under those hoods," Walter said and leaned up against the front door as if his thin, fragile frame could keep this ugliness and evil outside.

Something heavy hit the other side of the front door. Walter didn't budge.

"Where's a shotgun?" Annie asked.

"We don't have any guns," he said.

"I can shoot, Walter. Don't lie to me."

"Mrs. Witherspoon sold all her father's hunting guns after he died."

"Well, I'm not hiding in here waiting for those bastards to burn us out," Annie said and strode with such force toward the door that Walter instinctively stepped aside. Annie unlocked the door, opened it and walked out onto the portico. Walter followed.

The boisterous crowd of hooded men quieted for a moment. Then one voice called out, "Well, look what we got here. An old nigger and pregnant white trash." The crowd laughed and began to move closer.

Annie immediately realized her mistake. These animals didn't see her or Walter as human beings. They were completely invisible to the approaching mob. Fear ripped through her like an exploding scream but no sound came from her throat. Then the baby kicked hard inside her and jolted her into action.

"Stop!" she shouted.

The crowd hovered just off the edge of the brick steps, only feet from her and Walter. Annie tasted vomit in her throat.

"I'm Delia Witherspoon's great-granddaughter." She raised her voice above the swirling nausea.

"That don't mean shit if this old boy thinks he's going to own her property," another voice called out of the darkness.

"He doesn't," Annie lied. Her knees were caving in, and her head spun.

"We heard different," a familiar voice said.

"You heard wrong. I own this property, and I asked Mr. Walter to continue to work for me as he has for my family for years," Annie said but avoided looking at Walter.

There were murmurs in the group.

Then as if in a dream, Annie saw Drew's car pull into the long drive, followed by several other cars.

One hooded voice called out, "Come on, boys, let's go."

The crowd began to break up.

Drew drove past the vehicles now filling up with Klansmen. His car barreled across the grass right up to the steps where Annie stood with Walter. Drew leapt out of his car, leaving the door open, and Annie felt herself collapse into his arms just as he reached her. He lifted her up and carried her into the house.

A brief smile came to his lips as Walter watched several young men and women, presumably students of Professor Bidwell's, pour out of the other cars left willy nilly all over Delia Witherspoon's pristine lawn. Two young men began pushing the burning cross over with a crow bar. Walter tottered in to help Drew with Annie. He directed the professor into the main parlor where he laid his now trembling wife onto a sofa.

"My darling, my darling," Drew repeated, kneeling on the floor next to Annie. He kissed her face and hands over and over. "My Annie, my dearest."

Walter backed out of the room, closing the double doors to give the young couple some privacy. When he turned to face the hall, a group of a dozen students crowded in the front doorway. They stood silently watching him as he stared back at them.

After a moment, one young woman began applauding. Then another and another joined in. The students began approaching Walter one at a time, shaking his hand and saying how brave he was and how sorry they were that this had happened. One young man said to tell Dr. Bidwell that they'd be outside if he or his wife needed anything. They all filed out until one young black man was left. He spoke to Walter in a soft, foreign accent.

"I come to America to study. I learn more about this country outside the class room."

In Delia Witherspoon's parlor, Drew held Annie close. She was still shaking.

"Let me take you home," he told her.

"I can't get warm," she chattered.

He began rubbing her arms. "What kind of a place is this?"

"How did you know to come?" she asked.

"Before I started to lecture, one of my students said that he heard some guys talking about it at a gas station. When I left to race up here, the entire class followed me."

"I lied! I usurped Walter's rights because those bastards scared me. I told them it was my property."

"You saved Walter's life and your own and our baby's." Drew held her tight again. He felt her body beginning to calm down. "Under the circumstances, you did the right thing."

"They wouldn't have killed us." Annie tried to sound convincing.

"You don't know that," Drew said, stroking Annie's hair, her dark curls catching his fingers.

"They wanted to intimidate me into taking the estate away from Walter, and I caved in."

"You're being too harsh with yourself. I'm sure that Walter understands."

"I've never been frightened like that! It made me feel sick."

"Let me take you home, Annie," Drew said again.

"Do you think that Walter will be all right here?"

"I mean to Oregon."

It took a moment before Annie could comprehend what Drew meant. "I can't live in Oregon!" she said sharply.

"Shh, shh." Drew touched her hair again. "We'll talk about it later."

Annie pushed his hand away. "Don't patronize me. I may be hugely pregnant, but I'm not helpless."

Drew stood. The full fury of his feelings rose to the surface.

"I've never been so frightened either. You don't know what I felt when I first drove in and saw you surrounded by those crazy men with burning torches!" His voice grew louder.

"I felt helpless, and I won't feel that way again! I don't care if you think this is ridiculous or old-fashioned, but it's my job to protect you. To protect our baby. I don't know how to deal with—with this," he said and gestured helplessly out toward the front lawn where the cross now laid smoking. "This is insanity!"

"I have a responsibility, too," Annie said quietly but certainly. "I grew up here, and the only way to change what's wrong is to stay and make a difference. Running away isn't going to fix things. Hiding from what's ugly in this world won't make it go away."

"Let's go back to the Knoll," Drew finally said. "I'm exhausted."

Walter was waiting for them in the hall when Drew and Annie emerged from the parlor.

"Miss Annie, I don't want all this. If it were important to me, I'd fight for it, but I never wanted any of it."

"I understand," Annie said, too tired to argue.

"I have a great-niece who has a place for me with her and her children in Baltimore. We've always been close. She told me that she really wants me to live with her. Her husband died suddenly last year, and I can help with the two boys. They can be a handful for her."

"What are you saying?" Annie asked.

"I'm giving it all back. It's all yours. You can't make me keep it," Walter said firmly.

"I'll talk to J.J. Finch tomorrow. But I am going to insist that you get enough to take care of yourself, your great-niece, and to put those boys through college."

"Thank you, I'd appreciate that," Walter said.

"I expect to be invited to their college graduations."

"Yes, ma'am." Walter winked. "Do you mind if I take the dog?"

"You can take anything you want," Annie replied.

"Would you like to stay with us?" Drew asked.

"No, thank you. I'll be fine."

"I'm driving Annie home in her truck. We'll leave my car here so if anyone gets another bug up their butt, they might be discouraged if they think that someone else is still here," Drew said.

"By the way, I'm Walter Barns."

"Pleased to meet you, Mr. Barns. I'm—"

"I know who you are, sir. Thank you."

After Drew pulled Annie's truck off the property and the last student cars followed, Walter locked the door. He staggered over to the staircase and lowered his stiff bones down onto the bottom step. For a moment, his paper-thin hands danced in front of his face like translucent birds. Then he let go, lowering his face into his lap to cry. The old Pekinese, with nails clicking, wandered over and lay down, resting his chin on Walter's right shoe.

The amount of wealth and responsibility that was being handed over to Annie would not hit her for some time. She really didn't know what Delia had owned. But during the drive back to Annie Crow Knoll, some of the possibilities of her new financial independence suddenly dawned on her.

"You're going to get moved up now!" she blurted out impulsively.

"I don't want to be moved up," Drew snapped.

"But you deserve it. Now Delia isn't around to cheat you out of it, and I'll be the one donating or not donating money to that college."

"I won't be moved up because you can buy it for me!"

Annie fell silent. She never intended to insult her husband.

"But we can fund your new Folklore curriculum. We can publish your textbook," she tried again.

"No, Annie. I don't want any of your money."

"It's our money."

"No, it's not. It's yours, and I'm begging you to leave me out of it. I'd be nothing but humiliated if I were promoted or published or funded now that you hold some of the purse strings on campus."

"It's my fault that you've been overlooked. Can't I make it up to you?"

"No." Drew's face was stern.

Annie didn't like the look of it.

"Fine," she said. "I'll find other projects to fund. That college needs a minority program and women's studies."

"That would be wonderful," Drew said with restraint in his voice.

Annie longed to tell her husband all that Walter had revealed about her mother and grandmother, but now was not the time. They were silent on the rest of the drive back to Promise and out Baycliff Road to Annie Crow Knoll.

Annie's water broke as she was standing in the kitchen making a shopping list for Thanksgiving dinner.

"Well, that was convenient," she said to herself with relief that she hadn't let loose on the new living room rug.

"Bo?" she hollered out the front door.

Bo was heading to his car which was parked in the circle by the flagpole. Annie had invited him out to discuss capital improvements she wanted him to make on the Knoll. The sun had set, and he had just finished checking all the cottages on the property before he headed home.

When Bo heard his name, he turned to see Annie waving from the front porch.

Suddenly her face squeezed tight, and he ran to her.

"Can you take me to the hospital?" she asked when she caught her breath. "I'm going into labor."

He took her arm to lead her to his car, but she stopped.

"Not yet. There are a couple things we have to do first," she insisted, and they headed back into the cottage. "Please get the overnight bag by the table and put it in the car while I call Drew at the college. He can meet us there after his last class."

After carrying Annie's bag to his car, Bo hurried back into the cottage expecting her to be ready to go, but she was still on the phone.

"We'd best be going, Annie," Bo said anxiously.

"Just one minute, Bo. I'm having trouble getting through."

"You can call him from the hospital," Bo insisted when he noticed the puddle on the kitchen floor.

"Hello?" Annie said into the receiver. "Yes, this is Drew Bidwell's wife. Please tell him to meet me at the hospital. The baby is coming."

Finally when Bo had Annie in his car and was pulling out of the Knoll, she grabbed the dashboard with both hands and a tiny cry escaped her throat.

"Go ahead and scream, Annie," Bo advised. "And keep breathing. Don't go holdin' your breath like that."

The contraction passed, and Annie slumped back in the car seat with sweat rolling down her face.

"I'm not one for screaming, Bo," she said bravely.

"Well, you'll be hollering before the night's over," Bo said with a laugh and sped up a bit when he turned onto Center Street. The hospital in Chester Landing was at least forty-five minutes away, and he was not going to deliver this baby! Then he saw the red lights flashing in the rear view window.

"Damn," Bo said.

Bo never cursed, so Annie pulled herself up to see what was behind them. Bo slowed down, and then stopped on the side of the road.

"Oh, no," Annie said when she saw Bunky Watson step

out of the patrol car.

Patrolman Watson pounded his fist on the top of Big Black Bo's car and then directed the blinding beam of his flashlight into the driver's side window.

"Roll down your window, boy," he demanded.

Bo obliged, and Annie noticed that he immediately put his left hand back up on the steering wheel next to his right.

Bunky Watson's face then appeared in the open window.

"What are you doing here in town, boy?" he snapped.

Before Bo could say anything, Annie leaned forward.

"For God's sake, Bunky, he's drivin' me to the hospital."

"Annie, what are you doing in this Negro's car?"

"What I'm going to be doin' is having a baby if you don't let us get on to the hospital."

"Is it his baby?" Bunky asked sarcastically.

"Now Bunky, you know that my husband is Drew Bidwell, and he's at the college so Mr. Bo, who works for me as I'm sure you also know, was kind enough to drive me into the hospital where Drew will meet me."

"Why aren't you sittin' in the back seat?" Bunky asked.

"I-I don't know, Bunky. I was having a contraction when he helped me into the car so I just sat where he put me." Annie immediately regretted the wording of her explanation.

"You put her in the front seat with you, boy? What were you thinking?" Bunky asked and waited for an answer.

"I thought I could keep an eye on her up here," Bo explained.

"You know the sun set fifteen minutes ago?" Bunky stated with authority.

"Yes," Bo answered.

"And you were going ten miles over the speed limit."

Annie saw Bo's hands grip the steering wheel tighter just when pain started again deep in her spine. She leaned forward in her seat.

"Bunky, you stupid ass, I'm about to have a baby, and if

you don't let us pass now, you and Bo are going to be delivering it together right here on Center Street." Annie seethed between her teeth, and then she let out a blood-curdling scream as the contraction peaked.

"Go!" Bunky ordered and stepped back from the car.

Bo threw the car back into drive and pulled away. Annie leaned back against her seat again, panting. After a moment, she started to laugh.

"You were right about the screaming, Bo. It does help."

Bo smiled. He reached over and squeezed her hand. Annie held onto it, and he let her. In all these years, they had never touched.

Annie couldn't remember a time in her life when she didn't know Bo. He'd been her father's closest friend, but there was always a boundary. It hadn't stopped the connection, the trust, or the love, but it had made physical displays of any emotion taboo. Annie thought of the time that she had discovered her mother and Bo embracing. What made it wrong? Bo's race? Her parents' marriage? Annie didn't know and was almost relieved when another contraction came and erased any more thoughts of her mother in Bo's arms. The baby was coming soon.

When the pain subsided, Annie realized that she had been crushing Bo's hand. When she released her death grip, he didn't remove his hand, so she continued to hold on. It was like when she was little and her mama would have to pull out a splinter or take off a Band-Aid, and her daddy would let her squeeze his hand as tightly as she wanted. Daddy never complained.

Her parents had always been there whenever she was hurt or scared. Annie felt the full weight of their absence during this important moment in her life. But Bo was there. He always was. She trusted him as if he were her father. But there was no one to mother Annie now. Who could she talk to when she needed advice about the baby? There was no woman to reassure her now when the wave of pain started again. Annie cried and gripped Bo's hand again until the contraction ended. "It's all right, Annie," Bo reassured.

Annie could barely hear his voice. It was as if she were under water, and Bo was calling from the beach.

"Don't worry," Bo continued. "We're almost to the hospital, and Drew will be there."

Bo kept talking to Annie. Even during the contractions, he spoke calmly through her screams. Bo knew that everything would be fine because Annie was white. She'd be rushed right into the hospital and into a clean, sterile, safe delivery room with all the doctors and medical procedures necessary to bring this little baby into the world. There'd be no delay, no questions raised, no "But we don't take coloreds at this hospital" while she bled on the floor with the staff looking at the blood as if it were urine.

Bo heard Annie let out a whimper. He was squeezing her hand back and hadn't stopped. He let go and used both hands to steer the car up to the hospital entrance. Drew was waiting out front with an orderly and a wheel chair. When the orderly wheeled Annie toward the door, Drew started to go, but then suddenly turned back and threw his arms around Bo.

"Thank you, Bo." Drew said.

"You're welcome."

"Well, come on. There's no time to waste," Drew said, as he nudged Bo toward the door.

"No, I'll wait out here in the car," Bo said. He wasn't going into that hospital even if he could now. It didn't matter to Bo that the orderly was black, and so were ten percent of the other staff, including several nurses.

"Suit yourself. I'll come right out and tell you as soon as

I know anything," Drew hollered as he ran into the hospital.

Bo got back into his car. No one was around, and as Annie gave birth to Drew's son, Bo let himself shudder with deep sobs that rose over him.

An hour and a half later, Drew approached Bo's car. "It's a boy!" he yelled.

Bo jumped out of the car. "Is she all right?" he asked.

"Yes, Annie is fine! The baby is fine! Here, have a cigar."

Bo took the cigar with one hand and shook Drew's hand with the other.

"Congratulations!" Bo laughed. "What's his name?"

"Nathan. Nathan Bo Bidwell," Drew told him.

Bo didn't move. He couldn't speak.

Then Drew slapped Bo on the back and said, "Congratulations!"

"Are you sure?" Bo asked.

"Of course!"

"It does have a ring to it, doesn't it?" Bo responded and took a bandanna out of his back pocket to dab his eyes.

"Annie's the one who sent me out here to you as soon as I was willing to leave her, but I'd better get back in there."

"Go!"

"Thank you, Bo. Thank you for getting her here safely."

They shook hands again, and Bo watched Drew hurry back into the hospital.

There was a white child whose middle name was his own. Bo shook his head in amazement. How surprising life could be.

Chapter Seventeen
Winter 1967-68

THE FIRST MORNING DREW HAD to go back to classes and left Annie alone with this tiny creature, she thought she'd lose her mind. This was supposed to be the happiest time in her life, but instead Annie felt out of control. One minute she was fine and the next all she felt were waves of despair followed by fear of when the despair would hit again.

"Annie! The baby is crying!" Drew shouted when he came home that afternoon.

"What?" Annie had been sitting oblivious to anything for she wasn't sure how long, perhaps hours.

Drew brushed past her toward little Nate's room. Filled with guilt, Annie followed him into the nursery.

"Hey there, buddy? What's the matter with my boy?" Drew cooed as he picked his son up out of his crib and rocked the child gently. Nate immediately settled down.

"I'm sorry," Annie began to cry. "I don't know how I

couldn't have heard him."

"I could hear him all the way from my car," Drew snapped as he carried Nate over to the changing table.

"Let me do it," Annie said.

Drew took a good look at her. "Annie, you're exhausted. Go lie down and nap. I'll take care of Nate."

"But—"

"Go."

Annie slept for a long time. When she awoke, it was past dinnertime and both Drew and the baby were gone. She found a note.

I'm taking Nate with me over to play chess with Pack tonight. You were sleeping so soundly that I didn't want to wake you. Love, Drew

Annie went back to bed and slept again until Drew woke her in the morning.

"I'm leaving for school, Annie," he called from the kitchen.

"Okay," Annie wandered out of the bedroom. Nate was in his highchair.

"How are you?"

"Fine."

"Oh, I invited Packard and Sheila to Christmas dinner," he told her as he put on his coat.

"I don't want them here," Annie said flatly.

Drew was taken aback. "Why not?" he finally asked.

"I have more than enough to handle with the baby, the decorating, the shopping and wrapping."

"Can't Grace help?"

"She's not flying in until Christmas Eve. I don't want any more company."

"Okay, okay. I'll un-invite them, I guess," Drew said and kissed Nate's head on his way out the door.

As Grace drove her rental car through the entrance to Annie Crow Knoll, she smiled at the cement crows atop the stone columns. Packard's sign had been taken in for the winter, and also missing was Liz's famous mistletoe garland that customarily decorated the front gates. Grace had rarely been on the Knoll in winter, and her senses were immediately flooded by the familiar yet different view of the bay, nearly frozen except where the Coast Guard ice breaker kept the shipping lanes open to the Chesapeake and Delaware Canal. A giddiness washed over her as she stepped out of the car. She felt the power of the cold air hit her as it blew off the water, moving loose, brittle leaves across the lawn.

"Merry Christmas!" Grace heard Drew shout as he dashed out without a coat to help her unload the car of her suitcases and several packages to be put under the tree. He looked as handsome as ever but tired.

"Annie in with the baby?" Grace asked, as she closed the car trunk.

"No, he's napping, and Annie is running an errand. I offered to go so she could be here when you arrived, but she insisted on going herself."

Grace hid her disappointment that Annie wasn't there to greet her.

There was a wreath on the porch door, and inside Sunrise Cottage, a haphazardly decorated Christmas tree stood in the corner of the living room.

Drew took her coat and hung it in the closet.

"Want some hot chocolate to warm up?" he asked.

"Can I see the baby first?"

"Sure. We made Annie's old room into the nursery," he explained as they walked back. "Annie is beside herself that you'll be sleeping on the sofa."

"Are you kidding? I'll love waking up next to the tree on Christmas morning!"

Drew gently eased the bedroom door open and led Grace over to the crib. Nathan was still sound asleep.

"An angel," Grace whispered with tears choking her voice.

"Most of the time," Drew said quietly.

The baby moved his mouth a little allowing a tiny bubble to escape.

"Ahh," Grace cooed.

"Yeah." Drew smiled with great pride.

"He's perfect!" Grace said. "Absolutely perfect and gorgeous."

"Like his mother," Drew said.

"He smells so good, too."

"His poop doesn't smell so good," Drew observed.

Grace laughed. "I can't wait to hold him."

"Let's let him sleep a little longer. I'll make you some cocoa."

Grace and Drew tiptoed out of the nursery.

"I don't know what is taking Annie so long," Drew said, as he pulled the bedroom door shut.

"Is she all right? I mean, is she doing okay?" Grace asked.

"I think so," Drew said. "She's a little tired. We both are. He's not sleeping through the night, so it's tough."

Grace sat at the familiar kitchen table. She remembered all the meals she had eaten here as a child with Annie and her parents.

"I'll get up with him while I'm here. You two should sleep."

"After taking all your finals, you probably need some sleep, too!" Drew poured milk into a pot and lit the stove.

"I caught up on the plane."

"God, I can never sleep on a plane."

Annie appeared at the kitchen door with a bag of groceries, which she handed to Drew.

"Merry Christmas!" Grace said and jumped up to hug her dear friend. "Let me look at the new mother!"

Annie's eyes seemed vacant. Then she looked away from Grace and took off her coat.

"How was your flight?" she asked.

"It was fine. I slept through most of it."

"Can you imagine that?" Drew said. "Now that she's all caught up, she's offering to get up with the baby at night."

"I'm going to take a nap," Annie said and suddenly disappeared from the kitchen.

Drew busied himself with putting the groceries away. Grace began to follow Annie, but the door to the master bedroom was already shut.

All of Drew's body language was telling Grace that he didn't want to listen to any more, but she felt compelled.

"Annie is depressed," Grace insisted in a low voice while Annie was in the other room putting Nate down for a nap.

"It'll even out soon. It's been a big adjustment," Drew whispered.

"You're not listening to me! I want Maizie to take a look at her."

"You're overreacting. You've only been here a few days."

"Open your eyes, Drew!"

"Doc says that she's fine. He'd recognize if Annie wasn't right."

"He doesn't know her like I do," Grace said.

"And I don't?" Drew was defensive.

"Apparently not!" Grace let her frustration get the best of her and immediately regretted it. She realized that isolating Drew was not going to help.

"What the hell are you two talking about?" Annie shouted from across the living room.

Her voice woke the baby, but instead of returning to the nursery, Annie went straight into the bedroom and slammed the door shut.

Drew shot Grace an annoyed look as he went to care for Nate.

Grace ignored him and walked right in to find Annie lying across the bed on her stomach with her head buried in her arms. She crossed the room and sat next to her.

"Annie, Drew and I have been talking about you. We're concerned about you and didn't know how to tell you. You're not well, honey, and I want to take you to Baltimore to see Dr. Maizie."

"I'm a terrible mother," a little voice said from the covers.

"No, you're not. You love Nate very much, don't you?"

Annie nodded but no words came out.

"I think that it's some kind of depression from having the baby that's keeping you from being yourself."

Annie raised her head. "Just lock me up, I guess." She smiled a little.

"That's a girl," Grace said and handed her the tissue box.

"Let Grace take you to Maizie," Drew said from the doorway. Nate was now lying quietly in his arms.

Grace had no idea how long Drew had been there.

Annie's chin shook, and she could hardly form the words. "I've failed you, Drew."

Drew rushed to the bed, throwing his arms around Annie and crushing Nate between them. The baby didn't seem to mind.

"Never, my Annie, never," Drew said.

Grace rose to leave them alone. Before she could close the door, she heard Annie say, "I'll make this up to you, little Nate. I'll make it up to both of you. I'll be the best mother in the world."

"Is there any history of depression in your family?" Maizie asked.

She was still so beautiful, Annie thought. The silver streaks in the doctor's strawberry hair made her look distinguished.

"My maternal grandmother committed suicide. I guess you could say that she was depressed," Annie answered.

"How about your mother or father?"

That question came from Dr. Edith Osborne, the psychiatrist Maizie had asked to consult. Annie found it surprising that Dr. Osborne appeared younger than Maizie. She had expected someone much older.

"You knew them," Annie responded, looking at Maizie. "Did they ever seem depressed to you?"

"Some people are very good at disguising their symptoms, but no, I don't recall ever thinking that either of them did ."

"My mother thought that Liz was depressed sometimes," Grace spoke up.

"What?" Annie snapped.

"Of course, my mother could have been wrong," Grace back-peddled.

"Depression sometimes runs in families. We have to distinguish whether this is totally related to the pregnancy or other mental illness," Dr. Osborne said patiently.

"Great. You think that I'm nuts?"

"No, but before I can suggest anything, I want as full a picture as possible."

"I understand," Annie told her. "I'm sorry," she said to both the doctors and to Grace.

Grace took hold of Annie's hand.

"Now, I'm going to ask you something, Annie, and I want you to be totally honest," Maizie said.

"I'll try."

"Do you want to have other children?"

"No, absolutely not."

"Did you always plan on just one?"

"No."

"Why do you feel this way now?"

"I'm not going to go through this again."

"Your mother only had one child?" Dr. Osborne asked. Annie nodded. "Do you know why?"

"I guess that I was enough to test the patience of Job."

Dr. Osborne looked at her colleague and then said, "After we run some urine and blood tests, we're going to try some medication. This is going to be trial and error, Annie, so you have to be patient. It may take some time to find the right combination to get you feeling better so try not to be discouraged if things don't improve right away."

"Why can't you be more specific about the treatment?" Grace asked.

"Frankly, we don't know a whole lot about this. Millions of women have suffered, but it's always been brushed off—until recently. Dr. Osborne is doing groundbreaking research, as long as she continues to get funding," Maizie explained.

"Dr. Osborne, I'll be a guinea pig, and I'll make a donation to your research, too," Annie said. "All I know is that I want to feel better fast so I can start making it up to Nate for the first month of his life."

"Don't be too hard on yourself. I'm sure Nate is doing fine. I doubt that there will be any long term effects on him," Maizie reassured.

During their drive back to the Eastern Shore, Annie looked down again at the dark water as they crossed the Susquehanna

River. On the trip to Dr. Maizie's office in Baltimore, the gray, wintry water had looked inviting. Now Annie had been given hope again. She could hang on for the time being.

"You'll never guess who I ran into on my walk yesterday." Grace interrupted Annie's thoughts.

"Packard and his girlfriend," Annie answered.

"How'd you know?"

"Drew told me. Why didn't you tell me when it happened?"

"You don't like her much so I didn't bring it up."

"But you did just now."

"You don't seem on the verge of suicide now."

"Cute. Very cute."

"Do you think they'll get married?" Grace asked.

"God, I hope not. It's probably just a casual thing. Drew says that Packard refuses to stay at her place in the city. If she wants to see him, she has to come out here, and she does a couple of times a month."

"Yeah, sounds casual," Grace agreed.

"I don't think she's about to give up her high powered career to live in Promise, and Pack sure isn't going anywhere." *I'm not going anywhere either*, Annie thought to herself, and she found that comforting.

The women drove in silence for a while. The closer they got to Annie Crow Knoll, the calmer Annie felt.

"I can stay a few more days if you need me to," Grace said suddenly.

"I'd love you to stay, but aren't your parents expecting you for New Year's Eve?" Annie asked, remembering that Grace had a morning flight booked out of Philadelphia.

"Not really, but someone else is," Grace admitted with a slight smile.

"Who?"

"I've met someone special," Grace said.

"You have a lover and you haven't told me anything all

these days you've been here?" Annie gave Grace a hard smack on the arm.

"I wanted to tell you, but the time never seemed right."

"I'm sorry. This hasn't been much of a Christmas vacation for you."

"I wanted to come."

"But you could have been in sunny California with what's his name?"

"Pete!"

"Really?" Annie laughed. It felt so good to laugh.

"I told you that I'd marry a Pete."

"Marry? Are you engaged?"

"Not officially, but we're discussing the possibility."

"Pete!" Annie said out loud.

"But you didn't find an Oliver."

"No."

"Drew is okay. He loves you beyond reason. He just doesn't know what to do sometimes," Grace said.

"I know," Annie reassured Grace and herself. "You don't have to worry about us."

"Are you sure?" Grace asked. "I don't mind staying longer."

"Look, Pete may have an engagement ring wrapped up under the tree, you silly girl! Stop taking care of me and go live your life."

"I will."

"Promise?"

"Cross my heart."

"Call me the minute he asks."

"Don't worry; you'll be the first to know."

"Grace?" Annie paused a moment. "I don't know what I'd do without you."

"Me either."

Part Three

CHAPTER EIGHTEEN
SUMMER 1980

DURING AN EVENING SOFTBALL GAME, Grace's eight-year-old son Petey managed to hit the ball clear through one of the porch screens on Cockatiel Cottage.

"Lucky I wasn't sitting on the porch, or I might have been knocked out," Grace complained as she helped Annie work on the repair.

Bo had started the job that morning, but when he couldn't stop coughing, Annie had insisted he go home and rest.

"Quite a swing young Petey has," Annie told her.

"Nate was pitching," Grace said.

"Don't try to blame the pitcher," Annie teased.

"Petey may make the big league, yet."

Just as the women were inserting the repaired screen into place, Petey and his sister Beth Ann raced through the entrance to the Knoll.

Grace's ten-year-old daughter got there first. "Nate's been

in a fight!" she announced.

"And he's got blood all over his face," Petey added breathlessly.

"What?" Annie looked anxiously for her twelve-year-old son, who appeared at the entrance to Annie Crow Knoll. The front tire of Nate's bike wobbled with several broken spokes repeatedly hitting the drive as he pushed it past the stone pillars.

"Nate!" Annie called as she ran toward him. Beneath drying blood, his face was dark with anger, and it looked like he had a black eye coming. His clothes were covered with dirt.

"What happened?" she asked and tried to touch his face.

"Not now, Mom," he said, pulling away.

Annie knew he'd go straight to his father, he always did. She let him go. When he reached Sunrise Cottage, he threw his damaged bike down on the ground and ran inside.

"Is Nate going to be all right, Aunt Annie?" Beth Ann asked.

"Sure, sweetie," Annie said and put her hand on the little girl's shoulder.

"Beth Ann, do you know what happened?" Grace asked.

"He wouldn't tell us. Petey and I saw him coming up the street. We asked him, but he just shook his head. Then we ran to tell you."

"Anything I can do?" Grace asked Annie.

"Maybe later. I'm going to see what Drew is getting out of him."

Annie hurried over to her cottage. When she came inside, she heard Nate's voice in the kitchen.

"They were pushing a little black girl around behind that barn on Swamp Road near Coletown," her son explained.

Annie winced when she heard Nate had been riding his bike on the road where her parents were killed in the car accident. She stopped in the doorway between the kitchen and dining room and watched Drew put ice cubes into a dishtowel.

"Here, put this on your eye." Drew handed Nate the ice.

Annie wished her son would come to her once in a while. Thankfully Drew was home today. Otherwise Nate would have just seethed until his father arrived.

"She fell on the ground, and I didn't know what they were going to do next so I told them to leave her alone. Then they called me a …"

"Yeah, I know." Drew glanced over and met Annie's eyes. She knew that look.

It meant either "don't interfere" or "why do we continue to live in a place where this sort of thing still happens." Annie stayed put and silent.

Nate winced when he put the ice on his face.

"Keep it there," Drew instructed as he sat across from his son. "Go on."

"Well, I didn't care what they called me, but I couldn't let them hurt her. She was crying. I just wanted to help her, you know," Nate explained.

"You did the right thing, son."

"I told her to run, and she did. Froggy shoved me off my bike and jumped on the front wheel while Rusty Watson came after me. I was doing pretty good, I think. I mean I was really pissed so I was punching like crazy, but then Froggy started in on me, too."

Annie's mind raced. Two against one, and Bunky Watson's kid was older and much bigger than Nate. They were bullies who had tried before to give Nate—no doubt other children, too—trouble.

Annie didn't like to think what those two hoodlums were planning on doing to that girl.

"I think I blacked out for a second because they were gone when I got up off the ground."

"My God!" Drew got up and paced.

Now Annie crossed to where her son sat. She knelt down to check his eyes.

"I think Doc better take a look at you," she said.

Nate immediately turned to his father.

"Absolutely. Nate, you're going to the doctor with your mother."

"Where are you going?" Annie asked as Drew grabbed his car keys.

"To find Sheriff Bunky Watson."

"Doc said Nate will be okay. No concussion. His eye will be fine once the swelling goes down," Annie told Drew when he returned a couple of hours later.

"This time," Drew said with sarcasm.

"Well, what did the sheriff have to say for his son?"

"Bunky claims his kid and Froggy Ferguson were with him all day. They were nowhere near Colctown."

"His word against our son's."

"We all know how that goes in this wasteland."

"I wish you wouldn't do that," Annie said.

"Well, it is. This whole county is…"

Annie interrupted. "What about Coletown? Anyone there know who this little girl is?"

"I stopped at Bo's, and he said there wasn't a word about it," Drew explained as he grabbed a couple of cold beers from the refrigerator.

"Poor kid is probably too afraid to say anything to anyone."

"Can you blame her around here?" Drew started for the back door and then stopped. "You'd better get Bo to see Doc. That cough of his sounds like it's coming from his toes."

Annie would have told Drew that Bo refused to go to doctors, but he was out the back door and headed to Packard's before she could say a word.

Nate runs to Drew and Drew runs to Packard. Does anyone need me? She wondered.

Annie heard a knock on the front door.

"Annie?" Grace came in. "Nate said he's alright, but he looks awful."

"Doc said he checks out okay. He'll be hurting for a few days, though."

"He's sitting on my porch with Beth and Petey. They asked him to take them out in the dinghy. I told them to let him rest."

"If we could just keep everyone here on the Knoll where life is safe and happy."

"He was very brave to intervene the way he did," Grace told Annie.

"I know. He's a good kid. He doesn't deserve this. Those two boys are the same ones that gave him a hard time when he cooked an entire Mexican meal for his class report on Mexico. They aren't even in his grade, but they heard about it and tried to push him around. He stood his ground though, and it just turned into some name-calling."

"They're jealous they don't know how to turn on a stove."

"No one in Bunky's family has trouble opening the refrigerator though," Annie joked. She sighed. "Nate was so little that he had to stand on a chair to reach the counter when he first wanted to cook with me. It's the only time he preferred to be with me," she said with a catch in her voice. "Otherwise, it's always Drew."

"I'm relieved when the kids want Pete. Gives me a break."

"I know I sound ungrateful and jealous. It's selfish of me."

"Remember the time we discovered Nate, Beth Ann and Petey trying to bake a cake a few years back?" Grace laughed.

"God, there were eggs all over the floor."

"Beth Ann was crying."

"Petey was covered with flour."

"And Chef Nate was mixing up some concoction in a bowl that was almost too big for him to hold."

"Didn't I take pictures?"

"Yes, you did. You should dig them up. Give us a laugh."

"You always get me to laugh, Grace," Annie said with some relief.

"I hate to bring it up, but did Drew get anywhere with Bunky?"

"Nope. Nothing but another reason not to stay here."

"What?"

"Want some ice tea?" Annie asked.

"No. What are you saying?"

"Look, Grace. He stays away as much as possible on his research trips, and then complains when he is here. He's not happy. Hasn't been for a long time." Annie poured herself a glass of ice tea.

"But he decided to teach here in the first place. He had other offers."

"Maybe it wouldn't be so bad if he'd married someone willing to live in Chester Landing, but I don't think it even holds any excitement for him anymore. The college is so small, and they haven't treated him well despite all the prestige he's brought them with his text books and a nationally recognized curriculum, for God's sake," Annie said with resentment.

"I'm sure being passed over for department chair when Dr. Leonard retired this spring didn't help," Grace noted.

"Losing the position to an outsider was just the icing on the cake…and to a woman," Annie added.

"Drew wouldn't hold that against her," Grace defended.

"Well, he'd never admit to it."

"Not and live to tell the tale around here," Grace joked. "But he used to love the Knoll."

"That was when he was young and idealistic." Annie took a sip of her ice tea.

"Pete and I still love it, so do the kids," Grace said cheerfully.

"You're here two months out of the year. Pete's only here

for a few weeks of vacation. Full time is different for someone who needs more stimulation. He never would have stayed at Queen Anne College if he hadn't met me."

"So move," Grace advised.

Annie looked at Grace as if she was insane.

"I guess not," Grace remarked.

"He knew when he married me I'd never live anywhere else."

Annie thought about how happy she and Drew had been when he first came to the Knoll. He'd seemed totally content with living on the bay, with his teaching and with her. Now he looked like he was heading for a mid-life crisis and what would that mean for their marriage, she couldn't imagine.

Chapter Nineteen
Winter 1980-81

THE LIGHT FROM THE KEROSENE lantern flickered over Bo's dark face. Annie shifted in the hard chair next to his bed. He opened his eyes.

"What are you doing here?"

"I'm sorry. I didn't mean to wake you," Annie said.

"Why don't you go home and leave an old man to die in peace?"

The persistent cough Bo had fought most of the summer had turned into something Annie wasn't willing to accept. She didn't want to believe Bo was actually dying, but instinct told her that he was telling her the truth. The seemingly indestructible giant of a man was failing and quickly.

"Let me take you back to the Knoll, Bo. Let me take care of you at home."

"This here's my home."

"But there's no decent heat!" Annie said, losing her patience.

"Listen, missy. If you don't like it, go!"

Annie felt struck. She hadn't meant to be rude about Bo's little house, which consisted of a living room, kitchen, one bedroom, a bathroom, drafty windows, and at the moment, no electricity, due to an ice storm. The only light and heat were coming from the backup lantern and an old wood stove.

"All I meant was—"

"I know what you meant. White people always tryin' to save us from ourselves."

"I'm not white people! You're my family, Bo."

"You are white people, and we ain't family," he said, shifting uncomfortably in his bed.

She knew this was the pain and not Bo talking, but it hurt her to hear it.

"You're all I have, Bo."

"No, I am not. Leave it to you to make this about you."

"I can't stop myself from reacting to the fact that you're fixin' on dying."

"Well, it's my dyin', and I'm doin' it my way, in my place."

Annie grabbed his hand and forced her fingers between his.

"I'm sorry." Annie looked straight into his face. Her eyes were filled with tears, but she fought for control. "I won't cry," she added as one tear fell onto Bo's leathery hand in hers and turned the spot darker. "Don't make me leave, Bo."

"You can stay. But no more tellin' me what I ought to be doin'. Your father was the boss and then you were the boss on the Knoll. Now, we're here, and I'm boss."

"Okay," Annie said as she released Bo's hand.

"Let me sleep as long as I want to sleep. Don't be fussin' around me. God, you wear me out, girl."

"Yes, sir," Annie said quietly. "You want to sleep now?"

"I do," Bo said and rolled over onto his other side.

Annie started to pull the blanket up over his bulky shoulder. Bo turned his head and stared at her.

"Sorry," Annie said as she let go of the blanket and sat back down in the hard chair.

Annie watched Bo's breathing while he slept. His large chest and shoulders rose with air and then receded. It reminded Annie of the tide at the Knoll. Whenever there was an interruption in this ebb and flow, she feared the worst.

What am I ever going to do without you ? she asked herself. Slowly his breathing evened out, and Annie was lulled to sleep.

Annie awoke with a start. She thought that she had heard someone scream. The kerosene lamp had gone out, and she couldn't see a thing. She started stumbling around to find more fuel when she heard Bo move.

"There's another lamp filled up out on the kitchen table," he told her.

Annie walked gingerly into the other room, felt around for matches and lit the lamp.

When she carried the light back into his bedroom, Bo smiled at her.

"What put you in a better mood?"

"You looked like your mother a little just now."

Annie didn't say anything but set the lamp down on a nightstand. She wanted to ask the question but couldn't.

"Your mother and I never had relations," Bo said softly.

"I don't want to hear about that," she snapped.

"You've always wondered, haven't you?"

Annie nodded.

"Your mother asked me not to interfere."

"So let's leave it that way," Annie interrupted.

"When she and Luke died so young and sudden, I thought about bringing it up. I don't know what, but something kept me quiet all these years. But I can't die peaceful without clearing this up. You should know that your mother was always faithful to your father."

"I don't care anymore."

"Yes, you do. You were too hard on her, Annie. She was a good woman."

"Oh, yeah. Just perfect."

"No, she wasn't perfect. No one is, including you. You can't hurt her anymore. Now you're just hurting yourself with this hardness. Miss Liz and I never had relations," Bo stated again.

"But you would have if I hadn't seen you."

"You were a child. What did you know about such things?" Bo asked.

"Nothing, I suppose."

"Your mama loved your father. I loved your father, too."

"Then what were you doing with his wife?"

"I wasn't with her. It was nothin' more than a hug."

Annie looked away.

"You can believe me or not. That's up to you." Bo continued. "You know how hard marriage can be, even when people love each other like you and Drew or your parents. Sometimes, I got your mother's meaning when Luke didn't or couldn't. But Miss Liz was always a lady. She was beside herself when you ran away from her that day."

"I didn't talk to her for weeks."

"She knew that you were mad at her."

"No, I was mad at myself, really. Mama cried for days after that. I thought it was my fault. I'd ruined something special between you."

"Your mama was cryin' over you, not me," Bo said.

Always vigilant never to fall into a depression like she'd had when Nate was born, Annie fought to keep her tears from returning.

"She had it rough growing up. You realize that, don't you?" Bo asked.

Annie only nodded.

"I think that she did good for someone coming up like that. Her mother wasn't right in the head, and her grandmother was downright evil."

"You've always known about that?"

"We used to talk."

Annie fell silent.

"What is it?" Bo asked.

"Do you—do you know why I was an only child?"

"No, I don't. What I can tell you is that when I started working on the Knoll the spring after you were born, your mother was very quiet. She stayed in the cottage all the time. It wasn't unusual for a white woman to keep a distance, plus with a new baby and all. But when I did see her, she looked sad. She seemed that way for a long time," Bo explained, and then he started to cough.

Annie ran to the kitchen sink for some water.

For a while, the coughing wouldn't stop. It was hard and deep. Annie stood with the glass, helpless.

Eventually, Bo pulled himself up on one arm and was able to take a sip. When he lay back down, his breathing was hard.

"I wish this weren't happening to you," Annie said and with her usual frankness added, "I wish you weren't dying."

"Me, too. But the lungs aren't going to last. That's just the way of it. Probably those good smokes with your dad."

"If he hadn't been killed, do you think he'd be going this way?"

"I'm glad he's not. Better to die sudden."

"I guess you'll be seeing him soon—and Mama, too."

"How do you know I'm goin' to the same place they are?"

"Heaven isn't segregated," Annie said.

"Maybe I'm not goin' to heaven," Bo answered with a wink and then exhausted, he rolled over to sleep again.

Annie had more questions. She wondered why she hadn't the courage to bring them up all these years. Now, there might not be time to get the answers.

Various people came by to sit with Bo. None of them were surprised to see Annie. It seemed they knew about her, but she hadn't ever met them. Bo had always been private. Annie felt sad that she'd rarely asked about his life off the Knoll.

Two young men came by twice a day, once in the morning and once in the early evening. Annie assumed this was around their work schedule. They were identical twins, and they told Annie that their names were Jerome and Jamal. Neither said much, and Annie didn't force any conversation. They brought in firewood for the stove in case the electric heat quit again, and they moved Bo to change the sheets and wash him up, as much as he'd allow them.

The most frequent visitor was Viola Granger, an exquisitely handsome woman in her fifties. She carried herself with such pride and dignity that she might have been an African queen. Annie always felt herself stand up straighter whenever Viola came by to visit Bo.

During her first visit, Viola said she had met Annie before.

"Don't you remember? There was a wedding out at the Knoll," she explained.

With that prompting, Annie immediately recognized Viola as the dignified server to whom Lois Renker had given so much trouble at Maizie's wedding.

"I was just a girl, but I do remember you. You made quite an impression on me."

"Nearly got myself fired but that lovely bride came over."

"Maizie."

"Yes, she handled it."

Annie always made tea when Viola stopped in because she usually stayed longer than anyone else did, and Annie liked her company. Bo enjoyed her visits too, and when he would nod off, the women would wander into the kitchen and talk.

"My sister was married to Big Black Bo back when we were young," Viola told Annie.

"I never knew that he was married!"

"Yes, to my twin sister, Olivia."

"Twins? Are those two young men related to you?"

"They're my grandsons," Viola said with pride.

"They never told me why they come and help."

"Those boys love their great uncle."

"What happened to your sister?"

"Bo and Livi were very much in love," Viola said and paused. After a moment, she continued, "This place was a very happy home, but my sister died tryin' to birth their little girl."

"And the baby?" Annie asked.

"She didn't make it either. Maybe if they'd been able to be in the hospital, things could have been different, but the whites-only hospital wouldn't take her."

"I'm sorry," Annie said, feeling that the words sounded hollow. "He never married again?"

"No. Livi was his true love. Not to say that he didn't keep company."

Viola walked over to the doorway to check that Bo was still asleep.

"I sure hope he can't hear me," she continued in a whisper. "But Big Black Bo was very popular with the ladies."

"When my parents died, and I came to Coletown for the first time, I was surprised that folks here called him Big Black Bo."

"Why?"

"I figured white people had named him that."

Viola shook her head. "When he was a kid, he was bigger than anyone else. His friends started teasing him with that, and it stuck. I think he liked the alliteration."

"Do you know how he got that big scar on his arm?" Annie asked.

"He would never reveal the truth about that. Bo always got along with folks so it was unusual. All I know is his mama was fit to be tied when he came home cut like that."

When Bo's pain was becoming unbearable, an elderly woman arrived at the door. She was tiny, with a gnome-like appearance. At first, Annie wondered if the stress and exhaustion of caring for Bo had finally pushed her over the edge and that she might be imagining this little elf.

"Hello, Annie," she said carrying a large tapestry bag when she entered Bo's house. "I'm Granny. It's good of you to stay with Bo, but it ain't necessary."

"It's necessary for me," Annie said.

So far, everyone had tolerated Annie's presence in their community. She didn't want to be rude, but no one could make her leave now.

Bo called out in pain again.

"He won't let me take him to the hospital where they could do something for his pain," Annie explained.

"Of course not. He's in no need of a hospital. All he needs is right in here," she said, patting the side of her bag. "Now you go on home to your family and get some rest."

Drew had come by every day to check on Bo and bring in food. Bo wasn't eating anymore, but Annie appreciated the support and ate something to keep up her own strength. Exhausted, Annie wanted to sleep in her own bed, not in the hard chair next to Bo.

"I'll go home for a little while, but I'm coming back."

"If you come back, I'll have this brewed up and tell you how much to give him."

"I'll be back," Annie said firmly.

"You'll have to be careful with this," Granny said as she started pulling various leaves and herbs out of her carpetbag. "We don't want to kill him. Only the Lord decides when we die, but Big Black Bo needs a little help while he waits."

Annie returned the next morning to find Bo sleeping peacefully and Granny knitting.

"That's the calmest he's been for days," Annie said.

"Old Granny knows what she's doin'. Now, you give him a sip, only a sip, of this every time he stirs or moans. I'll be back with more the day after tomorrow, but I doubt he'll last that much longer. Soon he'll be with Livi and his little baby. I only wish I could have done something for them, but it was out of my hands," the old woman said and shook her head.

Annie walked with her to the door. "Thank you," she said.

"For what?" Granny asked.

"For helping Bo."

"That's what I do for all our folk."

"Are you Bo's Granny?" Annie asked.

"I'm everyone's Granny."

"But how did you know to come?" Annie asked.

The older woman shrugged her birdlike shoulders. "Granny just knows," she said with a smile and slipped out disappearing into the morning fog.

Drew looked up from his undergraduate Introduction to American Folklore lecture notes to see a woman slink into the back row of the packed hall. Dr. Bidwell's students were rarely late. It was something that he did not tolerate. He cleared his throat and continued teaching. As Drew moved away from the podium and across the stage in order to make his point more dramatically, he glanced up to the back row and recognized the latecomer to be the new chairperson of his department. He wondered what she was doing there but continued talking while his students furiously took notes.

At the end of the lecture as the students filed out, his new boss waited. When the aisle was clear, she moved cat-like toward Drew. She wore her blond hair short, but there was something very feminine and sensual in her form-fitted suit jacket and skirt.

"Hello, Dr. Palmer," Drew said briefly looking up over his glasses as he placed his notes and texts into a briefcase.

"Please, call me Susan," she told him.

Drew didn't respond.

"I was just admiring your notes for your Urban American Folklore book."

Drew was startled. With the help of his secretary, he was still transcribing all the interview tapes he'd made last summer in Harlem, Chicago and Detroit.

"Oh, I persuaded Mrs. Swain to let me take a peek," she told him as she sat in the front row and crossed her long, graceful legs just the right way.

Still licking his wounds from losing the chair to this woman, Drew didn't appreciate his physical reaction to her movements. He had hoped that with the change of pace the promotion would bring, he'd feel happier about staying here. However, the selection committee snubbed him. Now this woman seemed to want to play some game.

"Ask my permission next time," he told her.

"I didn't think you'd mind."

"I do."

Drew recognized when someone was interested in him. With students, over the years, he had learned to skillfully shift the misplaced sexual tension within appropriate boundaries. But this was no student. She was a grown woman, and whatever her motivation, Drew was attracted to her despite, or maybe because she had stolen the chairmanship right out from under him.

"My son has a junior high basketball playoff this afternoon. Please excuse me," Drew said as he stepped past where she was perched and walked out of the lecture hall.

Thankfully it was Drew's last class of the day. He'd planned on going back to his office to grade papers before Nate's game, but he headed straight for his car instead. He needed to find Annie. She'd be where she'd been every day and almost every night for the past weeks, in Coletown at Bo's side.

Drew practiced what he'd say to her in his head. This distance between them wasn't anything new or related in any way to her absence since Bo was dying. It had been developing for years. Drew respected Annie's need to grieve and be with Bo during his last hours. Drew, himself, was coping with his own loss of Bo, but there were plenty of others who could stay with the man tonight. Drew needed to speak with Annie about something. They needed to talk about their future, and she shouldn't miss Nate's game.

However, when Drew pulled up in front of Big Black Bo's place, people were standing outside and in the doorway. The tiny house was crowded with more people, too. Bo had died.

The morning of Bo's funeral, the sun shone brightly. Most of the night's light snowfall had melted leaving only tiny patches of white encircling bushes and shrubs.

Drew was in the shower when Annie heard a quiet rap at the front door. Then a louder one before she reached it.

Viola stood on the front porch of Sunrise Cottage in her Sunday best, which included a beautiful red velvet hat with black feathers.

"Come in," Annie told her.

Nate appeared from his bedroom dressed in his suit for Bo's funeral.

"Mrs. Granger, this is my son Nate. Nate, this is Mrs. Granger."

Nate shook Viola's hand. "Hello."

"I'm sorry your mama missed your game. How'd you do?" Viola asked.

"We lost."

"That's too bad."

"Doesn't matter."

"Big Black Bo told me how you helped that girl from Coletown last summer."

"Yes, ma'am." Nate turned to his mother. "I'm going to

see if Dad's ready. Okay?"

"Sure, honey," Annie told him.

Viola carried two hatboxes with her.

"Come sit down." Annie led Viola to the living room.

Viola put the hatboxes on the coffee table. "Here, you need to wear one of these," she said as she took the lid off each box.

"They're lovely," Annie said, trying to keep the confusion from her voice.

"They belong to Jerome's wife. They're the calmest hats in the house."

One was a pillbox of soft green, and the sensual rim on the other hat reminded Annie of something Ingrid Bergman might have worn in *Casablanca,* though this one had rhinestones encircling the base.

"Why do I need a hat?" Annie asked.

"Because no self-respecting female over the age of sixteen shows up at the Coletown Church of God without a hat, and I don't mean any old hat. I mean a hat!"

"I never wear anything but baseball caps," Annie told her.

"Haven't been inside a church for a long time either, I suspect," Viola said.

"Well, no," Annie admitted.

Viola made a clucking noise with her tongue and shook her head but then said, "Try one on."

Annie selected the Ingrid Bergman hat and admired herself in the nearby hall mirror. "It looks beautiful!" Annie said.

"And so do you. See what a hat does for a woman."

"But it's such a festive hat." Annie observed Viola's feathers and asked anyway, "Shouldn't I be wearing black?"

"We're celebrating Big Black Bo's life. He loved women, and he loved our hats so we need to strut our best this morning."

There was to be a luncheon held in the basement of the Coletown Church of God following the funeral.

After walking the short distance from the cemetery to the church, Drew turned to Annie and said, "Let's not stay. It's cold. I'd like to go home and get warm."

"We can warm up in the church," Annie replied. "I want to see Viola and return her hat."

"You can return it later. I want to get out of this suit and into something comfortable."

Since Annie was quite ready to shed her dress and heels, she acquiesced.

During the drive home, Drew didn't talk. Annie recognized what she thought was the familiar quiet before the storm. Nate was silent as well.

In an effort to fill the void, Annie said, "I'm going to create another scholarship at the college. It'll be in Bo's memory."

"That should be well received," Drew responded.

"I don't care if it is or it isn't. There are local kids, blacks, who could benefit from the opportunity. And it'd be nice if you could be more supportive about this."

"I mean to be. It's just that you never do anything that doesn't ruffle feathers."

Annie continually gave away large amounts of Delia Witherspoon's money. It was as if she were managing a grant and not her own inheritance. Right after things were settled with Walter and his beneficiaries, Annie had sold off all the businesses to the struggling employees at prices they could afford and at half the value. In doing so, she had transformed the lives of several families, who before had had little hope of financial solvency.

When Drew had refused any donation toward his American Folklore curriculum, Annie had made gifts to the college for several women's scholarships and funded the new Women's Studies Department.

She never bought expensive cars or clothes but set enough aside and invested wisely to make the Knoll solvent, Nate's future secure, and their old age comfortable. They had traveled a little when Drew could convince her that it was for Nate's education and development.

"Sorry if how I choose to disperse Delia's money makes things uncomfortable for you," Annie said finally.

"Don't worry. I can handle it. I always have," Drew answered.

After a long silence, Nate said from the backseat, "Dad, why don't you put on the radio?"

"Good idea."

When they reached the Knoll and Nate had bolted from the car, disappearing into Sunrise Cottage to change out of his suit, Drew turned to Annie and said, "I'm thinking about taking next summer off."

Drew hadn't taken a summer off in years. He either taught classes or did research and wrote.

"That'd be great! I could really use the help on the Knoll. I don't know how I'm going to cope without Bo."

"I'm not doing it to work here!" Drew said sharply.

"Oh," Annie replied quietly.

"Annie, I want us to go to the West Coast next summer," he said desperately.

"How's the Knoll supposed to be run?" she asked out of habit.

"It can run itself. What's to run?" Annie looked hurt, but Drew continued. "Hire someone."

"You think it's no big deal, but I love to do it myself. I enjoy the preparation. I anticipate the work."

Drew knew that she did. Annie worked just as hard as she had at nineteen. It didn't matter that she could afford to hire three people to do the work of one woman; she preferred to do it herself. Bo had been the only other person she trusted to work with her.

"I get great pleasure from seeing people enjoy themselves here," Annie went on.

"I like making it nice for them. Most of them are dear, dear friends. It's a community, a respite from their worldly cares, a safe haven for their children. Memories are made here. People make lifetime friendships. Some even fall in love here."

"As we did," Drew interrupted, "but we don't get our own time, our own respite to reconnect."

"It's been fifteen years since Mom and Dad died, and I held on to this place and made it my own Annie Crow Knoll. The Finches, the Slims and Mrs. Waters have been coming here for over thirty years. They're like family. They need me."

"Nate and I are your family, Annie!" Drew knew that he should say that he needed her, too, but his anger got the best of him. "When is it our turn? Nate's and mine?"

"This is a hell of a time to dump this on me, Drew." Annie got out of the car and walked into Sunrise Cottage.

Drew stayed in the car. Then he started it again, pulled out of the Knoll and drove to Chester Landing. When his stomach growled, he checked his watch. Two in the afternoon, and he hadn't eaten lunch. He passed the college and parked around the corner from Randi's, a casual pub on College Avenue. He wanted a cheeseburger and a beer in the worst way. He figured there was very little chance of running into students, who frequented the Blue Crab closer to campus.

Randi's was pretty quiet since the lunch rush was over, but a group of faculty members was breaking up from a luncheon meeting when he entered. In order to avoid them, Drew went to a secluded booth in the back. He had canceled all of today's classes because of Bo's funeral, and it was no one's business why he was here drinking a beer instead of lecturing in Adams Hall.

Suddenly he realized someone was slipping into the other side of his booth.

Dr. Susan Palmer set a cold, brimming beer in front of him. Then she unwrapped her straw, dropped it into her Diet Pepsi and placed her lips around it to suck the soda up into her mouth. Drew forgot his beer and watched her every move. She looked up at him and smiled.

"I want us to be friends, Drew."

"You're my boss, Dr. Palmer."

"Susan. Please call me Susan. I know you applied for my job and were passed over."

"I'm sure you are fully qualified."

"Look, I'd like to make it up to you," she said and pulled a pen out of her shoulder bag and wrote her phone number on a cocktail napkin. Then she stood and leaned over the table.

"It'd just be sex, Drew. Great sex. That's all. No strings," she whispered into his ear.

He didn't look up as she stepped out of the booth and walked toward the door.

Drew did, however, slip the napkin into his pocket. Then he drained the beer mug and ordered another.

Too unsteady to drive safely, Drew walked the four blocks over to his office on campus. No one noticed him, and he was able to sneak in the door, leave the lights off and collapse on the broken down sofa across from his desk where he fell asleep. He awoke with a start, unsure where he was or what time it had gotten to be. As he began to focus, recalling how he'd found his way to the closest and safest place to crash after drinking too much at Randi's, he noticed the time. Drew was late for his weekly chess game with Packard.

He pulled on his coat and trudged back down College Avenue to retrieve his car. The air had grown colder since the sun had set some time ago. He hunched his shoulders against the wind and jammed his hands into his coat pockets. Where was the cocktail napkin? He checked his pants pocket. It was there.

A strong gust blew dirt into Drew's eyes when he rounded the corner toward his car. Turning his back on the wind, he took off his glasses and dabbed at his eyes with the napkin. There was a trash receptacle steps away, but he shoved the napkin back into his coat pocket.

Packard was searching for matches to start a fire in the wood stove when Drew came through the door of the Schoolhouse Studio.

"I thought you might stay with Annie this evening," he said as he finally located a matchbox under a pile of clean brushes. It contained one match.

"Damn, it's cold in here," Drew grumbled.

"I just got back," he explained.

"Back?"

"The installation of my show up in Philadelphia," Pack said as he lit the fire.

"Oh, God, I forgot. Bo's funeral today. I'm kind of crazy." Drew ran his hand through his hair.

"I'm sorry I couldn't make it because I had to be at the gallery. Bo was a good man."

"Yes." Drew took a seat by the fire.

"How's Annie taking it?" Packard asked.

"Okay, I guess. You know Annie." Then changing the subject, Drew asked, "How did the installation go?"

"The usual bull, but it looks okay. Beer?" Pack asked as he opened the mini-fridge and grabbed a bottle for himself.

Drew shook his head. The cold schoolhouse was beginning to warm, but Drew was too chilled to take off his coat.

"Want anything else?" Packard asked.

"Coffee."

Packard set his beer down and lumbered over to the electric coffee maker.

"When's the opening?" Drew asked.

"Tomorrow night."

"Why the hell didn't you stay up there?"

"Didn't want to miss our chess game. I've been plotting my next move for days," Pack joked and nodded toward the chessboard left exactly as it was from last week.

"That's crazy. You'll have to drive all the way back to Philadelphia tomorrow."

Packard collapsed his big frame into the large easy chair across from Drew and stretched his long legs out onto a hassock.

"This way I can stop by the cemetery and pay my respects to Bo tomorrow morning."

"You won't stay in the city tomorrow night either, will you," Drew remarked.

"I like to sleep in my own bed." Pack smiled and sipped his beer.

Hot water began dripping into the glass coffee pot.

"What is it with you and my wife? Never wanting to go anywhere else, always staying here."

Packard shrugged.

"How can you prefer to sit here in Promise and read about the world from one of your hundreds of books rather than taste it first hand?"

"What's wrong, Drew?" he asked. "You look more tossed about than usual."

"I've been drinking."

"Oh?"

"Is that coffee ready yet? I could use it," Drew said and rose to find a mug.

"There's a clean one by the coffee machine."

Drew located the mug and blew dust out of it.

"Well, relatively clean," Pack said and drank more of his beer.

The coffee smelled rich and the hot liquid began to warm Drew.

"I'm wondering why you aren't home with Annie tonight?" Packard asked, knowing that's where he'd be if his wife just buried someone she loved.

"It's chess night. Are we going to play or not?" Drew said

and crossed over to the board to take his seat.

"All right." Pack decided to let the subject drop. "You want a cigar?" he asked, hauling himself out of his comfortable chair.

"Sure, why not."

Packard's shadow loomed over the board when he walked in front of the wood stove with two cigars in his hand. "Do you have any matches? I'm out."

Drew stood, searching his pockets and pulled out the cocktail napkin. He looked at the number a moment and then tossed it into the fire.

"What was that?" Packard asked.

"One of the reasons I was drinking," Drew said sarcastically.

"One?"

"Yeah. It was a woman's number."

Packard paused and then asked, "What's the other reason?"

"Annie," Drew answered.

Pack's hand came down hard on the table, rattling the chess pieces. Drew's queen toppled over.

The men's eyes met briefly before Drew looked down at the board. He gently set his queen upright. "Aren't we playing?" he asked quietly.

Packard moved back to the wood stove, adding another log to the fire. The flames lit up his face.

"Not tonight, Drew. You go home now," he said in a steady, unemotional voice.

Drew did not move. "Look, I'm getting nowhere at Queen Anne College. It's time I moved on."

"What the hell does that have to do with another woman?"

"Nothing but a passing thought. That's why it's ash now. I wouldn't do that to Annie."

Packard felt some of the tension across his shoulders relax.

"I have a job lined up for next year at Berkeley, and my mentor there from undergraduate days said with my reputation and his recommendation, there will be no question about me taking his chairmanship when he retires in a couple of years."

"This is about a title?"

"You know it's more than that."

"But you're going to put Annie in the position of choosing between you and the Knoll."

"There's no contest. She'll never leave."

"So you're ending your marriage?"

"I've sacrificed close to fifteen years living here for her. I can't do it anymore."

"Sacrificed?" Packard's voice was raised. "Do you still love her?"

Drew's eyes softened. "I'll always love Annie, but she takes too much for granted."

Packard knitted his eyebrows.

"I know that doesn't make sense. It's not exactly what I mean, but it's always all about her. The Knoll takes up all her focus and energy. I can't even get her to take a trip to Europe with Nate and me. I know I sound like a selfish ass, but I'm tired of second best. Even when Bo was sick, she had to be there practically every minute. She missed Nate's playoff game, for God's sake! I cared for Bo. I understand that he was sort of a surrogate father figure, but he had people to sit with him. It became all about her again, didn't it?"

Packard shifted his position by the woodstove but said nothing.

"And that episode with Bunky Watson's kid and that other Neanderthal getting away with beating up Nate last summer. I want my son out of this environment."

"You're taking Nate with you?"

"If he wants to go, yes. I'll put him in a good private school."

"Drew, boys get into fights. Aren't you overreacting a little?"

"He can come back here to no man's land every summer and regress all he wants."

"My God." Packard shook his head.

Drew took a swig of his coffee that was now getting cold.

"You're going to abandon Annie and make her son choose between his mother and you," Packard said out loud as if he was trying to make it clearer to Drew.

"She can come with us, but she won't."

"But she loves you both."

"Not enough."

"What does that mean?"

Drew stood up. "I'll be completely honest, my friend. Annie will hardly notice we're gone because she has the Knoll, and she has you."

Packard couldn't speak.

Drew gazed up to the two giant mobiles of the planets circling a crow and crows circling the earth and then looked back at Packard.

"I know you've been in love with her for years," he said. "Take good care of her."

"But she loves you. Not me, you fool," Packard said.

"It's not enough anymore, Pack." Drew walked out the door and never looked back.

CHAPTER TWENTY
FALL 1981

AROUND MIDMORNING ON THE SATURDAY before Thanksgiving, Annie was in bed and dreaming that her father was building the Crow's Nest. It was a fitful sleep with the sound of hammering pounding as her dream continued. She never rose for lunch or dinner but slept on through the night.

After Drew and Nate had left, Annie had kept up a brave front until the end of the season. Once the cottagers had departed and Grace, with her family, had reluctantly flown home, Annie had nothing to distract her from the pain. Every day she faced an empty cottage and an empty life.

Two days ago had been Nate's fourteenth birthday. Annie had mailed his presents to California and called on the day, but for the first time in her son's life, she wasn't with him to bake his cake and celebrate his birth. After saying goodbye to him on the phone, she went to bed and cried herself to sleep.

Finally Annie woke. The temperatures had dropped during

the night and just before dawn, a light frost covered the Knoll. There was no possibility of getting back to sleep, so she put a jacket on over her pajamas and walked outside. The cold air made Annie more aware of everything around her. All the cottage porches wore their winter sheets of white plywood. She realized that Packard must have done all this for her. Upon later inspection, she'd find that he'd also turned off the water and disconnected the gas to each cottage, and poured antifreeze into every sink, toilet and shower drain. A twinge of guilt hit her stomach, but she quickly let that go numb. She didn't want to feel anything.

Annie wandered down and sat on the end of the dock, which was covered with a thin layer of ice. She didn't feel the cold or the damp through her pajama bottoms. A smoky mist hung along the edge of Cattail where the warm marsh water hit the cold air. The sun rose, turning the water a silver-pink. Ribbons of satiny rose floated toward Annie as the current rippled by. If she slipped off the dock, she'd float forever into that deep, endless abyss. The ancient, yet familiar, drums seducing her into oblivion became crystal clear when she looked into the water that morning.

"No!" Annie said out loud to herself. The dock suddenly felt cold against her skin, and her pajamas were wet from sitting on the frosty wood. After weeks of slipping into a place she had resisted since Nate was a baby, Annie realized there in the dawn that she had to go on in whatever fashion she could manage. It might not be anything resembling normal, but she would do it. She had to do it.

Annie went inside, took a hot shower, dressed in clean sweatpants and a T-shirt and forced down some cereal and half a cup of coffee. She had finished the milk up and realized she needed to go to the food store. The project seemed overwhelming so she phoned Turner's Market and asked to get some groceries delivered. Then she called the florist and ordered a fruit basket to be delivered to Packard.

Annie felt good about accomplishing something and decided to gather up the laundry that was strewn around her bedroom. She opened the closet; seeing all of Drew's clothes gone still took her breath away. She found herself stumbling into Nate's room, which was only partially empty. He would be back in the summers and at Christmas.

J.J. Finch had talked to her about fighting Drew for custody, but she didn't want Nate to suffer from that battle. Grace had strongly advised Annie to move out to California with Drew and Nate, to live there for a while and see if she could adjust. However, Annie thought it would only give Nate false hope for his parents' marriage. Annie knew the marriage was over. This had little to do with her resistance to leave the Knoll. Drew could say it was her fault, but how could her unwillingness to leave be any more to blame that his unwillingness to stay?

Annie opened Nate's closet and took in a deep breath. The smell of her child caused her to slump to the floor and sob. Her body took over as she allowed the pain to rise out of her into a howl. Letting herself go was both frightening and freeing. It didn't stop. Annie began to cough and then gag. She raced to the toilet and threw up the cereal and coffee. Finally purged, she sank completely onto the floor and slept again.

She woke up when one of the high school boys working down at Turner's knocked on the front door with her food delivery. He was quick about leaving, and she was grateful not to have to talk to anyone for very long. In the bottom of one of the bags was a box of chocolates that she hadn't ordered. She opened it and ate two; one with caramel in the middle and the other with a cherry center. They tasted good. After eating a third one, Annie went back into the bedroom to sleep again.

There were no lights on in Sunrise Cottage when Packard pulled into the circle drive. After carrying the large carton it took to transport a complete Thanksgiving Day dinner up to her porch, Pack tapped lightly on the front door. There was no sign of life anywhere. Then he realized that he should have telephoned. He forced himself to knock harder. Still nothing. Even his hammering the plywood over the porch screens hadn't roused her several days ago. He sat for twenty minutes or so on the front porch hoping she'd make a sound in there. He couldn't bring himself to knock again, so he simply left the feast on the porch. It was plenty cold to keep the food from spoiling. She'd find it in the morning.

A light snow began to fall as Packard drove out through the gates of the Knoll and down the road to his house.

What am I going to eat? he asked himself now that he had left the entire turkey, all the potatoes and every single string bean on Annie's porch. He'd baked six apples and only had room to pack four. He'd have to warm up the two remaining apples covered in brown sugar and raisins and call it Thanksgiving dinner.

He laughed out loud. This hadn't been good planning on his part.

Chapter Twenty-One
Winter 1981-82

SINCE IT WAS NATE'S FIRST visit home, Annie forced herself to decorate a Christmas tree. She couldn't bring herself to shop, so she ordered his gifts from catalogues. She would put on her best face. She desperately needed to wrap her arms around her son but didn't want to scare him to death. Annie tried to be optimistic about his stay because although his notes and brief phone calls had been stiff, they were pleasant. She hoped he didn't resent her for her choice to stay on the Knoll and end the marriage.

When the airport shuttle service dropped Nate off in the circle drive, Annie waited just a moment to watch him get out of the van. He must have grown two inches since last summer. Then she bolted out the front door.

"Nate!" she called, running to him. She grabbed him into a hug but his arms remained limp at his sides. Immediately fear and hesitation rose in her, and she stepped back, searching her fourteen-year-old son's face. He scowled.

The van pulled away after Annie paid the driver.

"Merry Christmas, Nate," she said softly.

"Yeah, great. Let's get this over with," he mumbled, picked up his suitcase and walked into the cottage without her.

Tears immediately welled up in Annie's eyes. *No!* she told herself and fought them off. *I can deal with this.* She marched right into the cottage after him.

"You obviously don't want to be here. Would you like to call your father and arrange a flight home tomorrow?"

It looked like that threw him for a moment. He had surely expected her to try to please him or beg for his forgiveness. However, he regained his momentum quickly.

"That would be fine with me except that Dad insisted that I come, and I don't want to piss him off."

Annie was tempted to criticize his language but bit her tongue.

"Why did he insist you come if you didn't want to?" she asked.

"He had other plans and needed me out of the way."

Annie's mind was in a whirl. "Nate, I'm sure your dad wanted to spend Christmas with you. He just knew how much I missed you. You must have misunderstood his intention."

"I didn't misunderstand shit. He's got a girlfriend, and she's got two kids. He's spending Christmas with his new family," Nate spit out.

"That was quick," Annie said and collapsed into a nearby chair.

As angry tears began to roll down Nate's face, he said, "If you'd just come to California with us, none of this would have happened, and I'd still have a family."

Annie couldn't catch her breath. Then she heard a door slam. From Nate's bedroom she heard things being smashed against the walls.

Somehow she propelled herself to his room. "Nate, honey?" She knocked. It sounded like he threw his suitcase against the door. She tried the knob, but he had locked it.

"Nate, please open up . Your father loves you. He'll never replace you."

She heard a thud; maybe he'd pushed his desk chair over.

"You're irreplaceable," Annie said louder. "I, on the other hand, am very replaceable," she whispered. There was one more thump, perhaps a shoe against the wall.

Annie could hear him crying. "Nate, please let me in?"

Silence. Well, maybe he had worn himself out.

"I love you, Nate."

The crisis over for the moment, Annie began to shiver. Again she couldn't catch her breath, which caused strange sounds to come out of her mouth.

"Mom?"

"Ye ... yes."

"Are you okay?"

"I... I j... just have to lie down."

Annie stumbled to her bed. After several minutes, the panic subsided, and she began to breathe normally. She thought about trying to make another effort with Nate, but exhaustion took over and she fell asleep.

As winter wore on, Annie couldn't put enough food into her mouth. She'd open a bag of potato chips, promising herself just one handful, and by the time that pleasant numbness took over, the bag was empty. Mouthful after mouthful, trying to stuff up the hole inside her. A banana covered with chunky peanut butter languished on her tongue. All she needed now was some chocolate. Where had she stashed the leftover Hershey Kisses she kept on hand for the kids who stayed on the Knoll during the summer? Annie gained weight, and her stomach strained against her waistband. She started wearing baggy shirts to cover the pants she left unfastened over her expanding belly. Annie enjoyed the feeling, imagining herself pregnant, once again carrying Nate inside her.

Climbing up into the Crow's Nest became a daily habit. Annie loaded chocolates and a thermos of hot tea into the basket. With her binoculars slung over her shoulder and a blanket draped over one arm, she climbed up into the place that felt the safest and the least lonely. For hours, Annie watched the world from her perch. She noted the birds that were staying through the winter and listed the ships which followed the Coast Guard ice breaker keeping the shipping lanes open to the C & D Canal. And she watched Packard Marlboro.

Without leaves on the trees separating the Knoll from the Marlboro property, Annie had a clear view of Packard's dock, his house and even the Schoolhouse Studio. From the Crow's Nest and from her cottage windows, she found herself keeping track of his comings and goings. Annie smelled the wood fire smoke floating out of the Schoolhouse Studio chimney when Packard was painting. At night, she felt better seeing the lamps come on in his house across the field that separated them. When the ice thawed, she liked hearing *Sophie's* motor and seeing her running lights pull back in after dark. Annie considered going over for a visit, but she didn't want to talk. It was enough knowing that he was over there.

Chapter Twenty-Two
Spring 1982

THERE WERE TIMES WHEN THE tide changed directions so quickly and with such force that it seemed as if someone had flipped a switch. The water surged back from the bay in a great rush up into the river and under the Knoll dock. Today was one of those days, and from up in the Crow's Nest, Annie felt it. A large kettle of gulls that had circled above the bay all morning suddenly broke up and started calling and flying up river. The wind settled down, and Annie trained her binoculars on the trees bordering the Marlboro property to look for spring warblers. The trees were budding now, but she could still see most of Packard's field from her perch in the Crow's Nest. Annie moved her binoculars and discovered Packard walking toward the Knoll. She didn't know what to do. Still in her pajamas and robe, she couldn't make it down in time to change.

When she saw Pack hesitate in the field and look as if he might change his mind, Annie felt both relief and disappointment. She needed company, but it had been so long that she wasn't sure how to be sociable.

As Packard stood frozen midway across, Annie considered staying in the Crow's Nest until he knocked on her cottage door, waited for her to answer and finally gave up. But he would see her car parked in the circle out front. He might become alarmed and start calling and searching for her. What could she say if he discovered her hiding in the tree house wearing pajamas and a robe in the middle of the day? How would she explain not answering him?

But Packard turned around to head back to his house, and the wind picked up again. Annie went down the ladder to go in and dress. Maybe he'd be back later? He could have forgotten something. One way or the other, he had certainly raised her curiosity.

It took another full week before Packard got his courage up once again to cross the field. This time, he carried fresh daffodils picked from his front yard. When Pack rounded Annie's cottage and discovered hundreds of blooming daffodils, he nearly dropped his bunch. But he didn't want to show up empty handed, so he gripped them tightly and knocked on her front door.

Should have bought candy, he thought to himself.

Annie was on the waterside of the cottage raking her garden beds and didn't see him come over or hear him knocking. When Pack went around Annie's porch in search of her, he came up on her so suddenly she jumped.

Packard wore a new denim shirt and a pair of jeans. His face was clean-shaven, and he'd put some water on his unmanageable locks of salt and pepper hair. They had stayed in place for half the walk over, but by the time the wind had done its job, he was back to his usual wild look. The nervousness in his dark eyes added to the affect. Not exactly what he'd had in mind, scaring her to death.

"Oh, Packard," Annie let out as she tried to catch her breath.

"I scared you. I'm sorry." Pack shoved the flowers out in front of him. He hoped the gesture would relieve her, but it seemed to startle her more, and she moved back a step.

"These are lovely. Thank you," Annie said as she took the flowers from him.

"I forgot that you had so many of your own." Packard gestured, wishing he still had the flowers to hold. Then he shoved both hands into his pockets.

"But I hate to cut them in order to bring them into the house. Now I won't have to," Annie said.

"I have more if you want them for inside," he offered.

"Thank you. These will be plenty. Do you want to come in while I get these into a vase?" Annie asked.

"No, thank you." Packard wasn't sure what to say next. "I came over to see how you were doing."

"I'm fine. Glad winter is over. It'll feel good to start preparing for the season," Annie paused. "Packard, I never thanked you properly for all you did last fall."

"It was nothing."

"No, it was incredible."

"And you did thank me. I enjoyed the fruit basket very much," he told her.

"I should have come over myself," Annie said.

"No 'shoulds', Annie. You have always done your best."

"I just couldn't."

"I understood."

"Thank you."

Annie and Packard were silent for a moment.

"Do you have plans for this Easter Sunday?" Packard asked suddenly.

"Well, no, actually I don't," Annie told him.

"Would you like to come to dinner at my house?" Pack finally got it out. "If Nate is coming home, he is welcome, too," he added, wishing that he hadn't.

"No, spending Christmas with his dysfunctional mother was more than enough for him. He's staying in California with Drew during his Easter break."

"I don't think you're dysfunctional. You're brave and wonderful." The words spilled out before he could stop them. "However you were at Christmas was to be expected."

"Oh, God," she suddenly let out.

Packard didn't think that he had done anything else to startle her.

"The Thanksgiving dinner you left on my porch."

"You explained in your thank you note that you had been asleep."

"Yes, I know, but I felt so badly that I didn't wake up when you knocked. The turkey was delicious. Everything was."

"I'll prepare something else."

"Something else?"

"If you're free?" Pack finally asked.

"Free?" Annie seemed to be having trouble following Packard's train of thought.

"For Easter dinner?"

"Oh, yes, I'd love to come," Annie answered.

"Great!" Packard said and started to rush off as if the meal had to be started right this minute. Then he turned back for a moment standing by the fence. "Is seven o'clock all right?"

"Fine," Annie smiled.

"It's not too late?" Pack asked.

"No, it's fine."

"I mean, families usually eat Easter dinner earlier."

"Seven is perfect," Annie reassured him.

"Then it's a date." Pack hollered as he cleared the fence and started across the field.

Was it a date? Did she have a date with Packard Marlboro for Easter dinner?

No. I'm imagining things, Annie told herself, while rooting through her closet and chest of drawers. Annie considered canceling with Packard. She literally had nothing to wear. "I've never had trouble with my weight in my life," she had complained to Grace during their last phone call.

"Welcome to the real world," Grace had answered and followed with a sarcastic laugh.

Annie's bedroom was now strewn with clothes that didn't fit properly. She had worn nothing but baggy sweat pants and old shirts all winter and couldn't very well show up in those for Easter dinner.

Since a checkup with Doc the previous month, Annie had made an effort to exercise and eat regular meals again. She had lost a few pounds, but that was no significant help at the moment.

Pulling off the last pair of pants she owned, Annie thought she'd tell Packard that she was sick, but she wanted to go. It was a step. A step toward what, she wasn't sure. And at the same time, it was a step away from Drew, which seemed unimaginable even though he had walked away from her.

Ironically, seeing Packard also felt like being close to Drew again. They had him in common. The connection was palpable. Whatever it was, Annie felt ready for something, at least a holiday meal with another human being.

Just then, Gus, the UPS man, tooted the horn of his brown truck as he came to a screeching halt in the circle drive.

"Looks like a package from your son in California, Mrs. Bidwell," he said as Annie signed for the package.

She couldn't get inside fast enough to open it. Fortunately, as always, Gus was in his usual hurry, and he didn't hold her up.

Inside the box, Annie discovered a note, which read,

Dear Mom,

I thought about buying you an Easter bonnet, but you aren't much for hats.

Since you liked the birthday present I sent you in January, I went back to the same store for this.

Hope you like it!

Happy Easter!
Nate

Annie tore open the tissue, which covered the blues and purples of an exquisite silk, wrap-around skirt. The colors flowed and intertwined like delphiniums in a wild French garden. Best yet, it fit and would still fit a size down when she lost the weight. Her son's gift had solved her clothing crisis, at least for this day. She had in her closet a lovely, loose, pale purple blouse that worked, and the scarf that Nate had sent for her birthday would go nicely with the neckline. The outfit might be a bit summery for April, but it was her only option. She hoped she wouldn't have to crush it all under a coat in order to stay warm during her walk across the field.

Packard lit candles on the buffet beneath the painting of eleven-year-old Annie holding her dead crow. He stepped back around the dining room table and looked up at the child's pained eyes.

He wondered how Annie would react. She had never seen this painting. She didn't know of its existence, unless Drew had told her. That seemed unlikely, but even if he had, actually seeing herself holding her dead pet could make Annie uncomfortable during dinner. Although this worried Pack, he laughed out loud, thinking that a picture of dead crow would put anyone off their meal. Yet it had hung on the dining room wall in the direction of the Knoll for twenty-five years. There was no one to complain because Packard never had dinner guests. Even back when he was seeing Sheila Van Bruen, she had only admired the painting.

Where to put it? Packard thought. First he considered taking it upstairs to a bedroom where Annie wouldn't see it. However, was there any possibility that she'd go up there and find the painting hidden away? She would think that he didn't like it. She'd ask why it wasn't hanging down stairs where people could enjoy it. What people? Packard laughed again. Having someone, other than Drew, in his house was certainly an event. The fact that it wasn't just anyone, but "Annie Crow," wasn't lost on Packard.

Finally he decided to leave the damn thing where it was. That decision made, he did, however, blow out the candles. It looked too much like a shrine.

Annie realized, as she paused in front of the Schoolhouse Studio, that she hadn't gone any further onto Packard's property since she carried Oliver's remains in a shoebox.

Packard had never invited her, and she had never asked. It was his domain. The studio had been her boundary. This evening, she crossed over.

The Marlboro house was older than any of the cottages on the Knoll. Its perfect positioning on the peninsula was no accident. When Packard's great-grandfather had built the clapboard home, he knew how to angle it to take in the full effect of the Chesapeake. The expansive view, including the evening lights of Havre de Grace at the mouth of the Susquehanna River to the north and the dramatic curve of the bay to the southwest around Howell Point, took Annie's breath away.

"It's really something, isn't it?" Packard said to her as he opened the front door.

"I'd forgotten the view from here," Annie said, startled out of her amazement.

"Still, you've a darn good view from Annie Crow Knoll."

"I do, but this is unbelievable."

"You're welcome to come over and take it in anytime."

"Thank you. Now I know why Drew spent so many summer nights over here playing chess on the porch."

"Actually, I think it was because he relished all the times he beat me."

Annie smiled. She didn't often see Pack's sense of humor. There was a lot she didn't know about her reclusive neighbor.

"Come in." He held the door for her.

As Annie stepped toward the doorway, she saw the faded hummingbird still on the clapboard. It was obvious that over the years, Packard had painted the house a number of times, but he had brushed carefully around the ruby throat, never covering the tiny bird with fresh house paint.

"It's still here," Annie remarked.

"You remember."

"I haven't been on this porch in a long time."

"Well, that needs to change."

While many people who lived along the bay saved colored sea glass in a jar or two, Annie was totally surprised when she saw that every available surface in the living room was filled with various sized, clear glass bottles and jars. Each was filled with hundreds of pieces of broken glass rubbed smooth from the sand and water. Some jars were filled with mixed colors of green, amber, and clear white. Other bottles held only one color each. Annie did notice that this avid collector had only two jars of the prized color, blue.

"You don't have much blue."

"It's harder to find," he said.

"It seems that there was more of it when I was little. I have over four jars filled with it."

"You were lucky." He smiled.

"Apparently."

The walls were flanked with shelves packed with books. In any wall space not covered with bookcases, Packard's paintings were hanging.

Over the mantle, above another dozen jars and bottles filled with sea glass, hung a portrait of his parents. Annie stood looking at it for some time. Packard watched her take in the image.

"There's a sadness to them," Annie said. "A sad love."

"Yes. Thank you," he said, for she had noticed the truth in the portrait he had painted of his parents several years after their deaths.

"Would you like some wine?" he asked.

"Yes, that would be nice," Annie said as she walked to the bookcases lining the wall opposite of the fireplace.

Pack poured white wine from his grandmother's cut glass decanter into crystal glasses he'd set on a tray on the coffee table. He carried the two glasses over to Annie and held one out to her.

"So many books," she said taking the glass. "*History of World Art*, *Religions of the World*."

"I didn't feel able to travel, but a painter needs to see the world—" He interrupted himself. "No, experience the world. I've done that the only way I could."

"You never really needed to go anywhere else?"

"I know that I've limited myself, but all I need is here on the bay," Packard answered.

"Me, too."

"Yes, I know."

Annie moved on to the next set of book titles.

"*Yoga and Meditation*?" Annie said with a surprised tone.

"You are full of surprises."

"You have no idea," he answered and finished the wine in his glass.

Annie sipped her wine and then looked directly at Packard. The salt and pepper in his hair only hinted that he was in his early fifties. He appeared younger. Annie realized that he looked devastatingly handsome tonight. She didn't know when it had actually happened, but her life-long feelings for Packard Marlboro shifted. Or perhaps she had always been attracted to him and had been in denial for years. Either way, it was an incredible relief to feel alive again, to attract a man and feel attracted to him.

A timer went off in the kitchen.

"Will you excuse me?" he said.

Packard disappeared through the adjoining dining room and into the kitchen to see to dinner, and Annie sat down by the fire. The flames took the chill off the evening air. She drank more of her wine. It was delicious. Why had she assumed he only drank beer and whiskey? He was a fisherman. Well, he was an artist, too. She knew that, but still everything about him seemed new. He was a self-educated man. A Renaissance man. Then Drew came to her mind. Her husband had known the real Packard Marlboro. Suddenly she felt fidgety and rose to go see if he wanted help or company in the kitchen. Carrying her wineglass with her, Annie walked into the dining room.

Packard came out of the kitchen to find Annie frozen in front of her portrait. As she took in the image of herself as a child holding the dead body of her beloved pet crow, the wineglass shook gently in her hand. Pack studied her face. He couldn't tell what she was thinking. She looked about to cry, but then, she looked like she could laugh, too. Between her silence and not knowing how this was affecting her, Pack felt every alarm button in his body poised to go off. But he took a deep breath and waited.

Finally she asked, "When did you paint this?"

"I finished it after we—" He didn't know what words to say.

"—buried him at sea?" Annie said, bursting into a smile with tears immediately following.

Oh, God, Packard thought to himself.

Annie set down her glass and stepped toward him.

"It's perfect," she said and put her arms around his waist just as she had when she was eleven years old and Oliver's burning remains had floated out into the bay.

Pack instinctively put his arms around her shoulders. Her head rested on his chest as the crying eased.

Packard lightly touched her soft curls with one hand. After a moment, she looked up at him. He wanted to kiss her but didn't.

She didn't apologize for crying but stopped it with practiced discipline.

"Dinner smells delicious," she said as she untangled her arms from around him.

"It's ready, if you're hungry."

They feasted on salmon that tasted like nothing Annie had eaten before.

"What is on the fish?" she asked.

"It's rubbed with a chili and sage paste."

"And what do I taste in the tomato chutney?"

"A little jalapeno pepper and mango."

"I haven't eaten this well since—" Annie broke off.

"I don't often cook like this for myself," Pack rescued her. "But during the long winter months when I need a break from painting and I can't go fishing, I watch cooking shows on PBS."

"You're kidding, aren't you?"

"No. I love to watch other people cook."

"I loved to watch Nate cook, but since they left—" Annie trailed off again.

"I should have checked on you. Made sure you were eating," Packard said.

"Oh, I ate. Junk food. I've gained fifteen pounds."

"It suits you."

"No, it's got to go. Now that I'm beginning to feel better, I can control myself and get some exercise again."

"You're feeling better?" Pack asked.

"Yes. Doc thought I should try an anti-depressant, but I resisted. I mean, there was a reason I was down, for God's sake. It's not something that a pill can fix."

Packard didn't interrupt her.

"But I do have some history of depression, and Doc felt a little medication could help me to process my loss," Annie explained, surprised at how comfortable she felt revealing this information.

"So it's helping?" was all Pack asked.

"Yes, I'm beginning to think about what to do with the rest of my life. I need things to look forward to."

"What are you considering?"

"I haven't gotten that far." Annie paused and looked at her empty plate. "That was delicious."

"Why don't you go out and relax by the fire. We'll have dessert in the living room."

"Sure I can't help?"

"I'll only be a minute."

"The diet starts tomorrow," Annie laughed.

When Pack came in with a tray of dessert and tea, he heard Coltrane on the stereo.

Annie was kneeling, putting more wood on the fire. The glow lit her face and played across her mop of curls. Packard thought his homemade vanilla almond ice cream would melt from the heat of his hands holding the tray. He hoped that Annie wouldn't notice him shake a little as he set the tray down on the coffee table.

"Anything wrong?" she asked and took a seat on the sofa.

"No. I was noticing how beautiful you look," he said and

sat next to her to pour the tea.

When he finished pouring, he didn't pick up either teacup. Instead, Annie watched with excited anticipation as he reached for her hand.

Unfortunately, when his skin touched hers, she felt panic.

"Annie, I care a great deal for you. I know that I'm older than you, but I'm in good health. My grandparents were vital well into their nineties. My parents were the exception, not the rule in my family."

"What are you saying, Packard?"

"I'm not putting this very well," he said and cleared his throat. "I still have a lot to offer you, Annie."

This was sounding more like a marriage proposal than a seduction, Annie suddenly thought. She had to stop him before he said any more.

"I know you do, Packard. You have a lot to offer any woman lucky enough to gain your affection," Annie interrupted.

A smart, if not socially adept man, Pack heard the "but" in her voice.

"But?" he asked.

"I'm not ready to share my life with anyone," she said delicately.

He waited.

"It would be an injustice to you if I let myself get involved with you in order to fill the void I feel inside. I'm still…grieving," Annie said, regretting that this might be the only time that Packard would broach the topic.

"I understand."

"Maybe it's time that I head back," Annie said uncomfortably.

"I'll walk you home."

"Thank you, but it's not necessary."

They both rose and moved toward the front door.

"I had a wonderful evening. Dinner was delicious. I'm glad I wasn't alone tonight. I mean, it was helpful to spend the holiday with you," Annie said.

"You'll need this to find your way in the dark," Packard said, handing her a flashlight that he kept hanging on a hook by the door.

"Thanks. I'll return it in the morning," Annie said.

"There's no hurry. I have others."

"Good night, and thanks again."

"Good night, Annie."

From the porch, he watched the flashlight beam travel through the trees and lost it once she reached the field. He ran upstairs to his bedroom window and caught sight of her pausing for a moment. Annie stood looking out at the lights across the bay. The wind blew up across the water. He watched as the beam continued on to the Knoll. The lamps came on in Annie's cottage. When he knew she was safely home, Packard went downstairs to clean up. The fire was dying down, and the ice cream was melting.

"I've got to get out of here," he muttered to himself.

In the kitchen, he threw containers of the leftovers into his ice chest. He poured the melted ice cream down the drain and washed up the dirty dishes, pots and pans. After tossing some clothes into his duffel bag, grabbing his sketch pad and pencils, he headed for his dock.

The next morning, when Annie came by to return the flashlight, *Sophie* was missing from the dock. She sat on Packard's porch steps sinking down into her warm jacket in the cold spring air. She stayed there for some time, staring out at the bay.

Several days later when Packard pulled into his dock, cleaned up *Sophie* and lugged his gear to the porch, he found a note from Annie taped to his front door.

Dear Packard,

Thanks for a delicious Easter dinner. It was a lovely evening.

I've decided to go visit Grace. Hoping Nate might be willing to come down to San Diego to see me, too. No idea how long I'll be gone. Please keep an eye on the Knoll.
Thanks, Annie

Packard crumpled the note up in his hand as he carried his gear into the house. He wished he hadn't left so abruptly after Easter dinner and hadn't stayed away so long. During the first day that he was out on the bay, he had replayed the evening with Annie over in his head a million times. He sensed that she was attracted to him that night. He felt the combined chemistry and knew that it wasn't just his own longing creating something false. Although he understood that she was still sorting out her life and didn't want to get involved, he had taken off as usual. He had run when Drew had first appeared, when her wedding date had arrived, when she was pregnant with Nate and when Drew left her.

"What the hell do I keep running away from?" he mumbled to himself. At the very least, he could be a friend to her.

Packard decided he would resist the impulse to leave Annie alone. But she was nearly three thousand miles away, so for now there was nothing he could do but paint. After a shower and a quick bite to eat, he headed directly over to the Schoolhouse Studio to start preliminary studies from the sketches he'd done while out on *Sophie*. Images of his sister Sophia flooded him. It was going to be a long night of work.

After several weeks in California with Grace and her family, Annie hesitantly pulled her car onto the Knoll. The moment she parked on the circle drive and gazed out at the bay, she broke into tears. She retrieved a tissue and was blowing her nose when Packard appeared. He opened the car door, took her by the arm, and eased her out of the seat, into the Sunrise Cottage and onto a chair at her kitchen table. Without saying a word, he lit the stove under her kettle and began opening cabinets in search of a teacup.

"Second door over," Annie said.

He opened the right cabinet and took out a mug.

"Aren't you having any?" she asked.

Pack grabbed a second mug. As the kettle heated up, he began opening each canister lined up on the counter in hopes of finding the tea bags.

"Last one."

He pulled two bags from the canister and poured the hot water.

"I didn't want to come back," she said and then couldn't continue for a moment.

She took several deep breaths before she could speak again.

Packard moved the box of tissues that he noticed on the counter over to the table. He sat across from her. Steam rose from both mugs of hot tea water.

"I didn't want to come back to the Knoll." Annie shook her head in disbelief.

"I've never felt like this. Like this wasn't my home, wasn't where I longed to be. But they're everywhere. Drew and Nate are everywhere here."

Suddenly Annie's hand came down hard on the table.

"I'm so angry with Drew. I can never look out at the dock

without seeing him and Nate smile and wave up at me while they're fishing. I can't see a Sunfish without picturing Drew teaching Nate to sail. I can't drive past those cement crows at the entrance without thinking of the day Drew gave them to me when I opened Annie Crow Knoll. I can't go into Honeymoon Cottage where he and I made love for the first time. I've never wanted to leave this place before, but then, it was such a relief to be at Grace's. I felt like I could breathe because I wasn't constantly reminded. Grace's family distracted me. I helped Petey and Beth Ann with their homework. Grace and I repainted her living room. Pete was thrilled to be relieved of that job. It felt so good to be needed."

"I need you, Annie. So do Nate and all your friends who will be coming back soon to stay in this beautiful place that you provide."

"Thank you, Packard." Annie briefly touched his hand that rested on the table next to his untouched tea. "But Nate doesn't need me anymore."

"Did you get to see him out there?"

"No, he was too busy at school."

"He's adjusting, just as you are. I am, too. Maybe it's something we have to accept. This altered state that Drew has left us in."

"You miss him, too?"

"Of course."

"I keep waiting for it to end."

"Perhaps it isn't something that ever goes away, not completely anyway."

"God, don't say that!" She dropped her head into her arms on the table.

"Be with it, Annie," he said, lightly touching the top of her curly hair.

She lifted her head and nodded it.

Then Packard rose to go get her suitcases out of the car.

"Be with it," she repeated out loud to herself as she sat

alone.

She imagined the possibility of neither waiting for the future when the pain stops nor living in the past when Drew and Nate were here.

Packard came back in and set the suitcases on the floor. Annie turned to see him standing in the doorway.

"I have new work to show you when you're up to it. Drew always got the first look. Now I'd like you to be the one."

"I'd be honored."

"You're probably tired right now."

"No, let's go. It'll do me good."

When they entered the Schoolhouse Studio, Annie was immediately drawn to the large canvas of a young woman dressed in skins and furs. Her hair was made up of Mourning Doves that circled her face and sat upon her shoulders. Their coal black eyes, both piercing and warm at the same time, matched the woman's eyes. They also matched Packard's eyes.

"This is your sister."

Packard took in a surprised breath.

Sophia stood in a lush forest and was surrounded by various wild animals. To her right stood a black bear and cub. A pair of Bald Eagles sat on a tree branch to her left. A raccoon curled up comfortably in the crook of her left arm. A small Eastern Screech-Owl sat on her extended right arm. Most prominent was a red fox that rested at her feet. All of the creatures looked directly at Annie.

"She's magnificent," Annie said after a long silence. "It's like nothing you've done before."

"When I was a little boy, after my sister died, I used to pretend that she had been kidnapped by gypsies, and she escaped them in the wilderness. I imagined that she was raised by wild animals and was safe and happy in this existence, free from the responsibilities and constraints of regular family," Packard explained. "I had forgotten this until I saw her image on the canvas."

"You took care of your sick parents all by yourself, didn't you?"

He nodded.

"When did they pass?"

"They were both gone before I was twenty."

"Same as me."

Annie turned away from the painting and looked into his eyes. He paused and then led her to a nearly completed canvas. Big Black Bo and his wife Olivia walked hand in hand on the water of the Chesapeake Bay. Their daughter was a laughing toddler perched on Bo's shoulders as the couple crossed to the other side.

"Oh, Packard," Annie whispered.

"It's nearly finished."

"Have you met Bo's sister-in-law Viola Granger?"

"No, I haven't had the pleasure."

"Bo's wife was her twin sister. If you haven't met Viola, how did you know what Olivia looked like?"

"I don't know," he said simply.

"Packard, this is amazing. It's absolutely spiritual to me. May I come back and see it when it's done?"

"Come over anytime you like."

Annie did make frequent visits, and as the days wore on, she noticed that Packard did nothing but work on the new series. It was a major collection that he created at breakneck pace. *Sophie* sat at the dock unused. He rarely seemed to leave the studio to sleep or eat. Occasionally, she'd find the studio empty, but Packard would show up momentarily freshly showered and eating an apple. Once she discovered him sound asleep on the old sofa still wearing the reading glasses he needed to see details clearly.

Although Annie realized Packard always had and always would thrive without her, she began bringing food to the studio. She quickly abandoned large meals that he barely touched and brought fresh fruit and vegetables, cheeses and breads, which he gratefully devoured, sometimes while still holding a paintbrush in one hand. Along with giving Annie a sense of purpose, she relished watching Packard work and the images that emerged on the canvas. To her surprise, he did not seem to mind her presence while he worked.

She felt welcomed.

Chapter Twenty-Three
Summer 1982

DALI-LIKE CLOUDS DOTTED A CRYSTAL blue sky. A stiff breeze flapped the Maryland State flag atop its post at the end of the dock. Annie straightened up after applying a fresh coat of thick, white paint to the top of each piling. It felt good to work. After a brief break, Annie picked up the brush again and knelt down to paint a five-inch wide safety line along the very end of the dock. While cutting the brush along the heavy pencil line she'd drawn earlier, the wind blew some loose strands of Annie's hair across her face, and she smudged white paint across her nose when she pushed it out of the way. The breeze died down, and she heard a distant buzzing sound in its place.

Annie looked up river and saw a bright, yellow object flying along the tree line. Being a woman who seldom allowed distractions to keep her from completing a task, Annie returned her attention to painting the neat, straight line along the edge of the boards. The sound grew louder and closer. Annie looked up again and the buzzing, yellow object was an ultralight air craft. It was coming so close to the end of the dock that Annie could almost shake hands with the pilot. The intense sound forced her to her feet, paintbrush in hand, as a man flew past. His white shirt billowed around him. His brown hair was wildly blowing about his tan face.

It was Tommy Reynolds, and he was looking at her, pointing at his nose and laughing. Then he flashed a smile at her and waved. Annie waved back and then looked down to see white paint spattered across the dock.

"Damn it!" she yelled out loud. "Damn him!"

She looked up as the yellow flying machine continued down the bay.

"Damn, damn, damn!"

Annie marched up the dock to find paint thinner and a rag.

About two hours later, after Annie had connected every heavy-duty extension cord she owned and two she borrowed from Packard, she had successfully removed the last drops of paint from the planks with her electric sander. As she dragged the last heavy cord up the steps from the dock, Annie heard Chicago's *Does Anybody Really Know What Time It Is* blasting from a Corvette convertible coming down the drive toward her. When Tommy Reynolds turned off his car, he flashed that smile again, beautiful white teeth against light almond skin. He'd obviously spent the winter someplace sunny. He lowered his sunglasses and looked directly at Annie with his beautiful green eyes. The longing she felt surprised her.

"Annie Crow," he said and stepped out of the car.

"Tommy Reynolds."

He walked to her with his arms held open. She dropped the extension cord and let him pull her close. It felt good to be hugged and to hug back.

When Annie looked up at him, Tom began gently rubbing at the paint still stuck on her nose.

She didn't feel any instinct to pull away but did ask,

"What are you doing?"

"I can't possibly talk to you seriously with this stuff across your nose," he said, still rubbing.

"What stuff? Oh, is that why you were pointing at your nose when you flew by in that contraption?"

"There, all gone."

"I've been running around here with paint on my face for hours."

"Apparently."

Tom took Annie by the arm and walked to the edge of the Knoll.

"Dock looks nice."

"I just finished removing all the paint that you made me spill!"

"I made you spill?" Tom asked.

"Yes, you! You startled me flying so close to the dock."

"It isn't my fault that you can't—" He paused and started laughing.

Annie laughed, too.

"God, we're ten years old again," she said.

"I'm sorry that I scared you."

"I wasn't scared. I was startled," Annie said defensively.

"There you go again, ten years old."

"Okay, okay."

"I apologize for whatever I did that caused you extra labor, and I will find a way to make it up to you."

"You are a charmer."

"Always have been."

"No, I'm sorry, but you weren't. Something is different about you."

"After two failed marriages, I've learned to acquiesce."

"I bet your mother doesn't recognize you."

"Aren't you sweet!" Tom said and gave her a light punch in the arm.

Packard appeared at the top of the steps after a hike from

Cattail.

"Tide's coming back in," he said as he crossed over to them and extended his hand to Tom. "How are you?"

"I'm well. Good to see you," Tom responded, shaking his hand.

"Was that your ultralight earlier?"

"Yes."

"Must be terrific to see this place from up there."

"I'd be happy to take you up in it some time."

"That'd be great."

"You interested in a ride, too, Annie?" Tom asked.

"Sure!"

"You going to be around this summer, Tom?" Packard asked.

"Yes. I'm renting a place in Kingstown for the season. Signed the lease this morning."

"We'll be seeing you then," Pack noted.

"I hope so," he answered.

Pack nodded and headed on across to his place.

Tommy turned to Annie. "He's come out of his shell."

"Hmm," was all Annie replied as she watched Packard climb over the fence.

"How are you doing, Annie?" Tom asked.

She looked at him. "Getting back on my feet."

"Sorry to hear about your divorce."

"Yeah," Annie said and pushed the ground with the toe of her sneaker. "In a couple weeks, my son is coming back for the summer."

"My oldest goes to college this fall. It makes me feel so old," Tom joked.

"You don't look it."

"Neither do you, Annie." His gaze met hers. "You look wonderful."

"So can I interest you in some ice tea or a beer?" she asked.

"A beer would be great."

"Sure. I'll meet you down on the dock."

Annie appreciated the few minutes alone while she grabbed a couple of beers from the refrigerator. Realizing that she was in old paint clothes, she dashed into the bedroom and threw on a clean shirt and some jeans. She ran a brush though her stubborn curls and decided that she'd better wash her face, too. After adding a little lipstick, a few seconds passed as she debated on a splash of perfume. Finally she dabbed some on and then forced herself to go back out there.

As Annie approached the end of the dock, Tom was looking up river through binoculars that he'd grabbed from his car.

"It doesn't seem the same," he said as she approached. "Cattail doesn't come out as far into the river as I remember."

"No," Annie answered. "Lots of storms and erosion."

"Do kids still go over there to build forts?"

"Yes, but only at low tide. There's no beach at high tide anymore."

"Things don't last."

"They change," Annie responded.

Annie was about to ask why, after all these years, he was suddenly back on the bay, when he glanced at his watch.

"I'm sorry, Annie, but I've got to go. My oldest is singing in her last high school choir concert tonight. I have a two hour drive to New Jersey."

As they walked back up to his car, Annie said, "You didn't get to drink your beer."

"I'll take a rain check. In fact, I'd like to take you to dinner once I get settled down here. That is, if you'd want to," Tom asked gently.

"Yes, that would be nice."

After he settled into the driver's seat, he said, "I'll give you a call next week."

"Great."

"It was good to see you, Annie."

Tom touched the hand that she unconsciously had resting

on his car door.

"Good to see you, too."

Tom let go of her hand and started the car. He put his sunglasses back on. Annie stepped back, and he pulled around the circle and up the drive. She smiled when she heard the Spinners' version of *Working My Way Back to You* blasting up Baycliff Road.

Grace managed to coordinate her family's flight from San Diego to land in Philadelphia an hour before Nate's flight arrived there from San Francisco. She drove her kids and Annie's son to the Knoll in her rental car.

When Nate jumped out of the car, he gave his mother a quick hello kiss on the cheek and without one thought of unpacking, ran down to the dock with Beth Ann and Petey.

"Looks like the drive here with your kids helped him to acclimate," Annie told Grace. "Thanks for arranging all this."

"He said that he really wanted to come to the Knoll this summer. Drew apparently is dating someone new who doesn't have children. Maybe he's less threatened," Grace explained.

Watching the three kids horse playing on the dock, Annie said, "They'll end up in the water any minute."

"Before I start unloading all this stuff into Cockatiel Cottage, tell me how your date went with dreamy Tommy Reynolds," Grace asked.

"We didn't have sex, if that's what you're wondering."

"Me?" Grace said with mock innocence.

"It was lovely. I hadn't been on a date since I was nineteen!"

"What about your dinner with Packard?"

"At Easter?"

"Duh!"

"Well, yes, I guess that was sort of a date."

"Like bees to honey," Grace teased.

"Well, there isn't going to be any 'birds and bees' this summer with Nate here. I don't want to upset him."

"I've got him covered if you want to sneak off for a rendezvous with Tommy. God knows, I wouldn't pass up the opportunity if I were in your position."

"My position this summer is mother."

"What are you going to do, live like a nun until he's twenty-five?"

"Come on, let's get you settled," Annie said.

Grace threw her arm over Annie's shoulders, "You're doing all right now, aren't you?"

"Yes, I'm getting there."

Everyone, and especially Packard, noticed Tom Reynolds was a frequent visitor to Annie Crow Knoll. Whenever there was an impromptu barbecue, as if by magic, Tom would show up in his boat. Or perhaps, he would arrive, and an impromptu barbecue would follow. Several of the cottagers remembered him as a boy on the Knoll, and everyone liked him.

Often Tom brought his children with him. Whether his little one was pestering Tom to take him swimming or the teens were begging to go water skiing, Tom was never far from Annie's side. But neither was Packard. He made sure of that. He noticed Annie seemed happier than she'd been in a long time. Perhaps the cloud of Drew's leaving was lifting. If Tom was helping that to happen, Pack was grateful and patiently waiting.

Packard heard the screen door to the studio open. He paused from painting a moment, turned and saw young Nate standing inside the doorway.

"Welcome," Packard said simply and began working again.

Nate wandered around the studio, looking at paintings and fingering brushes.

"Want to take up painting?" Packard asked suddenly.

Startled, Nate managed to knock over a jar of brushes.

"Sorry," he said as he righted them.

"No damage done."

"I was wondering if you'd take me out fishing like we used to with Dad."

"Sure."

Nate seemed a little surprised that the answer had come so quickly and surely. He wandered around again.

"There's some soda in the fridge. Help yourself," Packard told him.

"Thanks."

Nate opened a can of Coke and settled on a stool next to Packard's worktable. He was looking more like his father by the day, Pack noted. The blue eyes and glasses had something to do with it, but also the shape of his face. He did look like he'd have a huskier build though. Drew was thinner.

As if reading his mind, Nate asked, "Do you miss my dad?"

"Very much." Packard paused from working and peered over his reading glasses at Nate. "Missed you, too." He turned back to assess his painting. "You've been coming to the studio since your dad brought you over in a stroller."

Nate blushed.

Packard decided it was time to stop. "How do you like your new school?" he asked as he started to clean his brush.

"It's good," Nate answered. "Lot more art and music classes."

"I'd like that."

"I do. And when I get to the high school classes, they've got Culinary Arts that even boys take and also theatre."

"Sounds like you made the right move."

Nate shifted on the stool. "Dad talks about you a lot. Quotes you even. Tells facts and says you're the expert."

Packard chuckled.

"He does! Stuff like—" Nate changed his voice to a deeper, serious tone, "—red dog is a haze before a storm."

"Does he think I sound like that?"

Nate continued the imitation. "Means you'd better get off the water and fast."

"You're kidding, right?" Pack asked.

"Will you ever come out to California to visit? I doubt that Dad will ever come back here."

"We'll see. For now, you and I can go fishing."

"Cool."

"Do you play chess?"

"Sure. I've even beat Dad a couple of times. I don't think he just let me win either."

"I can guarantee that he didn't." Packard smiled.

Distant thunder rumbled just after sunset. From the porch of Sunrise Cottage, Annie checked the sky and watched Nate come up the steps from the dock followed by Chicky Zebler from Kingfisher Cottage and Cathy Martino, nicknamed Chatty Cathy for obvious reasons, from Tockwogh Cottage. She could hear them complimenting him on his water skiing. Tom Reynolds often asked Nate to join his two teenage daughters and him when they went skiing. Annie noticed Grace's little Beth Ann, who was only eleven, trail behind the teens looking forlorn. She couldn't compete with Tom's gorgeous daughters or Chicky and Cathy. Her buddy Nate was outgrowing her now. It looked like he'd had quite an audience for his skills on the water this evening.

God, Annie laughed to herself, *these girls act like he walked on the water*.

When Nate said good night to his fans, he didn't come into Sunrise Cottage but climbed up into the Crow's Nest. It only took ten minutes before the night air was charged with electricity. Overlapping flashes of lightning flickered every second as the storm moved up the bay toward Promise. Annie hadn't been in the Crow's Nest since spring. The light show would be great from up there.

"Mind if I join you?" Annie called up to her son.

When Nate's face appeared at the top of the ladder, he looked so much like Drew it took Annie's breath away.

"Come on up," he hollered down.

When she reached the top of the ladder, Nate gave her a hand into the tree house.

"Cold front coming in," he said knowingly.

"We'll take it. It's been too hot for too long," Annie said as she sat across from him to watch the approaching storm.

"Mr. Packard said this morning that we'd feel a big change after this line of storms pass tonight."

More flashes of lightning lit up the sky followed by rolls of thunder several miles away.

Nate looked at Annie. "Who do you like more, Mr. Packard or Mr. Reynolds?"

"What?" Annie couldn't hide her surprise.

"Well, it's pretty obvious they both like you," he stated like she had to be stupid.

"You sound like your Aunt Grace."

"See, she gets it, too."

"What makes you ask this?"

"Mr. Reynolds is always asking questions about you. I mean, he's nice and all, but he's just trying to get to you through me."

"How does that make you feel?" Annie asked.

"I don't care. I get to water ski and hang out with his babe daughters. It's great. He even lets me drive the boat when Jessica is skiing. I can't drive when Jenny skis because she's not as good as her older sister. Jess loves it when I make sharp turns and she has to cross the wake. She can handle that stuff."

The wind suddenly picked up and rain poured in through the opening. Nate lowered a canvas flap but it just blew open again.

"We're going to get soaked," he said over the storm.

"We already are anyway." Annie moved against the wall.

Nate crawled over and sat next to her like he used to when he was little. Annie longed to put her arm around him, but she wasn't sure he'd let her.

After a moment, he asked, "Do you still love Dad?"

"I do love him, but not the married kind anymore."

Lightning flashed closer and a clap of thunder cracked almost immediately. Annie and Nate grabbed each other instinctively.

"Holy cow!" Annie cried.

"It's just the angels bowling, Mom. Remember?"

They both laughed and hugged each other as the tree holding the Crow's Nest swayed in the wind. Annie knew they ought to make a run for it to the safer, dry cottage, but she wasn't willing to end this moment with her son. Maybe when he was far away again and maybe when he was feeling angry with her again, he'd remember this moment and think she wasn't all that bad.

When a bolt of lightning hit the bay joined by a deafening clap of thunder, she kissed the top of his head.

"Come on, it's too close now."

They scurried down the ladder and into Sunrise Cottage soaking wet and laughing.

Chapter Twenty-Four

Fall 1982

THE KNOLL WAS DESERTED MIDWEEK. Nate and Grace's family had returned to the West Coast. Slim and his wife had driven to Cape May for a few days. Mrs. Waters was spending the week with Sam and Maizie in Baltimore because Jim Finch was recovering from some surgery. The rest of the Finch clan was sticking close to home until Jim was on his feet again.

It seemed funny to have the place to herself, but Annie didn't mind. She had one chore before she could take a swim and enjoy the warm, sunny day. That was to clean Fish Tale Cottage after weekend renters had left two days before. Just as she was dragging the vacuum cleaner across the lawn to Tommy Reynolds' old cottage, he pulled in the drive, blasting the Eagles' *One of These Nights* on his car stereo.

When he turned his ignition off, peacefulness folded over the Knoll again.

"You're as bad as the kids with that music so loud," Annie

hollered over to him.

"I've come to kidnap Cinderella and take her to Rock Harbor for lunch," he announced as he hopped out of his car and quickly joined her.

"Sounds nice, but I'm cleaning."

"Why don't you pay someone to do this?" he asked and lifted the vacuum cleaner to follow her into Fish Tale.

"I have on and off, but right now, I enjoy doing it myself."

"My God, this is like going into a time machine," he said, setting the vacuum down on the living room floor of his old cottage.

"Hasn't changed much. We've painted, and there are different rugs and blinds, but things are pretty much the same around here."

"Painted?" Tom didn't stay for the answer but quickly walked to the bedroom he'd shared with his brother. He looked at the woodwork framing the closet door with disappointment. "You painted over the measurements."

"What?" Annie followed him.

"My parents measured Jack and me the first weekend of every season and marked our heights and the year in pencil on this door frame."

"I'm really sorry. If your folks had kept renting, I would have left it," Annie explained apologetically.

Tom turned to her. His face looked vulnerable and young. Then he crossed to Annie and kissed her. When she responded, he pushed her firmly to the wall, kissing her again.

It felt good to have his strong body pinning her against the old plaster, his hips leaning into hers.

Annie lifted her arms up and around his neck. She ran her fingers through his hair as she let his tongue inside her mouth.

Tom moaned softly and lifted her up with his hands cradling her buttocks. Annie instinctively wrapped her legs around his waist.

With her balanced between his hips and the wall, he unbuttoned her shirt and ran his tongue along the top edge of her bra.

"Annie Crow, I've dreamed of your breasts many times since we went skinny dipping as kids," he whispered.

Silly boy, she heard her fourteen-year-old self think. *He would never be her lover. He was beautiful but not worthy. By morning his ego would have him bragging to everyone how he'd seen Miss Annie Crow naked. No, someone else would be her first lover. Someone who deserved her.*

Immediately aware of the change in Annie, Tom gently lowered her so she was standing on the floor, and he stepped away.

"I'm sorry," he said.

"It's okay," Annie told him, still breathless.

"It's too soon. What the hell was I thinking? You just looked so—."

"I'm sure I did. You were simply responding to what I was putting out there."

"I can't tell you how sorry I am."

"Don't be! It was lovely, really, to feel so excited again."

"Good," Tom said a little confused. "But?"

Annie couldn't explain why she hesitated.

"When you are ready," he said, "let me know…never mind. I'm going before I do or say something else stupid."

Tom walked to the door and then turned back.

"I'm sorry that my parents bailed out on you when your folks died," he added. "I don't know why they didn't rent again. They've spent their whole lives regretting it, reminiscing about all the fun we had here."

"Tell them that they are welcome to rent again."

"I will."

"You're a very nice man, Tommy Reynolds."

It sounded like "good bye," but he forced a smile and left Fish Tale Cottage.

Annie heard his Corvette pull slowly out of the drive and

then speed up after he turned onto Baycliff Road. Then the music came on. She listened as *Heartache Tonight* faded up the road.

Annie felt like she was about to burst open. She abandoned her cleaning project and went down to the dock. Since no one was around, she stripped off her clothes and dove into the bay. It was exhilarating to feel the incoming tide glide over her naked body. A crow called from a limb above the Crow's Nest. It flew over her as she floated on her back toward the beach looking up at the white puffy clouds.

Annie wondered why she hadn't corrected Tom Reynolds when he assumed that it was the break up with Drew that stopped her from what had promised to be a lovely afternoon. She couldn't quite understand the strength of the pull away from Tom, but they had both felt it. Then she stood up in the water and smiled.

It was Packard.

Annie showered, dressed and began walking across Packard's field to his studio. She stopped only once on her way, and the grasshoppers that went flying with each of her steps settled down. The pause was not one of doubt, simply preparation. After a deep breath, she continued, and the insects leaped wildly out of her way.

Packard knew she was coming. He'd sensed it for days and showered and shaved each morning.

When she appeared in the door, he wasn't surprised, but the sight of her made him drop his paintbrush to the floor. He didn't even wipe his hands clean on a towel. He immediately moved toward her.

"I want to discuss—" she started to say.

"We'll figure it out later," he said, easily picking her up in his big arms, pushing the door shut with one hip and clicking the latch over with an elbow.

"But there are things—" she began again.

Packard laid her down on the old sofa, and she couldn't say another word or think another thought because he was covering her mouth with kisses that drove any concerns swiftly out of her head.

In caressing her, he smudged paint from his fingers on her face and in her hair.

She didn't mind or didn't notice.

When she opened his shirt and pulled it off his shoulders, she smeared red ocher from her cheek down his neck as she kissed her way to his chest.

Above, two huge mobiles of black crows and heavenly planets spun in the heat.

Below, slowly, ritually, these two souls met as their bodies merged. Paint and sweet sweat mingled. Nothing was rushed. Every deep, sensual moment was fully realized before they moved to experience the next moment and the next.

By the following day, hunger finally won out over more lovemaking. They stumbled over to Packard's house and collapsed into the huge, claw footed bathtub upstairs. While soaking and washing paint off each other, they ate fruit, cheese and bread. They sipped wine and waited for the hot water heater to catch up to refill the tub when it cooled.

On the third day, while lying in his bed with Annie in his arms, Pack said, "I wonder why no one has come looking for you?"

"I took care of that. I left a note on my door that said, 'I'm with Packard. Unless there's a fire or someone drowns, don't interrupt us.'"

She loved how the lines wrinkled around his rich, brown eyes when he laughed.

"I guess the cat is out of the bag then," he said.

"You don't think for one minute we could keep this a secret, do you?"

"No, not around here."

"Do you want it to be a secret?"

"I'd shout it from the roof top, except I'm sure the whole town knows by now anyway."

He loved how her mouth turned up slowly when she smiled. Then she pounced on top of him again. He loved that, too.

Unwillingly, on the fourth day, Annie forced herself to bring up what she'd wanted to discuss before they did anything. She trusted Packard when he said that they'd figure it all out later. Later had arrived, and she didn't want to hurt him.

"Packard?" she said, as they lazed naked on the floor in a pool of light pouring in through his bedroom window. Pack was gently tracing his finger along the line of her thigh, up her hip, to her waist.

"Yes?"

She adjusted her position so she could see his face. He traced her collarbone and her shoulder.

"I don't want to marry again."

"I know." His finger traveled down her arm.

Annie paused.

"I'm sorry, did I interrupt you?" he asked and let his hand rest on her hip.

"You amaze me. I don't get how you seem to know things before I do."

"That's what you wanted to tell me when you came to the studio."

"Yes. Do you know why?'

"If you'd like to tell me, I'll listen," he said calmly and without judgment.

"Something happens to a woman when she gets married. I don't know if it's social conditioning or hormones, but no matter how strong a person she may be or how clear she is about herself, she begins to give away parts of herself to her husband. Little, tiny pieces that aren't even noticeable at first, given up freely because it actually feels good, right, womanly to sacrifice for him. She steps aside for his sake, his career, his desires, his problems. Flick, there goes another part of her, like flakes floating away, and she thinks, if she thinks, I'll never miss that. But over time, she starts to notice whole chunks of herself gone. After years of this, she gives resentfully. It's a habit now, a condition, an addiction, which she has no idea how to stop. Even if she knew how to stop it, she's afraid. Afraid he'll hate her if she doesn't continue to disintegrate before his blind eyes. One good wind, she'll blow away like so much sand, but she goes on doing it. He didn't ask her to do it, but she does. I did. I watched my mother do it. Grace does it.

"I'm sure Drew compromised for me as well. Men give and sacrifice, but they aren't predisposed to losing themselves. They realize when they give in. It's a choice they make, not a requirement of their gender. They keep track of their compromises, measuring them out like money. Women minimize their sacrifices, give without thinking. Women bend. They lean in toward their husband and family. Giving in is natural to us, almost like a knee jerk reaction."

"I don't want you to give up anything," Packard said.

"I don't think Drew did either, at least not consciously, but as his wife, I did."

"It's a choice."

"Yes, but marriage changed that for me. I lost sense of my own boundaries. I want my—separateness."

"We're past separateness," he said gently.

"I know. However, I want my own place. I don't want to marry or live together."

"Let's be with it each day, each moment. Nothing is permanent, Annie. Not even what we have right now, with or without a marriage license."

"You're not disappointed?"

"How could I possibly be disappointed?" Packard said,

taking her back into his arms. "I'm so happy right now."

"What about the future?" Annie asked.

"There is no future. We have this second. Right now, that's it."

Annie thought for a moment. "That's very liberating, isn't it?" she remarked.

"Yep." Pack smiled.

"No ownership. No Mr. and Mrs. No clinging."

"None."

"And yet, I love you," Annie said.

"I love you, too."

"In ways, I've loved you all my life."

"I've loved you in many lives."

As they lingered over breakfast the fifth day, Packard said, "I have a new painting I'd like you to see."

"In the studio?" Annie asked.

"Yes."

"I didn't see it the other night."

Annie could easily have missed it amid the various canvases and projects Pack had strewn about. But honestly, there could have been a gorilla in the studio, and she wouldn't have noticed it when Packard swept her off her feet at the door.

"We had other priorities," he joked.

"Let's go. I can't wait."

If they hadn't been carrying their full coffee mugs, Annie would have run to the studio.

Sheila Van Bruen, who still represented Packard, had mounted a touring show of what she good-naturedly referred to as "Packard's Grateful Dead." His many spiritual portraits, beginning first with his sister and then Bo, had all been of people who had died. After the tour hit some key locations, Packard started receiving commissions for new portraits of dearly departed ones. People sent photographs of and stories about their loved ones, but Pack usually had a sketch finished before they arrived.

Through a dream, he'd see an elderly woman covered with vines and flowers. Then the phone would ring the next day with a new client whose grandmother had been an avid gardener. Pack never questioned this new gift. He had learned how to flow with life rather than struggle against it.

When they entered the studio, Packard picked up the brush he'd dropped five days ago. The light had been better at the back end of the studio on the last day he had worked, so the large easel faced away from the door and the couch. Pack asked Annie to wait until he turned the painting to face her in the morning light. Then he paused. He considered warning her but didn't want to control her reaction.

Annie's parents were wrapped in pale ivory-colored fabric. Huge white wings extended from their backs. The background was a dark sky filled with stars. Below them were the cottages, beach and dock of the Knoll. They flew with arms linked, and in their hands, Luke held two crow feathers while Liz held locks of hair.

"The locks of hair!" Annie said.

"Yes?" Packard didn't know their significance.

"Mama saved locks of my hair from when I was little."

"Well, that explains it, then."

Annie took a stool to sit down.

"Are you all right?"

"I could use some water or something cold."

Pack ran the tap a moment before filling a glass for her. When he handed the glass to her, she pressed it against her cheek.

"It's beautiful, Packard." Annie looked at every detail of the painting for a long time.

Finally she decided to share what she'd never spoken to anyone about, except Bo, and not until he was dying.

"I resented my mother for too long," she began as she looked into Liz's gray eyes staring at her from the painting.

Packard simply pulled up a chair next to her and waited.

"I believed that she and Bo had an affair." She expected Packard to at least shift in his chair, but he was completely still. She turned to him. "I found them embracing when I was still a kid. It tormented me. My 'perfect' mother, who seemed to continually find fault with me, was unfaithful to my father. Of course, it wasn't true. Bo swore to me right before he passed. But even now, I still feel the edge of resentment."

"May I ask a question?" Packard said softly.

"Yes."

"Did you gain any benefit from holding onto this?"

"Benefit? How could I possibly benefit from something that destroyed my image of my mother?" Annie asked.

"What about this image of your mother?"

"She was flawless while I was always a disappointment to her."

"Were you relieved to find out she wasn't perfect?"

"It gave me power over her; I can tell you that."

"Power?"

"She stopped criticizing me, well, out loud anyway. I could still tell by her look when she wasn't pleased with me, but she couldn't say anything anymore because I had the power to completely change her life, her marriage, her reputation, everything by simply telling what I saw."

"But what you thought you saw wasn't true."

Annie considered that for a moment. "So why did she give me that control?" she asked.

Packard shrugged.

"My power was actually an illusion."

"So was your image of her."

Annie struggled for a moment to grasp what he was saying. Then she realized. "That's absolutely right! She put forth this image of properness, and it was all for show. She was illegitimate, did you know that?"

"No."

"Neither did I until Delia died. Walter told me."

"All the more reason for being so proper and expecting a great deal from you," Packard reflected.

"Why?"

"She had a lot to make up for."

"I just wish she'd told me the truth."

"Maybe she was embarrassed. Maybe she was afraid of letting you down."

"That would have been better than being lied to for years," Annie argued.

"She couldn't know that, Annie."

"True."

"Either way, she didn't want to hurt you."

"No, I guess not." Annie paused. "I know she and Dad loved me, and I loved them. I believe Bo…"

"But…" Packard filled in.

"Something still bothers me, and I don't understand what."

"It is possible to love someone and also have other feelings that could hurt them."

"What do you mean?" Annie asked.

"It's possible that Bo and your mother had some mixed emotions for each other, but that didn't diminish their love for your father."

"If they did share something deeper, Bo never confessed that to me, but I suspected there was more."

"People can't help having feelings for each other."

Annie sighed. "I hope Nate figures this out sooner than I have."

"Figures out what?"

"That he doesn't have to hate his parents because he thinks they're perfect and he can't measure up. Only to hate us more when we prove to be screwed up human beings like everyone else."

Packard kissed her lightly on the head. "You are pretty hard on yourself, Annie Crow, even without your mother here to give you the 'look.'"

"I sometimes feel like I've completely blown it with Nate. I certainly did with Drew."

Packard put his arms around Annie and gave her a bear hug. "No regrets, my love. Only trust."

Annie leaned into his shoulder and looked up at her parents in the painting. She finally felt peaceful.

"Packard."

"Yes?" he asked.

"I want you to paint my spiritual portrait, now, while I'm alive."

"I'd love to."

"Nude," she continued.

"Even better."

EPILOGUE
LATE FALL 1982

LONG LINES OF SPIDER WEBS clinging to the eaves of Sunrise Cottage floated up and down in the breeze. The trees along the shoreline were turning golden and red. The black-eyed Susans were brown, and Annie had lots to do. It was a strange time for her, a mixed time, for as much as she enjoyed the solitude, she was sad to see the season end. All the cottages had to be closed up. No welcoming lights would burn inside them now until May.

While carrying the lawn chairs toward the cellar for storage, Annie stepped over the unruly vines of her pumpkin patch. Still producing last minute yellow blossoms, the vines refused to stay behind the fence separating the garden from the path around her cottage. The fruits of Annie's patch sat lined up on her steps: big, round, orange reminders that it was time to prepare for winter.

Late that night, Annie saw a shooting star as she looked up into the crisp November sky. The wind had died down on the Knoll, and a few hardy cicadas were still humming their tunes. There was an eerie stillness when she paused partway onto the dock. The tide was fully out, and the water was motionless. It was as if nature were holding its breath, and Annie realized that she was, indeed, holding hers. Breathe, she told herself.

She continued walking and suddenly something moved farther out on the dock. She froze. It froze. Something orange that looked bigger than a stray cat. Annie pulled out a pocket flashlight and directed the beam down the dock.

A small fox stared back at her, probably out there looking for a scrap of bait. It dashed back a few steps, but it wasn't going to get too far in that direction. Annie retreated so the frightened creature could escape. The red fox crept past her and then dashed up the beach toward Cattail.

Annie laughed to herself. The fox was clearly more frightened than she was. At that moment, a flock of migrating Canadas flew overhead, honking. The tide shifted and a breeze picked up. Just like that, Annie felt herself settle.

When she came into Sunrise Cottage, her completed portrait sat in the living room leaning against the fireplace. Packard was asleep on her couch.

In the painting, Annie floated in water surrounded by large, flat lily pads. Her dark, auburn curls of hair swirled around her face. Her brown eyes looked directly at the viewer; however, one of her hands drifted out toward the golden torch of a blooming water lily. Standing on the wrist of her other arm was Oliver.

"I dreamed about a red fox," Packard told her when he woke up. Holding her in his arms, he added, "It came right up to me and let me pet it like a dog. I was a young boy in the dream, and the red fox followed me home."

ACKNOWLEDGEMENTS

I would like to thank Tawdra T. Kandle for her belief in this novel from our first discussion over lunch to her spot-on editing and finally to the realization of this dream. Thank you to both Tawdra and her partner Mandie Stevens at Hayson Publishing for all the support and encouragement. Their level of expertise is matchless.

I am eternally grateful to my husband Gary Collings for his unceasing support and honest opinions. His belief in me and my work nurtures my soul every day. My Solstice Sisters/ Oldsames-Anne, Patricia, Laurel, and Linda are the most magical of women who help to sustain both my creative life and personal life. The wisdom and teachings of Beverly Cassell and the Artist Conference Network showed me how to shift my way of being and discover possibilities. I want to thank everyone from the Mixed Media chapter of the Artist Conference Network who listened to and supported the early readings of this novel.

I am also grateful for the works of Julia Cameron that helped me to create a writing practice. Bonnie Newbauer's copious notes on draft two gave birth to the belief that I actually had a book. Anne Dubuisson's editing of drafts four and five led to discoveries beyond my dreams. I deeply thank Anne Knoll, Laurel Eckhardt Wilson, Bill Abrams, Shirlene Abrams and Patricia Osborne for reading and re-reading without complaint and always with honest feedback and sincere encouragement.

I appreciate the meals and discussions on Chesapeake watermen and workboats with Lorraine and Gary Whitehair along with conversations about art and artists with Murray (Desi) Dessner all of which led to the details of Packard Marlboro. Thank you to everyone at Sultana Projects for teaching me about the Chesapeake Bay, and the Cape May Bird Observatory, especially Bill Glazer, Sr. who taught me what I know about birds. I thank Richard Keephart for the many hours spent looking for sea glass and watching birds.

Thanks to all my Eastern Shore friends who have made me feel that the Chesapeake Bay is my second home. Thank you to all my students who inspire me every day.

Cover Photo: Gary Collings

Cover Design: Stephanie Nelson

Map: Shirlene Abrams

Author Photo: Gary Collings

About the Author

Gail Priest lives in New Jersey and summers in Maryland on the Chesapeake Bay with her husband and their cockatiel. In addition to writing novels, plays and screenplays, she teaches and directs in a high school performing arts program. She loves theatre, reading, birding and spending time in nature.

SUNSET

PART ONE

CHAPTER ONE

SUMMER 1980

NATE BIDWELL HEARD VOICES AS he bicycled by the abandoned barn on Swamp Road. He loved soaring down a series of hills out there past trees covered with kudzu vines that made them look like giant green topiary monsters. Nate stopped his bike at the barn near the border of Coletown, a small African American community. When he heard someone pleading, he rode off the pavement and across the grass at top speed, circling behind the dilapidated building. There he saw two familiar boys, Rusty Watson and Froggy Ferguson, shoving a young Coletown girl back and forth. They had isolated her where no one would see them. Anger shot up from Nate's gut when the girl fell and Rusty pinned her to the ground.

"Quit it," Nate hollered. He drove his bike across the dirt straight toward Froggy. The surprised boy jumped out of the way. Nate turned around and saw Rusty lumbering to his feet, while the little girl stayed on the ground crying. Now Nate could see that it was Ivy Green, whose mother occasionally worked cleaning cottages at Annie Crow Knoll, his home and his mother's community of summer cottages on the Chesapeake Bay. Her eyes were filled with panic, and her flat little chest heaved up and down with sobs. She wasn't more than seven years old. Rusty and Froggy were twice her age and older than Nate.

"Assholes," Nate said out loud.

Despite the bigger boys each weighing a good twenty pounds more than him, he barreled his bike toward Froggy, who caught hold of the handlebars and stopped Nate as if he had ridden into mud. They were face to face.

"We've always known your family loved nig…" Before he finished the word, Nate landed a clean punch into Froggy's gut. Then he felt Rusty plow into him from the side, and he smashed to the ground. Froggy jumped on the front tire of his bike.

"Run, Ivy, run!" Nate screamed as both boys fell on him. He punched wildly. His fist struck bone or teeth before he was hit in the face several times. Pain shot straight to the back of his head. Then another punch landed on his chest, and Nate was gasping for air. Somehow he was focused enough to look for Ivy. Thankfully there was no sign of her. The last thing he felt was another blow to his head.

When Nate woke up, he needed several moments to clear his mind enough to sit up. Blood trickled down his face from his nose. His right eye throbbed. When he closed his left eye, he could barely see and there was blood running into or out of the injured eye. At least Ivy had gotten away, he consoled himself as he stumbled up to examine his bike. Nearly half the spokes on the front tire were broken, and the rim was so badly bent, he wasn't sure he could even roll the bike home. Somehow that hurt worse than his physical injuries.

With some difficulty, Nate picked up his bike and canvassed his surroundings with his good eye. The other was quickly swelling shut, and he was a little unsteady on his feet. He slowly moved around the barn and back out to the road. No one was there to hurt him more, but there was no sign of anyone to help either.

Nate began wheeling his bike toward home on the rear tire, lifting the front wheel so it stayed off the surface of the road. He was several miles away from Annie Crow Knoll, the last property in the small Chesapeake Bay town of Promise.

He'd have to tell his mother he had been out on Swamp Road, the place where her parents were killed in a car accident years before he was born. Nate grimaced, anticipating her expression when she heard that. His dad, though, understood his attraction to speed and those hills. Nate thought his mother should get it, too. After all, their friend and employee Bo often told the story about Nate's mother at the Knoll, riding her bike down the hill, right off the end of the pier and into the bay when she was only nine years old. But his dad had asked him not to mention riding on Swamp Road in front of his mother, so Nate didn't. As with most things, Nate deferred to his father's advice.

After the first half mile of practically carrying his bike, Nate's shoulders began to ache, and his chest hurt when he breathed deeply. When his back tire also went flat, he tossed the bike down. In a fit of anger and frustration, he considered jumping on the back wheel and simply putting the bike out of its misery, but his head hurt too much to do anything that strenuous.

Just when he was about to start walking the rest of the way home without his bike, Bo's Ford pickup truck came down the road from Coletown and pulled over. The sheer relief of seeing the big man jump out of the cab with concern written all over his face nearly made Nate cry, but he'd never allow himself to do that at his age.

"Why aren't you on the Knoll?" Nate asked, surprised. Bo lived in Coletown, but today he should have been working at Annie Crow Knoll, as he had since Nate's mother was a baby. Bo had become like a surrogate father to his mom when Nate's grandparents died, and he was always like a grandfather to Nate.

"Never mind that. Are you okay?" Bo asked as he put his hands on Nate's shoulders.

"Been better."

"Good Lord," Bo said as he examined Nate's eye and pulled a clean bandanna out of his back pocket. "Here, you can put a little pressure on the cut under the brow but don't press directly on your eye."

"Yes, sir."

"You sure are gonna have a shiner. Let's get you back to the Knoll." Bo picked up Nate's bike and put it in the truck bed.

"Why aren't you there today?" Nate asked, rounding the cab and getting in.

"Your over-protective mom sent me home early. Man coughs a few times, and the hen starts clucking." Bo smiled and shook his head.

Nate knew both his parents were concerned about Bo's health, but he said nothing. Instead he asked, "How did you know to find me?"

Bo started up his truck, put it in gear and pulled out onto the road.

"Mrs. Green came to me. Poor little Ivy was more upset about you than herself. Kept telling her mama to make sure you were all right. You weren't at the barn so I kept driving toward the Knoll."

"It was Rusty Watson and Froggy Ferguson."

"Thanks. Ivy wouldn't tell her mom who they were, just that Nathan Bo Bidwell had saved her," Bo said, remembering the day Nate was born and his parents gave Bo the honor of using his name for their son's middle name.

"I'll tell whoever needs to know who they were," Nate insisted.

"Now, Nate. You did your part, and I'm so proud and grateful, but Mrs. Green doesn't want any trouble."

"She can't let them get away with this!"

"I agree with you, but Ivy won't say who the boys were because she's scared. Things could get ugly if she names the sheriff's son, and she and her mother would have no one there to help them."

"I don't believe this!" Nate was livid.

"Rusty's dad pulled me over when I was driving your mother to the hospital to give birth to you. Wanted to know why she was sitting in the front seat with a Negro."

"What happened?" Nate asked.

"You mama had a contraction and yelled bloody murder. Scared Bunky Watson half to death, and he let us go." Recalling it made Bo chuckle to himself.

"But that was twelve years ago. Things are different."

"Not that different."

"Still."

"I don't agree with Mrs. Green's decision, but I have to respect it. I'm asking you to respect it, too. Since you stopped them, let it go. If it had gone further, then she'd have to speak up."

"How am I supposed to explain my eye and my bike?" Nate asked.

"Tell the truth but leave out the girl's name."

"My father—"

"—will come right to me, I know. I'm going to do the lying, not you."

Nate was silent.

After a moment Bo added, "Ivy's older cousins will take care of this during football season now that I can tell them who it was."

When Bo saw Nate turn to him and smile, he laughed. However the laugh quickly turned into a deep cough that seemed to come from the big man's toes.

"Don't ever smoke, Nate," Bo said when he could speak again.

"No, sir."

"I'm serious."

"Yes, sir. I know."

"Good boy."

When they reached Promise, located on the tip of the peninsula between the Elk and Sassafras Rivers overlooking the headwaters of the bay, Nate said, "You'd better drop me off here. Since you're not supposed to know anything when my dad shows up in Coletown about an hour from now."

"You still have a half mile or so to walk out to the Knoll."

"I'll be all right. I'd rather go in alone anyway."

"Okay." Bo pulled his truck over on Center Street.

Nate jumped from the cab to help Bo get the bike out even though it hurt his head to move so fast, but he didn't want Bo to start coughing again.

"Thanks for coming to get me."

"I'm glad Ivy's mama came to me."

Bo climbed back into his truck and made a U-turn to head back out of town. He waved when he passed Nate.

Rather than continuing down Center Street, which ran past the Promise United Methodist Church, Turner's Market and directly to the town beach on the Chesapeake Bay, Nate took the back streets. He cut across to Baycliff Road in order to avoid people who might be picking up their mail or groceries or coming up from the beach. He couldn't begin to deal with the questions anyone would ask. Nate regretted not trying to sneak into the doctor's office across from the market. Maybe if he arrived home already checked out by Doc, his parents would be less alarmed. But he had to dodge people.

When he passed the driveway to Mr. Packard's, the last property in Promise before Annie Crow Knoll without detection, Nate breathed a sigh of relief. However it was short-lived, because Beth Ann and Petey caught sight of him and came running from where they were playing in the field on which Packard's School House Studio stood.

At first they were both just glad to see him along the road, because for them the world began and ended with Nate. Every summer they couldn't wait to fly from California with their mother, Nate's mother's best friend, and spend their vacation on the bay with him. He helped them when they caught fish out on the pier. He took them out in the canoe. He taught them about the birds they saw, and as far as they were concerned, Nate knew everything.

With her blond ponytail swinging, Beth Ann raced to him first. The smile on her cute face disappeared when she realized Nate was hurt.

"What happened?" she asked breathlessly.

Petey, of course, noticed the damaged bike first. "What happened to your wheel?"

"I got in a fight."

"With your bike?" Petey asked, wide-eyed.

Nate pushed ahead toward the entrance to Annie Crow Knoll without answering. Both younger kids raced passed him, sprinting between the two stone pillars topped with cement crows.

Nate trudged on behind them. He spotted his mother repairing a screen window on the porch of Cockatiel Cottage; Petey had managed to hit a softball right through it. Beth Ann and Petey's mom, whom Nate affectionately called Aunt Grace, was helping Annie with the job. Beth Ann reached their mothers first, squealing about Nate getting into a fight. Petey, clamoring to be heard, chimed in about the bike.

His mother's concerned eyes met his as sounds of broken wheel spokes repeatedly hit the drive that ran down the middle of Annie Crow Knoll, dividing the property with seven pale yellow cottages on each side.

"Nate!" She ran to him. "What happened?" She tried to touch his face.

"Not now, Mom," he said and pulled away.

If Aunt Grace, Beth Ann and Petey hadn't been watching, he might have let her take him into her arms. He needed reassurance, but he preferred to get it from his father, who would be in Sunrise Cottage working on his latest book of American Folklore. His mother let him go. When he reached his cottage, Nate threw his damaged bike down on the ground and ran inside.

All For Hope

The captivating contemporary romance from

OLIVIA HARDIN

Author of *The Bend-Bite-Shift series*

TO PROTECT HER HEART, HE left her behind. To protect her life, he'll leave the life he's made behind. Sometimes the safest distance between two hearts is no distance at all...

Kidnapping a baby wasn't something Hope ever dreamed she would do. But she's been burned by the legal system before, so when the court places her friend's child into the custody of an abuser, she takes matters into her own hands. She steals the baby and fakes her death, hoping to make a clean getaway. She planned every detail, except one. Her high school sweetheart and best friend, who left her years before, sees her at a gas station. Hope thinks all is lost, until he offers to help them. Brennan had always been the love of Hope's life, but he never wanted to be. She knows she cannot depend on him for long. However, as each day passes, it becomes painfully obvious that she is in way over her head. She goes with him, intending to keep him always an arm's length away to protect her heart. But being on the run together sparks the old flames that once burned between Brennan and Hope. Families, friends, and lovers must band together to save an innocent baby and a daring woman or both of their lives will be destroyed. Together, they'll do it All for Hope...

Other Books by Hayson Publishing

Through the Valley Love Endures by Eddie David Santiago

All for Hope by Olivia Hardin

The King Series by Tawdra Kandle
Fearless
Breathless
Restless
Endless

The Posse by Tawdra Kandle
Best Served Cold by Tawdra Kandle
Just Desserts by Tawdra Kandle
Undeniable by Tawdra Kandle
Unquenchable by Tawdra Kandle
The Last One by Tawdra Kandle
Stardust on the Sea by Tawdra Kandle

Imperfection by Phaedra Seabolt

Annie Crow Knoll: Sunrise by Gail Priest
Annie Crow Knoll: Sunset by Gail Priest

Tough Love by Marcie A. Bridges

Haunted U by Jessica Gibson

The Praefortis by Michelle Ferguson

CPSIA information can be obtained at www.ICGtesting.com
Printed in the USA
BVOW04s0244010916

460832BV00001B/13/P